By AUGUST LI & EON DE BEAUMONT

STEAMCRAFT AND SORCERY
Boots for the Gentleman
A Grimoire for the Baron
Snowdrop

By AUGUST LI

Coal to Diamonds
Neskaya
On Tinsel Wings • This Same Flower
Steamed Up (Dreamspinner Anthology)
Wine and Roses

By EON DE BEAUMONT

Hedgehogs Are Everywhen
Men of Steel (Dreamspinner Anthology)
Rum and Ginger
The Vanguard's Gift
Wayward Grace

Published by DREAMSPINNER PRESS
http://www.dreamspinnerpress.com

A GRIMOIRE FOR THE BARON

AUGUST LI AND EON DE BEAUMONT

Steamcraft and Sorcery Book Two

Dreamspinner Press

Published by
DREAMSPINNER PRESS

5032 Capital Circle SW, Suite 2, PMB# 279, Tallahassee, FL 32305-7886 USA
http://www.dreamspinnerpress.com/

A Grimoire for the Baron
© 2014 August Li and Eon de Beaumont.

Cover Art
© 2012 Anne Cain.
annecain.art@gmail.com
Cover content is for illustrative purposes only and any person depicted on the cover is a model.

ISBN: 978-1-63216-631-9
Digital ISBN: 978-1-63216-632-6
Library of Congress Control Number: 2014947750
Second Edition August 2014
First edition published by Dreamspinner Press, October 2012

Printed in the United States of America
∞
This paper meets the requirements of
ANSI/NISO Z39.48-1992 (Permanence of Paper).

Chapter 1

QUERRILOUS KNOTTE had never been anything but a thief. He'd been a thief since he'd come to understand certain objects could be traded for food, for clothing, for weapons to defend himself, or for a night of safety behind a sturdy door. Early on, Querry had realized no one in the world would give him the things he needed to survive. If he wanted to live, he had to take them, and so he had. Over time, he'd become quite good at it and had grown to like it. It felt good to show the privileged minority their wealth and station didn't keep them as secure as they deluded themselves into thinking.

Querry smirked as he leaned against the wall of The Mermaid's Tail, the local tavern. He watched Frolic pack his steamer trunk with the clockwork toys that hadn't sold throughout the day. Querry pushed off the wall and strode across the street to help his friend with his burden. Frolic's pale face lit up when he turned his golden eyes on Querry.

"Need a hand?" Querry asked.

Frolic shook his head. "I can manage. I'm stronger than I look," Frolic responded with a wink. Although Frolic looked like a young man in his late teens, he was actually a highly sophisticated clockwork himself. Querry had seen him best men twice his size with ease.

"Is it time?" Frolic asked with obvious glee.

Querry lifted his hand to shield his eyes as he looked out over the ocean. The sun was just beginning to set, and the throngs of dockworkers, sailors, and fishermen started home for the night alongside the more well-to-do of the village, who'd been shopping at the markets and fishmongers or just enjoying the beach. Querry smiled and nodded. "It certainly is." Crowds made a wonderful place to do some light thievery, with all those bodies jostling about, tired from the day's labor, thinking about dinner, distracted.

Frolic skipped into position a few feet ahead of Querry, making a colossal show of pretending his trunk was just a little too heavy for him. He tripped, knocking a gentleman into Querry, who caught the man, then expertly slipped his hand into the man's coat, relieving him of his coin purse.

"Pardon me, sir," Frolic simpered, fixing the man with a puppy dog expression. The whole scene appeared genuinely accidental. The slightly rumpled gentleman only huffed as he hurried away.

Frolic and Querry exchanged glances as they moved on to their next mark. Querry smiled. He loved that Frolic shared his taste for adventure and danger. Lately it seemed that Frolic liked it even more than before his accident. Perhaps the faerie magic used to repair him had made him reckless and wilder than before. Perhaps his brush with his mortality had made him eager to squeeze every drop of experience and excitement out of life. Either way, he clearly enjoyed the game as much as Querry. They played out the Bump and Snatch on a well-dressed lady, who was obviously from out of town. Querry knew they couldn't go overboard. They only did this once or twice a month, just to keep their skills sharp. Any more than that, and people might start to get suspicious. But it was just too much fun, and after the trouble they'd managed to survive in Halcyon, Querry felt like there wasn't anything they couldn't accomplish together.

Frolic bumped, Querry snatched, and the target was none the wiser. The crowd gradually thinned, and Querry sighed. "Looks like we're done here," Querry lamented.

Frolic nodded and fell into step next to him. As they walked, Querry noticed a perfect mark. The man emerged from a brothel with a vacant smirk, still holding his billfold. Querry elbowed Frolic, and they shared a silent communication. Frolic smiled and meandered over toward the target. The smaller man slipped, tossing his trunk into the air. It landed just in front of the big man and burst open, spilling its contents. "Oh no!" Frolic exclaimed in his best helpless youth voice. Unaccustomed to deception, Frolic almost always went too far, but it usually worked for him.

"Here now, don't worry, little fella," the larger gentleman said as he absently stuffed his billfold into his back pocket. "Let me help you."

Querry sidled up behind the man, plucked the billfold from his pocket, and emptied it. He replaced it just as Frolic secured his trunk.

"Oy," the man exclaimed, spinning on Querry. "What're you doing there?"

"Sorry, sir. Just thought I could help you and the young fellow," Querry crooned, hoping he could diffuse the man's sudden suspicion. Frolic moved off as they'd always practiced, but his gaze locked with Querry's. Then Querry noticed the man reaching into his back pocket, and he knew the situation was about to explode. He gave Frolic the signal to run, and Frolic obeyed, hefting the trunk onto his back as he went. Querry dashed off in the opposite direction, the angry man in hot pursuit.

"Come back here, you filthy cutpurse!"

Querry easily outdistanced the larger, slower man, ducking into an alley so he could slow down, so he appeared less conspicuous. He pulled a hat from his pocket and plopped it over his distinctive black curls. He slipped off his red vest and turned it inside out, making it a black vest. The tiny flat he and Frolic shared with Reg was just ahead now. He skipped happily across the street, and a hurtling form crashed into him. Querry almost fell, but managed to stay on his feet. When he looked up, his eyes grew wide with surprise. The big, bald man from the brothel stood in front of him, heaving great gulps of the fishy air.

"Sorry, mate. Chasin' a thief," he gasped. "Red vest. Seen him?" Querry only nodded and pointed up the street. "Thanks, mate," the man said, giving Querry a friendly clap on the shoulder before running off. Querry laughed heartily as he ascended the stairs to their flat.

He was a thief, had always been a thief, and a bloody brilliant one, at that. Now Querry's beloved partner wanted him to be something else. He could see it on Reg's face the moment he closed the door. Querry was still laughing, but when he saw the looks on Reg's and Frolic's faces, he stopped abruptly.

"You seem pretty pleased with yourself," Reg fumed.

"Is it wrong for me to be proud of my talents?" Querry stamped his foot and raked his black curls out of his eyes, pushing the hat off and letting it fall to the floor. He paced the length of their tiny, seaside hovel in a Thalacean port, resisting his desire to kick the rickety table or the iron frame of the bed. He spun on the ball of his foot and crossed the little room again. It smelled of the flowers Reg had bought fresh earlier in the day but underneath lurked the scent of rancid fish and sea water polluted by steamships. "I'm good at what I do, and I'm not ashamed. Are you ashamed of me, Reg?"

Reg collapsed on the edge of their wrought iron bed, all the tensions dropping from his slight form and his anger deflating in a drawn-out sigh. He leaned his elbows on his knees, and his gaze dropped to the chipped, blue tile floor. At Reg's despair, more disturbing than his passionate arguments, Querry swallowed his annoyance and affront and took a step toward him. Reg looked up and pushed his long fringe out of his hazel eyes. The half a year they'd spent under the strong sun of the Thalacean beach had lightened Reg's hair to the color of sunlit wheat and brought a healthy, bronze tint to his face. With his darker coloring, Querry easily passed for a native. No amount of heat or sun could alter Frolic's complexion, and he remained a flawless ivory, kissed with traces of pastel rose. His large golden eyes widened with concern as he watched Querry and Reg, and he rested his delicate hand on the hilt of his enchanted sword.

"I'm not ashamed, Querry, I'm worried," Reg said in a voice left scratchy by his previous tirade. "The three of us are wanted criminals. We barely managed to escape Halcyon with our lives. I just don't think it's prudent to tempt fate. What if you get caught?"

"I won't," Querry said, crossing his arms over his chest and lifting his chin. He couldn't quite suppress the smug smile pulling at the corners of his lips. "Never do."

"You are not invulnerable!" Reg's voice raised as a scrap of his former anger returned.

"I never said I was invulnerable. Only that I'm good."

"Damn it!" Reg stood and smacked the white, plaster wall. Frolic flinched, and Querry recoiled. Reg never lost his temper. He won his debates through reason, calm, and cool, and Querry usually relented just because what Reg said made sense. But Querry had been reluctantly treading the cautious path for months now, and he itched for the night air on a rooftop, the way his senses fine-tuned to everything as he worked. He needed to feel that thrill, to remind himself how much more talented he was than the privileged he robbed. He couldn't help longing for excitement and the challenge his illicit activities provided him. Though he'd never tell Reg, the chance of getting caught made it all the more delicious.

"I'm going crazy here," he said as gently as he could, hoping to make his partner understand. "I have to stretch my legs, test my tools."

It didn't work. Reg stood a few inches from Querry's chest, his fists balled beside his hips and his full lips trembling. "Try thinking about someone other than yourself for a change! What do you think would happen to me and Frolic if you got caught? What if Frolic is with you? Do you think it'll take long before they realize he isn't human? What do you suppose they'll do to him?"

"I taught Frolic! He knows what to do. Besides, I'm not forcing him to come with me. I've kept Frolic safe since I found him!"

"Stop it." Frolic interrupted them and positioned his small body between them, looking from Querry's face to Reg's. "Don't talk about me like I'm not in the room. Please, just stop fighting."

His obvious distress neutralized Querry's anger, and Reg's tight expression softened with sympathy. Both of them went to Frolic's side and took up one of his hands. They apologized in unison, but Frolic still looked miserable. Reg stroked Frolic's smooth cheek with the back of his hand, and Frolic's white eyelashes fluttered with momentary contentment. Querry took his hand and led him to the large table that occupied over half of their living space. The three of them sat down, and Querry poured some strong, local wine for Reg and himself, wishing Frolic could partake of the simple comfort a potent drink offered. With Frolic, everything was much more complex.

"Let's try to talk like people who love each other." Sometimes, naïve little Frolic astounded Querry with his insight. Querry and Reg both nodded and looked at the rough, wooden surface of the table, ashamed at their behavior.

Querry reached across the table to take each of their hands in one of his. He closed his eyes for a moment, breathing deeply to calm himself and just savoring the connection they shared. "I'm sorry," he said softly, squeezing their fingers and delighting in the warmth and slight dampness of their skin. Here by the southern sea, even Frolic seemed to don a perpetual sheen of moisture, though Querry knew he couldn't sweat. Even so, his white, ringlet curls wound tighter and springier than ever, curlicuing out from his face in every direction. Querry found the disorder enchanting. Frolic always looked as if he'd just tumbled out of bed after a bout of lovemaking.

"I'm not sorry."

Reg's statement surprised Querry. "What?"

"I think you're being foolish, Querry, and I can't begin to imagine why you want to take this risk. We aren't desperate for money."

Querry glanced around their single-room dwelling, with the bed in the corner, the table at the center, some cracked crockery on a shelf on the wall, and a small, iron stove barely large enough to heat a kettle. When they tried to cook on it, suffocating smoke filled the space. Other than that, little filled the room beyond the bits of scrap Frolic used to make clockwork toys to sell to tourists or entrepreneurial sailors. A half-completed cat, with a jointed neck, hips, spine, and legs that would move as if alive when complete, waited on the board resting across two stone blocks that Frolic used as a workbench. Its green eyes, indistinguishable from life, would move and roll about when Frolic wound the toy. Bits of other, more fantastical creatures lay strewn across the floor nearby. Unlike other toymakers, Frolic made no effort to hide the elaborate, clockwork joints of his creations. Instead, he integrated them into his designs, making the functional aspects part of the aesthetic appeal. He flaunted his mechanical artistry rather than hiding it, to devastating effect. In Halcyon, such amazing items, far superior to anything else available, would have sold in fine boutiques for high prices. Here, Frolic barely managed to trade his wondrous creations for enough coin to buy a meal.

Being poor didn't bother Querry. He'd always been poor, had never had more to his name than a simple room such as this. The idea of submitting to another's authority grated on him, though. He didn't mind having little in the way of material possessions, so long as he could say no one owned him. After being an indentured laborer as a child, being beholden to no one was very important to Querry.

As if he read Querry's mind, Reg said, "You could find legitimate work, you know."

Querry bristled and sat up straighter in his wooden chair. "You really want me to spend my days gutting fish or hauling crates? Why should I?"

Reg rubbed his forehead. "It's an honest living, and it's good enough for most people. It wouldn't put us in danger."

Reg didn't understand. Querry had no intention of spending his life shoveling shit for a domineering employer. He possessed talents that said he didn't need to. Querry had never been indebted to anyone, and he wasn't about to change that. He didn't need wealth, but he needed his freedom more than his next breath. After their childhood of virtual slavery in Halcyon's factories, why couldn't Reg appreciate that?

"Why do you have to make it sound as if I'm choosing between my love for you and Frolic and giving up my ideals?" Querry asked.

"Because, in a way, you are," Reg answered, his gaze steady. "Which one will you sacrifice, Querry?"

"Neither. Stop doubting me. I've been doing this for as long as I can remember, and I've always been fine. God, Reg. Look at what we've done.

We brought down a corrupt Grande Chancellor with an army of clockwork automatons and a magical weapon. I think I can manage a little simple burglary, don't you?"

"But we don't need the money," Reg protested. Then his eyes widened with realization, and his cheeks colored with outrage. "Burglary? You don't mean to say you're going back out. You can't be serious!"

Querry shook his head and stared into Reg's gentle, hazel eyes, willing him to understand, wishing he could find the words to convey his desires. "I need this."

"Must you take Frolic?"

"I want to go," Frolic quickly interrupted.

"Why?" Reg asked.

Frolic drew his hands out of theirs and folded them in front of himself, staring intently at his knuckles. "I just want to go with Querry. And it's fun."

"Fine." Reg looked absolutely defeated as he circled the rim of his wine glass with his finger, not looking at either of them. He didn't rise from his chair as Querry and Frolic stood and prepared for their evening's adventure.

Querry checked his gear: his mechanical grapple, clockwork pistol, sword, and lock picks in place above the black leather trousers, sturdy boots reinforced with rivets and steel plates, armored waistcoat, and ensorcelled goggles. He secured his weapons and tools to the three thick belts draping his hips. In this warm climate, he'd discarded the seamen's coat he normally wore over his working attire. In the dark leather, he'd melt into the night. He'd finally managed to break it in enough that it didn't creak when he bent and twisted. As Querry looked across the table, Frolic tucked his striking, light hair beneath a black hood and pulled his armored gloves over his pale hands. The snug, dark coat with the double rows of brass buttons and epaulets and matching pants he wore would blend with the darkness as well as Querry's garments. His knee-high boots with the quartet of buckles and reinforced padding would make no sound on the street, or moving across a rooftop or floor.

The two of them stood and moved toward the door.

Reg's chair screeched against the tiles as he got to his feet to join them. Clasping one of their gloved hands in each of his, he whispered, "Be careful."

"Always," Querry said.

"I still wish you wouldn't go. I have a very bad feeling about this."

"It'll be fine, Reggie. It's always fine. Trust me. I've been doing this for a long time."

Reg pinned Querry's dark curls behind his ear before kissing his cheek and dragging his sweet, swollen lips down Querry's face. His breath smelled of the rich wine they'd shared. "Don't make me sorry."

"Never." Querry twined his arms around Reg's small waist and pulled him close enough to bury his face in Reg's blond hair and breathe in his clean scent. It made Querry want to stay in. He closed his eyes and rested his face against his oldest friend's soft hair. "I love you, Reggie."

"Come back to me, Querry, or I won't forgive you."

"Nothing in this world can keep me from coming back to you," Querry breathed, his lips pressed against Reg's forehead where he could taste a hint of Reg's salty perspiration.

"And take care of Frolic."

Frolic giggled and broke away from Querry to embrace Reg and kiss him hard, standing on his tiptoes to reach Reg's lips. Querry grinned as he watched Reg and Frolic's mouths and hands roaming and exploring, as if they hadn't touched each other hundreds of times. He stood to the side and put his arms around both of them, drawing them tight against his chest. He nuzzled his face into their hair and held their different but complementary fragrances in along with his breath. As much as he needed to test his skills, he wished the three of them need never separate. Reluctantly, he let them go and moved toward the simple, wooden door.

"We'll be back soon, Reggie."

"I hope so."

"Everything will be fine, Reggie," Frolic said, turning back to hold Reg close a little longer. He nibbled Reg's bee-stung lips with obvious bliss, his eyelids fluttering shut as their tongues joined. Frolic scraped his nails down the back of Reggie's white, linen shirt until he could cup his ass over his worn, gray trousers. Reg pulled Frolic hard against his chest as he plunged his tongue deep into Frolic's mouth.

As much as Querry enjoyed watching them together, as much as he felt his body react to the sight of his two beautiful lovers enjoying each other's charms and becoming aroused, he cleared his throat theatrically. Reg and Frolic grudgingly pulled away from one another, their chests and bellies separating, then their faces, until finally just their hands remained joined. They gazed at each other with obvious longing, shared a final, quick kiss, and disengaged. While Frolic looked as he always did, Reg's cheeks burned a deep red. Querry couldn't resist pressing his mouth to that heated flesh before he caught Frolic's hand and led him out into the night, toward the danger and uncertainty he and Frolic somehow needed.

CHAPTER 2

QUERRY STOOD staring at the simple, wooden door of their rented home as it closed. He couldn't banish the visions of his beloved Reg waiting within, worrying the night away, until he and Frolic returned. Suddenly, his need to indulge in his skills felt utterly selfish. The compulsion to test his talents didn't diminish, though. He needed this. Querry took a deep breath and tasted the saltwater beneath the toxic, industrial fumes. It felt familiar, though this wasn't Halcyon. If anything, the people here lacked the silly pretenses Querry had always despised. Most of them fished or farmed for a living. Few of them possessed anything like wealth, but those who did occupied exorbitant villas on the hillside. Querry and Frolic headed in that direction.

They passed simple, whitewashed homes similar to their own. Windows were dark; almost everyone slept within. Few people wandered the streets, so Querry and Frolic didn't worry over their attire. Even so, they kept to the shadows as much as possible as they traveled the ancient, winding dirt paths which grew steeper as they ascended. Sweating beneath his leather and a little out of breath, Querry envied Frolic, walking beside him without even a bead of perspiration on his pale face. Querry smiled at his beauty and the graceful way he moved. Though constructed from a combination of complex clockwork and powerful enchantments, only Frolic's utter perfection and unusual coloring betrayed his origins. Querry had learned shortly after meeting his companion that Frolic's heritage made him no less human. He was inquisitive, kind, loyal, and passionate.

"What is it?" Frolic asked, stopping beneath a cypress tree to watch Querry with his huge, golden eyes darting back and forth. "Why are you looking at me like that?"

No one was around, so Querry reached out to stroke Frolic's cheek and run the pad of his thumb over Frolic's pastel, rosebud lips. "I was just thinking. Remembering everything we've been through this year. I'm glad to have you with me."

"It's strange," Frolic said, leaning his head into Querry's palm. "It all feels so far away, and yet it feels like it only happened yesterday. Am I different, Querry?"

Querry hesitated. "We all are. After everything that happened, how could we not be?"

Frolic nodded and looked out toward the sea, his expression distant and melancholy. Nothing but the sound of the waves and the calls of the birds broke the silence. Frolic *was* different, after the faerie magic had been used to repair him, and he'd seen the only other creatures of his kind destroyed. He'd become much more contemplative, given to long spells of silence. He'd also become rather rash, as if he didn't value his own safety sometimes. Watching him, Querry wondered for the hundredth time if he'd done the right thing. He tried to reassure himself he'd done the best he could at the time.

"Right, then," Querry said to end the oppressive silence and drive out his doubts. Nothing could distract him like a job, when he needed to focus all his attention on his surroundings. "Come on. We're almost there."

"Do you have a place in mind?" Frolic fell into step beside Querry.

Querry nodded. "I've been watching it for weeks now. There's never anyone about, not even servants. If I had to guess, I'd say it's a holiday house, and it's not being used at the moment. Listen, when we get inside, don't take anything obvious. It'll be better if the owners don't realize we've been here for a bit."

"I'd like to find something for Reggie, to make him feel better. I think he feels left out, not being able to come with us."

"He just worries too much. He's never been any different, not even when we were boys. Always worrying if I was eating properly and getting enough sleep." He shook his head, grinning at the reminiscence. "I think he was born an old woman."

After an arduous climb that left Querry's thighs aching, they reached a wooden door in a stucco wall. Ivy grew in thick sheets across the whitewashed surface. Querry and Frolic glanced at each other and each nodded once. There would be no more small talk now. They both spared a moment to take in the majestic view of the quaint village below them and the rocky coast beyond. The sea foam stood in stark contrast to the dark water and sky. Here, away from the streetlights and clouds of pollution from the factories, the stars shined brightly and looked as large as penny coins. They hesitantly turned their attention back to the task at hand. After drawing a pick from a hidden pocket in his waistcoat, Querry made short work of the simple, rusty lock and pushed the door open with a soft creak, just wide enough for him and Frolic to enter the courtyard.

Once inside, they pressed their backs flat against the wall. The light of the moon allowed Querry to scan around without the need for the ensorcelled goggles that allowed him to see in the dark. He detected no movement among the groves of fragrant lemon trees lining the long, gravel drive leading to the single-story, sand-colored villa with the red, tiled roof. Not even a lantern burned along the exterior, and all of the windows stood completely dark. A fountain tinkled softly to the left of the arched doors of the main entrance. Querry's pulse increased as he canted his head to indicate a path leading around the side of the house. Exhilaration sang in his veins as his senses grew acute. He could see almost perfectly, and his hearing sharpened until he felt he could isolate the rustle of every leaf and blade of grass.

Frolic nodded his understanding, and the two of them crouched low as they made their way around the side of the villa, mindful of the crunch of gravel beneath their boots, just in case someone was about. The idea didn't worry Querry. He'd looted plenty of houses in Halcyon while their owners slept, had dinner, or sipped their expensive cognac in their studies. Once, he'd cleaned out an attic while hundreds of people, the Grand Chancellor included, attended a party just beneath. Tonight, he almost wished for a little more of a challenge. Maybe, after Reg realized he had nothing to worry about, Querry would seek a more lucrative, higher-stakes job. For now, it just felt good to be out in the shadows, with the cool, night breeze ruffling his hair and Frolic at his side.

They reached a side door, probably a tradesmen's entrance to the kitchen or cellars. A clockwork mechanism more complex than the lock on the gate secured it, but with his innate understanding of such machinery, Frolic had it open in moments. He shot Querry a proud little smile, looking for a second as he had before the events in Halcyon: innocent, eager to please, and in awe of everything.

Querry smiled back. To him, every locked door was like a wrapped package topped with a ribbon, just waiting to be ripped open. At least he assumed so; he'd never had gifts to open on holidays as an orphaned child.

Once inside, Querry slipped his heavy goggles over his eyes and turned the levers near his temple until the enchanted glass that let him see in the dark clicked into place. Everything instantly sprung alight in grainy, grayish greens. Querry blinked a few times to adjust to it. They stood in a small storeroom or pantry, surrounded by sacks of flour, crates of turnips and potatoes, and some dusty barrels probably containing the heavy, Thalacean wine native to the area. Beyond it lay a tidy kitchen with neat rows of dishes and pots and pans hanging from the ceiling. The hearth was completely clean of ashes, as if it hadn't been used for quite some time. It even smelled deserted; no aromas of recently prepared meals lingered in the stale air. Querry felt even more confident the house was empty, and even stood upright and walked through the dining room and into the hall, instead of creeping quietly and hugging the wall.

Querry found the villa sparsely furnished, even by the standards of Thalacean aesthetic. Back in Anglica, the wealthy covered every inch of their brocade walls with artwork in gaudy, gilded frames and crammed every inch of every room with upholstered furniture, foreign rugs, vases, statuary, bookstands, and fringed cushions. Here, open space seemed more coveted. The villa displayed beautiful and intricately tiled floors, and a few lovely landscapes adorned the walls, but many of the rooms stood empty. Others held only a few odd bits of furniture: mismatched chairs or reclining benches covered in sheets. So far, Querry and Frolic had found only an antique-looking dagger with an ivory handle, a silver candle snuffer cast to look like an owl, an enameled box, and a handful of coins in a desk drawer. Frolic was delighted when he discovered a fancy writing kit with colored inks, a few sheets of vellum, quills, and blotters. Better yet, he found a small, green, leather book with a faerie embossed in gold on the cover. Though the edges of the pages crumbled, gorgeous woodcut prints illustrated the stories. Frolic slipped the treasures inside his coat with a wide grin.

They entered the expansive courtyard at the center of the villa and passed the potted shrubs and large, marble statue of the sea god, Neptus, with his nymphs at the center. A thick layer of algae covered the ring of water around the sculpture. They'd check a few more rooms before going home, Querry decided. It didn't seem the owners of the house stored any valuables here. He doubted they'd get the equivalent of a few pounds for the trinkets they'd acquired. At least Frolic had found his gifts for Reg. It might not be so bad to get home early after all, Querry thought as he imagined Reg showing Frolic his gratitude.

We live together, Querry thought. Once, not long ago, living with Reg and Frolic, always having them close and being able to show them his affection whenever he liked, had seemed like an impossible dream. He'd thought he wanted nothing else. Why wasn't it enough?

Querry pushed it to the back of his mind to ponder later. It wasn't like him to get sidetracked while working, but he and Frolic weren't in any danger here. A set of double doors with brass handles caught Querry's attention, and he jutted his chin in its direction. He didn't wait for Frolic to acknowledge him. They'd worked together enough Querry felt confident Frolic understood. He grasped the handles and prepared to throw the doors open.

"Wait," Frolic hissed so close to Querry's ear his breath brushed across Querry's cheek.

"What?" Querry mouthed the word and shrugged.

Frolic raised his shoulders, mirroring Querry's motion. He pointed toward the doors and turned his palms toward the ceiling, his eyes wide and confused.

"What?" Querry mouthed again, more theatrically.

Frolic shook his head. "Nothing. I, I don't know what I was thinking. I had a funny feeling, but—nothing. Go ahead."

Querry gripped him by the shoulders and looked into his eyes, not at all comforted when Frolic wouldn't meet his gaze. "Are you sure?"

Frolic clamped his eyes shut. "It was the faerie influence again. I get… confused. I thought—I'm sure it's nothing."

"Should we go?" Querry whispered. "We can go. There's nothing here, anyway."

"Let's check this one last room. It would be nice to bring something worthwhile back to Reggie. He works so hard, keeping the books for that disagreeable harbormaster. He makes far more than I do selling toys, but I know he isn't happy."

"All right, then." Querry sighed. Frolic hadn't said it, but Querry contributed nothing beyond the few coins he could pinch from the drunken sailors in the dockside taverns. What if this last room contained a chest full of gold and priceless jewels? One never knew until one tore the bow off the package….

Querry couldn't resist. He flung the double doors open and strode into the room, noticing instantly the clutter the rest of the house lacked. He almost laughed out loud. Shelves of books lined the walls, and sat in stacks all over the floor. Glass cabinets held all manner of curiosities, and several sturdy-looking chests stood along the edge of the room. An assortment of papers covered the Anglican-style, rolltop desk, and even the candelabra looked expensive. Querry couldn't wait to spend a good few hours picking through the chaos and finding the choice pieces, almost like a treasure hunt. He hurried toward the center of the room, where some mahogany boxes full of glittering things stood open on a table between two leather armchairs. Even through the imperfect vision his goggles offered, he recognized a few strings of pearls as big as grapes and some faceted jewels the size of his fingernails.

Compelled by greed, Querry approached the enticing stash with his hands already reaching for the riches. Then he stopped, not out of doubt or fear, but because he suddenly couldn't move. His feet felt nailed to the floor, and his limbs seemed made of cement. He couldn't even turn his head when he heard a little whimper from Frolic.

"Querry?"

"What the hell? What's happening?"

"It's a spell. I knew I sensed magic."

"Well, do something about it," Querry said. Panic twisted his guts into knots.

"I can perceive magic, and understand magic, but I can't perform magic, Querry."

Querry tried to reach for his sword or pistol, but couldn't move his arms. He swore, desperately trying to formulate some sort of escape strategy. Though he'd dealt with faeries back in Halcyon, he'd never paid enough attention to magic to know what sort of a spell could have such an effect. He'd seen wards drawn on the ground that immobilized anyone who crossed them. Had he and Frolic stumbled over such a thing? If they had, how would they get free of it? He'd been careful to make sure no one would know they were here, which meant no one would ever come looking for them. If his guess proved right, the owners of this house didn't use it for months at a time. Frolic would survive the wait, but Querry would starve to death. What would watching that do to Frolic? Querry couldn't bear the thought of damaging him any further than he already had.

He'd figure something out. He was too good to let it end like this. He searched for the tiny vestige of fey perception he'd acquired from his gentleman. Before he could trigger his fey sense, the dozens of stubby candles around the room sprung alight, searing Querry's vision underneath his goggles. He squeezed his eyes shut and groaned, the brightness burning through his eyelids.

Querry felt his goggles gently brushed up onto his hairline. He sensed the presence of someone standing in front of him, smelled brandy, tobacco, and expensive cologne. As a hand caressed the back of his head, he slowly opened his eyes.

The dark, blurry shape before him came into focus: an attractive, older man with dark hair, wearing an Auriental robe and holding a curved pipe. He tilted his head a few inches to the side as he regarded Querry. Black hair, as dark as Querry's own but streaked with silver at the temples, grazed the man's shoulders. His skin, while tanned, didn't appear of Thalacean complexion, and he had deep blue eyes like the sky at twilight. His lips trembled and twitched as he suppressed his smirk.

"Who the hell are you?" Querry snarled, barely able to even move his lips, struggling against the mystic restraints to no avail.

The man, tall and lank, retreated a few steps, crossed his arms, and chewed on the stem of his pipe. Some dark stubble lined his wine-darkened, full lips. "I'll ask the questions, Mr. Knotte. After all, you're the one who's broken into my villa and robbed me. It seems I've caught you in the act. Whatever shall I do with you now?"

His inflection and nonchalance recalled to Querry an Anglican noble. This man was used to being obeyed, flattered, and catered to. He clearly expected to be fawned over. He'd be disappointed. Querry didn't acknowledge such status. In truth, he despised it.

"You son of a bitch! Let us go!"

"Why would I do that? I've apprehended you burglarizing me. You won't get off so easily, I'm afraid."

"What do you want?" Querry noticed another figure cowering in the corner of the room, a slight young man with gnarled spikes of golden brown hair and bright, emerald eyes. His long, slender ears protruded past his tangled tresses. A fey. Accustomed to the mercy of the Fair Folk, Querry appealed to him.

"Help me."

The faerie shook his head and focused on his worn boots.

The dark man waved his hand in the faerie's direction. "Mr. Knotte, Mr. Frolic, this is Tom Teezle, my... assistant."

16

Querry detected a faint curl of the fey's lips at that explanation. "So what? What do you want from us?"

The man sauntered over to a cupboard, took out a crystal glass, poured himself a generous share of the clear, local, licorice-flavored liqueur, and downed a large swallow. He squinted at the burn and wiped his lips with his silk sleeve.

"I have a proposal for you and your accomplice, Mr. Knotte," he said.

"How do you know my name? Nobody knows me here."

"I do." He stroked Querry's face, but it didn't feel sexual. Still, Querry recoiled as much as the spell allowed.

"What do you want?" Querry repeated, unused to feeling helpless and not at all fond of the sensation.

The man backed away and sat on the edge of the desk with one thigh on the surface and his bare calf hanging over. "As I see it, I have two options. One, I can hold you immobilized here until the authorities arrive. They'll certainly cart you off to Solanopolis to stand trial. I wonder what they'll make of your unique companion, or if they'll recognize the man wanted for questioning in regards to the death of the Anglican Grande Chancellor. I assume many inventors would like to study the intricacies of your Frolic. So far, they can't manage to duplicate him. And they want to. They want to very much."

"Let Frolic go," Querry said. "He had nothing to do with this. Turn me over, if you must, but let him go."

"You don't get to make demands, Mr. Knotte. You have very little to bargain with."

"But not nothing?" Querry grasped at the slim possibility.

"Not nothing."

"Querry, be careful," Frolic warned.

"Tell me what you want from me," Querry demanded.

"It's simple. I'm organizing an expedition, and I'm in need of people with certain talents. Skilled help, if you will."

Querry glared. If this man wanted his talents, it likely wasn't for anything legitimate, and Querry didn't like being called "help."

"What's the nature of this expedition?" he asked.

"Archaeological. I have been researching an artifact, and I think I've located it. I'm putting together a team to help me retrieve it. I think your skills will be very valuable to me. It's not much of a choice, Mr. Knotte. You and your associate can agree to help me, continuing to do all the things you enjoy doing anyway, finding the adventure you seem to covet, and probably making some profit along the way. I'll even pay you for your time. If you refuse, I'll have little choice but to alert the authorities of your, shall we say, activities."

"What exactly would we have to do?" Querry asked, feeling a thrill at the prospect of treasure and exploration.

"Querry?" Frolic sounded uncertain.

"I'm traveling to the jungles south of Allied Libertania. The forests are largely uncharted, full of savages and wild beasts. There's also political unrest between the Portalegrese and Belvaisian rulers, and there are frequent slave revolts. Basically, it will be fairly dangerous, and the more men I can conscript who know how to use pistols and rapiers, the better. Come on, Mr. Knotte. I can see it in your eyes. It sounds like grand fun, doesn't it? You *want* to say yes."

"Damn it. What's this artifact you're after, then? And what's in it for us?"

The man's eyes narrowed, and Querry watched the stranger size him up, wondering how far he could trust him and deciding just how much to reveal. The older man chewed his pipe again, clearly a frustrated or nervous gesture. Finally he said, "You don't need to know that. As for what you'll receive in return, I've already explained. Travel, treasure, and the adventure of a lifetime. I'm asking for your skills with a sword and pistol, your companion's knowledge of clockwork, and your gifts in regards to… infiltration. The rest need not concern you."

"I'm afraid it concerns me very much. I'm not willing to put Frolic or myself in this situation without all the information. Who are you, by the way? What's your name, and how do you know so much about us?"

"I'm Lord Gavindale Starling, Mr. Knotte, and I apologize for my reprehensible manners, but this is an unusual situation, is it not? I trust you can see fit to forgive my faux pas. So, are you and Mr. Frolic interested?"

"Frolic," Frolic said softly. "Just Frolic."

"Wait," Querry said. "Lord?"

Lord Starling sighed dramatically. "Yes. I am a baron. I'm also a magician of considerable talent, as you can see, so I find myself no longer welcome in Anglica. May I have your answer now, Mr. Knotte?"

"It's Querry. And no, not until you answer my questions. Otherwise I'll take my chances with your so-called authorities. They've never been able to hold me before."

"I know," Lord Starling said with a hint of admiration. "Very well. I'm seeking a source of magical energy, a fabled font of arcane power that's been mentioned in mystic manuscripts for centuries. You're an astute man, Querry. Surely you can see the world is standing on a precipice. Either magic or technology will rule men's lives and provide their resources. I've seen the devastating effect industrialization has had on this world, and I'd like to provide a viable alternative. Magical energy doesn't require slave labor or pollute our precious water and air. If I can find this well, I'll be able to offer the people of the world a clean and harmless source of power. Will you help me?"

"It's not one or the other," Frolic said softly. "Magic and clockwork can exist side by side."

"I want to give the world this energy source," Lord Starling said, ignoring Frolic. "Magic can do so much. It can create items without workers risking their safety in factories. It can provide light and heat without spewing toxic fumes. It can heal injuries and illness. The possibilities are endless. Please, Querry. Please help me do this. If you won't help for the benefit to humanity, help for the exotic treasures you're likely to find in the jungle. I assure you, you'll return from this excursion a wealthy man. Beyond that, you'll have the opportunity to see parts of the world where no civilized man has ever set foot."

"What do you think, Frolic?" Querry asked, fighting the spell to try to look over his shoulder at his partner. He couldn't manage to twist his neck enough to see Frolic's face, but he couldn't miss Frolic's deep sigh.

"I don't know, Querry. Reg is going to be furious. But I've been a prisoner before, and I'm not eager to be one again. It sounds like he wants to do some good. I like the idea of doing something beneficial, after all the destruction we've caused."

Querry didn't bother arguing over what Frolic saw as destruction. They'd destroyed the clockworks similar to Frolic out of absolute necessity, though Querry knew Frolic felt their loss keenly. His clockwork love felt alone without them, the last of his kind. Querry simply asked, "Do you say we agree?"

"We have no choice," Frolic said. "And I can't help feeling a little excited. It'll be a more fun challenge than picking pockets down by the tavern. I say we show them what we can do."

"Very well. What do you need from us?"

Starling smirked. "Tom?"

The small fey nodded his understanding and took some a vellum scroll from a small, ebony box on the desk. Resting it on his outstretched palms, he held it out to his master. Starling unrolled it.

"This is a binding, magical contract. You will sign it in your blood and be released from it only when our mission is completed."

Querry hadn't been expecting anything so extreme. Damn, why hadn't he paid more attention to how magic worked while he'd spent all that time with the faeries? He imagined his gentleman having a good laugh at his expense.

"I don't have blood," Frolic said.

"No matter," Starling said, waving the small complication away as trivial with a flip of his hand. "My servant will see to it. As long as your intentions are honest, you will be bound by the contract. Violate it, and both of you will die."

"That's a bit much, isn't it?" Querry protested.

"You'll have nothing to worry about so long as you do your jobs."

"Show me this bargain," Querry demanded. "And for goodness sake, let us out of this silly enchantment. My muscles are cramping."

Starling rolled his eyes and waved his hand again, as if brushing away a minor annoyance.

Querry felt a tingling sensation as circulation returned to his limbs. He lifted his foot gingerly, smiling as his body followed the commands of his brain. He stretched his fingers and curled them into fists. Then he stretched his arms over his head, just because he could. He hurried to take his place by Frolic's side. Both of their hands went to the weapons they wore at their hips, though they knew the swords would do them little good.

"The contract," Querry repeated, reaching out his hand.

Starling placed the parchment in his palm, and Querry unrolled it to read:

We, the undersigned, hereafter referred to as "agents," do willingly, in good faith, and without ulterior motives pertaining to personal profit, profits to other parties, which are defined as goods, services, or the exchange of information of possible benefit to outside persons, organizations, government bodies, or religious or political establishments, do agree to assist the undersigned, hereafter referred to as "the patron" to the best of our abilities. The agents further agree to protect the patron's interest, in terms of physical safety, financial stability and personal information of both an arcane and mundane nature. Such information shall include, but is not limited to notes, scrolls, manuscripts, maps, grimoires, and privileged information exchanged verbally or overheard.

The agents further agree to use any and all skills available to them to further the patron's mission, inquiries, and interests. To this end, the agents swear, through a binding, magical agreement, wherein the well-being and physical comfort of said agents shall be directly tied to their continued, good-faith efforts to ensure the success of the patron and his expedition. To this end, agents willingly agree to carry out any and all direct orders issued by said patron, excepting those which can reasonably be assumed to lead to serious injury or death. Superficial injury, defined as injury from which agents can recover with minimal treatment, is excluded from this exception.

Should said agents willingly, with malicious intent or in pursuit of interests separate from the patron, fail to perform their duties to the best of their talents and abilities, by arcane bond, they shall suffer physical pain and injury up to and including death. Upon agents' renewed cooperation and adherence to the previous terms, all arcane penalties shall be revoked.

This contract is rendered complete upon successful fulfillment of the patron's goals, and is rendered null and void upon death of the patron or agent. If, in a period of five years, both the patron and agents are living but the mission has not been completed, agents are released from the agreement.

Querry massaged his temples as he tried to make sense of the obtuse language. He wished he could ask Reg to take a look at it, but he didn't think Starling would entertain that idea. Much of what the contract said escaped him, but words like death, serious injury, and physical pain did not. He didn't worry so much for himself; he'd survived worse. He didn't like the idea of subjecting Frolic to such danger, though, and he hated being toyed with and left in the dark. He'd hated that most about working for the faeries back in

Halcyon, never knowing their real motivations or his part in their games. It might be worse than what Frolic could face at the hands of the authorities. At least with them, they'd know what they stood against. But the authorities weren't the problem; the people who would bribe or threaten them to obtain Frolic, who would take him apart piece by piece to learn how he worked and how to duplicate him posed the real danger.

Querry made his decision in an instant. "I agree. Where do I sign?"

Lord Starling handed him a small, sharp dagger, and Querry wriggled out of his leather glove to drag the thin blade across his wrist. The aristocrat caught his blood in a shallow, sterling dish. Then he dipped a fancy, feather quill and handed it to Querry. Before Querry could change his mind, he wrote his name in large, looping letters across the bottom of the document. As he did, he caught the faerie, Tom Teezle's, gaze and watched his reaction. Tom's eyes narrowed ever so slightly, but exposed nothing more than the slightest interest. Faeries could be completely clear in their opinions, Querry knew, but only if they so desired.

"I need to sign as well," Frolic said.

Querry realized he'd decided for Frolic, had been deciding for him since he'd found Frolic in the inventor's basement. Querry hadn't meant to, but it was done.

The fey, Tom Teezle, stood close to Frolic. "Magic is your life-essence. You know this. It is what flows through you like blood. Sign in magic."

Tom lifted Frolic's slender wrist to his chin and regarded the bluish tubes mimicking veins. He drew in a deep breath, harvesting Frolic's scent. To Querry's deep shock, Tom Teezle ran his tongue up the soft inside of Frolic's arm, and his gaze never left Frolic's honey-gold eyes as he did. Frolic shivered, whether from discomfort or pleasure, Querry couldn't be sure. Querry might have been jealous had a human taken such liberties, but he'd been around faeries enough to know they didn't regulate physical interaction the same way as his people, if they regulated it at all. Most couldn't begin to comprehend human rules in regards to such things, so Querry felt no offense as he watched them. As Frolic's white lashes fluttered with sensation, Tom Teezle stepped back and regarded Frolic through narrowed eyes.

"The resonance of this enchantment is familiar to me. I can't imagine how or why he—"

"Tom, attend to the task at hand," Starling said, an edge to his proper voice.

Murder flashed in the fey's eyes for less than a second, but Querry caught it. He restated his theory about magic being Frolic's essence and waited for Frolic's reply. Frolic simply stood with his white brows knit together and a miniscule crease between them.

"Do you agree?" the fey asked again in a breathy, husky tone.

"Yes," Frolic whispered.

"Then sign." The small faerie held the inside of Frolic's wrist against the contract. A thin thread of sparkling gold spread from Frolic's delicate wrist to the scroll. For a moment, the golden light in Frolic's large eyes dimmed, but by the time he blinked everything had returned to normal. The filigree of magic twisted in the air like a serpent caught by the tail, winding and looping over itself until it formed Frolic's name in an elaborate script full of unnecessary flourish. It sank into the parchment with a hiss and a puff of ochre smoke, searing the signature there next to Querry's.

A loud pop tore Querry's attention away from the spectacle. As he turned to see Lord Starling opening a large bottle of Belvaisian sparkling wine, he noticed from the corner of his eye Tom Teezle sliding the scroll inside his shirt.

Starling poured the foaming, pale gold liquid into four crystal glasses and passed them around. He raised his, and the others reluctantly followed his example. After a quartet of clinks, all of them but Frolic downed the wine. The clockwork boy merely watched the tiny bubbles rise to the surface of the liquid so nearly matching the shade of his eyes. The undoubtedly expensive wine was wasted on Querry. Reg would have appreciated it more with his refined tastes, and thinking of him robbed Querry of any enjoyment he might have gleaned. In his excitement over Starling's grand expedition, he hadn't considered his partner's reaction. From the time he'd been a boy and first glimpsed Reg, Querry had wanted nothing else. He never thought life would let him have Reg, and now it had, but Querry, by being a self-absorbed and bloody stupid bastard, had probably just lost him. His head swam, and he felt suddenly sick. What had he done? Reg had given up his whole life to save Querry; asking him to wait until he and Frolic completed this quest was too much. Reg was the gentlest, most compassionate man Querry knew, but he'd never been one to suffer an insult from anyone. Growing up as they had, they'd learned to look out for themselves. They'd learned to defend their pride because they possessed precious little else. Reg never forgot those lessons. Even from Querry, he would only take so much.

Feeling like he'd fall over, Querry stumbled to the ornate leather chair behind Starling's desk and collapsed. He couldn't catch his breath. Though he'd been chased by armed men dozens of times, scaled walls, fought and destroyed terrifying devices, ventured into the Otherworld of the fey, and even defeated Halcyon's former Grande Chancellor and his clockwork soldiers, he'd never been so afraid or felt as miserable and hopeless as he did now.

CHAPTER 3

WHEN HE got tired of sitting in the one-room dwelling he shared with Querry and Frolic, Reg decided to take a walk along the rocky coastline. He'd swept out the hearth, washed the glasses, wiped down the table, and dusted off their few possessions. Basically, he'd exhausted every distraction the humble dwelling provided.

One thing he missed about Halcyon was the availability of books and newspapers. As Chief Royal Archivist, he'd had access to an amazing diversity of material, and his status allowed him to line the walls of his study in handsome, leather-bound volumes. After work, he'd often sat with a brandy, reading late into the night. His interests were eclectic: he enjoyed treatises on scientific theory, travel anecdotes, biographies, history, especially of the ancient world, and of course, fiction, anything that could capture his mind and whisk him away from his mundane and unsatisfying life for an evening.

His life wasn't mundane any longer, and now he had Querry and Frolic. As Reg wandered along the coast, past an overturned rowboat and nets left out to dry, nothing broke the silence but the roar of the high tide crashing against the cliffs farther off and rolling over the gravelly shore. He'd always found the seaside calming, and here it was cleaner and quieter than in Halcyon. The stars burned brighter than he could have ever imagined back beneath the gaslight and smog. He liked the little Thalacean port, could see them making a life together here. Even so, he couldn't calm his mind tonight as he picked his way along the beach.

He missed his books. Without them to occupy his mind, Reg's thoughts wandered. He made his way across a smooth, flat stone jutting out a few feet over the water, sat on the surface, still slightly warm from the intense heat of the day, slipped off his shoes and socks, and let his feet dangle into the tepid, foamy surf. In the distance, a foghorn sounded from some unseen ship. Reg looked out over the water and thought about his home so far across it. For Querry and Frolic, he'd given up the sweet, green fields of Anglica, the muted, gray skies and rich loam that fed the old trees, thick brush, moss, and ferns beneath it. Never, in the rest of his life, would he walk across a meadow in the cool, silver fog of an Anglican morning. He didn't regret it—he convinced himself he wasn't sorry—but he couldn't help reminiscing about his home, his real home, before he'd come to the filthy back alleys of Halcyon.

Reg had only one real memory of his father. He returned to it tonight as he sometimes did. It was late summer, and for some reason Reggie senior hadn't left for the fields before his son awoke. They spent a rare day together, wandering through the forest with shafts of golden light breaking through the thick leaves, Reg searching the ground for a suitable branch to use as a sword, and his father filling a metal pail with berries. They chased frogs across the little streams tumbling over the round, gray stones and ate bread and sausages for lunch. Afterward, Reg hid among the high wheat, crouched low with his hand pressed over his mouth so his father wouldn't hear him giggle. After what seemed like an excruciating period of time, Reg's father swooped down and tickled his ribs until Reg couldn't breathe from laughing.

Then he kissed Reg's sweaty, slightly sunburned forehead and said, "I love ya, boy."

They laid there looking at the sky. Reg would never forget the way the wheat looked in the late-day sun: hazy, golden, and almost glowing as it swayed in the soft breeze. His father's hair was just that color, as was Reg's now. Finally, Reg's father scooped him up and sat Reg on his shoulder to walk back to their simple cottage. Reg thought he could see the whole world from his perch.

Whenever he remembered that perfect day, Reg wondered how he might be different if he'd had his parents to raise him, his father to teach him to be a good man. How would he have turned out had he been protected and cherished? Would he be the same person as today?

Back then, he'd never imagined life could be a crushing monotony of toil or that people could be so cruel. After the fever took his parents, some relatives kept him for a time because they needed help with the autumn harvest. Then they passed him off to other short-handed farms. Reg learned quickly his only value lay in the crops he could sow or the hay he could cut down. They viewed him as little more than a piece of equipment. Eventually, they all threw him away. Reg didn't fear being abandoned, but he'd come to expect it. With his parents gone, he knew no one would ever care about him or want him just for him. To others, he was something to use.

He learned suspicion and to defend himself. No one else cared what happened to him, not until he met a black-haired boy with gem-like blue eyes, burning with so much passion it scared Reg at first, like it might scorch him if he got too close. But he got close, because he knew Querry would protect him with his life. He knew Querry would never leave him. Querry wanted him exactly as he was. Back then, Reg thought Querry almost supernatural, and doubted even death could stand in his way. Reg was self-reliant; he didn't need Querry, but he wanted him, and almost as soon as he saw him, he loved him.

Then Querry'd found Frolic, so extraordinarily beautiful, so innocent and full of wonder at the world. The clockwork boy had desired Reg so earnestly and made him feel so special. Frolic gave Reg something he hadn't even known was missing. Now, he had people to treasure and protect, who'd adore him and keep him safe in return. He had so much love in his life now, when he'd never expected any at all.

Still, when they went off without him and put themselves in danger, Reg felt alone again. They ignored his need to feel included, not that he wanted to learn to grapple up walls or pick locks. He wondered if they knew how much he worried while they were gone. After the events in Halcyon, Querry considered himself untouchable. Reg sometimes thought Querry would have gone to the noose years ago if not for Reg to make him see reason.

Reg wriggled his toes in the briny water. All he wanted was a long, safe life with the men he loved. He'd be satisfied spending it here, as long as they could be together. Querry couldn't be satisfied. He needed adventure, danger even, and now Frolic did too. It felt unfair. Reg's desires, while simple compared to their grandiose schemes, were no less valid, and he needed to make them understand.

Still, he knew what Querry and Frolic were, and he had to accept it on some level. He'd chosen to be with them, and he couldn't pick the traits he admired in them and cut away the rest. In truth, he wouldn't want to change anything about them. Reg took a deep breath and pushed his sea-damp fringe out of his eyes. Then he stood and stretched before hopping from the rock to the beach below. The jagged stones bit his soles, and he chuckled at his own foolishness as he slipped into his stockings and boots. His partners would be fine. Querry could be reckless, but he wasn't a fool. Reg decided to accept his partners and stop judging them. They had never judged him or told him what to do. He owed them his approval and understanding, and they owed him theirs. They'd give it, he felt certain. They'd gotten through worse together.

A candle burned in their single window when Reg reached the house. He'd snuffed them all before he left. He grinned like a boy with a pocketful of sweets, and his pulse sped up. Querry and Frolic had come home early. Visions of how they might spend the evening hours filled Reg's head until they spilled down his spine, all the way to the root of his body, making him tremble in anticipation. Perhaps talking could wait awhile. He hurried inside, but the sight of his partners doused the flicker of arousal he'd felt.

Querry stood with his gloved palm resting on the table, beads of sweat sparkling on his upper lip and high cheekbones. Frolic sat in the corner by the hearth with his arms wrapped around his calves and his face buried between his knees. He didn't lift his head as Reg closed the door, and Reg went to kneel down beside him and find out what bothered him. He'd made it about halfway across the small room when Querry spoke.

"We need to talk."

A chill overtook Reg, as if he'd fallen into icy water. He struggled to catch his breath at the anxiety he heard in Querry's voice. Querry didn't get worried; he got angry. With his throat closed and his stomach tight, Reg couldn't even ask Querry what he meant.

Frolic slowly lifted his head and met Reg's gaze. His wide, golden eyes flitted to Querry, then back to Reg. If possible, he looked even paler as he rocked on the floor and worried his lower lip with his perfect teeth.

"Tell me," Reg finally managed to croak.

Querry splashed some wine into a chipped cup with a shaking hand, spilling some over the smooth surface of the table. He downed it in a few deep gulps and wiped his mouth with the back of his bare, left hand. Some bloody gauze wound around his wrist.

"I—we had a spot of trouble, Reg. Nothing major. Nothing I couldn't handle."

"Trouble?" Reg's voice sounded strangled and unfamiliar to him. "You couldn't have been caught, or you wouldn't be here, right? Unless you escaped? Are they looking for you? Oh hell. Querry, did you— Are they dead?"

"You automatically think I killed someone?" Querry scrunched his brows together, frowned, and crossed his arms over his chest. "That's what you think of me?"

"I— No. You two are scaring me, though. Tell me everything's fine."

"I can't quite say that." Querry poured more wine with a slightly steadier hand and drank. It left his lips shiny and stained. He relayed the events of the evening gingerly at first, but as his tale continued, his confidence grew until it sounded almost like bragging. He gestured with his hands, demonstrating how he or Frolic had opened a lock or dipped into a shadow. When he described pearls the size of hen's eggs and chests overflowing with gold and jewels, Reg felt a bit incredulous, but also a little bit proud.

Frolic smiled and said, "I still can't understand why some things are worth so much more than others. I used to think beauty determined value, but the shells and sea glass I find on the beach are far lovelier than dull copper coins. I can't comprehend how they can be worthless."

Reg returned his smile. A glass jar of bits he'd scavenged along the coastline sat on the hearth, truly beautiful in the firelight. Still, Reg wouldn't let them wiggle out of this so easily. "Let's hear about the trouble."

Querry explained about the magical trap, the exiled, aristocratic wizard, and the faerie servant. He described the details of the contract he and Frolic had entered into, summarizing it for his lover. At some point, Reg slumped into one of their rickety chairs, and Frolic stood behind him with his hand curled around Reg's shoulder. Reg reached up and grasped Frolic's warm, slender fingers, though he wasn't really aware of moving at all as he tried to digest Querry's words. They'd entered into an arrangement. It would last five years. Five years, or until one of them, or all of them, died. *Died, in some hot, fetid jungle surrounded by savages.* No, it had to be a joke—

Querry's chuckle broke into Reg's musings like a wave crashing against the beach and tossing the stones and shells into disarray. Reg's thoughts flew into chaos. How could Querry find this horrifying situation amusing?

"So in the end, it might be a bit of fun after all. And we certainly stand to make some money. I won't spend any of it. I'll bring all of it back to you." Querry said it like he'd be doing Reg a favor.

Reg couldn't think. He couldn't even hear anything but the blood rushing rhythmically through his veins, faster and faster as his anger increased to a point he'd never experienced. He balled his fists to stop his hands shaking. Before Reg's mind could formulate an argument, his body responded. He leapt out of his chair, crossed the space separating him from Querry in two long strides, drew back, and hit Querry as hard as he could, splitting his skin against Querry's teeth.

Querry's head jerked back, and he stumbled a few steps before his knees hit the edge of a chair, and he tumbled over it, landing hard on his back. Querry lay still for a few seconds before he sat up and mopped the blood from his split and swollen lower lip.

It took all the willpower Reg possessed not to dive on him and pummel him until his knuckles bled. Somewhere at the periphery of his anger, he felt Frolic's hold on his elbow and heard Frolic's pleading voice. Reg tore his arm out of Frolic's grip and stood over Querry.

"You absolute ass! You think I want your money? Damn it, Querry! I *had* money. I was engaged to the daughter of a damned earl! I gave it up so you'd be safe. That's all I want. You obviously don't know anything about me, and you clearly don't care what I want."

He raised his torn, throbbing hand to strike Querry's beautiful face again. Querry didn't flinch or try to shield himself with his arms. It just made Reg angrier, the idea Querry would just sit back and take it. He wasn't afraid.

"You think I can't hurt you?" Reg shouted as he bent down to seize a handful of Querry's black hair.

"I know you can hurt me," Querry said, his gaze locking with Reg's. "You can destroy me. You might be the only thing that can."

"Damn it." Reg let go of Querry's locks and raked his fingers through his own as he staggered back to his feet. "After all the boasting you do about being beholden to no one, as free as an alley cat, you do something like this. This bastard owns you, Querry. Frolic too. You expect me not to be upset about that?"

"Reggie, I didn't have much choice."

"You could have chosen not to go in the first place. You just think too bloody well of yourself to get honest work like everyone else. I'd wager you've finally realized you aren't untouchable. A shame you dragged Frolic down with you. You've really done it this time. You know that, Querry?"

"I know."

Reg turned away from him, betrayal, fear, and anger pulling him in every direction. He tore a shard from his thumbnail and spit it into the fireplace.

Frolic caught his arms, pulled him close, and nestled his face against Reg's chest. "I'm sorry," he whispered. "I never want to be away from you, Reggie. You mean everything to me. You and Querry are everything."

Reg softened, his rage ebbing away like the tide at Frolic's sweet voice. He let Frolic pull him into an embrace, and he kissed Frolic's forehead just where his ivory skin met his silver hair. Frolic made a little sound of delight and satisfaction, and Reg whispered, "I don't blame *you*."

Though Frolic didn't pull away, he stiffened. "You should. I can make decisions for myself, the same as Querry. I'm not just his little clockwork sidekick."

"I didn't mean—" Reg pulled away from Frolic so he could look into Frolic's eyes. He saw so many conflicting emotions behind them he didn't know how to begin sorting them out. "Damn it, Frolic, I love you."

"I know, Reggie. Talk to Querry. Please."

Reg looked at Querry, the person he'd counted on since he'd been a boy, the person he almost idolized as invincible, sprawled on the dusty, chipped tile floor. Querry licked his broken lip, and his bright blue eyes sparkled with unshed tears. Overall, he looked terrified. For the first time, Reg realized how much power he wielded over Querry. Nothing had influence over Querry, yet he did. If he so chose, Reg could shatter Querry's world. He didn't want such a power, so he surrendered it. In that moment, Reg chose not to ever use Querry's devotion to him to hurt his oldest friend.

"Reggie?" Querry whispered, reaching out but not attempting to touch Reg. "You mean so much to me. You'll never know. Shit, I don't expect you to wait five years for us. I can't ask you to do that."

Reg kneaded his lower back with his thumbs. He dug around inside himself, searching for his anger, but he couldn't find it. The people he loved were hurting, and he felt only sympathy.

"No, Querry, you can't ask me to wait. I certainly won't wait." Reg crouched by the bed and dragged out a wooden ammunition box left over from the war with the Belvaisian emperor. He tossed the lid back and took from within his two antique pistols with the mother of pearl handles. Digging through the contents, through everything left of his life in Anglica, Reg found the stiff, leather belt and holster. He stood and strapped it around his hips, and then he placed the guns in their positions at his sides. Turning to Querry and Frolic, he said, "When do we leave, then?"

Querry struggled to his feet with the help of the tabletop. He gripped it hard to stop his swaying. "What are you saying, love?"

Reg draped his arm across Querry's slender but strong shoulders. He reached out, and Frolic insinuated himself beneath Reg's other arm, his face resting against Reg's chest. Reg kissed the top of Frolic's head, burying his face in the chaos of his curls. Then he pressed his lips to Querry's fine, dark brow.

"I'm a part of this," Reg said. "I'm coming with you so that I can keep your damned fool asses out of trouble. I can't believe you thought you could leave me behind."

Both of them wrapped their arms around Reg's neck and waist, pulling them together until their hipbones jabbed into each other, and their groins stood only a few maddening inches apart. All at once, their lips came together, and their mouths opened, all three tongues twining together in a hot, wet knot. Reg pulled away when he tasted blood.

"I'm sorry I hit you, Querry," he said, looking at his sand-caked boots.

"I deserved it. I know I messed up. But we can do this, especially the three of us together. Look what we've managed before. We'll come back rich."

"Let's just ensure we come back at all," Reg said, still uneasy about the prospect.

"I'll make sure of it, Reggie." Querry clutched Reg's wrist fiercely, possessively. "I swear, I'll never let anything happen to you. Nothing will stop me from protecting you."

"Or me," Frolic said. "I can't lose either of you. I won't let anything take you from me."

Chapter 4

Frolic spent the next week and a half in the cluttered corner of their home serving as his workshop, surrounded by wires, gears, metal tubing, leather, and canvas. Today, he sat with his legs crossed in front of a wooden plank propped on two cement blocks and a large needle in his hand, inlaying a brown leather vest with strips of thin metal for Reg. He'd already fashioned a similar pair of trousers, reinforcing the knees and seat and adding a row of brass rivets up the sides of the legs. Before they left on their excursion with Lord Starling, he wanted to make Reg a matching pair of gloves with metal knobs on the knuckles and design a way for his pistols to load automatically and carry more ammunition. He didn't think designing a clockwork delivery system would be difficult, but it would take time to implement without destroying the aesthetic of the antique guns, and they'd be leaving the following morning. Reg still needed goggles, and the spring mechanism on Querry's grapple had been catching. Frolic stitched up the seam on the vest, set it aside, spread a fresh piece of leather over his bench, and picked up the scissors.

He looked wistfully over his shoulder at a rusted anvil. A little bird sat on top, small enough to nestle in Frolic's palm. He set the shears down, picked it up, and wound the little knob hidden beneath the engraved, brass feathers of its tail. When Frolic set it on the floor, it gave a little hop, cocked its head, and blinked its eyes. Frolic smiled as his creation stepped lightly over the floor, but his smile dropped away as it spread its wings and beat them twice. He'd been trying for months to figure out how to make it fly, but despite the gears within being as small as flies' wings, it was still too heavy to get off the ground. Even with his enhanced vision, Frolic didn't think he could construct clockwork any smaller. He looked down at his knuckles and moved his fingers, watching the play of artificial bone and sinew beneath his skin. Some of the gears within him were only a fraction of the size of those within his bird. How had his creator managed it? Not for the first time, Frolic wished he could speak with the man who made him. He had so many questions about his existence no one else could ever answer. Why had he been made as he had? Were his thoughts and feelings his own, or had they been engineered by his creator? Did he respond to things around him as he did simply because he'd been built to do so?

Querry would tell him there was no order to life; it was just a string of random, chaotic, and unrelated events to be exploited by the clever and talented. He would tell Frolic to do what made him happy. Reg would stroke his curls, smile his gentle smile, and admit he didn't know. Frolic needed more. He needed to understand how much of him had been predetermined by his maker, and how much he could claim as his own identity.

Frolic reached beneath his shirt and fondled the detailed metal feather he wore on a chain around his neck, remembering the beautiful clockwork angels that frightening faerie Querry knew had destroyed. They, like Frolic, had been designed as part of a magic-syphoning device, a horrifying weapon. For some reason, Frolic's creator had given him alone the will to choose, made him look completely human, and given him perfect, functioning human anatomy. Querry and Reg suspected he'd done it to thwart the men who'd forced him to construct the horrible weapon, that perhaps he'd done it out of a love he'd formed for Frolic as he built him. They said he'd wanted Frolic free and happy. Frolic just couldn't be sure.

To distract himself, Frolic returned to his work, wishing he had some music to keep him company. By the time Querry and Reg returned home just as the sun started to set, he'd finished everything but Querry's grapple. If needs be, he could continue working on it during the voyage. After all, it would be a long one. Maybe it would give him time to work out his little bird. He hated unoccupied time; it encouraged thinking, which led to confusion. He loved working with Querry, because it didn't leave him even a second to get lost in his head.

Querry punched Reg playfully in the shoulder as he pushed the door shut with the side of his foot. Both of them looked pleased, and Frolic felt relieved they weren't quarreling anymore. Querry set a basket full of cucumbers, tomatoes, and spinach on the table. Reg, his cheeks and the bridge of his nose painted pink by the sun, set down a few bottles of wine and a fishy-smelling package wrapped in brown paper. They'd all agreed to share a special meal before leaving yet another home behind. Reg walked over to Frolic and bent his waist to kiss the top of Frolic's head. He smelled of warm skin and the sea. Frolic liked it.

"I finished the things I've been working on for you," Frolic said as he stood up, proud of all he'd accomplished. "Try them on." He handed Reg the trousers, vest, and gloves.

"Go on, then," Querry said with a mischievous smile.

Reg looked around the room. They'd been lovers for almost a year, but Reg still flushed at changing in front of them. Frolic had never understood the human notion of hiding their bodies, but he found Reg's shyness endearing. Slowly, Reg stepped out of his shoes and worn trousers and put on the garments Frolic made.

Querry whistled when Reg'd finished, and Frolic admired his partner's lean body beneath the snug, armored leather. He looked absolutely dashing, and Frolic said so.

"Damn," Querry agreed. "Seeing you in that gear might make this whole ordeal worthwhile." He ran the tip of his tongue across his upper lip and his hand over the swell of Reg's leather-encased ass.

"Thank you," Reg said, reaching for Frolic and drawing him near. "These are quite beautiful."

"They're to keep you safe," Frolic said, stroking Reg's hot cheek.

From behind Reg's shoulder, Querry gave Frolic a wink and a grin. Frolic returned it and stretched his neck to give first Querry, then Reg, a quick peck before showing them how he'd improved the guns.

"I'm so glad you two are back," Frolic admitted. "I get lonely faster than I should."

"You should have come with us to the market," Querry said.

Reg nodded. "We had quite a lovely time. It would have been better with you there, though."

"Well, I wanted to finish," Frolic said. "We'll still have to find you some better boots, though, Reggie."

"And a sword," Querry added.

"Another time," Reg said. "I'm famished, and the seafood won't keep. Let's get dinner going."

Preparing the evening meal together was one of Frolic's favorite parts of the day, even though he didn't eat. He liked the way they all worked together, Querry slicing the loaf of dark bread, while Frolic rinsed the vegetables in a pail and dried them on a cloth. Reg built a fire, peeled a bulb of garlic, and heated some oil in a skillet. After he finished with the bread,

Querry opened one of the bottles of wine and poured some for Reg and himself. As they worked, they touched each other's hands, grazed each other's waists, and even kissed when they passed one another. Though they'd only just met around this time last year, they worked together perfectly.

Frolic made the salad, cutting a few of the tomatoes into little rosettes. He liked details, liked creating beauty anywhere he could. Querry stood behind him and said, "It looks wonderful," before giving Frolic a playful smack on the ass. Reg chuckled as he poured some of the bright, amethyst wine into the pot with the mussels, pieces of chopped octopus, and garlic. It sizzled and steamed. A sweet, savory aroma filled the room. Frolic smiled as Querry's stomach rumbled. He arranged the vegetables in two wooden bowls and set them on the table. Outside, the sun fell toward the sea, chased closely by the cobalt of the night sky, so Frolic lit the candles at the center of the table before sitting down.

Reg served the seafood and poured more wine for Querry and himself. They took their places across from Frolic and ate, soaking up the fragrant broth with their bread. Frolic liked watching their jaws move as they chewed, liked the way they licked their lips and the small sounds of satisfaction they made. Watching Querry and Reg eat also got him in the mood for what usually followed. To him, it served almost as foreplay to watch the pleasure they took in their food and wine. Throughout the meal, Frolic caught himself licking and touching his own mouth as he watched his lovers mop the flavors from theirs.

Reg dabbed his lips with a napkin and took a sip of his wine. "Is this so bad?" he asked.

Querry shook his head. "It's delicious. I don't think I could ever go back to that over-processed, canned stuff I lived on back in Halcyon."

"You know that isn't what I mean." A little crease formed between Reg's eyebrows, indicating his annoyance. "I'm talking about simple pleasures: a good meal, a few glasses of wine, excellent company. It's enough for me, being here with you two, eating, talking, and going to bed. Will it ever be enough for you?"

"I—don't know." Querry looked deep into his glass as he swirled the jewel-like liquid around, reminding Frolic of a fortune teller divining over tea leaves he'd once seen at a market back in Halcyon.

"I don't want to settle," Querry said without looking up. "I have gifts. I don't want to waste them. I know you can't understand, Reg, but I like what I do."

"Frolic?"

"I want both you and Querry to be happy with me. It's hard to explain, but I like everything we do together. I love going off with Querry. It's exciting, and it helps me forget. But I love the quiet of sitting here like this too. There must be some way to reconcile the two."

"I have no problem reconciling anything." Querry poured himself more wine. "Besides, Reg, you never minded before. I've been picking pockets and cleaning out houses since we met, and you never asked me to stop. Why the sudden concern?"

Reg looked up from his plate and caught Frolic's gaze with his gentle, hazel eyes. "It isn't just you anymore. You know what could happen to Frolic if he's caught. I'm no longer a boy, either. I used to believe nothing could happen to you. Now I realize that's not true. You nearly died of a fever in my guest room, Querry. You'd still be languishing in that filthy prison if I hadn't saved you. I'm sorry, Querry, but you're as mortal as the rest of us. I love you, and I don't want to lose you."

"What do you want me to do? I don't want to be anyone's whipping boy. I've had my fill of that for this lifetime."

"There's no point in worrying over all this now," Frolic said. "We should leave it until we get back from the expedition. Both of you are always telling me not to worry over things I can't control. We can decide what to do next after we get back. Can't we just enjoy our last night here? I'm going to miss this little house. Someday, I'd like somewhere permanent, somewhere we can call our own."

"We'll never have it if we're constantly on the run," Reg said.

"I don't want to think about it anymore," Frolic said. "Not tonight. I've done enough thinking this afternoon while I was alone."

"Oh, love, I'm sorry." Reg reached across the table to take Frolic's hand. "What can we do?"

As much as Frolic resented Reg finding him fragile, he needed the comfort. Why was everything so skewed? Why could a question never just be answered with a single, logical solution? Frolic supposed that might make existence dull and predictable. He didn't know if it might be a fair trade, though, if it rid him of all his confusion.

He ran his fingertips over the back of Reg's hand. "I just want to forget for a time. Reg, Querry, please—"

Querry stood and came around behind Frolic, lifting Frolic's curls to kiss the back of his neck. His warm, slick lips moved from Frolic's collarbone to his earlobe. "My beauty, give me a chance, and I'll make you forget your own name."

"You already are." Frolic's eyelids fluttered shut, all his attention focused on the meeting of Querry's lips to his skin and his hand over Reg's across the table. "Let's give our little house a proper farewell, so we always remember our time here."

"Yes." Reg's chair screeched against the tile. Before Frolic could open his eyes, Reg dropped onto his lap, straddling Frolic's pelvis. He scooted closer until their bellies pressed together. He brushed his lips across Frolic's as Querry nibbled the edge of Frolic's ear. Frolic seized Reg by the back of the neck with one hand, pulling him closer, while he reached behind him to grasp Querry's waves of dark hair with the other. He thrust his tongue between Reg's teeth and found an eager greeting.

When Reg pulled his lips away, Frolic opened his eyes to Reg and Querry kissing enthusiastically just above his head. Both of them moaned and grunted with delight as they explored each other's mouths. The sweet sounds aroused Frolic, as did Querry's hand down his shirt and Reg's moving up his thigh. With trembling hands, Frolic unbuttoned Reg's plain white, linen shirt and let it fall open to expose his lean chest and belly. Though he lacked Querry's wiry musculature, Reg was firm, fit, and beautiful. His skin felt warm beneath Frolic's fervently roaming hands. Frolic grasped Reg's waist just above his hipbones and tugged him near. He captured one of Reg's pale nipples between his lips and sucked it into his mouth. Reg arched into Frolic, and Querry's arm wound around both of them. He found Frolic's nipple and circled it with the fingers of his other hand. Frolic cried out.

"Damn, Frolic, it's like music, the sounds you make," Querry panted, his breath moistening Frolic's neck.

"It is," Reg agreed, kneading Frolic's balls through his pants while he fondled Querry's ear. "It's so delightful. I'll never grow tired of it."

"You're both so perfect," Querry said, right before his teeth dented the globe of Frolic's shoulder through his coarse shirt. "I love you, Frolic. Reggie, love you...."

Reg stood slowly with his belly only a few inches from Frolic's nose. Frolic pulled at Reg's waistband until the buttons popped open. He pushed them down until he freed Reg's erection. The dusky, rose-purple head poked past his foreskin, already leaking clear-white seed. Frolic thumbed the hood back to expose his partner's swollen crown before circling it with his tongue. Reg groaned, and his hips bucked forward. Frolic opened his mouth to accept him, relishing the feeling of Reg's hard, silken dick against his tongue. Reg took a few steps back, and Frolic fell to his knees to chase him, the chair falling over as he left it.

On his hands and knees, Frolic sucked Reg's erection into his mouth, his throat. Querry tugged at the waistband of his trousers, growling with frustration. Reluctantly, Frolic released Reg's delicious cock with a slurp and sat on his heels.

Reg grumbled and stroked himself.

"Damn it, let me," Querry said, walking past Frolic to kiss Reg and jerk him. Reg's hands traversed Querry's body, clutching at the fabric of his clothes, pulling his shirt tails free of his pants to get at his skin beneath.

Frolic knew what he wanted. He slid his bracers over his arms and unbuttoned his shirt. "Take your clothes off. Please."

Querry and Reg complied without hesitation. As soon as they all stood naked, their clothes tossed haphazardly across the room, Frolic dropped back onto his hands and crawled toward Reg, slowly, looking up at them from beneath his lashes, teasing them with the sway of his hips. He sat on his heels and cupped Reg's balls, massaging them, as he ran his tongue up the length of Reg's shaft. He felt the raised veins beneath his tongue before he closed his lips around the crown. It skipped within his mouth.

Frolic pushed himself up on his knees, raising his ass to Querry in invitation. Of course, Querry intuited Frolic's desire. The three of them knew each other well. Querry knelt and pulled Frolic's cheeks apart to run his tongue over Frolic's opening. An electric jolt of pleasure shot from the point of contact up through Frolic's body. He groaned, his throat vibrating around Reg's shaft.

"Oh, God, love." Reg turned his face to the ceiling and buried his fingers in Frolic's hair, holding onto it as he circled his hips, thrusting into Frolic's mouth.

Frolic loved pleasuring Reg and Querry this way, tasting them, exploring the weight and texture of their flesh with his lips and tongue, feeling every twitch and tremble of their bliss up close, but it had one disadvantage. He couldn't reciprocate the sweet, jumbled words of affection tumbling from Reg. He couldn't tell either of them how beautiful they were or how much he loved them without stopping. He didn't want to stop; his attentions brought Reggie closer and closer. Frolic knew by now just what his partners liked, and Reg didn't like it when he stopped. So, as much as Frolic wanted to tell Querry to get on with it, to quit making him wait, he kept sucking hard on Reg's crown instead.

Finally, Querry went to the stand by their bed and found the vial of oil in the top drawer. Just hearing him unscrew the cap made Frolic shiver. He slowed the movements of his mouth, still exploring the veins and ridges of Reg's erection but with less urgency, hoping he might last, because what Frolic truly wanted was both of them inside him at the same time.

Querry circled Frolic's opening with a cool, slick finger, tracing around the rim and making Frolic twitch with anticipation. He groaned and pushed back against Querry, which made Querry chuckle and kiss the crescent of his cheek.

"Can't wait, beauty?"

Frolic shook his head and spread his legs a little wider. Still laughing, Querry wriggled his fingers inside Frolic and spread them open against the instinctive resistance of the muscles. Frolic had learned how to open himself to his lovers, and he relaxed to take another of Querry's fingers. Reg raked his hair out of his face and stroked Frolic's cheek as Querry pushed a little deeper, grazing the magic spot inside that sent bolts of intense sensation across Frolic's body. His erection suddenly demanded attention, and Frolic moved his hand from Reg's full, fuzzy balls to give the head a squeeze.

Querry grasped his wrist and pulled his hand away. "I'll take care of that for you, love. Please let me." His warm hand closed around the root of Frolic's cock just as he slid his fingers out of Frolic and aligned the tip of his erection with Frolic's hole.

A little squeal escaped Frolic at the tearing sensation when Querry pushed past the last vestiges of resistance and entered him. It always hurt a little at first, but Querry knew to wait for Frolic to become accustomed to it. It didn't take long for him to push back against Querry, encouraging him. As he did, Reg grasped the back of his head, muttering nonsense as his thrusts grew short and quick. Frolic worked his tongue against the belly of Reg's cock as Querry slid slowly in and out of him. After only a few minutes, Reg pulled out of Frolic's mouth.

"Oh God. Oh, my beautiful, sweet—oh, loves!" His seed splashed across Frolic's cheek and chin, some of it getting into his hair.

Frolic didn't care, though, because watching Reg flush, tremble, and fall apart in the bliss of his release summoned the familiar tightening across

Frolic's pelvis. His muscles clenched and released erratically, his own pleasure imminent. Reg dropped down in front of him and reached for a discarded shirt to wipe Frolic's face. Frolic couldn't miss the love and adoration in Reg's eyes as he smiled languidly and said, "You're always so wonderful. Perfect every time. I love you so much."

He bent down and kissed Frolic gently, running his tongue over Frolic's lips and teeth, then swirling it around Frolic's tongue. He kissed each of Frolic's eyes before moving around him toward Querry. Frolic looked over his shoulder to watch them kissing, Reg's hand tickling down the side of Querry's waist. Then Reg broke away and looked down, to where Querry and Frolic's bodies joined.

"Like what you see?" Querry panted.

Reg just nodded, enthralled by the show before him. He touched the taut edge of Frolic's hole as Querry thrust in and out of it with deep, rhythmic strokes. Then he stretched his hand out, his thumb and finger framing Querry's shaft and Frolic's opening, while his other three fingers cradled Frolic's balls.

"Frolic, do you mind if I do this?" Reg asked.

"No. I like it when you touch me. Touch me anywhere you want. I want to share everything with you two."

"It's amazing to see you like this," Reg said, pecking up Frolic's back and massaging his balls as Querry stroked and fucked him. "It's so intimate."

"You have such a tight, sweet little ass," Querry said, circling his hips a little to make sure he hit Frolic's spot.

It worked. Frolic quaked with pleasure, shaking all over as it spread to every inch of his body, so intense it almost hurt. He moaned wantonly, almost crying, and dropped to his elbows. The first time he'd felt the release with Querry, he'd thought he'd die, burn up, just shake apart with the enormity of it. He felt it again now, like he wouldn't survive it; it was too good, too much. "Oh, Querry, yes! Reggie, I, I—God!"

He lay there panting, almost forgetting where they were, for many minutes until his lucidity started to return.

"Did I do it?" Querry asked, his strokes slow and shallow as he smiled at Frolic.

"What?"

"Did you forget your own name?" Querry asked. Beside him, Reg grinned as he toyed with Querry's nipple.

Frolic giggled and nodded. "I wasn't sure what country we were in for a few minutes. Thank you. I needed this."

"Need any more of it?" Querry asked with a deep stab that made Frolic gasp.

"Always."

"Oh, my love." Querry grabbed Frolic's hips and pounded into him with quick, deep strokes, obviously seeking his own release.

To Frolic's surprise, Reg lay down on his back and wriggled beneath him. He caressed Frolic's belly before taking hold of his erection and guiding it into his mouth. It couldn't have been an easy position to get into, but Reggie managed it, sucking voraciously on Frolic's crown. He also managed to bring Frolic off twice more before Querry spilled his seed across Frolic's back and then collapsed on top of it.

The three of them lay on their backs, side by side, sticky with sweat and fluids, and not caring in the least. "I'm so happy right now," Frolic told them, stretching his arm up and watching his fingers move in the firelight. "I feel like I could float away."

"Me too," Reg said. "This love we have... I don't know. Both of you mean so much to me. I love you, and it scares me."

"What, love?" Querry asked. "How do you mean?"

"I've always lost everything I care about. Being this happy makes me nervous, like I'm just waiting for it to be snatched away."

Querry pushed himself up on his elbow and reached across Frolic to catch Reg's chin with his finger and thumb. His blue eyes almost burned in the dark room as he looked down at Reg. "I won't let that happen. I won't let anything keep us apart, any of us, ever. I swear, it, Reg."

"So do I," Frolic hurried to say.

Reg smiled. "There's still a part of me that believes you two can do it, can do anything. Just make sure you don't prove me wrong."

All of them giggled, and before long they were kissing again, Frolic on his side facing Reg and Querry curled up behind him, dividing his attention between Frolic's back and shoulders and Reggie's sweet, bee-stung lips. Frolic grew hard again and reached down to stroke himself. Querry swatted his hand away, and both he and Reg took its place, both of them tugging, twisting and jerking until Frolic felt like he exploded, and whimpered through another climax.

Querry flopped onto his back. "What is that, four of them? I think I'm a little jealous."

Reg snuggled closer and wrapped his arms and legs around Frolic's smaller body. "It is certainly special. You should thank whoever made you for that little perk."

Frolic chewed his lower lip. "But why did he make me this way? I was designed as part of the clock tower, to direct the angels. I never should have had the chance to know I can feel this way. Why does it feel so good when one of you is inside me? Why would he have made me this way? Did he know I'd want that one day? Did he design me to want it?"

"He never wanted you to be a weapon," Reg said for probably the hundredth time. "He gave you free will, made you look human, and hid you away so you couldn't be exploited. The rest of it—I don't know. He clearly wanted you to experience all life's pleasures."

"No one made you want to be with us, Frolic," Querry said. "You chose us. Your creator couldn't have known we'd all meet one day."

"I just want to know why I am the way I am," Frolic whispered. Then he let the subject drop. Querry and Reg knew no more of his creator's intentions than he did.

A few more minutes passed before Querry stood. He stretched and rubbed his knees, which were covered in small scrapes, cuts, and bruises. "A tile floor isn't the best place for this kind of thing, I suppose. Not that it bothered me at the time." He dressed, went outside, and returned with two pails of water: one for them to clean up and another to wash the dishes. After they'd tidied up and cleaned the evidence of their union from their bodies, they got into bed together and adjusted until they found agreeable positions. Before long, Querry and Reg fell asleep, their limbs wound around Frolic and each other like a tangled fishing net and their breath warm and moist against Frolic's cheeks. Frolic didn't require sleep, but he enjoyed it, found it an almost decadent pleasure to lay idle for hours, accomplishing nothing but watching the strange pictures and stories play out inside his head. Tonight it eluded him. He thought about Querry's knees, and his own, uninjured body. They were so fragile, his companions. What if something happened to them on this expedition? Frolic couldn't help worrying as he listened to the song of the sea and the secrets whispered by the wind.

CHAPTER 5

THE NEXT morning, Querry, Reg, and Frolic left their small house before dawn, leaving everything behind but their clothing, weapons, and packs. Frolic pulled his trunk, stuffed full of diversions for the long voyage, and to which he'd attached a small axle and wheels, down the hill. He stopped and looked back at the salt-encrusted, white walls and simple, blue wooden door of their little home. In spite of everything, and though he looked forward to their adventure, knowing he'd probably never see the little place again left him feeling hollow. He consoled himself by imagining the valuable things they'd find, the challenges they'd face. When the expedition began, he'd have no spare time for rumination.

Soon they reached the docks and the army of dinghies transporting supplies to the great ship waiting farther out in the bay. Frolic squinted at it; it appeared to be a hybrid, a traditional sailing ship augmented with steam engines. He felt a surge of excitement at the prospect of examining how it worked. He bet he could improve it if the sailors didn't object. Frolic encountered precious little machinery he couldn't develop. Humans didn't understand it as he did. To him, clockwork lived; it spoke to him, told him what it needed. He hoped they'd let him have a look. It would pass the time.

The three of them made their way to one of the waiting vessels, and Frolic heaved his trunk over the side before getting in. A native Thalacean, a scrawny boy in nothing but loose trousers and a red vest, started the motor. In moments, Frolic's home lay far behind him, and he found himself climbing a rope ladder to the deck. People, mostly locals, milled about, unloading wooden crates larger than themselves. Frolic wondered what the crates contained as the workers quickly spirited them below deck. He also saw more mundane things like barrels of lamp oil and sacks of wool, presumably intended for trade. Lord Starling had amassed quite a company, but most of them looked like hired labor. A trio of others, heavily armed and wearing pieced together bits of military uniforms, stood near the helm. One of them jutted his chin toward Frolic and his companions, saying something and making the other two laugh. Frolic became acutely aware of how everyone stared at them, at him. Not long ago, when Querry had taken him from the doll maker's cellar, he hadn't realized anything distinguished him from others. Now, though, he knew his white hair and yellow eyes inspired fear and suspicion in the people who saw him. Why hadn't his creator made him look a little more ordinary? He would never know.

"All right, beauty?" Querry whispered as he clutched Frolic's wrist.

"They know I don't belong here. All of them do. They're wondering what I am." Frolic didn't add how he wondered the same about himself.

"You have as much right to be anywhere as anyone," Reg said, his eyes full of sympathy and understanding. "Don't let them make you uncomfortable."

Frolic nodded. For now, none of them could do much but wait to be directed. Eventually, Tom Teezle wove his way through the throng, standing out among the simply dressed workers in his green, tweed trousers, clean shirt, paisley cravat, and emerald, Auriental-printed waistcoat. Frolic felt the magic wafting off Tom Teezle like heat from the afternoon sand as he stood before them and crossed his arms. His expression remained unreadable.

"I'll show you to your cabin," Tom said. "Am I wrong to assume you don't mind sharing?"

Just then, as the sailors prepared to set off, the previously clear sky darkened, and sheets of rain poured down. The crew shrieked and covered their heads with their arms. The workers hurried to protect the cargo as the rain struck the deck like bullets, too cold for the Thalacean clime. Thunder shook Frolic to his gold-alloy bones. Tom grabbed Frolic's elbow and dragged him toward a hatch. The three of them followed the fey down a ladder into murky, humid darkness. Frolic barely noticed his surroundings; the words of the sea and sky echoed in his head. They offered a warning, told them not to proceed, to abandon their mission. Everything in creation seemed to hiss advisement at once, the myriad voices making Frolic clutch his head and shake it in an attempt to silence them.

"We can't do this," he said through clenched teeth. "Nothing wants us to. We've got to go home."

"Ignore them," Tom said without inflection. "It's just a storm. They're common this time of year."

"No," Frolic said. "The winds and the sea, they're warning us—"

"You're confused, friend."

"I know I'm confused!" Frolic's voice rose as he seized the fey's biceps. He just couldn't articulate everything the sea, sky, and wind said so urgently to him. They didn't relay their foreboding in words he could express. When he tried to say a few of them, Tom's eyes widened, and he clapped his hand over Frolic's lips.

"You shouldn't speak a language you don't understand. There's power in those words beyond your comprehension."

Frolic wrenched the faerie's arm away from his face and looked deep into his oddly angled, shifting green eyes. He found no hint of anything within, just his reflection staring back at him, as if he gazed into an emerald pool. He wished he could see Tom as he did a clockwork, see how his parts fit together, what made him work, his purpose. Since he couldn't, he said, "You know what's going on. You must."

Tom pulled away and rubbed his arms where Frolic had held him. "I can say no more. Much like you, I have terms I must adhere to. It is only a storm, and I can assure you it will pass. Try to get some rest." He pushed the latch up, and a metal door creaked open. With a sweep of his arm, the faerie indicated a small cell with a quartet of bunks riveted to the walls. It contained little else besides a large chest and some footlockers beneath the beds. The simple lanterns affixed to the beams overhead swayed with the motion of the ship, pulling shifting, eerie shadows from the sparse furnishings. It smelled of rust, damp wood, mildew, and disuse.

Reg groaned. "We'll be staying here for how many weeks, then?"

Frolic stroked Reg's waist, and he offered an appreciative smile in return. Querry had tried to explain how Reg craved the air and sky, because of his boyhood in the fields and forests. Frolic, who'd had no childhood, just a century of waiting in an abandoned cellar, couldn't really understand how one's early experiences shaped one's preferences later. He certainly didn't long for that cold, dark, and lonely room. He only knew he didn't want Reg to be unhappy, so he soothed him as best he could, by pulling him close and rubbing his cheek against Reg's chest.

Querry, of course, felt no distress. He took everything in stride, as always. Nothing bothered Querry, and he always knew what to do. It reassured Frolic as Tom shut the heavy, metal door and left them. If he followed Querry, Frolic knew he'd be all right.

"We don't have to stay here all the time," Querry said, stroking the back of Reg's and Frolic's heads. "We can go on deck and look at the sea whenever we like. It'll be beautiful. Think of it like a holiday." He pressed a kiss to each of their foreheads.

"A holiday?" Reg broke away from them and kicked the door. A metallic clang echoed through the small space.

"Reg, I thought you were onboard with this," Querry said cautiously. He reached for Reg's shoulder, but Reg shrugged his hand off.

"I didn't want this. You know I didn't. But it was either this or be left out again, left behind. I'm here now, and I don't intend to spend the entire journey complaining. Just don't expect me to pretend we're on holiday, either. All I want is to get through this and return somewhere I know we'll be safe."

"Reggie, I'm sorry," Frolic whispered. He'd hurt one of the people he loved most, and he hadn't even meant to. In the future, he'd make sure he didn't do anything to upset either of them if he could help it, but it was all so intricate: intentions, actions, reactions, and what provoked emotion. Sometimes the smallest things caused so much harm, and one could never predict when they would.

"Frolic, I don't—"

"You don't blame me. I know. You should. I wish you'd blame me."

"You blame me," Querry said in a voice thick with shame. "I don't know how many more times I can apologize."

"It doesn't matter," Reg said. "We're here. But, Querry, how long do you plan to carry on like this?"

"Like what?" Querry reached out for Reg, spreading his fingers within his shiny, black gloves.

For a long time, both Reg and Frolic stared at Querry's outstretched hand. Finally Reg took it and let himself be pulled against Querry. Querry folded his arms around him and buried his face in Reg's hair. "Tell me what you want."

Since the bunks were so narrow, they settled on the floor. Querry sat with his back against the damp, warped wood of the wall, and Reg settled between his legs with the back of his head against Querry's collarbone. Frolic nestled on his side, against Reggie's chest, enjoying the warm feeling of both of them toying with his curls.

Finally Reg answered Querry. "I want to be safe. I want to be free from worrying that everyone I love will be snatched away from me. God, I hate to sound like such a nonce, but you have to see reason. We won't be this young and fit forever. Honestly, can you picture us fighting our way through some jungle in our fifties, with our paunches, gray hair, and spectacles?"

"You already wear spectacles, Reg."

"Only for reading!"

"You'll still be beautiful to me," Querry said, "no matter how old and fat you become."

Though Querry and Reg chuckled at the absurd image, Frolic didn't. Querry and Reg were flesh; they'd grow old one day. They'd die. Nothing in the world could prevent it, not the most advanced machinery, not even magic. In less time than he'd spent waiting to be found in the doll maker's cellar, Querry and Reg would grow old and die. Frolic knew he'd be all alone again, just like the century he'd spent in the dark. He couldn't bear to think on it. He'd never survive without them; he didn't want to. The idea of facing the world without Querry and Reg by his side terrified him far more than oblivion.

"Frolic, beauty, what's wrong?" Reg said against the top of his head. "You're trembling."

In response, Frolic threw his head back, caught Reg's neck, and kissed him, then Querry. He wanted to forget.

EVEN AFTER they made love, Frolic couldn't sleep. He left the bunk the three of them had managed to squeeze into and quietly slipped into his clothes. The ship rocked back and forth as it made its way through the storm, stealing Frolic's balance as he moved into the hall beyond their room. Several times, he braced himself against the walls to keep from falling. The rain sounded like artillery fire against the decks above him as he wandered in the direction of the engine room. Before long, he opened a hatch and descended a metal ladder. It felt good to stand in the hot steam from the furnaces. The rhythmic pump and hiss of the engine, the motion of the crankshafts thrusting up and down, the flywheels spinning, and the gears turning soothed his mind. Unlike the weird language of the wind and sea he'd been able to perceive since Querry's faerie gentleman had resurrected him, these methodical sounds made sense to Frolic; he understood how it all worked, how the pieces came together and moved against one another to produce the power the ship needed. Magic made up half of him, but he couldn't begin to understand it as well. Machines were order, and magic unfathomable chaos.

Frolic meandered around the huge pistons, noting some ways to make the whole operation more efficient, when a small door caught his eye. Red-gold light spilled from beneath it, and the musical ping of a hammer against metal carried through from the other side. Frolic approached the metal portal apprehensively. He pushed the door open. It swung in without the rusty screech Frolic expected. Obviously someone had thought to oil the hinges. Frolic ventured into the chamber, toward the sound of the hammer. He found himself in a cluttered workshop dominated by an anvil and forge. Various gears and parts decorated the walls in an organized fashion. The metal glinted beautifully in the firelight.

A figure hunched over a heavy wooden workbench littered with bits of clockwork and items in various states of completion. Frolic hesitated. He watched the broad figure, silhouetted in the light of the lamp on the workbench, as he moved forward. A board creaked beneath his foot, and the person turned toward the sound.

"Who's there?" the figure asked. Frolic opened his mouth, but nothing came out. "Hello?" When the figure turned, Frolic could see her. She was plump, strong, with smooth, slightly tanned skin. She wore her strawberry hair in short pigtails that stood shockingly from her head. The strange woman wore a double-buttoned, leather waistcoat, modified goggles, and a complex tool belt. She still held her huge hammer in one hand, clearly ready to defend herself if she had to, and looking quite capable as well.

"Hello," Frolic whispered. "I'm Frolic."

"Cheers, Mr. Frolic." The woman relaxed, lowered the hammer, and smiled. "My name's Cornelia. In the employ of Lord Starling." She marched up and offered her hand. Frolic stared at the hand, unsure how to react to the unladylike gesture. He'd never really unraveled the complexities of interacting with women or understood why they should be treated differently, but he knew society imposed certain rules. He didn't want to misstep. His gaze traveled up to her warm expression and earnest smile. Frolic couldn't help but return the smile, and he shook her offered hand. Rough calluses covered Cornelia's palms.

Frolic felt a tad self-conscious. She studied him as she slowly pumped his hand. "Are you a faerie?" she asked.

"No." Frolic shook his head. *She thinks I'm lying*, Frolic thought. *I hope she doesn't start screaming. Maybe I should just go.* His fascination with the intricate items strewn over the bench, and with the woman who'd fashioned them, held him in place as she stared down at him.

"But there's something," Cornelia stated. She squinted at Frolic, still shaking his hand. "You're very pretty. A little too pretty, maybe."

"I'm—" Frolic paused, wondering if he should be honest with the odd girl. "I'm a—uh—well. I'm a clockwork. Kind of."

"Are you really?" she asked. She stretched Frolic's eyelid as she peered into his eye, still slowly shaking his hand. He started to feel slightly awkward and wondered how to politely reclaim his hand when she finally released it.

She circled Frolic excitedly, moving with more speed and frenetic energy than she seemed capable of at her size, lifting his arms, feeling his wrists, pinching and testing his skin. She flipped her goggles down and pulled Frolic's lips open, inspecting his teeth and mouth.

Her bizarrely magnified left eye made Frolic gasp. Normally he enjoyed being touched, loved being touched, but he didn't sense affection from her. Appreciation, maybe, but it felt rather degrading to be examined in such a manner. She had no right to press her sweaty fingers into his mouth.

Frolic grasped the young woman's wrist and pulled her hand from his mouth. He pushed her to arm's length and held her sturdy bones tight in his fist, knitting his brows as he looked into her light green eyes, one of them abnormally huge and detailed beneath her lens. "Just what do you think you're doing? Do you always stick your fingers down the throats of people you just met? Or do you think it's all right since I'm only a clockwork?"

Her round cheeks colored, and she stammered. "I—*only* a clockwork? Bloody hell you're strong. Look, I'm sorry. I—I didn't mean any offense. Sometimes I forget how to act around people, since I spend so much time on my own. It's just—you're *beautiful*. I've never even imagined anything— anyone—like you. I got carried away, and I apologize. Can we start again?"

Frolic released her arm and nodded. "Sorry. It's nice to meet you." He'd overreacted in a way he never would have before and almost hurt someone. Cornelia rubbed her wrist where he'd held it. But after a year of pursuit by people who saw him as nothing more than a tool or a weapon, who wanted to pick him apart without regards for his thoughts or feelings, self-preservation had become his instinctual response.

"The pleasure is all mine," she said, pushing the goggles back up over her hair. "Truly. But you are a marvel. If I might—that is, if you wouldn't mind—I'd love a closer look. Think of it like an apprentice artist admiring a painting."

He couldn't help but smile. Her respect felt sincere, and he noticed she tripped on her words when she grew nervous or excited. Still, she spoke well, more like Reg than Querry—

"You won't mind if I have a look at your work? Or bring some of mine down to see what you make of it?"

"No, not at all," she answered absently and retrieved an odd, cone-shaped implement from her table. "This is what they've given me as a temporary workspace on the voyage. It's not much, but I'll make do." She turned with the strange instrument, lifting Frolic's hair and poking it into Frolic's ear. "Hmm." She replaced the cone and grabbed a small, rubber mallet. "May I?" she asked.

"I suppose so," Frolic reluctantly agreed. No sooner had the words left his mouth than Cornelia had a stool hooked with her heavily booted foot, sliding it under his bum as she pushed him to a seated position. She laid her ear against Frolic's thigh and used the mallet to strike his knee. His foot jumped slightly.

"Fantastic," Cornelia whispered. She moved her ear to Frolic's bicep and struck his elbow. "First rate," she commented. Cornelia abandoned his arm and leaned into Frolic's chest. She used the mallet on Frolic's ribs, and he started giggling. She sprang up, smiling. "You're ticklish?" she asked, her eyes wide.

"Apparently," Frolic answered after catching his breath.

"Brilliant!" Cornelia exclaimed and placed her ear on Frolic's head. She struck his skull gently with the little mallet and squealed like a young girl. Frolic heard the metal of his skull resonating pleasantly. He smiled, never having noticed that before.

"You. Are. Amazing." Cornelia breathlessly enunciated each word and gathered Frolic into a powerful hug.

"Thank you." Frolic hugged her back. "You're not so bad yourself, Cornelia. I'm sorry we got off to a rough start."

"Corny," she said.

"Pardon me?"

"Corny. My friends call me Corny."

"Are we friends now?"

"I should say so! This trip is going to be brilliant. I'm so glad we've met, Frolic."

"I'm pretty fair at clockworks and mechanics, if you should need a hand," Frolic offered.

"Grand. I was just straightening the tooth on this sprocket." Corny held up the item from her workbench. "Want to help me install it in the engine?"

"Definitely," Frolic replied. Cornelia grabbed Frolic's hand and led him to the engine room.

Chapter 6

For the next week or so, it rained constantly. Querry could scarcely believe the world contained as much water as the ever-present clouds dumped on the ship. He'd spent the better part of that week sick as a dog, emptying the contents of his stomach over the railing. By midweek he'd decided to just stop eating, and he was annoyed neither Reg nor Frolic had the same trouble. He supposed Frolic couldn't get seasick, and Reg's adoptive parents had been able to afford a few sea voyages, giving Reg the advantage of having gotten used to the rocking of the boat. Querry had only ever been on one other boat, a huge, passenger steamship. Compared to this small vessel and the way it bobbed on the waves and pitched relentlessly from side to side, the steamship seemed as stable as dry land. Querry finally felt safe enough to try a bit of the hard bread from the galley. He sat picking small bits off and eating them as he pondered the ominous weather. It was as if the storm followed them, always overhead like an umbrella. No matter how hard the sporadic winds propelled them, how far they pushed the engines, or how many times they altered course, they couldn't break away from it. Querry swore he hadn't seen the sun since leaving Thalacea. For their entire voyage, they'd been suspended in a dank, dusk-like gloom.

A dark splotch spread across the ceiling of their cabin, where it leaked like an old faucet into a rusted metal pail. Everything reeked of dampness. The coarse sheets and blankets felt heavy and soggy when Querry, Reg, and Frolic got into bed. Querry's clothes seemed to cling to him, and some of the rivets of the outsides of his trousers started to rust. Worst of all, worse even than the seasickness, he felt restless. The weather kept them inside. Frolic spent time with the tinkerer, an awkward young woman with some brilliant theories about steamcraft and clockwork, but little charm or skill at conversation. Querry found Cornelia a little dull, but Frolic seemed content to work with her for silent hours on end. He worried about Reg. With little else to do, Reg slept much of the day, and when he wasn't dozing or just lying in his bunk half-dressed, he talked of their inevitable aging and even demise. Sometimes he spoke wistfully of his childhood, talking more to himself about what might have been, ignoring any response from Querry or Frolic. Nothing they said or did banished his melancholy. Frolic looked like he'd been slapped every time he failed to cheer their companion.

Now, they were sleeping face to face, their limbs twisted up beneath the sodden sheets, their foreheads pressed together. Querry bent and kissed each of them on the cheek. Frolic stirred, smiled, and puckered his lips as if to return the kiss, though his glorious eyes didn't open. Reg didn't move at all, even when Querry clutched his hair and tilted his head to look at his face. He swiped the back of his hand down Reg's cheek. Querry loved Reg so much, had loved him for almost all he could remember of his life, and he just wanted to soothe his dark mood. Querry wanted to appease his dear Frolic's confusion over his origins and purpose just as desperately, but he couldn't do that, either. Not finding a solution to something he wished to accomplish felt very novel to Querry. It was so easy just to take what he wanted, or beat down something opposing him. It had been so much simpler on his own, not that he'd ever trade those lonely, meaningless days for what he had with Reg and Frolic. Being powerless just left a sour taste in his mouth, even worse than the one left by his illness.

Querry pulled on his trousers, rumpled shirt, bracers, and boots. He didn't bother with a cravat or even a jacket; as wet and miserable as they all were, nobody cared about formality. He made his way to the deck, deserted except for the most essential crewmen. He crossed the saturated planks, ignoring the tepid droplets pelting him. He'd been trying for a week to speak to his mysterious patron. Something difficult to acquire only made Querry desire it more; he knew and accepted this about himself. Therefore, when he reached the door to Lord Starling's cabin, he didn't knock and wait to be turned away. He simply entered.

The aristocrat sat at his rolltop desk in nothing but a pair of loose, Auriental pants. A young, olive-skinned, Thalacean man, as perfect and beautiful as the statues his ancient ancestors cut from marble, reclined nude on the canopied bed. When Querry entered, the young man started, wrapped Starling's brocade coverlet around his waist, and hurried from the cabin. Querry knew his surprise showed on his face, but the baron remained unaffected. Tom Teezle sat on the floor in the corner, arranging some colored ribbons across his folded knee. When he saw Querry, he quickly balled them up and stuffed them in his waistcoat pocket.

"Mr. Knotte," Starling said, raising an empty glass.

"Please, call me Querry."

"Very well. Very well, Querry. Absinthe?"

Querry shrugged, compelled by sheer boredom to accept.

"Or can your stomach not take it?" Starling chided.

"I'm fine now, damn it." Querry almost growled. "And thirsty," he added defiantly.

Starling indicated a wooden chair in front of the desk, and Querry sat. Starling positioned the slotted spoons across the glasses, set a sugar cube on top of each one, and poured the chartreuse liqueur over them. He lit the cubes and let them burn for a moment, careful not to let the flame touch the alcohol in the goblets, before splashing some water over them and dousing the bluish fire. The liquid turned a milky, greenish white, and the baron slid a glass across the desk to Querry.

Lifting his cup, Starling asked, "To what shall we drink?"

Querry rolled his eyes. "Can't think of much to toast so far on this job, to tell the truth. Bit of a mucky mess, isn't it?"

He didn't know why, but Querry looked at Tom, sitting cross-legged in the corner. The fey showed him a satisfied smile, his green eyes glistening.

"Why not offer Tom a drink?" Querry asked, again unsure of his intentions. Tom's clever grin, beautiful in the way only a faerie could manage, made it worthwhile.

"If it pleases you," Starling said slowly, repeating the absinthe ritual a third time.

When he finished, Querry took the glass to Tom, kneeling to his level, and then deciding to sit on the floor in front of him with his back to the aristocrat. If unattached, Querry might have been quite captivated by Tom and probably even pursued him. "Cheers, Tom," he said, lifting his glass. Then, remembering something his gentleman had once said, he made a toast. "To the Endless Summer."

Genuine delight lit the small fey's face, multiplying his beauty, as he raised his glass. "The Endless Summer."

"Does it give you a feeling of power to dismiss me, Querry? To ignore me so blatantly?" Starling said in a flat voice.

"Does it give you a feeling of power to keep Tom as a servant?" Querry countered. As a barb, he added, "Do you feel superior by keeping him in bondage? Can't you find yourself loyal, willing followers? Maybe there's not much to inspire others to follow you, though."

"It would satisfy you if I got angry, if I retaliated, wouldn't it? I won't besmirch myself so."

"Arrogant prick," Querry muttered.

"I beg your pardon?"

"You heard me."

"Why the animosity all of a sudden, Mr.—Querry?"

"All of a sudden? You trapped me, us, into this mess. Just like I'm sure you snared poor Tom here. Go on, deny it."

"I will not. There is a long tradition of wizards taking fey servants. That's not why you hate me, though, is it? You hate the aristocracy, the rich."

"And why not? A few of you live off the suffering of thousands, and you couldn't care less." Querry downed his drink in three large gulps. It left his throat and nostrils burning. He wondered if his stomach could take it, though he'd never give Starling the satisfaction of knowing that. "You don't even care. You think it's your due, because of the silly title you inherited. Bollocks. I think I'll go. I'm sorry I wasted your time. Tom, I hope we'll speak again sometime."

Without waiting for a response from either of them, Querry stood, dropped his glass on Starling's desk, and left the cabin in a far fouler mood than he'd entered it. More rain greeted him outside, drenching his clothing in only a few minutes. Querry didn't care. He felt so confused. What had spurred his anger at Lord Starling? Sure, his oppression of Tom wasn't right, but why had it come out in such an uncontrollable current? Was it just Querry's boredom and frustration? He'd been so eager to find out more about his patron, but he'd spoiled it with his temper.

Damn it.

Querry shoved his hands into his trouser pockets and just stood on the deck, letting the rain soak him to his bones. How had he come to a point in his life where he found himself beneath the thumb of a self-important aristocrat? Had all his decisions led him here? Querry never puzzled over his choices; he simply did what he felt the moment dictated. So far it had served him, but now—

A sharp shove against his shoulder dragged Querry back to the present. He looked up to see one of the men in the mismatched military attire—one of the mercenaries, he wasn't a fool—glaring down at him.

"Outta my way, pretty boy," said the big man with the close-cropped, graying hair. His accent belayed a bit of the north of Anglica. His associates, two tall, lank men with dark hair and neat beards, obviously brothers, chuckled as they watched Querry through eyes squinted from decades of campaigns.

Querry reacted without thinking, as always. Almost on its own, his hand raised and shoved at the chest of a man half a foot taller and probably fifty pounds heavier than himself. "You have some sort of problem with me, mate?"

"Yeah, you might say that," the other man said. "You're a filthy sneak thief, ain't ya?"

"I've done what I had to," Querry said.

The three mercenaries traded grins, before their leader said, "Sad. Absolutely fucking sad, ain't it, lads? He thinks he's had such a rough life. Let me tell you something, boy. You ain't got no idea how hard life can be."

"You don't know me." Querry's voice rose as he drew his sword. "You've got less than no right to judge how I've lived my life."

"I know your type. Thinking you've had it so hard, using that to justify doing anything you want. You have no idea what hardship is, you whining brat. You've never seen war. I heard all about you, back in Halcyon, gamboling about with your grubby faerie mates. You're a traitor to your own kind. And don't think I don't know what you and your pretty little friends get up to when you're alone. So yeah, you might say I have a few small issues with you being here."

Words couldn't express Querry's anger. He lifted his blade and cut an *X* in the air before him, challenging the larger man with his eyes. He'd show the bastard how worthless he was while he knocked the teeth out of his smug mouth. How dare this prick insult Reggie and Frolic?

The big, bronzed mercenary threw his head back and laughed with his mouth open. "A feisty little piece of street trash, aren't we?"

"Shut your mouth and find out, if you've got the stones," Querry said.

One of the brothers slapped their commander's shoulder, and the mercenary leader grew serious as he drew a simple, sturdy sword of his own. He and Querry took a few steps back, raising and crossing their blades. The man thrust, and Querry parried. The rain beat down on them as they stared into each other's faces. Querry feigned an attack, waited for his opponent to block, and used the distraction to kick out with his right leg, sweeping the other's feet from beneath him and smiling as the larger man's backside smacked hard against the waterlogged wood of the deck.

Instead of pressing his advantage, Querry retreated a few feet, knowing it would insult and incense his adversary. This man might be a soldier, and a seasoned one, but Querry had fought for every scrap of sustenance since he'd been old enough to stand. He waited for the mercenary to get to his feet.

"A lucky strike," the man growled.

"Sure. If that makes you feel better."

With a roar, the big man rushed Querry, clearly planning to tackle him to the ground. While he didn't possess his enemy's bulk or raw strength, Querry was quick and agile. He stepped to the side at the last moment, and the other man pitched forward. Spinning on the ball of his foot, Querry moved behind him and kicked him hard in the bum, sending him sprawling on the deck. Some other sailors who'd been attracted by the noise cheered a little. Querry glowed as he waited for the prick to get up, so he could knock him down again.

"None of us are getting any younger," Querry taunted as his opponent pushed himself up on his hands and knees. "Especially not you, old man."

"You little son of a whore!"

"You think I don't know it? I'm not ashamed of what I am, what I've chosen to be. I'm bloody well better than you, after all. No matter who my mother was."

"We'll see." The mercenary raised his sword and brought it down in a sharp angle across Querry's waist.

Querry jumped backward just in time. He felt the current of air as the steel passed so close to his skin. Without thinking, he brought his foot between the other man's legs, hard. When his opponent crumpled to cradle his wounded goods, Querry circled around him and trapped his throat inside the crook of his arm.

"Tell me again how useless I am, you old tosser."

"Get your filthy hands off me, you dirty little, faerie-loving fa—"

Querry squeezed hard enough to strangle the hated insult. "As soon as you admit I've won. Go on, you toe-rag. Say the pretty boy, faerie-loving thief bested you. Be man enough to admit it."

"This isn't over. Mark my words."

"I'm shaking with fear," Querry said.

"You won't have time to shake, you little girl. You'll never see me coming."

"Really?" Querry tightened his grip on the other man's throat until he gagged and sputtered. "I dare you to try. Sneaking up on a thief isn't as easy as you might imagine, mate. And you'd be surprised at the nasty things I learned from my time with the fey. They almost make humans look civilized."

The mercenary's face purpled, and he went limp beneath Querry. Just as Querry prepared to release him, not wanting to cause actual harm, something strange happened.

The rain stopped abruptly. Querry had become so accustomed to the relentless rhythm of the downpour that he noticed its absence instantly. The squabble suddenly forgotten, he released his opponent in the wake of the weird silence. He stumbled back as the other man regained his breath and stood. The clouds retreated for a moment but returned immediately, doubling and congealing like the blood of the sky, the light that filtered through those bizarre clouds was oddly colored and unsettling. The waves tossing the ship stilled, and it stood motionless on calm waters. Querry barely felt balanced on the stable deck, as he'd become so familiarized with its rocking. He also noticed he wasn't nauseous at all anymore. Another feeling filled his stomach: dread.

"What the hell?" he muttered, with nothing but the distant call of sea birds to join him in breaking the silence.

Slowly, all of the crew came above to investigate the strange stillness. Laborers and sailors looked about, whispering in Thalacean, and pulling various religious talismans from beneath their shirts. Most of them, while submitting to the church, still held a firm belief in the old gods of their land, the gods of sunlight, thunder, and the sea. Of course the sailors revered Neptus in particular, and many of them called out to their patron god. The mariners tried desperately to get the ship moving. In some way Querry couldn't articulate, the odd, warm light glinting off the still, blue water disturbed him more than the perpetual rain had. He put his sword away in favor of the clockwork pistol Frolic had made him. As long as his arm from elbow to fingertips, the gun could fire a dozen times, reload automatically, and fire a dozen more. Looking down the thick barrel, Querry scanned around. He found no target, of course, only confused sailors standing beneath a calm, yet overcast sky. Why did it feel so wrong?

"Get down to the engine room," a man, maybe the first mate, said as he moved toward the hatch. Half a dozen men hurried to obey. "I want all the power we can squeeze out of this tub. The rest of you, hoist the sails."

"But's there's no wind, sir."

"Do what I say, damn it."

As they unfurled the canvas, Tom Teezle emerged from Lord Starling's cabin. Unlike everyone else, he seemed calm, maybe a little amused.

"What's going on, Tom?" Querry asked, hoping the fragile bond they'd formed earlier might yield something.

The faerie cocked his head, and his eyes narrowed at Querry. "Don't you have the sight? I thought for sure *someone* had kissed your eyes. Was I wrong?"

"No, but I can't always use it. It comes and goes."

"You should work on that," Tom said. "Now would be a very good time to start."

"What do you mean?" Querry grasped Tom's slender shoulder and stepped closer, almost bumping into his chest.

The fey raised his fine, golden eyebrows and smiled suggestively. "I must be very careful what I say, even down to the words I choose. You understand."

Querry looked past him to see Starling in the doorway, leaning against the frame with nothing but a formal, black, tailed coat, lined with red satin covering his bare torso. Though very decadent with his billowy trousers, it almost matched. He glared at his servant.

Tom spun on the ball of his foot. "Is there something you require, my lord?"

"An explanation, Tom. Why have we stopped?"

"You wish for me to tell you right now, sir?"

"Obviously," Starling snapped. "Speak."

"Very well. If that's what you want." Tom couldn't keep the delight from spilling out in his tone any more than the clouds could hold in the rain.

"The others, my people, are trying to impede you. You well knew they would."

"What the hell? Do you mean faeries are trying to stop us? And you knew they would? You knew, and didn't say anything to the rest of us? Damn it, you let me bring Reg and Frolic into something like this?" Querry stalked past Tom and seized Starling's lapel with the hand not clutching desperately to his gun.

"Take your hands off me, Querry."

"No! Not until you explain exactly—"

"No, now." Starling flicked his wrist, and an invisible force knocked Querry back. He stumbled to stay on his feet as his boots skidded across the deck. "Don't ever lay your hands on me again. Understood?"

"Don't order me around like a child, Starling! That magic doesn't make you invincible."

"Your contract does, at least in this case. Cause me harm or hinder me, and you and your clockwork friend will perish."

Querry curled his lips and prepared a retort, but he never got to voice it. Reg, Frolic, and Cornelia burst from the hatch.

"Somebody, do something!" the tinkerer yelled, waving a wrench almost the size of an oar. "They're destroying the engines."

"Who?" Starling demanded.

Her face reddened, and she stuttered. "I—them—those men. The sailors. They'll tear everything to pieces. Bloody, bloody hell!"

"Somebody stop them!" Starling hollered. "You men! Get down there and find out the meaning of this."

None of the crewmen moved. Most of them stood looking over the rails, out to sea, as if transfixed. No matter how much the baron blustered, they wouldn't stir, not even when he shook them or slapped their faces. Horrible sounds, banging, screeching, and grinding came from below. Soon, black smoke poured from the hatch. The steady sound of the engine grew irregular and then stopped.

Cornelia covered her face with her big hands. "Oh, those beautiful engines. Damn it all. I'll stop them myself." She lumbered toward the portal but stopped suddenly. "What is that music? Oh, isn't it lovely? Isn't it just the loveliest thing you ever heard?" She swayed to the tempo of her private serenade, her eyes glazing over. The enormous wrench clattered against the deck. Just then, one of the sailors climbed up on the rail, spread his arms, and leapt overboard with a joyous whoop.

Frolic turned to Tom. "Are you doing this?"

"Why would you think that?" The fey looked little more interested than if he watched the men swabbing the deck or adjusting the riggings.

"I saw one of you make people destroy something once," Frolic said, his eyes on his boots. "Is that what you're doing? Can you do that?"

"Well, had I the freedom to do so, I certainly *could*. That isn't to say I would, or I am—"

"Tom, come with me," Starling snapped. "Be ready. We have to save the engines by any means necessary. They're crucial to our mission. You and I will stop those men." He caught the fey by the elbow and dragged him toward the ladder leading below.

Querry swore. He looked around for a place to send Reg and Frolic, a place they'd be safe. Two more men dove into the sea, while a group of others tore at the sails and managed to shred their edges with their bare hands.

"Stay here," Querry said to his friends. Frolic bobbed his head, his small hand on the hilt of his sword. Reg, though, stared off at the horizon, his gentle, hazel eyes unfocused as he hummed softly to himself. "Watch him," Querry told Frolic. "Don't let him go off under any circumstances."

Frolic nodded his understanding and grasped Reg's hand. Querry ran to the starboard side of the ship and looked into the sea. He saw nothing but calm water, eerily calm, like a sheet of blue glass. He heard another splash, probably another sailor jumping into the surf. Somewhere, at the very edges of his perception, Querry felt the resonance of the music, though he couldn't hear it exactly. He felt it in his guts, in his bones, the vibration moving rhythmically through his body, creating a sensation akin to arousal and making him desperate for more. Down there, in the water, he'd find it. He needed to get down there. Nothing else mattered—

No! I've dealt with this before. My gentleman always made me feel this way, but I resisted him. Mostly. I can resist now. Nobody and nothing tells me what to do, damn it. He shook his head. He had to figure out what the hell was going on, so he'd know how to protect Reg and Frolic. Behind him, Reg screamed, and Frolic said soothing words Querry couldn't quite make out amidst the cacophony. Something on the deck caught fire, and some of the men brawled, others skipped, danced, and twirled around, while still others sought bliss and oblivion in the watery depths.

Querry drew a shattered breath and fumbled around for the gift his gentleman had left him. Something shook loose in his mind. He felt satisfied, as if he'd heard a lock click open. His vision changed, going blurry for a second before becoming excruciatingly clear. He saw the grain in the wood, every scuff on the deck, every fiber in the ropes. Gossamer, glowing threads of magic lay over the ship like a delicate net. Some of the bluish-white ribbons wrapped around the sailors, while others spiraled chaotically into, or maybe out of, the sea and sky. When he looked out across the water, Querry saw them: lithe, androgynous creatures with milky skin, bright eyes, and blue and green hair that lay across the surface of the ocean in intricate loops and curls. Their otherworldly beauty just made Querry want to reach them more, but he stamped the strong desire down. He saw at least a dozen of the beings on the starboard side alone.

"Let go of me, Frolic! I don't want to stay with you anymore. Why are you keeping me from being happy? You and Querry never give a damn about what I want. You're selfish. Let me go!"

"No, Reggie. You don't mean it."

Querry turned and sprinted across the deck, past the scuffling sailors, past the burning main mast, to where Frolic stood behind Reg, holding Reg's wrists behind his back.

"Frolic! Can you see it?" Chords of magic twined around Reg's limbs like creeping vines, moving over his body, wrapping around him until they nearly covered every inch of his skin. Querry drew his sword and swiped at them, but of course it did no good. He had an idea.

"It's everywhere, Querry," Frolic cried, clearly straining to keep hold of Reg. "We're in trouble, aren't we?"

"They haven't got us yet, beauty. Use your sword. Cut Reggie free."

"Are you sure?"

"Absolutely," Querry lied. Frolic's blade held some sort of enchantment. It chimed musically when he wielded it, and Querry often wondered if it was faerie-made. Something told him this would work, but he held his breath as Frolic released Reg and drew his weapon. As soon as he got free, Reg bolted for the railing. Querry dove, tackled him, and drove the wind from him as they hit the deck. Reg thrashed and swore, but Querry held him firmly as Frolic swung at the magical bonds. At first nothing happened, and Querry felt an encroaching despair. Then, slowly, the arcane fibers pulled apart where Frolic's sword passed through them and disintegrated, leaving behind only some sparkles, which soon dissipated into the ether. Querry exhaled.

Reg gasped, and his eyes darted back and forth as if he'd woken up in a strange and unexpected place. Querry kissed him hard, not caring who saw, and pushed the sweaty fringe out of his eyes.

"Reggie, just stay down. Please," Querry said.

"But—what's going on? I feel like I've been in the brandy—" Reg's gaze searched the deck. "It's the song, isn't it? It's driving us all mad."

"Reg, I need you to trust me. Stay here. Do you understand?"

"All right, Querry." Though he agreed, Reg didn't look happy. "But we have to block the music or it will take me again!"

Querry didn't have time to comfort him; he'd make it up to him later. He stood, looking for Frolic, ready to tell Frolic to use his weapon on the rest of the mystic threads. Frolic knew what to do. Before Querry could say a word, Frolic ran to the nearest sailor and lifted his blade. Men returned to lucidity as he cut them free. Reg, wool stuffed in his ears, followed Frolic with a sack of the fluffy white material stamped with the logo of a Libertanian trading company, helping the freed sailors. Briefly, Querry decided they'd found it in the storeroom along with the other goods Starling carried as chattel, to trade for supplies when they reached their destination. The crew was lucky his friends thought so quickly. Still, the sea faeries—Querry could comprehend them no other way—continued to weave their enchantment, replacing the shimmering ribbons faster than Frolic could sever them. The threads shifted from serene blue to angry, pulsing red.

One sailor, tangled in the malign enchantment, turned to Querry and smiled. That smile held madness and hunger. A growl grew faintly in the man's throat until he launched himself into the air at one of the crew members protected with cotton. To Querry's surprise and disgust, the ensorcelled man bit into the flesh of his shipmate, clawing at the protective material in the man's ears. The wool dislodged, and the second sailor screeched and clawed his way from his attacker, turning on another sailor. Querry knew magic came as naturally to fey as breath; they wouldn't tire out or run dry of sorcery. They had to be stopped before the crew tore each other to pieces.

Aiming his weapon and looking down the sights, Querry prepared to fire. He hated the idea of harming the beautiful creatures; fey had always treated him with more esteem than his human brethren. They respected craft, and a pleasing appearance, over wealth and titles. Querry couldn't take the shot. Despite the carnage blossoming on the deck behind him, he couldn't make his finger pull the trigger.

From the corner of his eye, Querry watched Frolic run and dive on the tinkerer, Cornelia. Frolic pinned her large form beneath his small body as he cut the chords surrounding her, while Reg wadded wool into her ears. When she came back to herself, she pressed Frolic's face against her ample bosom and kissed the top of his head. Both of them giggled. Then she stood, found her wrench, and looked about for something to pummel. She didn't have to look too long. One of the feral members of the crew lunged at her. She just managed to get her wrench up, preventing the madman from tearing out her throat. Cornelia batted the man away, striking him in the side of the head, and he fell unconscious. Reg tossed her the bag of wool, and she assumed his duties assisting Frolic, swatting the possessed away from them with ease.

Despite Querry's warning, Reg came and stood beside him, their shoulders touching, as Reg held his augmented pistols. Querry couldn't help being reassured at Reg's presence.

"What the hell are we shooting at?" Reg shouted over the noise.

"I told you to stay down."

"Since when are you in charge, Querry?"

"Since— Oh hell."

"Right. What am I shooting at?"

"I don't know." Querry lied to his partner, lied to someone who loved and trusted him for the second time in less than an hour.

"Querry?" Reg suspected; he knew Querry too well.

"I don't want to hurt the faeries, Reg."

"For the love of God, why not? Do you see what's happening here? People are dying because of them."

Querry couldn't answer. He looked at the lovely beings bobbing in the water, their smooth, lithe, upper bodies exposed, glistening with sea-spray. They belonged there, maybe, probably, more than the men aboard the ship. He didn't know why the sea fey impeded them, but perhaps they had legitimate reason. Should he trust them any less than Lord Starling? He wondered if his association with his gentleman would hold any water with the creatures surrounding the ship. As absurd as he knew it would sound to Reg or anyone else, Querry wished he could just speak with those faeries. His instinct for self-preservation clashed hard against his fondness for beings who'd treated him equitably, valued him when no one else did, and he didn't know which to choose.

He didn't get to decide. The mercenary leader Querry had quarreled with before, newly freed by Frolic and protected by Cornelia, joined them at the railing. The big man slipped some thick goggles over his eyes and lifted a huge, clockwork rifle to his shoulder. He took his shot, and Querry watched in horror as his bullet ripped through the chest of a gorgeous, male water fey. With a high-pitched shriek, the creature exploded in a spray of briny water. Querry tried to believe the fish-like man wasn't dead, just returned to his element.

"Haha! Take that, you bastards!" The mercenary shot at and vanquished another of the beings. Then he called out to his men. "Lads! Use the special lenses. And the iron bullets. Be quick. Move!"

The dark-haired brothers obeyed with the speed of any trained soldier, donning their eyewear and lifting their guns. Querry knew he couldn't stop them, as much as he wanted to. After a few more casualties, the ocean faeries opened their mouths impossibly wide, a discordant tone bellowing forth. The few sailors Frolic hadn't managed to liberate turned on the mercenaries. The unenchanted men grabbed pails to douse the fire on the main mast, while a few others tried to help the mercenaries. Querry noticed a couple of the men vomiting the blood and flesh of their shipmates onto the deck, and the bile rose in his throat.

Still, that single, bizarre note from the water fey drifted on the still air. Thunder clapped above, the air around the ship grew close and stifling. The mercenaries and the sailors, with Frolic and Cornelia, had managed to free the last few men who remained under the influence of the fey-song. Querry and Reg watched the scene unfold as the song swelled to an earsplitting pitch. The mercenaries retrieved their weapons, but even with the wool in their ears, their hands went to the sides of their heads, trying to block out the tone. Querry, Reg, and Cornelia did the same. Out of everyone, only Frolic remained upright and unaffected. He turned and shouted at his companions. Querry saw Frolic's mouth move, saw the horror in his eyes, but heard nothing but the ceaseless echo of that one, wavering note. Frolic's hand drifted up, pointing at something. Abruptly the song, like the rain, stopped.

"Querry, Reg," Frolic called. "You might want to have a look at this!" They immediately ran to the railing next to their love and sought out the object of the terror in Frolic's eyes.

"Dear God," Reg gasped, his hand going to his mouth.

CHAPTER 7

BEFORE QUERRY saw what Reg and Frolic were seeing, he looked at the sea fey. They all wore almost identical smirks. His gaze drifted up from them, focusing on a point just before the horizon. "That can't be good," he said, watching the spot of churning water in an otherwise calm sea headed straight for them. A strange, spiked fin crested the water, cutting a path directly to the ship.

"What is it?" The gray-haired mercenary asked. A crowd had gathered at the port railing. The water roiled around whatever it was. The beast rose slowly out of the salty, foaming water.

"Nothin' I've ever seen," answered an old sailor with a deep scar across the bridge of his nose.

"It's the devil," someone else offered as two vacant orbs as black as the void emerged above the waves it created. Something like giant sea snakes writhed in the wake the monster left behind.

No, Querry thought. *Not snakes, tentacles.* The sea fey bobbed on waves created by the rings preceding the beast's approach.

"To the cannons!" ordered the man Querry thought of as the first mate, finally breaking the spell of the monstrosity. Immediately men dashed about the deck, readying the portside cannons.

"It's not going to be enough," Cornelia murmured in awe. "I'll be back in a tick." She dashed to the portal leading to the hold and disappeared.

The ship rocked on the waves the creature created. The sea fey parted to make way for the beast they'd summoned. Its mouth rose into view, awful to behold, filled with strangely angled fangs at irregular intervals. The eyes blinked with two sets of eyelids, one set moving vertically, the other horizontally over those fathomless black orbs. Querry saw death in those globes, cold and indiscriminate.

"To arms, boys," the oldest mercenary barked, and his men knelt at the railing, pointing their guns and rifles at the beast. Querry and Reg exchanged a glance and did the same, using the rail to steady their weapons, though it did no good. The entire ship nodded on the now churning waters.

Odd light glinted off the scales of the monster, reminding Querry of the peacocks he'd once seen in a nobleman's menagerie back home. "It's not slowing down," he pointed out.

"It's going to ram us?" Reg asked. It suddenly occurred to Querry that this might not be the best place to be when those teeth reached the ship. He opened his mouth to tell the others, but the first mate gave the order to fire the cannons, and the world erupted around him. The mercenaries followed suit, firing at the beast.

The creature bellowed and rose out of the waves, launching itself at the ship. Querry saw the enormous beast in its entirety. Its huge mouth gaped hungrily. The body was that of some kind of abominable fish with scales and mean, spiky fins. Instead of a tail, the beast had a fan of tentacles that propelled it along. On either side of the creature's corpse-white belly were two sets of frog-like legs, the webbed feet ending in evil talons. The claws of the monster's front legs looked disturbingly similar to human hands.

The bullets had very little effect, and the few cannonballs that actually hit the beast did only slightly more damage. One or two of the tentacles were severed. Still, the abomination didn't slow, and one more leap would allow it to reach the ship. "Scatter!" Querry screamed, and to his surprise, nearly everyone listened to him. The few men who didn't were impaled by those nasty, crooked fangs.

The beast slid back into the ocean with the rock of the boat, though they felt it passing under the hull. "The guns aren't doing anything," Reg yelled as he leaned toward Querry.

"I noticed." Querry stowed his pistol and pulled out his sword. Reg did the same as Frolic joined them, the three of them standing shoulder to shoulder.

"What can we do against that thing?" Frolic asked.

"I don't know," Querry answered honestly. He couldn't bring himself to offer false assurances. They jumped back as the beast's giant claw landed on the deck, scratching into the boards as it dragged itself partially onto the ship. Its tentacles whipped around chaotically, smacking men around, coiling around them, crushing them. Most of the sailors dashed about trying to avoid the beast. The mercenaries, armed with blades, flanked the beast's arm.

A tentacle swept toward Querry, and he lashed out with his sword, slicing the appendage off. Black blood spattered across the boards of the deck. The creature roared and grabbed at Querry with the hand that wasn't holding it on the ship. Frolic leaped in front of his lover and lashed out with his magic blade, impaling the webbed hand. Frolic planted his feet, and when the beast pulled its hand back, it only succeeded in tearing its own flesh. More dark blood poured down Frolic's blade and coated his hands and arms.

"Heave!"

Querry's attention was drawn to the mercenaries.

Two of the men held blades over their heads, while the others lit the fuses of grenades. "Ho!" the leader shouted. Their blades flashed through the air, chopping at the beast's wrist, severing the hand. The loosed grenades exploded in the mouth of the monster as it dropped back into the sea. The mercenaries whooped with triumph, laughing and congratulating each other with slaps to the back.

The ship lurched, knocking everyone off balance as the beast leapt out of the boiling surf, its cadaver-white belly landing on the deck. Water poured over the rails as the ship dipped with the extra weight, close to capsizing. The tentacles crawled relentlessly toward the crew members. An angry war cry rent the air, and Querry turned in time to see Frolic leaping onto the face of the beast before plunging his enchanted blade into the monster's eye. Sickening, thick yellow liquid fountained out of the ruined sphere, knocking Frolic back to the ship.

The beast cried and flopped on the deck. Querry and Reg both hacked at the tentacles that came too close. It seemed as though each one they severed spawned two more. "This is getting us nowhere," Reg yelled.

"I'm open to suggestions!" Querry answered.

"Where's Frolic?"

"He's on the other side of the beast." Querry could see him hacking away at the tentacles as well, the monster's black blood splashing his fair skin and coating him in tar-like grime. "He's fighting like a man possessed."

The mercenaries were engaged similarly. One of the brothers lit another round of grenades. Before he could finish, the beast swept its abbreviated arm, knocking back the entire party of attackers, including Querry, Frolic, and Reg.

Querry slid across the deck, crashing into the starboard rail. He shook his head and looked up to see a flaming projectile lodge itself in the beast's scaly hide. Querry followed the smoke trail to Cornelia, standing with some sort of clockwork backpack. A copper tube the size of a small tree was attached to the apparatus, and she held it against her shoulder like a rifle. The projectile exploded, and the beast screeched, its ragged jaws snapping. The damage remained superficial, and the monster turned its attention to the defiant girl on the deck.

"Cornelia!" Frolic called to his newest friend. She fired another of the smoldering grenade-arrows. This one arched right into the beast's mouth. Querry suddenly had an idea. The monster's mouth snapped down on the incendiary object and muffled the ensuing explosion. When the beast opened its gaping maw again, smoke billowed out. Querry ran to Cornelia's side.

"How are you at aiming that thing?" he asked.

"Fair enough. I designed it myself, Mr. Knotte."

"Good." Querry patted her shoulder. "You'll know when to fire," he told her and dashed across the deck, avoiding the monster's tentacles. On his way, he scooped up a bit of fishing net. He reached his goal: three barrels of lamp oil lashed to the stern rail. He sliced the rope, and the barrels rolled free with the rocking of the ship. He tried to catch them all with the net but only managed two. Querry dragged the net with barrels back toward the beast, making no attempt to avoid the monster's tentacles. This was their only chance. If they didn't kill or drive the thing off soon, its weight alone would drag the ship to the bottom of the sea.

Querry's gamble paid off, and the beast swept him up, barrels and all, tossing him toward its mouth. Querry pulled out his grapple gun in midair, and fired. He thanked whatever deities might exist Frolic had found time to repair it. The grapple bit into the fin on the beast's back, and he reeled himself over the monster's mouth and onto its face, between its good and ruined eye. He released the grapple and pulled out his sword, stabbing it into one barrel then the other. Lamp oil spilled over the monster's face, and he gave Cornelia a high sign before diving off the beast. Seconds later, the grenade-arrow stuck fast in the monster's forehead as Querry rolled into his landing.

The grenade exploded, and the lamp oil burst into flames, coaxing strangled cries from the creature's throat as its flesh bubbled and cracked. The foul beast thrashed about the deck, splintering rails and booms, shredding sails. Finally, with one last, trumpeting bellow, the beast retreated into the sea.

The clouds dissipated with the disappearance of the creature. At some point the sea fey had departed as well.

Querry rose, cradling his shoulder, searching for Frolic and Reg. Frolic sat on the deck, covered in ichor but unscathed. Cornelia had run to check on him and now held his head in her lap. Reg lay just out of reach near the bow. Querry limped over.

"Are you all right, Reg?" Querry asked.

"Aside from having no idea what just happened, I suppose so." Reg rose, shakily.

"Fuck," Querry whispered. He grabbed the front of Reg's shirt and pulled him close, trembling as he wove his arms around Reg, just like the faerie magic had. He squeezed, feeling Reg's bones crack and grind under the pressure. He couldn't let go. Reg's scent aroused him as he buried his face in Reg's blond hair. Querry's body tingled with awareness, still ready to fight, still acute. It turned him on, made him seek an outlet for his energy, but his guilt and shame squelched it. He'd put his partner in such danger and barely managed to save him. He didn't deserve Reg's devotion.

"I'm sorry."

"Querry?"

"God, Reg. I love you so much."

"I love you too, Querry, but we should talk later, in private. Where's Frolic?"

Both of them turned, pulling away from one another, to see Frolic sheathing his blade as he crossed the deck. He looked shaken to his core, his golden eyes wide and wondering, and his sweet, swollen little lips turned down. Viscous black fluid clung to his skin and dripped from his curls. It saturated his clothing, reeking of rotted fish. He stopped a few feet short of Querry and Reg.

"What have we done?" Frolic whispered. "Why did we do this?"

Querry reached for him, but for the first time ever, Frolic didn't rush into his embrace. He just stood chewing his lip and said, "I felt like I was on the wrong side. Those creatures didn't deserve to die. If we'd have left them alone, they never would have summoned that thing."

"How can you say that?" Reg asked in a loud voice.

Frolic flinched. "Reg—what if they were right to try to stop us? We don't even know what we're doing."

"And who's to blame for that?" Reg snapped.

Querry's pulse raced. Anger replaced the hundred other conflicting emotions he experienced. His rage relieved his misunderstanding and felt almost like a reprieve. Here was something he understood. He'd been deceived, and the people he loved had been placed in danger. "I don't know who's at fault here. But I've an idea, and I'm bloody well going to find out. Wait here. I need to have a chat with our revered Lord Starling. I noticed he wasn't anywhere near the deck during that entire encounter! Yellow-bellied sod."

He strode toward the hatch, but Reg caught his arm. "You aren't going alone. I have some questions too."

"So do I," Frolic said, lifting his chin defiantly. "I'll have answers. I don't like what just happened, and I'll make him tell me why it did if I have to."

Querry nodded, glad for the support of his fellows as he descended into the smoke-filled hold in search of his employer. The time had come and then some for him to know what he and his companions really faced.

Chapter 8

REG, QUERRY, and Frolic found Lord Starling and Tom Teezle in the engine room, among stacks of smoking debris. Bent gears littered the floor, and steam hissed in spurts from damaged pipes. The intricate circuits of wheels and pistons that powered the ship stood still and silent. The furnace still burned, and the wizard and fey stood backlit by the red glow.

"You son of a bitch," Querry said, tensing, fists knotted tight, ready to lunge at Lord Starling.

Reg caught his friend's elbow. "Let's just hear what he has to say. Maybe it won't come to violence." Reg didn't add that if the baron didn't provide satisfactory answers to their questions, for once, he'd certainly advocate the use of a little force. This man had deceived them, and he'd put the people Reg loved in danger. Reg considered himself a patient and tolerant man, a man who valued reason over conflict, but he wouldn't abide anyone threatening Querry or Frolic.

Starling turned. "What is it?" he asked irritably. "Surely even the three of you are astute enough to see I have much to deal with at the moment."

"It will have to wait." Reg stepped in front of Querry and Frolic. "You owe us some explanations."

"I owe you nothing, Mr. Whitney. You have no right to demand anything of me. In fact, I don't recall ever requesting your presence here."

Reg struggled to control his outrage and keep his voice a polite volume. "That is beside the point, sir. I am here, and none of us, including you, have any way to leave, especially now. The secrets you've chosen to keep have cost several people their lives already. I simply cannot let the same thing happen to my friends. I will not, sir. One way or another, you will answer our questions. Remember, sir, you hold no contract over me. I remain free to act as I deem appropriate."

"Is that a threat?" Starling, instead of seeming offended, looked amused and a little in awe of Reg.

Reg resisted the compulsion to chew his thumbnail. He didn't want Starling to see his uncertainty. "I'm not threatening you, sir. I am simply stating a fact and hoping you'll behave like a gentleman and provide us the information we need to protect ourselves."

"Very well," Starling said. "You've convinced me. Let's go up to my cabin and discuss it over a bottle of wine or two."

"Wine?" Querry pushed past Reg and lifted his hands as if he'd choke the life out of the aristocrat, stopping himself only inches from Starling's throat. "Unlike you, we're bruised and covered in blood. And we're the lucky ones. Do you really think this is the time for a friendly drink?"

Starling shrugged. "What's done is done. It won't be undone whether I drink wine, water, gin, or nothing at all. Therefore, I'll drink wine. If you wish to have a conversation with me, you'll come to my cabin and accept my hospitality with some semblance of civility 'like a gentleman'." Starling smirked as he threw Reg's words back at them. "Oh, and do clean up a bit first. The smell is most disagreeable. Come along, Tom."

Querry ground his teeth audibly and trembled with rage as the baron, barely a smudge on his scandalous excuse for attire, strolled past them and climbed the ladder.

"What a strange man," Frolic said softly. "We need to be careful around him. His magic is very strong. I'm not sure even he can control it all the time. It spikes up when he's angry, so be careful what you say, Querry."

"I'm not afraid of that self-important bastard," Querry said.

"Nevertheless, it's sound advice, Querry." Reg almost felt the anger pumping through Querry when he touched Querry's shoulder. Reg knew Querry had no time to play by the rules of polite society. He knew his old friend didn't like such regulations, and certainly didn't like being bested. Querry liked having his hands tied least of all. Reg also knew Querry wanted to scream. He could practically hear his partner's thoughts: they'd just defeated a sea monster, a creature of mythic proportions, but they had to defer to a mere mortal. Though Reg didn't know where it came from or why he said it, he leaned in and whispered, "You can work off all your frustration soon, love. For the moment, let's find out what we need to know."

Frolic giggled and bounced on the balls of his feet. Querry turned to Reg, grinned, and ran the tip of his tongue over the edge of his teeth. "Be careful what you offer," he said in a low, gravelly voice that sent a shiver straight down Reg's spine to the root of his body. "I have a lot of frustration to work out after today."

"Luckily there are two of us," Frolic said. "But if both of you don't stop licking your mouths and chewing on your lips that way, I'm afraid we won't make it above deck."

Reg laughed, even though he knew how ridiculous and inappropriate it was to feel happy in that moment, after everything he'd seen and the danger he and his companions still faced. Maybe that was all the more reason to snatch up any moment of joy he could. He grabbed Querry and Frolic's hands, lifted them, and pressed a kiss to each of their palms. Frolic's remained soft and smooth despite the mechanical work he did. Little bloody crescents decorated Querry's rough skin where his nails bit down, probably while he'd listened to Starling imply his ignorance. The three of them stood smiling at each other like awkward children for a few minutes before climbing the ladder.

The sun still shined bright enough to make them squint as they emerged, but without the dazzling brilliance of before. The sky, while clear, didn't seem the blinding sapphire it had. Reg felt a twinge as he realized the world seemed less alive, somehow muted. He'd never felt such overwhelming desire as he had when he'd heard the faerie song. He remembered what he'd said to Frolic, and that he hadn't apologized. Later, he'd explain he hadn't been himself and hope his lovers understood.

The sailors bustled around the deck, replacing damaged ropes, pulling the sails down for mending, and clearing away debris. Some of them stared out across the water in silence, while others sat crying softly for lost friends and companions. Fans of foul, sticky blood like pitch sizzled under the hot sun as sailors with pails and mops hurried to swab them off. The trio of mercenaries who'd aided them cleaned their guns. Some other clockwork gear sat around them. Their leader looked up from his work to curl his lip at the three of them as they passed. They found one of the few pails of water not needed to douse the flames leftover from the battle and splashed the warm liquid over their faces and arms, washing as best they could.

"I can't stand this disgusting odor." Frolic slid his bracers down his arms, untied the ribbon around his neck, and flung it, along with his ink-soaked shirt, into the sea. Then he wet his hands and scrubbed at the ichor clinging to his slight body. He managed to wash most of it away, but a lock of his hair, just one ringlet on the left side of his face, between his eyebrow and his ear, remained stained as black as coal, in stark contrast to the rest of the silvery white waves.

Reg reached out to touch the ink-soaked lock, but something stopped him, and he let his hand fall on Frolic's bare shoulder. The three of them stood together, looking across the deck at Starling's closed door.

"Let's get this over with," Reg said.

THE INSIDE of Starling's luxurious cabin felt like another world. Reg swore he'd found himself back in Halcyon, in a gentleman's study after a dinner party. He expected someone to hand him a glass of single malt and maybe a cigar. Instead, Tom Teezle indicated a chair and an ottoman in front of Starling's cluttered desk. Reg sat in the chair while Querry and Frolic squeezed onto the bench. The baron took a dusty bottle from a drawer and served the golden wine in his fine, antique-looking, but mismatched glasses. Meanwhile, Tom offered them all a variety of cheeses, chocolates, and dried fruit from a tray.

"This is ridiculous," Querry said after he downed his wine, wasting the fine, complex vintage as he always did. For once, Reg couldn't blame him.

"No thank you," Frolic said as he offered Tom a smile. "In fact, why don't you have my share?"

"I am only serving the food," Tom told him. "I didn't prepare it, nor does it come from my people, so you need not be afraid."

"I'm not afraid," Frolic said. "Anyone can see there's no glamour at work on it."

His words caught Starling's attention. The baron's head snapped up. "Anyone could see that, you say. You are mistaken. Very few people can see such things. I myself cannot see them. Yet you can. How is that, Frolic?"

"Don't answer him," Querry said. "It's none of his business."

"I don't see the harm," Frolic said.

"No, I agree with Querry," Reg said quickly. He didn't trust Starling to know Frolic's workings, his vulnerabilities. "That is not our purpose here. We should not stray from our focus."

"What exactly would you like to know, Mr. Whitney?"

"Let's begin with our most recent encounter. Help me to understand it."

Starling swirled his wine in his glass, sniffed it, took a small sip, and closed his eyes with pleasure. For many minutes the liquid in his mouth occupied all his attention. Finally, he swallowed and said, "I don't know what you fail to grasp, Mr. Whitney. We were attacked, and luckily we were victorious, though the ship suffered heavy damage, damage that will likely add days or even weeks to our journey. It is unfortunate, but we're sailing through some very remote waters, and it is hard to know what to expect."

"That's not true," Querry said. "You were expecting them. You knew we'd be attacked eventually, by the fey. They were fey, weren't they? Different than fey like Tom and my—" Querry caught himself, apparently remembering how much Reg hated it when he called his former patron by the possessive. "—the gentleman I worked with back in Halcyon. But they felt Other."

Surprisingly, not Starling or Tom, but Frolic answered him. "You're right. They were fey. I understood the words of their song, just like I understood the gentleman and Kristof when they whispered to each other at night. They used the same words as the wind and the sea."

"My God," Starling said. "You understand their language? That's astonishing!"

"They've been begging us, warning us to turn around since we set out," Frolic said. "Tom, you must hear it too."

"Yes."

"Oh, Frolic," Reg said, his heart breaking for the understanding imposed upon his friend, an understanding Frolic didn't want and found very disturbing. "We should have listened to you."

"How could we?" Querry asked. "We have no choice but to be here."

"Unfortunately." Reg sipped his smooth, beautifully balanced, oak-mellowed wine. Even now, he could appreciate the nuances of the Belvaisian blend. "But we must find out what's going on so we can properly prepare ourselves. Am I wrong in thinking this is likely to happen again?"

"No," Frolic said.

"I want to know why," Querry said, his voice echoing in the posh chamber. "Why are the fey trying to stop you? Does it have something to do with Tom?"

"No. I acquired my fey servant through legitimate means, Mr. Knotte."

"It defies logic," Reg said. "From what I understand, you're hoping to find a source of magical energy. You claim to seek it for the good of everyone, to give humankind a clean, endless source of power. Why would the fey oppose that? Do they want the magic for themselves?"

Both Tom and Frolic chuckled before the fey answered. "Magic is as abundant in the Other World as air is in this place," Tom said. "It's likely the magic Lord Starling seeks is spilling from the Other Side, through a tear in the barrier between the two."

"Well, then they're clearly just protecting their magic from being stolen," Reg said. "I don't care for—" He wanted to say he didn't like fey, but understood their desire to protect their home, but he stopped himself when he remembered Tom's presence. "I don't care for the idea of stealing from them. We've no right."

"I have every right!" Starling's voice rose with passion. "I have to do this. Don't you see? Mankind needs energy. If it isn't provided by magic, it will be coal and steam, filthy machines and human misery. It will be one or the other. Industry will destroy this world unless I put a stop to it, show them another way. I don't want anyone else suffering." He slapped the desk, making his glasses and inkwell rattle and his haphazard maps and papers rustle. Reg ached for those ignored instruments. He longed to record their hardships, their impossible experiences. He didn't suppose Starling would offer him a quill and a few sheets of paper, though, so he didn't bother asking.

"You're wrong," Frolic said. "So wrong. Magic and industry can share a place in the world, exist together. How can you be so blind?"

"You know nothing of the world. Anyone can see, by the way you behave, you haven't lived in it for very long. I'd call you a child, if you were even human, so don't presume to advise me."

Before the intent even fully formed, Reg got to his feet. Querry also stood, his hand on the hilt of his sword.

"Oh, sit down, you fools. I haven't said anything that isn't true. This boy is a clockwork, and he's very naïve. The two of you are barely into manhood. I won't apologize if you find honesty so offensive, and I won't abandon my mission. This is my very life. I will find this place, and you will help me. Now, if that will be all, I have a great deal to do this afternoon. I must assess the damage to the ship, particularly to the engine, and delegate repair assignments. I must see what's left of the crew and make sure we can operate with a less than full retinue."

"My God, you speak of people's lives." Reg found he couldn't hold back. "People died out there. Horribly. Eaten by a monster. Do you suppose those simple sailors expected to face something like that?"

"People die," Starling said. "Nothing and no one can stand against death. Anyone who expects any kind of security from this life is deluded. For most, it's only a question of which of fate's whims proves fatal. Dumb luck allows some of us to survive while others are taken. I know this well, as will you when you've lived a few more years."

"I know it well enough. I've known it since before I could cut my own meat. But it doesn't mean any less when a life is lost. Every person matters. I hope I'll never think of flesh and blood men like supplies, as a means to an end, as you do. I find it reprehensible."

"Such sentiment will hardly bring them back."

Reg couldn't argue with that. He decided, as they stood to leave the fancy cabin, to help the sailors and laborers clean up if he could. He'd spent too many days wallowing in self-pity and feeling like a victim. It was time to do what he could to make sure the people he loved would be all right, to make sure they returned from this ill-fated adventure, though he wished he could record the lost men's stories. Something occurred to him, and he turned toward Starling again.

"There's just one more thing I require, if I may. I'd like to look over the contract Querry and Frolic signed."

"That's hardly necessary." Starling absently reached back and rolled the top of his desk shut.

"What don't you want me to see?" Reg persisted. "If everything is authentic, what do you have to hide? What's the harm in me looking it over?" Reg and Querry exchanged a glance. Querry inched behind Starling toward his desk.

"It has nothing to do with harm. Their contract is none of your business, Mr. Whitney," Starling said, clearly annoyed.

Frolic noticed Querry's intent. "Reg is our representative, like our solicitor," he said, drawing Starling's attention further from the desk.

"That's absurd." Starling sniffed. "It's been signed. Solicitors review contracts before they're signed, not after."

Querry reached tentatively toward the desk, but as soon as his hand came into contact with the roll top, biting energy sparked, clearly sending pain through Querry's arm. He yelped, and they all turned to look at him.

80

Tom Teezle smirked from his corner. "Sorry," Querry offered. "Stubbed my toe."

Starling looked at the thief suspiciously. "Yes well, I think it's time for you all to go," he stated, dismissing them. "You're stinking up my chambers." They filed from the room, and Reg noticed the smirking faerie.

"What was that?" Reg asked when they were safely on the deck and out of earshot of the baron.

"My guess would be neither Frolic nor I can get our hands on that contract," Querry said as he shook his still tingling, reddened hand. "Because we agreed not to work against Starling. Hell, that hurt. I hate to think of what would happen if we tried to harm him for real."

"I need to review the exact language of the agreement, see if I might find some hole in the wording, a way for you and Frolic to escape." Reg smacked his left fist into his right palm.

"We'll figure something out," Frolic offered, squeezing Reg's shoulder.

Reg calmed at Frolic's touch, an idea occurring to him. "I'll meet you down in our room," he said to Querry and Frolic. "We should have some lunch and talk. I'll give you a chance to wash up properly." He knew from the stories they told of Querry's and Frolic's first intimate encounter, that Querry had wiped nearly a century's worth of dust from Frolic's fair skin after finding him in an abandoned basement. It brought back fond memories for Querry; he still loved helping Frolic bathe, sometimes lingering over the task for an hour or more. Reg hoped it might have a calming effect on both of them.

Frolic captured Reg's gaze and smiled. "Hurry on, or I'll have to help Querry work out his frustration without you. It's much more pleasant when you're there too, Reggie. It's not the same without you." Frolic moved toward him, his perfect lips pursed, and Reg caught his shoulder to stop Frolic from kissing him. He found it endearing how Frolic didn't understand why they couldn't kiss whenever they wanted. He and Querry had tried to explain it to Frolic, but Frolic, by his nature, saw things as they should be instead of how they truly were.

"I'll be along soon," Reg said. "I'll bring something for me and Querry to eat."

They descended into the hold of the ship, and Reg took a deep breath, steeling himself as he approached the three mercenaries. The men still sat on the deck, fiddling with their equipment. Reg didn't know how he found the courage—he usually relied on Querry to deal with men like these—but he withdrew an engraved flask from his pocket and held it out to the gray-haired leader, a very serious and imposing man.

"What have you got there, son?"

"Highland single malt. Eighteen years old."

"Sounds fancy. Why would you share it with me, then?"

"As a trade." Reg sat down and crossed his legs. It was hot and humid, but thankfully, a light breeze ruffled his hair and cooled his burning cheeks. Querry always taunted him for blushing when he became nervous or aroused. He cursed it now; surely this experienced soldier noticed.

"A trade, you say? For what?"

"Only some answers. I'm Reginald, by the way. Reginald Whitney." He held out his hand, as was proper between gentlemen.

The other man looked at Reg's outstretched hand for a few seconds before grasping it in his huge, rough fist. "I ain't promising nothing. So, where from?"

"Halcyon."

"Yeah, a city boy. Saw that coming."

"And you?" Reg asked, optimistic about the conversation.

"Ravenshire. Been a long time since I been there, though."

Reg couldn't help grinning at the irony. He'd been engaged to the Earl of Ravenshire's daughter, before he rescued Querry and ran away with him and Frolic. He didn't regret it for a second, but he didn't think sharing that particular tale would aid his cause.

"Might I know your name?" Reg pressed.

"It's Jack. Jack Owens. These are me mates, Istvan and Attila, from Magyary. Veterans of their nation's failed war for independence." The brothers barely nodded to acknowledge Reg. "You're with that pretty boy thief, ain't you? And the white-haired faerie? Guess I know what that makes you."

"Oh, and what's that?"

Jack Owens made an obscene gesture, moving his fist in front of his lips while poking his tongue against the inside of his cheek.

"I beg your pardon!" Reg wanted to hit him, wished he could be Querry just long enough to put the mercenary in his place.

"You saying I'm wrong?"

"I'm saying it's not your affair. Now, we can talk like two civilized, Anglican men, or I can take my whiskey and go. I won't sit here and be insulted when I approached you honestly."

"Fine, lad. I s'pose you and your friends fought better than I expected of you, anyhow." Owens took another pull from the flask before passing it to Istvan. "What do you want to know?"

Reg took a deep breath and reminded himself he needed answers, not vengeance. "I'm curious about your gear, about your goggles especially. How do they work?"

"There's a fine layer of water from some special, Belvaisian spring between two panes of glass," Owens said. "The magic water reveals the fey, or anything they influence."

"Interesting. And how did you acquire them?"

"His Lordship provided 'em," Owens said.

"Which indicates he suspected we might face fey opposition on this expedition," Reg said, more to himself. "Did he tell you as much when you signed on?"

"He mentioned it might be a possibility. Why?"

Reg shook his head. "Did you sign a contract?"

"No need. Lordship knows what he'll get if we don't see our pay."

"And, and what did he tell you was the goal of this mission?"

"Something about a magical spring," Owens said, squinting at the burn of Reg's fine liquor. "Don't matter much. We're here to keep his Lordship alive. Basically, he's paying us to shoot anything what looks threatening. It's my kind of job. I don't need to know what he's after. Here's the thing about those fey, mate. Get some iron into 'em, and they're weak. Can't fling their silly spells around. You might talk to that handsome girl in the workshop too. I heard she's got plans to build some device to soak up their magic. Sounds well and truly useful. And as for that great, big fish? Well, shoot it and stab it enough and it dies like anything else, don't it?"

Having learned all he wanted to know and more, Reg snatched his flask back from the mercenary, pleased to find it not completely empty. "A pleasure meeting you," he said as he stood to leave.

"Aye, just stay out of my way, boy. Tell your fancy friends to do the same. And don't be eyeing up my cock."

Reg hurried toward the hatch, tired of Jack Owens after only ten minutes. Also, he couldn't wait to share what he'd learned with Querry and Frolic. He was so excited he almost forgot to stop by the galley and collect some bread, cheese, sausage, and canned carrots for their lunch.

Querry groaned with gratitude when Reg spread the food across the bunk they never used. "I'm starving. This looks all right, but I could really go for a kidney pie, just a cheap, greasy one from a cart back in Halcyon. And a gin. I miss gin."

"Do you think we'll return home one day?" Reg asked as he bent almost in half to sit on the bed they shared. "I miss the fog. Never imagined I'd say so, but there it is. I miss walking across a fallow field on a cool, misty morning. I remember the smell of the soil. How everything in the world seemed painted in barely different shades of gray."

They ate in silence with Frolic watching them. "I'm sorry you miss your homes," he said, looking intently as he curled and uncurled his delicate fingers, as if he saw some great mystery and meaning in the movement of his digits. "I've never really had a place of my own, so I suppose I feel at home anywhere you two are."

Querry rubbed circles over the center of Frolic's back. "I wouldn't do a thing differently, beauty. Not one."

"Well, I might," Reg said, thinking of the debacle they'd caused back home. "But as much as I miss Anglica at times, I wouldn't trade being with you for an estate and a title."

Querry laughed heartily at that. "You did give up an estate and a title for us, Reg. Don't think I'll ever forget it."

They moved onto the floor, folded their legs, and sat in a circle with their knees pressed together. Reg and Querry finished the whiskey in the flask, passing it back and forth as Reg explained what he'd learned from Jack Owens.

"I can't believe that prick even spoke to you," Querry said.

"Well, I suppose I bribed him. The important things are, they knew to expect fey opposition. Starling equipped them to deal with it. Further, they think he's after this magical wellspring. If he's after something else, he's deceived them also." Reg refilled his flask from the dusty bottle in his footlocker and replaced it in his pocket.

"I thought that might be the case," Frolic said. "I felt like he was lying about the energy source, and Tom Teezle looked away whenever he spoke of it."

"I'm afraid I've trained you up better than I should." Querry beamed at Frolic. "I noticed the same things."

"What if the magical spring is a lie and Starling's seeking something else, something he doesn't want us to know about?" Reg asked.

"I wish I could get Tom on his own, speak to him without Starling standing over us," Frolic said.

Querry nodded. "I might be able to distract Starling, keep him occupied for a bit. Let me think on just how."

"I worry," Reg said, picking at the peeling skin around his fingernails. "Will Frolic be safe alone with the fey? I don't like it. Those creatures are dangerous and unpredictable. And Tom seems to have some agenda of his own."

"I can't imagine why Tom would want to hurt me," Frolic said.

"No one knows or understands why they do any of the bizarre things they do. They just aren't like us. They don't think like us or value what we value. And their help never comes without a price. Isn't that right, Querry?"

"Usually, but—"

"Don't worry, Reggie. I won't agree to anything or make any deals with him. I just want to talk. Besides, part of me is fey now. I understand them a little, even if I wish I didn't sometimes. I'll be fine."

"I'd still feel better if one of us came with you," Reg said.

"Because I'm naïve and easy to fool?" Frolic had never sounded so bitter before.

Reg took his hand, stilling the erratic movement of his fingers. He captured Frolic's gaze and looked into his gorgeous, golden eyes so Frolic would see he meant what he said. "I love you. I have never lied to you, and I won't start now. You're brilliant, Frolic. You make things without any effort that simply astound me. All you have to do is glance at a bit of clockwork, and you understand everything about it. You can comprehend concepts I couldn't begin to understand on my best day. But there's a little truth to what Starling said. You are new to the world, and it can be more complex sometimes than any machine. You're just too pure to understand how cruel people can be to one another, what they'll do to others to get ahead. I love that about you. I'd protect you from anything that might change you if I could. But to be honest, there are things you don't understand, like why we can't kiss in public."

Frolic's lower lip jutted out, and he managed to look even more adorable, despite the unnerving stripe of black in his hair. "I really don't understand how expressing love can be a bad thing."

"Yet it can lead to all kinds of trouble for us," Querry said gently.

"I feel like I've lived," Frolic said. "I've known love and loss and fear and triumph. I know what's important to me, and I know what's right. I fight for what I believe in. I'm also confused a lot of the time, especially since that faerie used his magic to repair my heart, but I think humans are confused as often as I am."

"You're correct," Reg said. "I say none of this to hurt your feelings. The world and people refuse to work the way they should, and—"

A booming knock on the door cut Reg off. "Yes? Come in."

The door squeaked, and the tinkerer, Cornelia, stood there, nearly filling the frame. Her eyes grew wide and darted between Reg and Querry. "I, I—oh, dear. I didn't mean to interrupt. I didn't know you'd all be here—"

"Well, this is our cabin," Reg said gently. He couldn't imagine what the poor girl found so intimidating about Querry and himself.

"Right it is." She giggled nervously. "I didn't mean to say you shouldn't be here, only that I was surprised you are. But I shouldn't be surprised, should I? It is your cabin, after all, and it stands to reason—"

"Is there something we can do for you?" Querry asked, a little irritably it seemed to Reg.

"Right. Right to business, then. Well, the engines are a mess, all torn up, and it's going to take me days to put them back in order, especially without all the proper parts. Honestly, I'm going to have to get very creative with some of these repairs. There're gears so badly damaged they'll have to be bypassed entirely, which will mean rerouting entire circuits of the clockwork. I can't even begin to imagine how I'll fix some of the piston casings— But anyway, I was hoping I might borrow Frolic. No, not borrow! Not like a tool, or anything—"

Frolic stood and dusted off his bum. At least he wore a fresh set of clothes. His sweet, sincere smile calmed the agitated young woman a bit. "I'd be happy to help you, Corny."

They left together, Frolic looking even smaller and slighter next to the tinkerer's bulk. As soon as the door closed, Reg and Querry let out the laughter they'd been holding in. Reg rose to his knees and positioned himself above Querry's lap before dropping into it. He ran the tip of his nose over Querry's nose, then brushed his lips over Querry's mouth before saying, "It appears you'll have to take all that frustration out on me, then. I suppose I should ask you to be gentle."

Querry's blue eyes sparkled as he seized Reg by the hips and pulled him closer, his erection rubbing against Reg's ass through their trousers. With a low growl, Querry grabbed Reg by the back of the hair and pulled his head to the side so he could suck on the pulse-point just below Reg's jaw. Afterward, he whispered near Reg's ear, "You can ask anything you want. And if I thought for one minute, even half a minute that's what you really wanted, I might even agree."

Reg groaned with satisfaction and need as he opened his mouth to accept Querry's insistent tongue and submitted to the force of Querry's kiss.

CHAPTER 9

AS SOON as the door closed, Corny relaxed, letting out a long breath and deflating like an air sack on a flying ship when the burner turned off. Frolic thought maybe Reg had been right, and he didn't understand people so well, because Corny's reaction utterly perplexed him.

"They aren't so bad, you know. My friends. You'd probably actually like them if you gave them a chance. Querry loves clockwork, and Reg is the nicest man you'll ever meet. You really have no reason to be afraid of them."

She shook her head as they navigated the badly lit, twisting corridors, ducking to avoid pipes and gears. "It's not that I'm afraid. I just always seem to say the wrong things to people. All of a sudden my tongue feels three feet thick. It's so hard to guess how they might react. Now, give me a piece of machinery, and I can tell exactly what will happen if you move a part, add another, wind here or twist there. It's predictable, and it never varies. People, though. People confuse me."

"Me too," Frolic said. "I'm glad to finally have someone to talk to, though."

"Yeah, so am I." Corny stopped in front of a badly dented piece of metal paneling. She tossed Frolic a wrench and sat down on the ground to get started loosening the bolts. "Good a place as any to begin."

"Right." Frolic started on the bolts at the opposite side of the panel, and in a quarter of an hour or so, they'd nearly finished. Corny removed the bolts along the top of the section, since Frolic couldn't reach. Together, each of them taking a side of the pane, they shifted it, removed it, and laid it out of the way. The gears beneath looked badly damaged as Frolic leaned in to examine them.

Corny whistled through her teeth and slid her goggles over her eyes. "What a mess. Oh, I almost forgot!" She dashed over to an open metal toolbox and rooted through until she found an old pair of clunky goggles, which she handed to Frolic.

He looked at them with curiosity. "These needed fixed? Shouldn't we worry about the ship first?"

Corny giggled, a deep, rich sound, very different from her nervous titters. "They're for you, silly. Some of the gears in there are pretty small."

"Oh, I don't need them. I can see just fine." He sat down and got comfortable, anticipating many hours of precise adjustments.

"God, you're serious, aren't you? You can see them with your naked eyes?"

"Sure," Frolic said, loosening a screw with his fingernail.

"Amazing, you just—I think I might— Well then, here." Corny handed Frolic a few sheets of paper and a thin stick of charcoal.

"What's this for?" he asked.

With another laugh, she said, "To record the sequence of the gears as you take them apart? So you know how to put them back together after we've repaired them."

"I'll remember. In fact, I think I can make this all run more smoothly. Some of these gears are completely redundant. If I remove them and reroute some others, I can get the maximum output from the energy going into them. There's really no need to spread the power so thin. The tension on some of these springs is all wrong. Do you have an eighteen-gauge screwdriver?"

After she didn't respond for many minutes, Frolic looked over his shoulder to find the plump tinkerer beaming down at him, her hands pressed over her heart. "What's wrong?" he asked.

"Bloody hell, I think I'm in love." She pressed the tool he'd requested into his hand and sat down beside him. As they worked, she stopped often to ask Frolic's opinion on the configuration of various clockwork circuits. Together, they managed to streamline everything behind the metal wall so they didn't even have to repair any bent gears or straighten mangled teeth. They simply eliminated gears Frolic found unnecessary and replaced the damaged bits with superfluous pieces. They had to make some adjustments, as the extra parts weren't always the exact size of the damaged gears, but Frolic found it simple to compensate for the slight differences, and they finished in only a little over an hour.

"Brilliant!" Corny stood, stretched, and twisted her waist. Her bones cracked loudly.

"You don't dress like most women I've seen," Frolic observed as they made their way toward the next damaged panel.

"Well, I like breathing and moving around," she said as she crouched to start on the next round of bolts. "I like to be able to walk without teetering along like a fool. What's wrong with that?"

"Nothing. I just noticed it. I—really don't understand the need for people to dress differently from each other. It seems to me they'd want to wear clothes that protected them and helped them in their work. I appreciate beauty, but I don't understand wearing something that would slow you down or make it difficult to fight."

"Bless you, Frolic. Neither do I."

"So I'm not alone in being mixed up? You're a human, and you don't understand it either. Those corsets and heeled boots just seem stupid to me, and uncomfortable."

"Hear, hear. If there's one thing I understand about people, only one, it's that they don't think for themselves. I'll tell you this: if the magazines proclaimed it fashionable to dress as a rabbit, you'd see the ladies of Halcyon in bunny suits."

Frolic laughed until his sides hurt as he pictured noblewomen parading about in rabbit costumes. "I like you, Corny. I'm glad you're my friend. It's nice to know someone with such a good sense of humor and an understanding of clockwork. You're certainly someone I'd want at my back in a fight. Don't take offense, but I notice you don't halt or stutter when we're talking."

"I just feel comfortable with you. I don't have to put on airs or pretend to be someone else."

"Why would you have to do that for anyone?"

"You're so sweet, Frolic. I wish the rest of the world could see things the way you do. You really don't expect me to be anything else?"

"Like what? You're a brilliant tinkerer and a good friend to me. And like I mentioned, you can hold your own and then some if there's trouble."

"Right then. Let's get back to work. Another panel demands our attention. This is the easy part, especially with your insights. I have no idea how we'll repair the steam conduits and damaged pipes. We don't have the resources to replace them."

"I have a thought on that. Why don't we melt down all these spare parts and use the alloy to patch the cracks in the pipes? It will make them heavy, and won't be a permanent solution, but it might get us to a port where we can procure supplies. We'll have to take each section of pipe into your workshop. The molten steel won't last till we bring it here, but it's better than nothing."

"You are a marvel, Frolic. I'd like to know more about you, if you'd be willing." Corny sat down and adjusted her eyewear to inspect the clockwork.

"I'd like to know more about you too. You can ask me anything you want. I trust you, Corny."

"Thanks. I appreciate that. I can't help but wonder about how and why you were made. Why would someone make such an intricate clockwork? You seem so human. Do you know anything about the person who created you?"

"No. I wish I did. I'd give anything to know what he intended for me, why he made me as he did. I have to wonder how much of me is the result of what I've experienced and how much he designed."

Cornelia mopped her brow with the back of her hand. "I have to admit, I was wondering more about how your joints moved so smoothly. You have incredible range of motion."

"The gears within me are very small." Frolic hesitated, afraid to shatter the friendship he'd found, but needing to be honest with the tinkerer. "I'm as much magic as I am clockwork. It's the combination of the two that makes me what I am."

She pushed her goggles onto her hair and said, "How so?"

"I have a book that tells all about it. It took many people to construct me. My skin, hair, and eyes are mostly magical. Spelled. My heart too. I run on steam. Steam fuels all the gears that move every part of me. I draw air into my lungs, and my heart heats the vapor into steam. For my heart to remain hot, burning, takes very strong magic. It's a combination of things I don't really understand: fever dreams, oaths spoken during love, and elemental fire. The oaths Querry, Reg, and the others used to repair my heart when it broke were spoken between a powerful faerie and his wizard partner. Since then, I've understood the fey language. I've understood magic. Corny, I've never told anybody about this—"

"No worries." She clutched his shoulder, enveloping it in her large hand. "I won't speak a word of what you've said. I think I hate magic, anyway. It's the antithesis of what I do. What I do makes sense, works every time. Magic—damn, I don't even begin to understand how or why it works."

For a while, they worked on the gears within the panel in awkward silence. Finally, when he could take no more, Frolic asked, "How many people died today?"

Corny flinched. "I—I'm not sure. I think half a dozen jumped overboard, and we lost as many fighting that monster. Why?"

Though he knew he shouldn't, Frolic shared everything that had been troubling him with her. "My friends are human like you. As much as I love them, I can't stop them from growing old and dying. I don't want to be alone. I was alone for so long, Corny. You can't imagine. I was alone for almost eighty years, maybe more, in a dark, cold cellar. Do you think I could be replicated? Could I, with your help, make another like myself? Someone to keep me company, to save me from solitude? If we use the book, can we, you and I, make me a companion? Will you help me?"

"I—I guess I could try."

Frolic embraced her, burrowing his face into her fleshy neck. "Oh, thank you, Corny. You don't know how much this means to me."

"It's not going to be easy," she warned him. "And there's so much else to do with the engines and things."

"I know," Frolic said. "But I can't do it on my own. If we can work, plan, in our spare time, then maybe I can at least get started. I'm not deluding myself; I know it's probably going to take me many years. I just don't want to be left behind again when—when—" The thought of a world without Querry and Reg in it, where he'd never see their faces, hear their voices, or feel their hands upon him again made Frolic feel like every last one of his gears jammed at the same time. He couldn't move or breathe as he contemplated it.

"Oh, hey now." Corny put down the calipers she'd been using and pulled Frolic against her. She stroked his hair and shushed him until he calmed down a little. "That's years and years away, Frolic. Thinking about it now won't do you any good. What do you say we finish this work? It'll keep your mind off everything, yeah?"

"Yeah," he managed to whisper as he picked up his wrench with a shaking hand. He didn't speak anymore to Corny about his concerns, but he couldn't banish the dark thoughts as they worked well into evening. To distract himself, Frolic asked Corny how she'd learned to work with steam engines and gears.

"Self-taught, mostly. I convinced a few tinkerers to show me a thing or two here and there, but I learned most of it just by taking things apart. I've been doing that since I could pry a clock casing open with a butter knife. I'd love a look inside you— Damn, I didn't mean it like that. I'm sorry. I guess you can see why I had to run away."

"It's all right. I can let you look at my book. It describes how I work, and hopefully you'll get to see it while we build another clockwork. But why did you have to run away?"

"Because I didn't want the life my parents had planned out for me: a husband, children, planning luncheons and ladies' teas. Stuffed into a gown and looking like an upholstered couch. Dull. I wanted to see the world, use my skills, my brain. I didn't want some man telling me what to do for the rest of my days. Freedom and adventure, that's what I'm after."

"You're a little like my friend Querry, maybe just not as rash."

"Yeah, and as I'm sure you can imagine, my marriage prospects weren't encouraging."

"Why?" Frolic truly didn't understand. He thought Corny made a great companion. She was funny, kind, brilliant with machinery, and someone to depend on if things got ugly. What more could anyone want?

"Have a look, love. I'm not exactly a delicate flower. And I don't know how to talk to people or wave a fan around to give silly signals."

"But don't you miss being touched?"

She blushed and looked away.

"I've said something wrong, haven't I? I'm sorry."

"No, it's all right. It just isn't something most people are willing to discuss. You might not want to ask anyone else that question. To answer you, though... well sure, I guess. But I'm not willing to give up my freedom either. I won't pretend I'm simple or helpless just so a man feels valuable because he can take care of me. I can take care of myself just fine, and I won't pretend I can't. I suppose if I could find a man who saw me as an equal, just another person— Anyway. So your friends—do you love them? As in...."

"As in being touched? Wanting to be touched? That way? More than anything, but they say I shouldn't tell anyone. I don't understand why, but they say it's dangerous."

"You'd better listen to them, Frolic. You don't have to worry about me saying anything, though. Who would I even tell? For what it's worth, I think people should do what makes them happy. Touch them to your heart's content, but be careful. The world isn't fair. Come on, now. Let's get these tools packed up for the night. I'm starving."

Frolic hurried to gather their things, feeling much better after talking with his wonderful new friend, and very eager to see Querry and Reg again, to hold onto them and enjoy them as long as he could.

CHAPTER 10

"THIS IS the most ridiculous thing I've ever heard," Reg said as he paced the perimeter of their small cell. "Two master thieves, and who's supposed to break into Starling's desk? Me. Me, who's never so much as put a loose coin in my pocket."

"You'll be fine, Reg." Querry caught his hand and rubbed his thumb across Reg's knuckles. "Besides, Frolic and I can't do anything against Starling's interests. You saw what happened to me the last time I tried. Just discussing this plan is making me a bit nauseous."

Reg broke away from Querry and shot him an exasperated look. "Can't you just remember what the contract said? What about you, Frolic? Your memory's almost photographic."

"When it comes to clockwork and gears," Frolic said. "I barely understood most of those words when I read them, though. I understand the basic concept, but—no. I can't tell you exactly what it said. Sorry, Reg."

"If you two ever find yourselves in this situation again, for heaven's sake ask for a copy of the contract for yourselves. No, better yet, don't ever get yourselves into a situation like this again. Honestly. I can't believe I'm actually considering this. What will he do if he catches me?"

"No worries, Reggie. I'll distract Starling, and Frolic will keep Tom occupied. All you'll have to do is slip inside, grab it, and slip out. Easy as pie. It shouldn't take more than a minute or two. Although if you want to poke around for a few bottles of that lovely wine he keeps, I'll be sure to buy you a few extra minutes." Querry shot Reg a suggestive smile and wink, hoping it might amuse and arouse him as it usually did. Clearly, Querry'd made a mistake.

"Blast it, Querry! This is no joke. We're in obvious trouble here, and you have to take it seriously. For once in your life, you have to see we're not just playing some game. Won't you and Frolic distracting Starling and Tom count as working against him? Have you thought about that?"

"A little," Querry said. "I think we'll be fine. After all, nothing happened when we questioned him before. Nothing happened until I actually tried to steal from him. I really think we can get one over on the self-righteous bastard. And he deserves it. He thinks he's so bloody clever." The idea made Querry want to laugh out loud; he loved putting pompous asses in their places.

"Is that what this is about? Proving you're smarter than he is?"

"A little," Querry admitted cautiously. Reg's cheeks started to color, and his full lips pursed and turned down. "You were the one who said you wanted to see that contract."

"Yes, I want to find a way to get you and Frolic out of it. If I do, I want you to promise me we'll all leave Lord Starling's employ at the very next port. We're in danger as long as we continue to help that man. And then, I want to have a long and serious talk about our future. We just can't keep this up forever."

"I know," Querry said, putting his arguments aside for a more appropriate time. He had some difficulty imagining a time when he wouldn't be able to rob the privileged. Their complacency and false sense of security left them wide open, and Querry doubted they'd ever be any different.

"Wait," Frolic said, standing up from the bunk. "I don't want to leave yet. I don't care if we quit working for Lord Starling, but I want to stay on the ship. I'm working on something, and I need Corny's help."

"What?" Both Querry and Reg asked at once.

Frolic wouldn't look them in the eye. Querry couldn't ever remember Frolic keeping secrets, as he seemed to do now. If anything, he always erred on the side of bearing too much of his soul, even to his partners. Reg's brows arched up as he looked hard at Frolic's downturned face.

"It isn't anything important," he said in a thin whisper. "Just something I'm thinking of making. Something I want for myself."

Frolic looked so decimated, so broken for some reason Querry couldn't fathom, that he squeezed Frolic around the shoulders and kissed him on top of his head. At least Frolic returned Querry's smile when he finally faced him, but Querry almost felt like looking up into his face made Frolic sad. Since finding Frolic in the doll maker's cellar, all Querry had wanted was to shield him from the cruelty of the world and those who might want to take advantage of him. In some significant way, he'd failed.

"We can talk about all this later," Querry said. "We should do this as soon as we can."

Reg shook his head with resignation and flipped open the lid of the trunk at the foot of his bunk. He sorted through the few belongings he'd brought on their journey, including the weapons and armor Frolic had made, and the faerie book and writing set Frolic had given him. Finally, he found a few pieces of his precious paper and a quill and hid them in his trouser pockets.

"What are you planning to do with those?" Querry asked.

"I'm planning to copy down that contract, clearly. If Starling simply finds it missing, he won't have a hard time figuring out who took it, will he?"

"I'm impressed," Querry said. "I hadn't even thought of that."

With a sardonic smile, Reg said, "Of course you didn't, Querry. You didn't think of anything beyond making Starling look a fool."

Querry cringed inwardly as he realized Reg had the measure of him—of course he did. He knew Querry better than Querry knew himself sometimes. Reg was right too. Querry'd put humiliating Starling above all else—including the safety of the people he loved and swore to protect. Still, given what the three of them had accomplished in the past, he didn't think acquiring a copy of the contract would be difficult. For God's sake, they'd just defeated a ghastly leviathan, a creature straight out of a horrific story. How hard could it be to get a hold of a piece of paper?

"Don't forget what I said about the wine," he added in a last attempt to alleviate the tension he felt so unnecessary. "We'll use it to celebrate our success."

"I'm going to assist with the repairs to the riggings," Reg said, shaking his head.

"I'll come with you," Frolic offered. "I'm sure I can do something useful."

Querry followed them up to the deck, feeling queasy again as the planks seemed to undulate beneath his boots. The bloody seasickness was getting damned annoying, especially when he needed his wits sharp. Instead of concentrating on the roiling of his guts and the spinning of his head, he needed to concoct a compelling reason for Starling to leave his cabin without Tom. It had to be more than a desire for conversation; they could talk easily within the baron's chamber. He wandered over near the port side rail, just in case he couldn't hold his breakfast. Reg and Frolic met a group of sailors. Querry grinned when Reg followed the Thalaceans and stripped off his shirt. He looked so pale compared to them, and Querry hoped he wouldn't burn too badly, but he liked to see Reg break free of some of the uptight propriety imposed by his adoptive parents. Before abandoning that life, Reg, like any proper gentleman, refused to be seen without his coat, vest, cravat, hat, and gloves. Querry certainly liked watching Reg unfurl the lengths of heavy rope, his lithe muscles contracting and pulling against each other as he worked.

One of the sailors handed Frolic a gas-powered nail gun attached to a fuel tank, and he wandered away from the rest of the group, working to mend some of the broken rails closer to the stern. His fresh powder-blue shirt stayed tucked into his gray houndstooth trousers. Querry remembered how, when he'd first met Frolic, he'd had to impart to him the importance of not disrobing whenever he wished. He'd been delighted with Frolic's natural lack of shame or modesty over his beautiful form. Now, though, Frolic seemed uncomfortable when anyone looked at him at all. He was afraid they knew he was different, and Querry knew Frolic felt like an outcast. Querry hadn't noticed the change in his Frolic; it had obviously been gradual, and Frolic didn't seem self-conscious around Reggie and Querry. The idea Frolic might feel ashamed of his perfect body tore at Querry's heart.

Querry leaned his back on the railing, watching them work, watching the mercenaries playing a card game on an overturned barrel, tossing his thoughts about, trying to make sense of them, and trying to formulate some feasible way of occupying Starling. Every time he came up short, he grew more and more frustrated. The increasing heat and his increasing boredom plunged Querry into a fouler and fouler mood. Sweat dripped down the sides of his face and down his spine, and his stomach lurched every time a strong wave crashed against the vessel's hull. Minutes ticked by, stretching into half an hour, and Querry looked for something to occupy himself but found nothing.

Close to an hour wore on. Querry paced near the helm. How the bloody hell would he lure Starling away from Tom and his cabin? What could he say that wouldn't sound obvious? What could he do? It had seemed so simple when he'd explained it to Reg and Frolic. Now and then, the other two men paused in their labor to cast Querry wondering glances. Querry swore under his breath and pushed a clump of damp, rotting net back and forth with the armored toe of his boot.

A door slammed, and Querry turned toward the sound. Starling, in a pair of black, pinstriped trousers, matching waistcoat, and crisp, white shirt strode across the deck with Tom following closely behind. Querry cast around for some way to draw the baron's attention, and saw only one possibility. Without considering the consequences of his actions for too long, afraid to lose his opportunity, Querry hurried over to the mercenaries and shoved Jack Owens hard in the shoulder.

"What did you say to me?" Querry demanded.

"Piss off," Owens said without looking up from the cards he held, his teeth around the stump of a cigar.

"If you have something to say to me, say it to my face, if you're not a coward." Querry continued to taunt, planting his hands on his hips, widening his stance, and lifting his chin defiantly. He couldn't help enjoying himself just a bit. "Go on. Just what were you mumbling when I walked by?"

"I was talking to me mates. Now bugger off, lad."

"Make me."

To Querry's surprise, Owens never even looked up from his game. He simply dismissed Querry. Glancing over his shoulder, Querry saw Starling, who'd paused to observe, begin making his way to the hatch again. Querry had to act. He raised his arm and struck Jack Owens hard with the back of his hand. The larger man flew from the small pile of wood he sat upon and sprawled on his back on the deck, his cigar still clenched between his lips, though the smack of his body against the planks knocked the breath from his chest audibly. Still, he arched his back and got to his feet with a single smooth motion, spitting his smoke on the deck.

"You're fucking dead!" Owens lunged for Querry, and though Querry dodged, Owens caught him around the waist and tackled him to the deck, landing hard across Querry's chest.

Querry gasped for air and flicked his head just in time to avoid the blow aimed at his jaw. He tried to retaliate, but Owens grabbed his wrists and squeezed his bones until they felt like they cracked. "Not so clever now, are ya, pretty boy?"

"Bastard." Querry jerked his thigh up with all the force he could muster, driving into the other man's groin.

Owens's face reddened almost to purple, and he collapsed on the deck beside Querry. Querry wasted no time getting to his feet, but neither did the big mercenary. They faced off again as a crowd gathered around them.

Querry glanced to his left to find Frolic's gaze. During their nocturnal excursions, the two of them had learned to communicate without speech, almost without gesture, conveying intent just by looking in one another's eyes. Yet again, Querry knew in a second Frolic understood what he planned. The clockwork boy nodded almost imperceptibly. The momentary distraction cost Querry, though. As soon as he turned his head, Owens hit him in the eye with a roundhouse, and Querry's feet flew off the deck before he landed hard on his ass.

The older soldier advanced on Querry, and Querry just lay still until Owens reached him. Then he kicked out, hitting the other man in the shin with the heel of his boot. He doubted he broke the bone, but he knew he'd delivered at least a nasty bruise. Owens doubled over to grasp his leg, and Querry kicked up, hitting him square in the chest and knocking him back again. Some of the crewmen watching the brawl groaned with empathy. Querry twisted and pushed himself up on his hands and knees, not expecting Owens to recover as quickly as he did. Before Querry saw him coming, he drove his heel into Querry's ribs, flipping him to his back again.

Querry rolled before the mercenary could pin him a second time. He barely escaped Owens's dive, hurrying to his feet while the mercenary pitched forward, off balance. Before Owens regained his footing, Querry punched him in the lower back, three times in rapid succession, driving Owens down on his knees. Querry didn't really want to hurt the other man. Owens was a mouthy, judgmental prick, sure, but he didn't deserve serious injury, so Querry held back when he could have delivered a deciding strike. Owens wasn't so considerate. He swiped his arm out in a circle, hitting Querry in the knees and knocking him off his feet yet again. It had been a long time since Querry had faced such a formidable opponent.

Spittle flew from the mercenary's mouth as he drew one of the nasty, foot-long, serrated blades popular in the Empire's wildest colonies. "I'm gonna cut your balls off, you miserable little cocksucker. I'm finished with you and your faggot friends."

"Enough." A crack of thunder split the sky and silenced everyone present. As he strode to the center of the crowd, Starling, for once, looked regal and commanding instead of drunk and debauched. He stood proud and erect in his fine, fitted clothes, and his presence cowed all of them, even Querry. "I will not tolerate such behavior from those I have employed with the expectation of professionalism. You, sailors, get back to work. These repairs won't wait until tomorrow. We're adrift until they're complete, so use your time wisely, instead of standing around and gawking like idiots at two fools."

The baron reached down and seized Querry by his lapels, hauling him to his feet. Querry, too stunned to resist, let himself be dragged upright. Starling stared at him with deep blue eyes filled with such strong disappointment and disgust that Querry actually felt ashamed. He felt like a scolded child, and humbly followed the aristocrat into the galley to receive his punishment. Even Owens walked with his head bowed and his eyes on his scraped knuckles. Even so, Querry noticed Frolic catch Tom Teezle by the elbow and urge him away from the throng, toward a stack of crates near the helm. The two of them disappeared behind the pile of cargo as Querry, Owens, and Starling entered the shade of the galley.

Starling's cool, aristocratic demeanor disappeared as soon as they left the sight of the sailors. He grabbed Querry by the front of the shirt and shoved him against the wall, making the metal dishes, utensils, and cans of food rattle.

When Querry grabbed his wrists to push Starling off, currents of pain shot up his arms. Querry gritted his teeth against the shooting agony and said "Take your hands off me."

With a final shove that knocked tins of meat clattering to the floor, Starling released Querry. The baron took a few steps back and smoothed the points of his waistcoat. Then he crossed his arms and glared at both the thief and the mercenary. "What do you two think you're playing at?"

Both of them spoke at once. Querry said: "This bastard has been slandering and harassing me and my friends since we came aboard. If he wants to call us names and make implications, I have every right to defend against them. I won't suffer these insults."

At the same time, Owens bellowed: "These bummers have no place on this mission, sir. I don't mean to question your decisions, but do you realize the kind of men you've hired on? I saw their like by the Black Sea, and begging your pardon, your Lordship, but it ain't no good to employ men who'd rather bugger each other than use their guns!"

Starling raised his hand. "Both of you, shut up."

They did. Starling shook his head as he walked in small circles around the cramped room. "Are you children?"

"No, sir," Owens responded.

Querry curled his lip and said nothing.

"And should I have to watch over you like a nursemaid?"

"No, sir."

"Keep this belligerent bastard in line, and you'll have no worries from me, *majesty*," Querry said.

"Keep yourself in line, you little queer," Owens said, jabbing his thick finger in Querry's direction.

"Fuck off, Owens."

"Enough of this." Starling's voice echoed off the metal shelving and insubstantial, tin walls of the ship's kitchen. "You answer to me, both of you. The undertaking is the only thing of importance here. Nothing else matters. I don't care about the petty disputes you have with one another. You will do the jobs you're being paid to do, with minimal disruption. Do I make myself completely plain? Evans?"

"It's Owens, sir."

"Whatever." Starling flicked his wrist, as if to banish unseen cobwebs.

"Yes, sir," Owens said, hanging his head.

"Very well. You are dismissed." Starling waved toward the galley door, and Owens departed.

"You know, I'm not so accustomed to taking orders as he is," Querry said. "In fact, I take no orders but my own."

"And that's why I need you, Mr. Knotte. You have a completely different way of approaching a problem than the soldiers. I suspect I'll need it more than blind obedience soon enough. Still, I expect you to be civil."

"I'll be perfectly civil if he is. I won't have my friends slandered, Starling. I don't care much about myself—people have always seen me as trash—but Reg and Frolic don't deserve—"

"Certainly not. I understand your frustration, but one must always endeavor to be a gentleman, Querrilous."

"If you say so."

"I do." To Querry's utter bafflement, the baron grasped the back of his neck and kissed him hard between the eyes.

AS SOON as he saw Starling pull Querry into the galley, Frolic knew he had to seize the moment. He slipped behind the distracted sailors, calling on all

Querry had taught him of stealth, and touched Tom Teezle lightly on the shoulder. A warm current of magic flowed up Frolic's arm and made the parts within him vibrate pleasantly. He'd been nervous about dealing with the faerie without Querry or Reg; he didn't like acting without their guidance. Now, with the enchantment flowing through him, he felt calm, confident, and strong.

He met the faerie's gem-like eyes and smiled. "Would you mind talking to me for a few minutes, Tom?"

"Talk, then."

"Can we talk alone?" Frolic found a secluded corner of the deck hidden from the rest by some wooden crates. Tom followed him, and as they stood looking at one another, Frolic realized he didn't know what to say. He'd forgotten all the questions that had seemed so vital. In mere seconds the faerie looked bored, glancing over his shoulder every few minutes. Frolic worried if he didn't say something soon, Tom might leave.

"I'm curious about you," Frolic said without guile. He moved a little closer to Tom. The faerie's enormous eyes slanted in a way different from anyone Frolic had ever seen, and his skin differed too. It was a soft, golden brown, impossibly smooth, the pores barely visible. His tangled spikes of hair had an almost metallic quality.

"I'm a bit interested in you, as well. Specifically in the enchantment flowing through you. It was cast by someone *very* powerful. Did you know him well?"

Frolic nodded, remembering Querry's faerie companion. "He took something from me I cared about very much. I was afraid of him."

Tom giggled. "I should say so."

"You're very beautiful," Frolic said, touching the point of one of Tom's long ears. Then, remembering he couldn't touch anyone he wanted, that there were rules regarding it, he quickly pulled his hand away.

"Yes," Tom said.

"Are you happy working for Lord Starling? Is he good to you?"

"He is not a cruel man," Tom said as he spread his long, elegant fingers wide and held his hand less than an inch from Frolic's heart. "Still, we're better than them."

"Faeries?" Frolic felt the heat of Tom's palm through his shirt, felt enchantment pouring out of him. He supposed it made him feel similar to Querry and Reg when they had a few glasses of good wine.

"Creatures of magic. You and I."

"I'm not a creature of magic," Frolic said. "I'm a clockwork. Besides, isn't Starling a wizard?"

The fey sniffed. "That's the difference between dipping your toe in the ocean and being the ocean."

"So, you'd rather get away from him?"

"Of course. Wouldn't you?"

"What?" Frolic didn't understand.

"Wouldn't you rather be free than forced to serve humans? Don't you have things of your own to pursue?"

"No, you don't understand. I don't serve Querry and Reg. They're my friends. They teach me and keep me safe. I like being with them."

"You remain in the company of those dull creatures willingly?"

"That's unkind and untrue. You shouldn't say such things, Tom."

"I suppose it doesn't matter. The lives of these humans are brief compared to our own. We'll be free of them soon enough. Still, I wish it could be sooner. It's terribly tedious. Starling never lets me have any fun. With him, it's always useful things. Serving the purpose. You know, I might destroy him should I get the chance. I might not, but I might." Tom shrugged as if they discussed nothing more than the weather.

"The purpose," Frolic whispered. "Tom, is Starling really looking for a magical energy source? Or is it something else?"

"I'm forbidden to disclose his secrets by a contract rather like your own."

"Please, just tell me if he's lying to us. Just say yes or no."

"No." The fey grinned.

Frolic rubbed his forehead. "So the energy exists?"

"Starling believes it does."

"And what about you?"

"What does it matter?" Tom asked.

"It matters to me."

"The texts he's asked me to translate indicate something in that jungle. Something ancient and powerful. At the very least, we'll be well entertained for a change."

Frolic considered the flippant creature's words. "So, he learned of it from faerie manuscripts? How did he come by them?"

Tom laughed. "Not honestly."

"Is that why they—your people—are attacking us? Because he stole from them?"

"I don't believe so, no. But let me ask a question of you now, Frolic. If you aren't bound, why don't you use your magic? Why do you bother with all those inelegant machines?"

"I can't use magic. I can sense its presence. I feel it in you, Tom. But I can't control it. If I could, none of us would be here. I'd have been able to break Starling's spell."

"I wondered why you didn't."

They stood looking at one another in silence, Frolic's gaze steady while Tom's darted about, his hand still above Frolic's heart. Finally, Frolic reached up, slid his fingers between the fey's fingers, and curled his hand around Tom's. "I'll help you if I can, Tom. Help you free yourself."

Tom arched his brows, then narrowed his eyes. He mimicked Frolic's gesture and wound his fingers over Frolic's knuckles, amplifying the magic they traded. "Will you? And what will you ask of me in exchange?"

"Nothing!"

"I'd accuse anyone else of lying. But you... from you I believe it. I may not understand why you want to aid me, but I know you do. You are a very strange creature, unlike fey or man."

"I know." Frolic struggled to use his voice. Even Tom knew he didn't belong. He didn't belong anywhere. Why had he been made? Had his sole purpose been to control the clockwork angels, and if so, with those angels destroyed by the faerie gentleman, where did that leave him? Useless, unnecessary, and wrong?

"You're in a great deal of pain," Tom noted without sympathy but with a hint of interest in his voice.

"Maybe you can do something for me," Frolic proposed. "But only if you want to. I'll help you even if you refuse. I won't enter into any sort of bargain. If you help me, you have to do so as a friend."

Tom ran his fingertips over the back of Frolic's hand. It felt very pleasant. "What would you ask of me, Frolic?"

"Can you help me understand?"

"Understand what?"

Frolic didn't know how to explain it. He looked up at the sky and saw the clouds pushed slowly along by the light wind. The wind, clouds, and even the light had names he hadn't known before Querry's gentleman had used his magic to repair Frolic's heart. They held a profound significance, but Frolic couldn't quite grasp it. He closed his eyes, squeezed Tom's hand, and listened to the swish of the waves. They seemed to speak with the sky, conversing back and forth just beyond Frolic's comprehension. He sensed an entire, hidden realm beneath the waves, a realm beyond the boundaries of his experience. He sensed, all at once, the humans sweating as they toiled on the deck, talking about their midday meal or singing songs to soften their drudgery, and the Other Place existing beside it, beneath it, around it, and overlapping it. Everything lived and sang and spoke, yet Frolic stood outside all of it, neither man nor magic, but not fortunate enough to be a simple machine with a singular, irrefutable function.

"I see." Tom kissed Frolic's hand before releasing it.

"Can you help me understand what it all means?"

"Possibly. *You* must understand, I've never lived a moment without the voices of the wind and sea. Imagine not being able to understand language when your friends spoke to you. You can't. Nor can I comprehend the absence of their song. Still, if I am in a mood to sometime, I might speak with you further. There's precious little else to do on this slow, slovenly human transport. May I have this?" Tom caught the indigo ribbon about Frolic's neck between his thumb and finger and rubbed his pads over the silk in tight little circles.

As soon as Frolic nodded, he grasped the end, pulled the knot loose, and rubbed the ribbon against his cheek. The way his eyes fluttered shut reminded Frolic of his lovers in their most intimate and beautiful moments. His heart glowed a little warmer as he regarded the fey.

Finally, Tom slipped the cord into his pocket with a satisfied smile. "Can you get me more of these?"

"Probably," Frolic answered, too perplexed to even try to fathom it. Then again, Querry and Reg said the sea glass he loved held no value, so maybe Tom's desire for ribbon wasn't so ludicrous. Only people could assign value to objects; nothing held intrinsic worth. To a starving man, bread was more precious than gemstones or gold.

"Yes," he said and nodded once. "I'll get them if I can. Not to trade, but because I want you to have them. Everyone should have beautiful things, things they love. And maybe you'll choose to help me too."

"We shall see." Tom leaned in and kissed Frolic at the outer corner of his eyebrow. "We'll talk again, at any rate. You're much less tedious than the rest of these dirty, ignorant fools. Go on, now. I'm sure your friends have had time to accomplish everything they endeavored to do."

Without another word, the fey turned and walked gracefully away, his movements as perfect and beautiful as a spray of sea grass bending and swaying beneath the surf.

As soon as he saw Querry and Frolic lead Lord Starling and his fey away, Reg retrieved his shirt from the rail and slipped it on, fastening the buttons as he hurried toward the door to Starling's cabin. He couldn't help but feel everyone knew what he planned and watched him. Nor could he understand how Querry and Frolic took any pleasure in such risk. He felt like he'd be sick, and his hand shook so hard he barely managed to open the door.

Being alone in Starling's chamber, with the heavy door between him and the eyes of the others, made Reg feel a little bit better. He took a deep breath and approached the desk. Papers and maps littered the surface, covering it completely, all out of order. Several empty wine bottles weighted them down. Reg desperately wanted a look at the documents, as they probably held some clues to their destination, but he knew he didn't have time, so he went to the top drawer on the left-hand side, where he'd seen Starling stash the contract. It didn't budge an inch when Reg pulled on the ornate, brass handle. Reg swore under his breath.

Locked, of course.

Reg fumbled in his trouser pocket until he located the key Querry had given him, a skeleton key he'd called it, capable of opening most simple locks. Of course, they had no time for Querry to teach Reg to pick locks. According to him, it was a complex and subtle art. Reg didn't want to learn, anyway. Just this once, he'd do what he had to liberate his friends from Starling's grasp, but he didn't want to be a thief. Ever. He had little memory of his parents or their instructions, so he could only assume they'd been the ones to impart morality to him. Unlike his companions, Reg couldn't justify stealing by telling himself his victim had enough, or wouldn't miss it. But he'd spent many years enjoying the ill-gotten fruits of Querry's labors: drinks, meals, baubles, and blissful nights in inns away from the watchful eyes of his adoptive parents. He'd been content to let Querry brave the danger and sully himself while Reg had savored the profits without objection. *God, I never complained about anything Querry did.* Seeking solace from his stress and conflict, Reg drifted into those sweet memories. Querry had been so beautiful as a young man: lank and slender, his limbs and torso stretching faster than he could fill them out with his lack of good, regular meals. He'd been all bones, wiry muscle, and burning, blue eyes and coal-black hair, his skin pale and creamy from his nocturnal lifestyle and the Halcyon smog blocking the sun. Reg had never met anyone so demanding and giving at once—

He pushed the lovely recollections away. They'd sustained him for so many years, he saw them in his mind, felt the sensations, as if he'd traveled back almost a decade. Now, though, he needed to concentrate. With shaking hands, he tried to fit the key into the lock, iron clattering against iron. On his third try, Reg managed to slip the skeleton key into the hole. He held his breath as he turned it, doubting it would work and almost hoping it wouldn't. As much as he wanted a look at the contract, he didn't want to obtain it by such means. The mechanisms ground and clicked, then released. Reg slid the drawer open.

Querry and Frolic's contract lay atop a pile of parchment. Though he desperately wanted to unfurl it on the desk and read it then and there, Reg tried to think as his friends would. He couldn't consider the language of the agreement; he had to copy it as quickly as possible. Carefully, Reg untied the thin, black cord and let the sheet unroll. To his surprise, another, smaller sheet of paper nestled within. It had a greenish cast and contained strips of fibers, like bits of leaves and blades of grass. Reg smoothed it flat and read the words inscribed across it.

Gavindale Starling III, Baron of Greymont and Sele, also the Viscount du Marches, has hereby, through services rendered, procured the services of Our sworn vassal, from here upon called Thomas Teezle, until such time as the Servant's favorite bauble rests within a golden vessel, until such time as the child without a mother reunites with his father, until such time as Master and Servant soar beyond the Edge of the World, and a friend willingly places something in the Servant's hand which he cannot hold in his own.

For many minutes, longer than he dared spare, Reg stared at the odd scrap of paper and wondered how it found its way into his friends' sealed agreement. At last, he snapped out of his fugue and realized he could contemplate it later. He scrolled the words of Querry and Frolic's contract, the letters jagged since his hand shook so badly. Then, because it couldn't do any harm, he copied the short, cryptic verse binding Tom Teezle to Starling's service. Reg rolled the papers up, hoping the still wet ink wouldn't smudge too badly, and shoved them into his trouser pocket.

He stood among the chaos of familiar, Anglican things, missing home more than he'd ever admit to his partners. He'd given it up for them, and while he didn't regret it, not for a second, he did miss his homeland. It didn't matter, Reg decided. He'd done well—better than he'd expected, and he'd accept his small victory for now. Querry had mentioned a celebration. Reg slid a few more desk drawers open and found several dusty bottles of excellent, Belvaisian wine insulated by heaps of haphazard papers. He chose two of the best and shoved one of them between his waistband and underclothes. Then he untucked his shirt and slid the second bottle inside it, squeezing it against his ribs with his arm and feeling, in spite of his misgivings, rather clever. He couldn't help but anticipate his friends' gratitude for his successful work. For himself, he took a few more sheaves of parchment, so he could continue to record the events of their strange journey.

Just as Reg prepared to leave Starling's cabin, the door knob turned slowly, and the latch clicked open. Reg, relying on instinct, ducked beneath the desk as the door swung open, and the baron entered the room, followed by Tom. Reg curled into as small a ball as he could, the necks of the wine bottles poking him in the ribs. After a few seconds, he realized he couldn't hold his breath, so he tried to keep his breathing as shallow and soft as possible. Still, he shook from his fingertips to his toes, and he felt like his heart would explode out of his chest. Reg tried to concoct some excuse to tell Starling should he be caught, but every lie he considered sounded more ludicrous than the last.

"Where did you disappear to, faerie?" Starling asked. He sounded annoyed and exhausted, but not really angry.

"I spoke with the clockwork, Frolic," Tom answered, his tone betraying no emotion. "He is quite troubled."

"How so?"

Tom sighed dramatically. "You cannot understand. The poor creature received the perceptions of my people rather suddenly, and does not know quite how to take them. He asked for my assistance."

"And did you agree?"

"I can do nothing without my lord's blessing." The fey didn't even try to veil his sarcasm and mockery; if anything, he emphasized them.

Starling walked to the front edge of the desk. Reg recoiled and drew into a tighter knot. The baron lifted an empty bottle, exhaled with clear disappointment, and slammed it back down on the desk. "And the clockwork revealed nothing else?"

"Frolic," Tom said.

Reg couldn't help but smile, despite his distress.

"Don't toy with me," Starling said in a low, threatening tone. "What did you learn?"

"They're not fools. Would you have enlisted them if they were? They know there is danger. They know many things are left unsaid. That clockwork boy sees much. He will be an asset or a serious enemy. Above all, he loves his friends in that way you humans value certain other members of your race. But more. His passion is boundless. I believe that boy will do anything to keep his two humans safe. I believe, if he had to, he could draw upon the great power within him. He can't use it yet. He doesn't understand it, but don't test him."

"Good work, Tom." Starling continued to search around his desk, bed, and night table, presumably for a spare bottle. "Do you know anything else, as far as his goals?"

"No, my lord."

By Tom's tone, Reg sensed he was lying or holding something back. Surely Starling intuited the faerie's deception as well, and he said nothing for many minutes.

"Very well. Tell me, fey, how do we resist these attacks by your kindred?"

"We don't."

"Unacceptable!" Starling smacked the desk with his fist, rattling the inkwell and empty bottles and rustling the unorganized papers. "There are wards, charms against them, are there not?"

"Honestly." Tom snorted.

Reg dared to peer around the edge of the desk. Not two feet away, Starling tapped the toe of his expensive, leather shoe, and another few feet away the faerie waited, his slim legs tense beneath his snug, pale-green trousers. When Reg looked up, Tom caught his gaze, grinned slightly, and winked. It sent a shiver down Reg's spine.

"If you're so concerned, *my lord*, I suggest you speak with the human female who works on the engines. She is working on constructing a device to neutralize magic, if I'm not mistaken. Perhaps she's made progress, though of course you realize such a contraption will leave both you and me powerless. We'll be placing our fates in the hands of men who aren't loyal, some who are here under duress, and many who don't even care for us."

"Let me have a drink and think on this," Starling said, taking a step closer to the desk.

"That's not wise," Tom said a little too quickly. "We shouldn't hesitate. We don't know when the next attack will come. Let us speak to the woman now. The wine will not go to vinegar in a quarter of an hour, *sir*."

"Oh very well, you insufferable pest."

"I'm sure at least someone will be grateful we went below in a timely fashion," Tom said as the two of them left the cabin.

The door closed softly, and Reg waited a few minutes before emerging from his hiding place. He raked his sweaty hair off his forehead and tried to slow his breathing. While he knew he'd been fortunate, he absolutely abhorred the idea of being beholden to a faerie. Their help always came with a price. He'd watched Querry being toyed with and manipulated by the Fair Folk for too many years back in Halcyon. Still, Reg hadn't requested Tom's aid, and no bargain had passed between them. The faerie might expect Reg's future cooperation, but he couldn't demand it.

Still shaking, Reg readjusted the bottles beneath his shirt, left the cabin, hurried across the deck, and descended into the hold. He had much to discuss—and even more he couldn't say—with his companions.

CHAPTER 11

WHEN HE returned to the small room they shared, Reg found Querry and Frolic sitting on the floor, Frolic holding a wet cloth to Querry's eye. Querry sat straight up from the bunk he leaned against, giving Reg a good view of his swollen, blackened face. "Did you get it?" Querry asked.

Reg rolled his eyes as he opened his shirt and handed one of the wine bottles to his injured friend. "This should make you feel better."

"Brilliant! That means you did it, Reg! I knew you could!" Querry took a roll of leather from a pouch near his waist and unfurled it across his thigh. From the various tools and picks arranged neatly within, he selected a piece of curlicue metal and opened the wine. He took a long pull straight from the bottle and exhaled with satisfaction. "Everything tastes better if it's stolen."

Reg set the other bottle on top of a chest and joined them on the floor. Querry passed him the wine, and he drank. While creamy, smoky, and robust, the wine would have tasted better chilled. Still, Reg took a few more deep swallows to calm his nerves. "Your contract wasn't the only thing I found in that drawer. Somehow, the agreement binding that fey, Tom Teezle, to Lord Starling ended up sealed inside the parchment."

"Odd," Frolic said. "Or… maybe it isn't. I think Tom knew what we were up to. I think he even helped us as much as he could."

As Reg looked at Frolic, his sweet face and wide eyes as innocent as an angel's, he remembered what the fey had said about the terrible power within him. Should he mention it? How would he even breach the subject? Instead, he asked, "What do you mean he helped us?"

Frolic pursed his lips and toyed with the open collar of his shirt, running his fingers over the edge of the fabric. "When I spoke to him, he said you'd be done with your task before he left me. I think he knew. I think he wants our help to regain his freedom."

"I think you're right. He lured Starling away from the cabin while I was hidden under the desk. Tom made it possible for me to escape. And you think he expects his freedom in return?" Reg asked.

Querry drank, passed the wine back to Reg, and clapped his hands. "He'll make a very valuable ally! Well done, both of you."

"Wait just a minute, Querry. Have you forgotten so soon how that faerie back in Halcyon used you? They aren't to be trusted. They aren't like us."

"They still have a right to independence," Frolic said, with more passion than Reg had ever heard from him. "I think we should help Tom."

"Well, I think we should make a deal with him, enlist his power," Querry said. "Get him in our corner."

"No," Reg said firmly. "No, I don't think we should. Haven't obscure magical agreements led us into enough trouble already? We should have nothing to do with that creature. Under no circumstances should we enter into any kind of bargain with him. Please, swear to me we won't."

"I didn't say anything about a bargain, but if I can help him liberate himself, then I will," Frolic said. "It's only right."

Reg reached over to stroke Frolic's knee. "Beauty, you must be very careful. These creatures are old and experts at manipulation. He'll trick you if he can. Remember, he isn't human—"

"Neither am I!" Frolic sprung to his feet and strode to the door, standing with his arms crossed and his back to Querry and Reg. "No part of me is human, not a bit. If anything, I'm as much faerie as I am clockwork. You two made me that way. Don't forget that!"

Both of them stood. Reg sought Querry's gaze in the hopes of some suggestion as to how to undo what he'd unknowingly said. Querry merely shook his head and shrugged. Since he couldn't bear to see his dear Frolic hurting, Reg walked up behind him and wound his arms around Frolic's small waist. At first Frolic flinched and recoiled, but then he consented to be held, curving his back against Reg and relaxing into Reg's embrace. Frolic seemed so small and frail, yet Reg knew how much strength he possessed. Now, it seemed he possessed a power not even he knew of or understood. But it didn't matter. Reg knew what he loved about Frolic, and none of those things had changed.

"Ah, beauty. I'm so sorry." Reg rested his chin on the top of Frolic's head and closed his eyes. "You know it doesn't matter to me how you started out. You're still one of the finest people I've ever met. I only want to keep you safe. I'd give my life to protect you or Querry. But both of you seem susceptible to faerie glamour. I just wish you could see how deceitful they are. Frolic, my sweet Frolic, I didn't mean to upset you."

Frolic nuzzled against Reg's neck. "I'm sorry too, Reggie. I've been on edge. I can't say why."

"You had a right to be offended," Reg whispered, burrowing down into Frolic's hair just as Querry came to stand in front of Frolic and stroke his smooth face.

"The important thing is Reg got a copy of the contract," Querry said. "Maybe we'll get out of this mess after all. Until then, there's nothing much to do until the ship is repaired. For the time being, we're stuck where we are."

Frolic inclined his head to look at Querry, and Querry looked down at his face with a gentle, adoring expression. Then he looked at Reg with the same reverence on his features and his blue eyes shining, and Reg couldn't help himself. He reached over Frolic's shoulder, grasped Querry by the hair, and pulled his face close. He parted his lips and let Querry do the rest. Querry didn't disappoint him—he never did—as he pressed his mouth roughly against Reg's and forced his tongue past Reg's teeth. Frolic dropped his head onto Reg's shoulder, and Reg ran his hand up under Frolic's shirt while his other hand clawed at Querry's neck. Frolic flinched as Reg ran his fingertips lightly up his waist, and Querry broke free of Reg's lips to kiss Frolic. For the next several minutes they took turns kissing each other, their hands roving over each other's bodies as their breathing grew quick and heavy.

All the tension that had been coursing in Reg's veins since he'd woken up surged to a crescendo, making him tremble and writhe in the confines of Querry and Frolic's arms. He felt like he'd explode from the energy building within him. With a growl, he caught Querry's hair again, hauled him close, and bit his neck at his pulse-point.

Querry made a small, high-pitched sound of surprise and pain before pulling away and holding Reg's face between his palms. "Just what's gotten into you?" he asked with a mischievous smile on his swollen, shiny lips.

"I... I don't know. I've been so nervous, wound up so tight all day... I feel like it's tearing me in two. I've so much vigor at the moment, and I need this so much...."

Querry smiled knowingly and kissed Reg hard, their teeth knocking and scraping together. Meanwhile, Frolic nipped and suckled up the side of Querry's neck while he circled his sweet little ass against Reg's erection. Reg wriggled his arm between Querry and Frolic and ran his palm up Frolic's taut belly until he could capture a nipple between his thumb and finger. Frolic whimpered against Querry's skin and thrust against Querry. Reg grinned against Querry's lips, and Querry's eyes crinkled to crescents as they both felt Frolic go slack in their arms with the first of many climaxes. The wonderful sounds he made as he shivered with his release almost made Reg come in his trousers. Instead, he willed the release away and freed himself from Querry's mouth with a slurp. He pushed the white ringlets up and swiped his tongue from the prominent knob of Frolic's spine to his hairline. He tasted like a cool sunrise heavy with fog. Reg always expected a salty, human flavor, but Frolic's essence reminded him of morning rain.

Slowly, Reg dropped to his knees, rubbing his cheek and chin down Frolic's back and savoring the juts of bone and cords of sinew as he went. When he reached Frolic's waist Reg pulled his partner's shirttails loose and yanked the loose-fitting trousers to Frolic's knees. He peeled Frolic's undershorts down and kissed the half-moons of his slender ass before urging his cheeks apart. Frolic spread his legs a little wider and bent at the waist, leaning against Querry.

Reg burrowed his nose into Frolic's cleft, which lacked the expected musk, and pressed the tip against his wrinkled opening. It clenched in response.

"Oh, Reggie, yes!" Frolic almost sang.

Reg rested his forehead against Frolic's tailbone as Querry buried his fingers in Reg's hair. "Beauty...." Reg panted, his heart ready to leap out of his chest and his cock so hard it hurt. "Beauty... can I have you? Frolic, please...."

In response, Frolic turned, dropped to his knees, and kissed Reg. His kisses were so different from Querry's: enthusiastic but without the aggression. Though Reg relished Querry's dominance, he also enjoyed Frolic's innocent exploration. He wrapped Frolic in his arms and lay back against the metal floor of their cabin. In minutes, both Querry and Frolic lay across him, their bodies forming a slight peak above him as they kissed at opposite corners of his mouth, their tongues meeting his at the center. Both of their cocks, Frolic's bare and Querry's barely restrained by the fabric of his trousers, brushed alongside Reg's erection. Out of his mind with need, Reg bit at their lips as he struggled to get Querry's pants down. He pulled so hard he popped the buttons and sent them pinging against the steel-paneled floor. Finally, he managed to get his hand on Querry's cock and slide his foreskin back to reveal his rich, plum-colored head. Just the sight of it, the scent of it, made Reg desperate to feel it rubbing against his own penis, sliding across his belly, cleaving him, pushing inside him....

Ready to weep with frustration, Reg lifted his hips to pull his trousers down. He only got them to the tops of his thighs, but it was enough. Frolic, as if he could read Reg's mind, hurried to untie Reg's cravat and unbutton his shirt. Soon it fell open on either side of him, and both Querry and Frolic hurried to taste his exposed flesh.

"Oh dear God," Reg breathed, lost in the sensations of their warm, wet mouths on his chest and belly and their hard, velvety cocks sliding against his. He'd wanted to fuck Frolic, fuck him hard, but....

"I can't last. I'm going to.... Oh God!"

"It's all right," Querry said, wrapping his hand around all three of their cocks and pressing them tight together. "You need this, and I love you. Come for me."

Reg threw his head back and screwed his eyes shut as Frolic laid his hand over Querry's, increasing the pressure on their dicks. Lifting his hips, Reg thrust into the tight tunnel their fingers formed and felt their flesh catch against his own. Then he reached down and draped his hand over theirs, feeling the bumps of their knuckles before moving up to feel all three of their hot, hard, wet cockheads crushed against each other. He fondled the tips, spreading his and Querry's seed liberally over them all. As he continued to caress their slits and ridges, Querry and Frolic moved their hands to the bases and back up, jacking them with quick, urgent strokes.

Frolic dropped his mouth to Reg's nipple and encircled the rigid flesh with his hot tongue, while Querry kissed Reg and grabbed his balls, squeezing them rhythmically within his unoccupied fist.

"Go on, love," Querry said against his lips. "Show me how much you love me."

Frolic lifted his head, and his golden eyes caught and held Reg's gaze. "Yes, Reggie. I want to know I make you happy."

"Happy? God... I'm the luckiest man in the world.... Oh, yes. Grab me just like that. Your hands on me are all I need. Please... kiss me. Please, my loves."

Both of them descended on his mouth, and their three tongues twined together. All of them thrust hard, seeking their releases, finding it difficult to stay in each other's rhythm. None of them could really move freely with their pants barely to their knees. For Reg, it hardly mattered. The feeling of the men he loved on top of him, close against him, and kissing him while they held his cock next to theirs drove him over the edge he'd been trying to skirt. He plummeted into his release, screaming their names and slamming his head against the floor. He felt like he'd be shredded into ribbons as he shot his seed over Querry and Frolic's hands and his own stomach. Querry and Frolic held him together, gripping his cock tightly and joining their bodies. Their solid flesh against his grounded Reg until his ecstasy subsided, and he felt the floor beneath him again.

Querry and Frolic kissed an inch from his chin, and Querry's free hand massaged Frolic's ass and the back of his thigh. Frolic shivered with the aftershocks of however many orgasms he'd enjoyed. Sometimes it was hard to tell without any physical evidence. Reg realized Querry had come all over his belly and chest, and his semen coated the sparse hair up the center of Reg's stomach and chest. The smell made Reg's spent dick skip. He dipped a fingertip into the drying liquid and brought it to his mouth.

"I miss sucking your cock," he said to Querry.

"I can remedy that for you very easily, love," Querry said with a chuckle. "Anytime, truly."

"Look at the mess we've made," Reg said, raking his fingers through Frolic's hair. "We didn't even manage to undress properly. I... I'm afraid I've embarrassed myself. I didn't even last five minutes."

Querry turned on his side and nestled down against Reg's chest. Reg snaked an arm around his back and pulled him closer. "You were so excited, Reggie. Seeing you like that, seeing you like that because of us.... Well, you saw what it did to me. I'm glad you still have so much passion for me. That we all have so much passion for each other. Besides, it might have been quick, but it was good. It's always good."

Frolic wriggled closer, reached across Reg's chest despite the mess, knit his fingers with Querry's, pecked along Reg's jawline, and then said, "We'll always be like this, won't we?"

Reg couldn't answer. Frolic would never change, but he and Querry would. He couldn't help but wonder how Frolic would feel when their beauty faded. He didn't worry Frolic would abandon them; Frolic wasn't so shallow or disloyal, but his physical attraction might wane. What would happen to him when they were gone? He squeezed his lovers harder, as if he could prevent them being taken from him, as if he could stand against mortality and the passage of time. Of course he knew he couldn't; Querry was the one to fight such impossible odds. Some part of Reg still believed Querry, if anyone, could defeat anything.

"Reggie?"

"I can promise I'll always love you," Reg said. "Both of you."

Why was he thinking such morbid thoughts? They were only in their twenties, for God's sake. They had decades before them. Still, holding them now, feeling them stir against him and hearing the sound of their satisfied breathing, he wanted more. He wanted centuries, millennia, an eternity with these men. After everything he'd experienced, he still expected life to take them away. He felt like it was only a matter of time, and it terrified him.

Querry chuckled against his chest, pulling Reg out of the dark place he'd gone. "It's funny. You know, beauty, when Reg and I were just boys, we'd lay awake after our day of work in the factory and talk about running away and going off to exotic places on a ship. Remember, Reggie?"

Reg couldn't help but smile as he recalled feeling safe within Querry's lank limbs despite the danger and misery surrounding them. Their dream had felt close enough to touch, until growing up stole it away. *Until now*, Reg thought. "I suppose we did it. Here we are. I guess there's absolutely no stopping you when you want something, no matter how impossible it seems. You simply won't relent until you make it happen."

"If I've learned anything about this life, it's that you have to fight for everything. Take it. No one is ever going to give it to you."

"That's not true," Frolic said softly. "I didn't have to fight for either of you. All I had to do was ask, and you loved me and took care of me."

Reg couldn't bear to remind him of everything they'd battled against to remain free and together. Thankfully Querry didn't say it either. It was too lovely a sentiment to crush. They lay in silence for probably half an hour, gratified just to be together, even half-dressed and filthy as they were, even on a greasy metal floor.

"Do you think I can read over Tom's contract?" Frolic asked, shaking Reg out of his contented languor.

He'd completely overlooked the ill-gotten fruits of his adventure. His lovers sat up so he could move freely. He reached down and fished the crinkled copies from his trouser pocket. Reg supposed he'd rested long enough and should probably start studying Querry and Frolic's agreement. With a disgusted but amused grunt, he tried to brush the dry, flaky semen from his chest and torso before pulling up his trousers. In the heat of the cabin, he didn't bother buttoning his shirt. He and Frolic leaned back against the bunks and spread the papers across their laps. The verbose and meandering language instantly made his head ache. Something pressed against his palm, and he saw Querry smiling down at him as he pressed Reg's spectacles into his hand. Querry's blackened eye had swollen almost completely shut, his iris a cobalt slash in the bruised flesh. He watched both of them with clear adulation tinged with a trace of apology.

"I'll go see if I can find some coffee," Querry said. "Maybe some soap and water." He kissed each of them on the forehead before departing.

The door closed softly, and Frolic gasped. "I knew it! I can help Tom! I think this contract is talking about me."

Though he'd anticipated Frolic's reaction, it still struck Reg like a kick to the stomach.

CHAPTER 12

FROLIC, EXCITED to continue his work with Cornelia, hurried into the workshop. When he didn't see the tinkerer leaning over her bench, he picked his way around the partially completed projects they'd been experimenting with to the large door at the back of the room. The way their voyage had been going, Frolic needed some distraction. Storms assailed them almost daily. Essential parts of the ship broke or stopped functioning inexplicably. The sailors' instruments went missing. The ship's captain claimed ocean currents he'd sailed for decades had somehow changed course, or disappeared altogether. When they needed wind, the air stood as still and stale as the atmosphere within a tomb. Other times, it battered the vessel and threatened to capsize it. The crew suffered violent shifts in mood, sometimes so jolly and indolent they couldn't attend to their tasks, and at each other's throats moments later. All the while, Frolic heard the voices of the sky and sea begging them to turn back, swearing to stop them if they persisted. Both Reg and Querry had been on edge, and it made the last several weeks feel like half a year to Frolic.

Frolic entered the huge, empty part of the hold he and Corny had been given to work on their latest creation. Both gaslights and oil-burning lanterns hung from the walls. The light they cast fluctuated with the rocking of the ship, making Frolic doubt the solidity of the floor as he approached the large, rectangular construct that dwarfed even Cornelia.

At the sound of Frolic's boots echoing through the empty chamber, Corny stood and waved. The blue flame of the gas-powered torch she held went out with a soft whoosh, and she removed the metal mask from her head. With a wide smile, she waved Frolic over, and he hurried to see what had her in such high spirits.

As had become her habit, she set her tools down and clutched both of Frolic's hands before kissing him on top of his head. "Finally arrived, then," she said. "And not a moment too soon. I think she's almost ready, but I need your help to align some of the more delicate gears in the steering mechanism and regulate the fuel output. If we can't adjust it somehow, we'll find ourselves on the moon, I'm afraid."

"The moon talks in poetry. It's so pure and lonely," Frolic said.

She pushed playfully at his shoulder. "Enough of that. You know it gives me the shivers when you talk about that faerie stuff."

"I'm sorry. I really want you to like me." Frolic cursed himself for not having learned which of his thoughts to speak aloud and which to hold inside.

Corny threw her arm across his shoulders and gave him a squeeze. "Ah, Frolic, you know I love ya. Now, come see. I'm pretty pleased with the modifications I've done to the wings."

With her arm still around him, she guided him beneath one of the bat-like appendages. He looked up at the spines of the wings, which seemed much less angular and stiff than they had two days ago. Corny had added complex ball and socket joints at several places and multifaceted clockwork joints at others. They would afford the construct a much greater and more subtle range of motion. Above them, sheets of a brass alloy, so thin the light glowed through it, stretched across the framework. It rippled slightly when Corny went inside the vessel and adjusted some gauges, demonstrating how smoothly the wings lifted, stretched, angled back, and curled close to the ship.

Frolic gave a little hop and clapped his hands. "Oh, how wonderful, Corny! You reduced the choppiness of the movements and increased the, um, they can move in so many more directions now, and faster, I'll bet."

"You'd win that bet, mate. The new, smaller gears react much quicker to the controls. You'd think, at first, turning more gears would take longer than turning less, but it turns out the opposite is true, so long as everything is in balance. That way, the larger gears don't work so hard, and the load is more evenly distributed. Er, you know what I mean."

Frolic giggled and patted her arm. Both of them understood machines inside and out, knew the workings of their tiniest components, yet neither of them could properly articulate that knowledge to another. Fortunately, with each other, they felt no need. The steam conduits, engines, and gears spoke for themselves in a sort of beautiful, simplistic language. Unlike human words, nothing could be misunderstood. Nothing relied upon the listener's perceptions or prior experiences; clockwork existed and functioned without the need for interpretation. It expressed a single meaning, unlike all the other voices Frolic heard and struggled to comprehend.

"You've segmented the spines," Frolic said. "That was a brilliant idea. How did you come up with it?"

Corny removed her thick, leather gloves and shoved them into a pocket on her equally sturdy apron. "Well, I suppose I came up with them because of you. Ever since I met you, I've looked at machines in a different way. Nature knows best, it seems, and machines fashioned after living beings are much more efficient. I've been trying to make my clockworks more organic, make them move more like people and animals. It's proved a huge asset to my work. You know, Frolic, I designed the wings of this airship almost exactly after the little toy bird you brought me. I've never seen anything mechanical move so smoothly. Except for you, of course. So, I took a good close look at the way you'd constructed the wings, and pretty much just duplicated them. I've learned so much from the way you create your joints. I mean, one set of gears just doesn't do the job, does it?"

"Did you get my bird to fly?" Frolic asked. It sat on a stack of wooden crates a few dozen feet away, nothing more than a glimmer in the vast, brightly lit room.

Her face scrunched up in a wide grin. "Sure did, love."

She clasped his hand and led him toward his creation. "You just needed an energy source. The airship gave me the idea. See, unlike the airship you described to me, the one your friend built, ours doesn't rely on balloons of hot air to keep it afloat. Ours burns from the bottom, and while the heat helps to keep it in the sky, it's mostly used to keep the gears turning. Watch."

Corny wound Frolic's bird. It flapped its wings, and a few sparks shot from its beak and tail feathers. Then, to Frolic's astonishment and delight, it lifted off the crates and circled the large room three times before setting down again.

"How?"

"Well, the body is fairly hollow, so there was plenty of room to fit a small fuel source. I chose lamp oil, just because we have plenty onboard. It doesn't need much, just enough for the heat to lift the bird off the ground until the gears can get going. Then I outfitted it to keep them turning. I really think engines powered by burning fuel will be the rage one day. As long as the source doesn't run out, or is replenished, your bird could just about fly forever." As if to prove her words, Frolic's little avian fluttered up from its roost and came to perch on her shoulder.

"I don't like the idea of my toys depending on fuel," Frolic said. "Still, I'm quite impressed by what you've done. I spent months trying to figure out how to get it into the air."

The clockwork bird swiped a wing over its face before nesting down amidst the fabric and leather cover of Corny's shoulder. It blinked its eyes sleepily and lowered its head to its breast. She ran a thick finger down its back and over its small head. It nestled down as if contented. "I don't know, Frolic. Everything needs fuel. For us its food and sleep. For you, magic and heat and air. Don't really understand all that, truth be told. Machines need energy to operate, though, even the simplest of them. By winding a clockwork, aren't you giving it some of your energy? Wouldn't it be better if it had its own source?"

"Well, I suppose—"

"Lamp oil isn't going to cut it for our ship, though. After all, it has to be large enough to carry the entire expedition and all our supplies. Gas is expensive, but if we can get a hold of a few more tanks when we make port, I think we'll have enough to fly to our destination. It will shave weeks off this entire journey if we don't have to trek through the jungle. I understand there aren't even any roads. With this old girl, we won't have to worry about it, though. Lord Starling couldn't be happier."

"I can't wait to get her into the air." Frolic stepped back to look at what they'd managed to make in only a few weeks. They'd really accomplished something amazing, he thought. The airship he'd used as inspiration, the one built by Querry's friend, Dink, back in Halcyon, had more resembled a traditional carriage made from glass, wood, and polished brass. Theirs wasn't quite as pretty, made mostly from sheets of metal riveted together with only a row of small, square windows along each side and a larger one along the front. It shared the bat-like wings Dink had designed, and which allowed it, he hoped, the same maneuverability as the original. Instead of balloons floating above the passenger compartment, he and Corny had designed long, narrow bladders beneath the hull, which would fill with a mix of hot air and a recently discovered gas which was even lighter. Highlium, he thought he'd heard Corny call it. Apparently she'd learned the formula from a tinkerer onboard a pirate ship, of all places. Their ship also had a trio of gas furnaces along the back and another set beneath them to propel it up and forward.

Corny stroked the steel frame of the open door fondly. "Not bad, considering we weren't planning on making her and did so from mostly scrap. Still, I wish we had a few more weeks."

"Well, we don't. I heard some of the sailors say we'd be arriving within a day, at most. Should we get to work? Tell me what needs done first."

He followed her inside the ship to the helm. Both of them knelt down in front of the brass column beneath the helm. Cornelia pulled a metal toolbox across the floor, chose a screwdriver, and removed the casing to expose the gears within. They spent the next several hours refitting the clockwork within, as well as inside the conduits leading to the wings and rudders, making sure they all worked together in perfect synchronicity.

A rumbling sound distracted Frolic from his work. He looked up from the tip of one of the wings to Corny holding her stomach. Since he'd finished anyway, he stood up and tucked the wire-thin wrench he'd been using behind his ear, worried she might be feeling sick.

She smiled at him as she stashed her own tools in her apron pockets. A streak of black grease stretched from Corny's left cheek to the corner of her mouth. "Ah, Frolic. As much as I love this work, I don't enjoy missing a meal, obviously. We've come further than I could have hoped, so what do you say we stop for a bite and a spot of tea? My eyes are going crossed looking at gears, anyway."

Though he didn't eat and his eyes never tired, Frolic had come to understand the human need for food and respite. He rubbed the grime on his palms off on the thighs of his trousers and grinned his agreement. The two of them returned to the workshop, where Corny spread a dainty, flowered cloth across one of her large anvils. Frolic sat on the floor in front of it while she brought the kettle, a cup and saucer, a tin of sugar cubes, and a pitcher of cream. He knew she kept her teapot warm over the furnace, just in case she wanted a cup. He waited while she arranged her bread, canned ham, cheeses, preserved peas, butter, biscuits, silverware, and gold-edged plates on the makeshift table. Then she sat down across from him, licking her lips. She ate heartily, without stopping to make conversation, until she seemed to realize she might be neglecting her guest.

"Didn't mean to be rude, love." Corny dabbed the corners of her mouth with a lacey-edged napkin. "I'm afraid I was famished."

"I don't mind," Frolic said.

She soaked a biscuit in her tea. "So, how are your mates getting on?"

Frolic wondered what to say, how much information would be appropriate to share. He had such difficulty figuring it all out, but he trusted Corny. "Well, Reg is very frustrated. He wants to find a way out of our contract, but so far he can't come up with anything. He gets quite cross about it. Querry... well, Querry is restless. He gets bored easily. He always wants to be moving, working toward or against something. He hates waiting. It's made him very...."

"What?"

"I don't think I should tell you. I never know what to say and what to keep to myself."

Corny reached across their improvised table and squeezed Frolic's wrist. "Hell, love, I have no clue how to talk to people. But I can talk to you, and you can talk to me. To the devil with what anybody else thinks. It's just us here, so say what's on your mind."

"Querry wants to make love all the time. Two or three times a day, sometimes more."

She choked on the biscuit she'd been chewing. "Oh, well... oh my."

"I shouldn't have said it. I've upset you."

"No, not at all. I just wasn't expecting that. You're lucky to have a man who loves you so much. I'm happy for you, and... and a little envious."

"You would like a man to make love with?"

Corny blushed until her cheeks and nose looked bruised. "I wouldn't ever say this to anyone else, but... all right, yeah. I'd like to find a man who didn't expect me to be a servant or crank out babies, a man who might want to touch me. But that's not likely to happen, is it?"

"Why?"

"Look at me, Frolic."

"I am. I see a friend. I see someone who can build or fix almost anything, someone who can fight, and someone I like being with."

"If only the rest of the world—"

The ship pitched hard to the starboard side, cutting her off. Her lunch fell to the floor, the dishes shattering. Both of them got to their feet as the vessel lurched in the opposite direction. Frolic struggled not to fall over.

"What the hell is happening?" Corny yelled over the sounds of splitting wood and tearing metal. The ship rocked back and forth like a child's cradle.

Something cylindrical and pointed pierced the hull. Foamy water poured in from the rupture between the wall and ceiling. Another coral-colored tine pierced the other side of the workshop. The erratic motion of the ship threw Corny to her knees, and Frolic hurried to help her up as seawater flowed into the hold. Clutching each other's arms, they stumbled toward the hatch leading to the deck to find out what was going on. When they reached the ladder leading up, the ship dipped hard to port, knocking them on their sides, but not before Frolic heard the screams and frantic running of the sailors above him.

"Damn it," Corny said. "I already stashed all my weapons in the airship. If we're under attack—"

Frolic instinctively reached to his left hip, but he'd left his sword back in the cabin, seeing no need for it while working on their projects. "What are we going to do?" he cried. "I have to get to Querry and Reg, make sure they're safe—"

Corny wrapped her big, solid arms around his head and rolled, just in time to shield him from a falling ceiling beam. "We have to get out of here! I think the ship is going down." The briny water almost covered their prone bodies.

Gripping the wall for support, Frolic staggered to his feet and pulled Corny up with him. No sooner had they stood than the stern of the ship lifted into the air, pushing the vessel almost vertical, and tossing them toward the bow. Frolic clung to Corny as they somersaulted through the workshop, all their unfinished projects raining down upon them. He tried to cover her face and protect her from the worst of the falling metal. It might hurt if it struck him, but he wasn't flesh and wouldn't be so easily damaged.

The ship slammed down hard on its belly, tossing the remaining items in the workshop into the air. Frolic pulled Corny up, encircled her waist with his arms, and braced his back against the wall. The water reached their knees.

"We have to get off this tub!" Corny bellowed.

Frolic knew she was right. "How?"

"The airship's our only chance." She grabbed his hand and pulled him through the workshop, dodging bits of caving ceiling and falling debris.

"I won't leave without Reg and Querry!"

No sooner had Frolic uttered the words than he heard his friends calling for him from above. At the top of his voice, he shouted, "Down here! Come on! Bring anyone you can find. Please, please hurry!"

Corny dragged him toward the airship just as the entire bow of the ship ripped away beneath another spear of coral. Frolic broke away from her long enough to retrieve the leather satchel containing the book about how he was made. He couldn't leave it behind or he'd never truly understand himself or be able to build a companion. The sea and its rocky bed assailed the ship mercilessly, pulling it apart. With nothing to dam it, the water flowed into the hold. Corny dragged Frolic through the door as he struggled to look for his friends. The ship buckled at the center, and more water spilled in. Frolic clapped his hands over his mouth when he saw Querry and Reg sprinting toward the airship, their arms full of packs and equipment. Many more people, including Tom Teezle and the baron, followed close behind them. They, along with the three mercenaries and about a half a dozen of the sailors, hurried onboard the airship as the seafaring vessel sank lower into the water.

Frolic hurried over to his partners to make sure they were unharmed. Querry and Reg looked pale and worried, but he saw no injuries on them, no tears in their flesh. A few more sailors stumbled into the airship. The ocean submerged half of it now.

"We have to go!" Frolic shouted. "Now!"

Corny sealed the door and flipped some levers. The airship hummed as its furnaces tried to alight, but couldn't beneath the water. "Bloody hell, Frolic. We have to get someplace dry so we can take off."

"I'll see to it. Just keep the flow of gas steady and the wings going." Though Querry and Reg clutched at his elbows, trying to hold him back, Frolic pulled away and raced through the door and around the back of the airship. With all his might, Frolic pushed the vessel toward the gaping hole in the hull. To his surprise and relief, it moved toward the open air until it teetered on the edge of the chewed up hold, tilting precariously toward the churning ocean beneath it. The wet gas furnaces tried to alight, but only sputtered a few puffs of smoke. The airship tilted down toward the sea, ready to plunge bow-first into the roiling waves. Frolic grasped the stern-side but couldn't slow its decent. His feet slid across the wooden floor as he struggled to keep the airship and the entire crew, his lovers included, from plummeting into the depths of the sea.

Frolic tried to dig his nails into the metal hull to no avail. The vessel slipped through his fingers toward the angry waters awaiting it. He screamed and clutched at it, his nails leaving furrows across the steel sheeting. Just as the nose of the airship touched the water, the furnaces sprung to life. Frolic jumped away from the intense heat and dove through the door Corny held open. He landed on his belly as their ship soared toward the sun.

"Shit," Corny said. "Bloody, bloody hell! The fuel delivery system."

The airship ascended into the bright, blue sky. Corny hurried to the helm. "Somebody has to fly this thing!"

"You built it, girl," the baron snapped. "So fly it."

"I can't," Corny said, staring out the front window. "I know the mechanics, but—"

Reg pushed past her and grabbed the spokes of the wheel. "I've done this before. For the love of God, hold on." He jerked the helm back and forth, clearly trying to cease the vessel's ascent and establish a horizontal path. It finally straightened out, though it still rushed forward at a great speed.

Frolic saw nothing but a blue blur as the ship tossed from side to side, flinging the people and objects from one wall to the other. He didn't know whether the sky was above them and the sea beneath, or the opposite. A sudden burst from the lower fuel burners pitched the nose of the ship upward, almost vertical. Bright sunlight poured through the front window as the passengers were thrown toward the back. Frolic managed to grab one of the shelves they'd built into the wall and avoid tumbling over the others. Querry's back collided with his chest, and Frolic wrapped his other arm around his friend's waist. Reg struggled to keep hold of the helm and try to right the ship. He overcompensated, and the vessel did a barrel roll, pitching the passengers and their possessions against the ceiling and then back to the floor. Reg tugged on the controls, grasping the helm with one hand and flipping brass levers with the other, trying to get the ship horizontal again.

Querry's skin looked gray-green as Frolic guided him to a bolted-down, metal bench. "Just hold onto this. If there's trouble, get underneath."

Frolic used the walls and backs of the benches to stay on his feet as he pulled himself toward Reg. Through the front window, he saw the rocky coast about two miles away, rushing to meet them. "We have to slow down," Frolic yelled over the rush of the wind passing the hull, the noise of the gears, and the frantic voices of the terrified passengers.

"How?" Reg yelled back.

Frolic considered as the sharp rocks drew closer and closer. If they hit them at this speed, the ship would be demolished. He might survive, but the others, Querry and Reg—

"Spread the wings to their full span," he told Reg. "We'll have to glide in."

Though the look on his face said Reg didn't understand Frolic's plans, he nodded once and reached for the appropriate switches. Frolic hurried toward the back of the ship. On the way, he spared a moment to crouch next to Lord Starling and Tom Teezle. It surprised him to see the baron holding his faerie servant against his chest, protecting Tom's head with his arms.

"I need your help," he said to them. "It's going to be a bad landing no matter what, but if there's anything either of you can do with your magic to slow us down, it will help."

He didn't wait for their responses. The airship cut through the sky, nose down, as if intent upon destroying itself against the rocks. Thick, black smoke trailed from the stern like a twisted banner. The access door was damaged. Frolic looked at the tools, weapons, and equipment scattered across the floor. He didn't have time to be selective, so he picked up the first claw hammer he saw and crouched down. He forced the hammer's flattened tines into the seam of the damaged panel and pulled with all his strength. The ruined latch started to give, and the steel bent and tore, but after a moment he managed to dislodge the square of metal. The draft sucked his hair over his face, making it hard to see, but he managed to locate the copper pipes feeding gas to the burners. He turned the valves to the off position, but it wasn't enough. There would still be gas in the pipe feeding into the engine. Flipping the hammer in his hand, he struck at the tubing with none of the finesse he usually used when handling machinery. They'd built them to endure the elements, and they held no matter how hard Frolic hit them. It occurred to him if he'd managed to rupture the pipes and the hammer caused a spark, they'd all be in danger.

Instead, he wrapped his hand around the pipes and braced his feet against the side of the hull. The metal walls bent under the force, but the pipes still wouldn't give. Frolic took a deep breath and gave it everything he had. Finally the pipes pulled from their fittings. Gas hissed out through the holes, but Frolic didn't stop until he'd torn them completely from their tanks, and he flew across the cabin when they suddenly let go. The conduits flipped and snaked around, spewing noxious fumes. The ship finally slowed down.

Frolic raced back to the controls. A sharp updraft caught the wings, pushing the ship a few feet higher but impeding its forward momentum. As the ship rode the sudden current of wind, Frolic realized it hadn't been luck. He looked out the front window. They still plummeted toward the ragged stones dotting the shallow water and lining the beach. Reg flapped the wings down, lifting them into the air and buying them a few seconds, but Frolic worried it wouldn't be enough. Without the fuel to keep it aloft, the heavy ship succumbed to gravity. The wings couldn't hold it up. He'd made a fatal miscalculation.

"Reggie, get down."

"What?"

"Get down. Give me the helm. Try to protect yourself—" Frantic, more afraid than he'd ever been in his life, Frolic pushed Reg out of the way. "Go to Querry. Get under the bench."

If they didn't make it—No. He wouldn't let that happen, no matter what he had to do. Frolic looked over his shoulder and yelled to all those assembled. "Get on the floor. Cover your heads. We're coming in hard!"

He pulled the wings up and back, trying to create enough drag to slow them down. It helped, but not enough. Within seconds, they'd crash, and the sharp fangs of stone would tear through the hull and chew the ship apart. Frolic watched those lethal rocks draw near, and as fast as they came at them, it almost seemed to happen in slow motion. The ship spiraled down. No matter how Frolic configured the wings, he couldn't stop its haphazard descent. Without the furnaces to thrust it back into the air, he could do nothing but watch the rocks and sea come closer. He knew it wouldn't be pretty when they met.

Frolic braced himself for the collision, kneeling behind the control panel and covering his head. The impact he'd anticipated never came, and slowly, cautiously, he rose to peer out the window. A massive jet of seawater had caught the ship, embracing it like watery hands. It slid through the brine as tendrils of water clutched it, slowing its descent. Frolic sensed the ocean's desire to help, even if it had been compelled. He dropped back beneath the helm as the belly of the ship made contact with the shore, bouncing a few times before landing hard on its side. The water that had assisted them crashed down, breaking the windows and filling the compartment with foaming liquid. Frolic fought through the current to open the hatch, keeping his book clear of the water. Then he found Reg and Querry curled beneath a bench and hauled them through. The three of them dropped almost a dozen feet to the shore and pulled themselves away from the flooding vessel on their knees and elbows.

Frolic didn't relax until they'd made it a few hundred yards through the rough sand and gravel, almost to the tree line of the jungle. When he knew Querry and Reg were safe, he sat up, watching the other passengers running away from the doomed airship as it split in half, leaving part of it on the rocky shore while the rest sank into the ocean with a loud groan.

Querry leaned over a fallen tree and emptied his stomach.

Reg reached up with a trembling hand to cup Frolic's face. "Good thinking, beauty. You saved us."

"Did I?" Frolic looked back at the remains of the ship he and Corny had worked so hard to construct. Only a bent, shredded, and smoldering husk remained, but most of the people had survived. The sailors and crewman ran up the beach, dragging what supplies they could from the portion of the vessel not submerged in the churning tide.

Reg kissed Frolic's cheek briefly, as if afraid of being seen. "You did. You were brilliant, love," he whispered near Frolic's ear.

Frolic sighed. Reg and Querry were all right. But as he looked at the ruins of the airship, he couldn't help but wonder what they'd do next. The jungle behind them was so thick and dense it blotted out the sun. Frolic had never seen anything like the layers upon layers of vegetation. How would they get through it without the airship or any of their supplies?

CHAPTER 13

WHEN HE finished throwing up and felt like he could walk without stumbling, Querry went back to the wrecked airship to see what he could salvage. By the time he and Reg had realized what was happening, tines of coral and rock from the seabed had already pierced the hull, filling the ship with water. His only concern had been getting Reg and Frolic off the doomed vessel. Fortunately, Reg had thought to toss their weapons, clothing, and a few pieces of equipment into a sack. Querry found the burlap bag spilled over the wall of the airship, lying in two feet of water. He fished out his gun and Reggie's, though they'd probably be worthless until cleaned and dried out. He found Frolic's sword, his own grapple, picks, and dagger scattered among debris and bits of broken glass. The sea had completely destroyed Reg's faerie book and writing set, along with the meticulous records he'd been keeping of their journey.

Querry finally located the bag of canned foods he'd picked up from the hold as they'd run past. It reminded him they had no fresh water. He wished he could have washed the taste of being sick from his mouth. It had been worse, he told himself. At least they'd come through the crash unharmed. A little more poking about yielded some emergency rations and a metal locker full of weapons, undoubtedly placed there by the tinkerer, Cornelia. Querry sifted through the rubble a little longer, but when he didn't find much else, he dropped what he'd salvaged through the hatch and leapt lightly to the ground.

By the time he dragged the supplies and equipment back to the edge of the forest, the others sat in a circle, arguing loudly. Some of the crewmen had made it to the lifeboats and were just now coming ashore. After doing a quick count, Querry figured nearly everyone had survived. He hurried to see what the others debated so heatedly, coming to a stop behind Reg. Frolic sat on the other side of the ring next to the tinkerer and the three mercenaries.

"I will not delay this expedition under any circumstances," Starling said, smacking the side of his fist against his palm. "The sea voyage took twice as long as it should have."

"And whose fault was that?" Reg sat up straighter. "By withholding vital information, you put every man on that ship in danger. You knew what we faced, and you kept it to yourself. Perhaps if we'd been prepared—"

"I have no interest in your opinion, Mr. Whitney." Starling dismissed him with a flick of his wrist.

"I'm not finished—"

"Yes, you are."

One of the sailors—Querry thought he was the first mate—interrupted. "Let him speak."

The other seamen murmured their agreement. "We've lost our ship, our captain, and our livelihood to this madness already."

Starling sighed theatrically. "Very well, Mr. Whitney. What exactly do you propose?"

"I propose you tell us everything you know about what we're up against, what we're actually seeking, and what we can do to protect ourselves. We have the right to know!"

"I have said all I plan to say on the matter," Starling snarled. "If you don't like it, you're free to leave, boy."

"Watch yourself," Querry said, locking gazes with the baron and crossing his arms over his chest. Contract or not, no one was going to show Reg disrespect while he stood idle.

"Watch *yourself*, Mr. Knotte. You'd do well to remember your place."

Balling his fists, Querry stepped forward before he had a second to consider his reaction. Only Reg's outstretched arm stopped him from grabbing the cocky son of a bitch by his fancy collar.

"Further," Reg continued, "the course of action you propose is ludicrous at best. How do you expect us to continue forward without any supplies, or even a map to know where we're going? We need to make our way to a settlement, not into uncharted jungle. We must abandon this mission until we can prepare ourselves."

"The lad makes a fair point," Jack Owens said, without looking up from picking his fingernails with his knife.

The first mate spoke up. "We've come ashore a hundred miles or more south of the port city of Morazan. To reach it on foot will take forever."

"We continue on to the temple," Starling said idly.

"Temple?" Querry said to himself. He didn't recall Starling referring to it that way until now.

"With all due respect, sir," Owens said, "continue onward with no supplies, not even water? That's suicide."

"How vill ve find this place vith no map?" asked one of the dark-haired, mercenary brothers.

"I can find it," Starling said. "I assure you I can, and you don't need to know how."

"I think we do," Reg said.

"I'm afraid I agree," Owens said. "We ain't going no farther without food, water, and proper equipment."

"I'll pay you double," Starling offered.

"Won't do me no good if I'm dead," Owens replied.

"Then I shall continue on with only the aid of my servant, Frolic, and Mr. Knotte," Starling said. "The rest of you may do what you like."

"You will like hell!" Reg got to his feet. "You're not taking my friends anywhere unless we're ready for what we'll face. I won't let you."

"I've had enough of you." Starling waved his hand, and an invisible force knocked Reg to his back on the sand. Reg skidded a dozen feet before coming to a stop and lifting his head. A trickle of blood ran from one nostril, over his lips, and down his chin. "You can do nothing to stop me, Mr. Whitney."

At the sight of Reg bleeding on the ground, all rational thought abandoned Querry. He drew his pistol, flipped it in his hand, and holding it by the barrel, raised it to strike the baron. Tom hurried to stand between them.

"He has it coming, Tom," Querry said. He had no desire to harm the fey, and even less to battle against Tom's magic.

"I wish it mattered," Tom replied.

"Querry, stop," Reg said. "We'll beat him at his own game. I believe the exact words of the contract my friends signed are: *To this end, agents willingly agree to carry out any and all direct orders issued by said patron, excepting those which can reasonably be assumed to lead to serious injury or death. Superficial injury, defined as injury from which agents can recover with minimal treatment, is excluded from this exception."* I think starvation and lack of water constitute life-threatening conditions. Querry and Frolic don't have to agree."

"You little—" Starling gnashed his teeth. "How do you know that?"

"Frolic has a photographic memory," Reg said in a taunting tone, clearly not caring a fig if the baron believed him or not.

Querry felt so proud. Reg had Starling by the short and curlies. He met Tom's gaze and found the faerie grinning back at him with unabashed delight.

"I think… I, um…."

Querry spun on the ball of his foot to see Cornelia stammering, her face as red as her hair. Frolic reached over, squeezed her hand, and nodded. It seemed to lend her the courage to continue.

She took a deep breath before speaking. "I think we need time to do some repairs. The weapons are wet, and, um… and it's going to be hard to make it through the jungle on foot. In a few weeks, uh, if Frolic helps me, I can probably cobble something together from what's left of the ship."

"A few weeks?" Starling hissed.

"But, but, um, it will cut down our travel time later…."

"And where do you propose we make these repairs, girl?" the baron asked. "Do you see a workshop around here anywhere?"

"We have passed a small settlement on our way to Morazan," one of the sailors said. "We noticed it tucked into the trees as we sailed by. It sits on a hill enclosed by a fence of large trees sharpened to points. I have no idea who holds it, but it lies only about twenty miles to the north and maybe ten miles into the jungle."

"We should head there," Owens said. "Hopefully they'll be willing to trade."

"In that case, we should… ah, should salvage anything we can carry from the ship. For, um, collateral," Cornelia said.

"Brilliant!" Frolic got to his feet. "Let's get to work."

They spent the rest of the day reducing the beautiful airship to saleable parts, and since they had no shelter to rest beneath, at nightfall they set off for the walled settlement. Frolic and Cornelia had managed to cobble together a set of wheeled carts, which they pulled with great difficulty into the jungle.

Not long after darkness fell, it rained. The violent but brief storm left all of them soaked to the bones. A thick mist shrouded the forest and made Querry feel like he waded through warm water as their company made slow progress up the coast. Rocky, uneven terrain impeded them. Querry thought of little but the annoyance and his hunger, thirst, and desire to rest until they turned from the beach into the jungle. The broad, thick leaves of the native trees blotted out even the starlight, and they stumbled through the eerie shadows. Querry had expected the jungle to be silent at night and found it anything but. He didn't recognize the sounds of the insects and birds around them, and a few times he knew he heard larger animals moving in the thick bracken surrounding them and the branches above. He had no idea what manner of creatures called the bizarre land home, and he kept a hand waiting on his clockwork pistol. Odd cries and songs from things Querry couldn't even imagine filled the black spaces outside the weak glow of the few lanterns they'd salvaged.

All of Querry's muscles tensed and strained, awaiting some attack or confrontation. Every few seconds, he looked over his shoulder at Reg, helping to drag a cart, and Frolic, who carried far more than his share with his extraordinary strength and endurance. Querry kept expecting something to spring out and ambush them, and he had to be ready to defend them. He'd never imagined any area packed with so many living things; the Anglican forests stood silent at night save for the occasional call of an owl or the rustle of the underbrush as a badger or fox scurried past. Though he'd admit it to no one, not even his partners, Querry felt on edge. He'd grown up among towering smokestacks, crumbling boarding houses, brothels, factories the size of villages, and meandering alleyways. He felt out of place among the massive trees, rampant, flowering undergrowth, and vines the size of his ankles. Querry knew how to defend against pickpockets and thugs, but creatures he couldn't even picture made him uncomfortable. His senses reached the pinnacle of alertness, and his every fiber prepared to react.

Finally, in the middle of the night, after the half-moon had fallen below the ragged horizon, they reached the rough path leading up to the walled stronghold. Querry almost felt relief as they approached it; at least they'd be facing ordinary and predictable men.

They could see the gate, but Querry's eyes continued to scan the dark expanse of the trees on either side of the path. He and Reg walked just behind

Frolic and Cornelia. Reg had relinquished his post on the cart to another. They'd all been taking turns on the carts with the exception of Starling, the first mate, and Owens, who led the procession. The various crewmembers walked in small groups behind the carts while the mercenary brothers brought up the rear. Querry noted Tom Teezle walking just off the proper path near Starling but a few steps behind.

Querry still couldn't see anything. Although the wildlife in the trees seemed to have calmed somewhat, the sudden lack of noise made Querry even more uneasy than before. Reg was silent, scowling. Frolic and Cornelia conversed easily while the first mate and the baron discussed their plans in hushed tones. Owens and his men were silent, wearing grimaces similar to Reggie's, while the sailors whispered sporadically, obviously on edge in this foreign landscape.

Something loosed a high-pitched howl, causing Reg and a number of others to jump. "Monkey," Owens grumbled.

Maybe that's his way of comforting us, Querry thought. *If he even cares about our comfort.* Querry suspected the man didn't. Querry knew his type; Owens's first priority was his pay.

"Thank God. We made it," one of the sailors commented as the first rays of light from the torches on either side of the gate shone on their party.

Frolic stopped so suddenly Querry almost bumped into him. "Something's wrong," he whispered, casting his gaze about the road, straightening his back, and reaching for his sword.

"Nothing's wrong," Owens contradicted.

"No. He's right," Starling agreed, turning toward his indentured clockwork. "Something is wrong."

"Very wrong," Tom Teezle chimed in, finally joining the rest of the group.

The sailors crowded closer to the center of the road. Querry had just enough time to feel stifled by the sudden press of humanity when he heard a violent crashing. He snapped his head to the left, opening his eyes wider, trying desperately to penetrate the gloom.

"Oh, bugger," Corny exclaimed. The tinkerer had managed to shoulder her way to the edge of the crowd. She wore a set of elaborate goggles with dials and lenses that she fiddled with. Querry had once owned a similar pair ensorcelled to allow him to see in the dark during his work. They probably lay on the bottom of the ocean now.

"It's huge." Corny's tone sent goose bumps over the flesh on Querry's arms.

"What's huge?" Reg whispered the question. Querry shrugged without looking at him, instinctively moving closer to stand in front of him.

The crashing noise was steady, the sound of something bounding through the jungle. The mercenaries donned their own goggles, raised their rifles, and pointed them toward the crashing that was now joined by rhythmic grunting. Querry waited for the hail of gunfire, but the mercenaries must have been just as shocked as he was at the sight before them, so shocked they forgot the weapons in their hands.

The thing that emerged from the foliage sent chills up Querry's spine, renewing his dusting of goose flesh. It *was* huge, as Corny had observed. The beast had the body of a man but wrong and disproportionate. The arms were too long, more like an ape's, covered in thick muscle, the sinew beneath the skin bunching as it advanced on them. The beast's head was that of a wild boar, dangerous tusks protruding from the lower jaw. Dark, wiry hair grew from it, down its neck, thinning out to a sparse peppering over its shoulders. It wore a stained loincloth, hairy legs with cloven hooves visible beneath. In its massive right fist, it carried a spiked club.

"That's… not normal," Reg observed with obvious trepidation in his voice. His reaction might have been funny in a less dangerous situation. He pressed his shoulder flush with Querry's. "Is this another faerie creature?"

"Indeed," Teezle answered with an air of what Querry could only describe as nonchalance.

"I'll take care of this," Starling said, squaring his stance and spreading his arms in preparation for a spell. The Boar-man grunted like a railway train and pitched a rock at the baron, dropping the man instantly. Querry watched as his companions traded worried glances.

"Tom?" Frolic said the faerie's name like a prayer, tugging Tom's sleeve. Teezle curled his lip, preparing to strike, when the monster's club caught him in the chest, knocking him off his feet and batting him deep into the jungle. Frolic still held a scrap of Teezle's sleeve, though it was no longer attached to the faerie's shirt. The wind from the beast's bludgeon ruffled his hair.

"Get down," Querry called, reaching for Frolic as a floodgate opened. Whether it was the loss of their magic-users or Querry's exclamation, the sailors started screaming and scrambling from the monster. Abandoning the cart, they ran, pounding on the gate and calling for entry. A few raced toward the forest. Querry managed to get Frolic and Reg safely behind an upturned cart, though Frolic searched frantically for Cornelia.

"Shit," Owens spat. He must have remembered the big hunk of metal in his hand was a gun. "Boys!" The mercenaries leveled their weapons at the monster and promptly opened fire. The beast waded into the shower of bullets like it was nothing more than a pleasant, spring rain. The Boar-man trumpeted a great, snorting oink and swept the mercenaries aside with one pass of its enormous weapon.

The first mate rallied some of his men, and with a violent cry, the braver of the sailors charged the creature. Unfortunately, the beast was ready, batting the men away with its fists and club, snapping others up in its massive jaws. Within minutes, the first mate's squad lay scattered over the forest floor, injured or worse. A few of the sailors ran willy-nilly, frantic with fear. The beast plucked them from the ground or launched them into the trees with a swat from its club.

Owens got back on his feet, bellowing while he charged the beast with a knife the length of a man's forearm. He must have lost his gun when the beast smacked him, but he wasn't about to let that stop him. The Boar-man started to turn, but Owens was already in the air, leaping onto the monster's back. The blade bit into the meaty flesh of the Boar-man's right shoulder with a spurt of blood. Using the blade to pull himself up, Owens drew back and walloped the bellowing creature across the jaw. Querry had to admit the bastard had brass balls.

"He's mad," Reg said from behind Querry's shoulder.

"Maybe," Querry answered. "But look, it's dropped that bloody, big club." The creature's right arm hung limply, but it had already reached up with its left to wrench Owens from its back. To the man's credit, before he released the handle of the blade, he gave it a final, angry twist. The Boar-man squealed, raising Owens into the air, shaking him in its fist. All the beast's attention now focused on the mercenary.

Querry saw his window and made a quick inventory of the weapons at his disposal. While he formulated his most effective plan of attack, Cornelia's bellowing cry drew his attention. She cocked her arm back, hammer in hand, and let loose. The tool whistled through the air before it connected with the Boar-man's knee, shattering the joint and crippling the monster.

The beast dropped the man clutched in his fist and crumpled to the ground. Querry made a move toward the creature, but Frolic was over the cart, charging the beast before Querry could draw his pistol. Before he could cock the hammer back, Frolic was already on the monster's head. The clockwork boy grabbed the beast's tusks and pulled them, angling the monster toward a tree. Querry stood with his mouth gaping as he watched his perfect beauty steering the giant monster like some sort of horrific carriage. The creature bellowed as it slammed into the tree trunk. The Boar-man stumbled dizzily.

Pressing his advantage from his seat on the monster's snout, Frolic laced his fists together and raised them above his head. Querry thought he felt the force of that strike. The monster shook its head, dropped to its good knee, and tumbled forward. Querry hooted with pride. When he turned to share the moment with Reg, he found his oldest friend gone. The thrill of victory quickly turned to panic.

Reg reemerged in front of the collapsing Boar-man. Querry opened his mouth to say something; he didn't know what. Reggie had retrieved Frolic's sword. Querry's lovers exchanged glances, and Frolic nodded, leaping off the monster. Reg pushed his spectacles up the bridge of his nose and tightened his grip on the hilt before he swept the mystic sword through the air. The Boar-man's black eyes grew wide before his head separated from his body. Reg roared as the monster's blood fountained from its neck, splashing across him.

Querry ran to Reg, who still held Frolic's sword. Reggie drew deep, ragged breaths while Querry approached him. Querry wasn't used to being the one being protected. He was the protector, not the one who had to calm his companions afterward. Nonetheless, Querry tried to soothe his lover, encouraging him to release the weapon. Reg's limbs trembled with anger or fear, Querry couldn't know which, but Reg released the sword. "This is disgusting," Reg murmured, as if only now noticing the blood coating him.

"You saved us all, though," Querry said with a slight chuckle.

"I guess I did," Reg answered as he collapsed to the ground. Frolic crouched beside him and guided Reg's head to rest against his shoulder.

Starling and Teezle emerged from the forest. They looked disheveled, scraped but not seriously injured. The baron looked very angry as he picked his way over the broken bodies of the crew.

"Querry," Reg whispered. "I don't know what came over me."

"Hush." Querry reached down and smoothed Reg's bloody hair out of his face. "You were amazing. You did what needed done."

A small black boy appeared from the gate and joined the diminished party. Frolic gave Querry a significant look, and when Querry nodded, he left Reg in Querry's care and hurried to speak with the child.

"You fought like some kind of legendary warrior," Querry told Reg. Querry's tone was husky with arousal. "It was—" Querry paused to lick his lips. "—impressive."

Reg blushed bright red. "I just did what needed done, like you said." He offered Querry a small smile, and Querry kissed the corner of Reg's mouth at the only spot free of gore.

The native boy offered the mercenaries water as what was left of the party regrouped. Some of the sailors helped their wounded comrades toward the compound, while others dragged the bodies of their dead friends. Starling and Teezle examined the remains of the Boar-man, harvesting bits of the monster's corpse. Querry curled his lip. He made sure Reg recovered, helped him clean up, and when Frolic rejoined them with Corny in tow, Querry stood back while they embraced. Starling chuckled, drawing Querry's attention.

"You find something about this funny?" Querry stalked toward the baron and his faerie steward, wanting answers. The Boar-man encounter seemed like too much of a coincidence. Starling glared at Querry, interrupting the thief's approach. The two men stared each other down for a painful moment. Starling shook his head once. Querry decided in that instant he was going to punch that smug look off the baron's face, no matter what the consequences.

He took one more step before the pain shot through his limbs. He gritted his teeth and took another step. This time the pain brought him to his knees. Querry was sweating and panting. *One punch*, he thought. *Just one. The bastard deserves it.* He managed to stand, and his gaze fell on Tom Teezle, who wore a look of concern mixed with curiosity. Querry pleaded with his eyes, and the faerie shrugged almost imperceptibly and shook his head slowly. Despite his every instinct against it, Querry decided to abandon his current plan of action, and as soon as he finished the thought, the pain evaporated like it was never there. He'd get his chance. Reg would find the loophole in the contract, and Querry would get his chance.

Their young ambassador grabbed Querry's arm, drawing his attention from the baron and interrupting his vengeful train of thought. Reg, Frolic, and

Corny joined him. Querry was relieved when the scrawny black boy led them to and through the gate to the settlement. His relief quickly faded when he saw dozens of men in the towers lining the walls, their rifles trained on the diminished party. The gate closed behind them.

CHAPTER 14

THE SUN rose over the jagged edge of the barricade as Reg, Querry, Frolic, and the rest of them stepped into the yard. The pale, pink light of early morning touched their backs as probably fifty guns clicked above them. It all felt unreal to Reg, like they couldn't really be here, halfway across the world, covered in the blood of a monster with men ready to shoot them. It was all so ridiculous he almost wanted to laugh. The thick, mossy logs, muddy ground, and simple, wooden buildings looked as fuzzy and insubstantial in the dawn as if they'd walked into an impressionist's painting.

Out of habit, Reg looked over at Querry, expecting Querry to do something, to save them somehow. He quickly realized not even Querry could stop a bullet, though, and they had nowhere to go for cover. Reg pushed his way to the front of the group and raised his hands above his head. He looked up at the men in the towers, squinting to get a better view of them among the shadows still clinging to the walls. "We are not your enemies!" he called out. "We were shipwrecked and came here looking for help."

Only the twitter of birds in the trees beyond the compound answered him, and Reg cleared his dry throat to speak again. He had to make these people understand they had nothing to fear from his group, or they'd pick them off one by one, and nothing would save them. It might not save them anyway; these people could be savages for all he knew. Still, he had to try.

Lord Starling pushed past Reg as he decided what to say. Even dirty and disheveled, the baron exuded confidence and his ever-present dash of arrogance. "I am Lord Gavindale Starling, Baron of Greymont and Sele, and also the Viscount du Marches. I wish to speak with whoever is in charge here."

"Are you a Belvaisian?" one of the men yelled down.

"I am an Anglican noble," Starling answered.

"We ain't impressed," another man called in a lilting accent Reg couldn't identify. The rest of them laughed.

"I'm not asking you to be impressed. I'm merely requesting you behave like civilized human beings and cease pointing your weapons at us."

"And if we don't?"

"I may take offense," Starling said, provoking more laughter from the men. One of them even hurled a large, green fruit at the baron with a whoop and an insult. Starling calmly raised his hand, and the strange melon stopped in midair and hung there for a moment before exploding and showering the ground with its pulpy, pink innards. The laughter above them ceased abruptly.

"I wish to speak to the man in charge," the baron repeated.

A few minutes later, a gate similar to the one they'd entered swung open in front of them. Reg noted that the builders of the fortress had designed it much like a medieval castle, complete with a killing field between the outer wall and the inner. The realization did little to reassure him, and he wove through the throng to get near Querry and Frolic again.

Reg didn't expect what awaited them on the other side of the second wall. He'd envisioned crude shacks, maybe even tents, not the rows of well-built, if simple houses. Though the sun had just come up, men, women, and children busied themselves with daily chores as they might in any small village. As they followed the men who had opened the inner gate, Reg observed almost a proper city. Thousands probably called it home. Most of them were black, while a few looked like native people. Still, it felt distinctly military, with armed men patrolling the streets and watchtowers rising above the shops and homes.

Finally, they reached what appeared to be a central square. A large, rectangular, wooden house, three stories high with green shutters around the windows and even some baskets of flowers hanging from the eaves, stood across the dirt path. It might have seemed welcoming if not for the eight men with rifles standing in front of it. Their company stopped while one of the men leading them talked to the guards. Then he departed, leaving them standing beneath the heat of the strengthening sun for what felt like an hour.

Then the door opened, and the guard closest to it motioned them in with a cant of his head. Starling led the way into the large, empty interior. Reg blinked to adjust his vision to the cool, gray shadow, and realized they stood in some sort of meeting hall lined with simple, wooden benches. Four men sat at a table near the front of the room, backlit by a large, bay window. Starling strode up to them, his shoes clicking against the polished wooden floor. As he approached, one of the men stood. Little distinguished him from the guards outside; he was tall and muscular, had a clean-shaven head and a large gun strapped to his back.

The baron introduced himself and extended his hand. The other man clasped it. "My name is Abiya e Silva. Welcome. You and your friends should sit down, and then we can speak."

All of them pulled the benches closer to the table. Reg made sure he, Querry, and Frolic had a spot near the front, just to the left of Tom and the baron, where they would have a good view of the proceedings. "Just what is this place?" Reg asked.

Abiya e Silva looked a bit surprised. "You have not been here long," he observed.

"No," Reg said. "Our ship crashed about a day's walk from here. We lost all of our supplies and came here in search of aid."

The large man leaned his elbows on the table, angling his head closer to them. Reg could read no motivation or emotion in his large, dark eyes as he studied them. "You are here for our help?"

"That's right," Reg replied. "But you still haven't answered my question. Why did you draw weapons on us when we arrived?"

"You really don't know? Very well, then. We were simply being cautious. Our guards in the towers reported a group of armed, white men approaching the *quilombo*. That normally only means one thing."

"*Quilombo*?" Starling asked.

Abiya nodded. "It is what we call settlements such as this. All of us are runaway slaves."

Reg gasped with sudden understanding. He remembered reading vehement editorials against the slavery on the coffee and sugar plantations here. He also knew many opposed it, not for moral reasons, but because the cheap labor harmed profits from plantations on the Anglican island colonies. He'd had no idea the runaways had formed such elaborate garrisons as this one.

"I assure you, you have nothing to fear from us," Starling said. "We are on an archaeological expedition and have come here in the hopes of trading for some supplies. If any of your people are interested, I may also have need of skilled help, particularly guides familiar with the area. I can pay quite handsomely."

Reg wondered how the baron planned to get his hands on any funds in the middle of this jungle, but he said nothing.

"I am afraid we have no supplies to spare," Abiya said. "We are not as cruel as those we have fled from, however. We can offer you water, a meal, and a night of rest. After that, I'm afraid we must ask you to leave."

Jack Owens stood up. "Pardon me, mate, but all of you seemed pretty well-armed. You honestly expecting us to believe you can't spare any weapons?"

"We have cartloads of raw materials we can offer you in exchange," Starling added.

"And knowledge," Cornelia said. "If you have a place I can work, I can make you almost anything you want. Machinery, weapons—"

Their host held up a large hand. "I'm afraid we're not interested." The man to his right cupped a hand over his mouth and whispered in Abiya's ear. The rest of them waited in tense silence as the leader's eyes darted back and forth while he listened and considered. When his associate finished speaking, Abiya knit his brows and nodded. "We may be able to reach some sort of an arrangement after all."

"Go on," Starling said.

"There is a large plantation about thirty miles west of here, where hundreds of my people are kept in bondage. We have a small camp in the jungle outside it, and we have been trying for months to free them. To do that, we need to get weapons to that camp. The roads are watched, however, and we can't sneak past. A white, Anglican lord and his party of explorers might, though."

"If we do this for you, you'll provide us with provisions, weapons, supplies, and a guide for our expedition?" Starling asked.

"We'll offer you all we can spare."

"Then we agree."

"Wait," Reg said. "I sympathize with this cause, truly I do, but what will happen to us if we're caught?"

"We won't get caught," Querry said.

"I remember you saying that back in Thalacea," Reg reminded him. "The authorities here might just shoot us and leave us to rot in the jungle. Who would ever know? Or, they might construe it as sanctioned, Anglican aid to a slave revolt. This could lead to hostility between the two empires. We can't take this decision lightly."

"I think we must help them," Frolic said. "It's absolutely abhorrent that these people are kept as slaves. If we can help them be free, we must do it!"

"Frolic, I agree with you," Reg said. "But we won't do them any good by getting ourselves killed. I think this is very risky."

"It hardly matters," Starling said. "If doing this will facilitate the expedition, then we're going to do it. It's my decision, and I've decided."

"We won't be going with you," the first mate said. The other sailors voiced their agreement. "We've lost enough to this already. After we bury our dead comrades, me and the rest of the crew will head to the nearest port and hopefully find a ship we can serve aboard long enough to get us home, or at least away from here." With that, the remainder of the Thalacean seamen stood and left the hall.

"We'll need time to prepare," Owens said. "More than a day. More like a week or two. We need to make repairs and get ourselves a plan."

"Agreed," Querry said. "We'll need a way to transport these weapons."

"We should be ready to leave after we make the delivery," Starling said. "I have no wish to backtrack after losing so much time already. We should be ready to continue on, which means we'll need our supplies before we leave."

"Wait," Abiya said in his musical cadence. "If we give you food and weapons now, what guarantee do we have you'll make the delivery? What would stop you from just keeping our weapons for yourself?"

Starling looked absolutely affronted. "You have my word as a gentleman."

The big man laughed. "Forgive me if that is not enough. I have known too many so-called gentlemen who were the vilest of liars and tyrants. No, I will send some of my men with you."

"But that doesn't make any sense," Reg said. "Isn't the whole point to send white men so you won't be suspected?"

"I have a man I can send with you. The rest of my people will disguise themselves as your slaves. No one will doubt an Anglican lord owning half a dozen or so."

"I beg your pardon, sir!" Starling trembled with rage. "Anyone who has ever met an Anglican gentleman will know we would never stoop to something as vile as claiming ownership over another human being. How repulsive!"

"What about Tom?" Frolic asked, his indignation matching the baron's.

Starling spun on the ball of his foot and curled his lip at Frolic. "It's hardly the same thing. Keep your mouth shut, boy."

"No! It's exactly the same thing—"

Querry's bitter laughter interrupted Frolic's words. "Pretentious, hypocritical bastards, the lot of you bleeding aristocrats. I grew up in slavery. Reg grew up in slavery before he was adopted. We're your countrymen. Fellow Anglicans! Just because you don't call it slavery doesn't make it any better. Think about why me and Frolic are even here, you prick."

"Need I remind you, Mr. Knotte, that I apprehended you and your companion robbing my villa? Don't make me regret the mercy I showed you."

"Mercy?" Reg practically shouted.

"You know what I think of your opinions, Mr. Whitney, so save your strength for the mission."

"This is getting us nowhere," Abiya said, looking rather amused at the spectacle they created. "In this country, there are two types of people: rich, white, landowners and their black slaves. No one will wonder over your country of origin. It is not in my nature to compel you. I would like to be generous and offer you goods freely, but you cannot imagine the suffering of my people. I must ask this of you. I have no more to say. Wait here, and I will send one of my people to show you to rooms so you can prepare."

"I'll need a place to work," Corny said. "Er, that is, if I'm welcome to accompany you. I'd like to come along."

Starling nodded once as if he didn't care either way.

"I'll see you have access to a shop and tools," Abiya said as he stood from the table. He and the others left the hall.

Reg slumped back down on the bench, feeling utterly miserable. The blood drying on his shirt reeked in the intense heat. His empty stomach knotted up. He had a week to find a way out of Querry and Frolic's contract, or they'd have no choice but to go along with this fool's errand. He dropped his elbows to his knees and rubbed his temples. If only he could see something in the words, something he'd missed before…. Then they could join the sailors and try to find a way home. He shuddered to think what would happen to them if he failed. The idea of losing Querry and Frolic terrified him, but he didn't know how to prevent it.

AS SOON as the leaders of the *quilombo* left the room, the others split into groups: the three mercenaries in a corner near the window and Starling and

Tom near the door. Querry went to the benches where Reg, Cornelia, and Frolic sat talking in hushed tones. Reg looked devastated, and he flinched when Querry laid his hand across his shoulder.

"Reggie, we're doing the right thing," he said.

"I agree," Frolic added.

"This is foolish," Reg said, shaking his head and looking pale. "I agree with the sentiment, but we're involving ourselves with something far beyond the scope of the original mission. I don't like it, but it's not like anyone ever listens to me. If you did, none of us would be here at all. We'd be home fixing dinner. Safe. Damn it, I hate this."

Querry kneaded Reg's tense muscles as he considered what to say to reassure him. He wasn't worried about a handful of backwoods guards when he'd been eluding the constables in Halcyon since he'd been six. No way would these colonial fools outwit him. He wished Reg would give him a little more credit sometimes. What was he so worried about? Querry knew what he was doing.

Querry bent his waist and wriggled his face into the hair above Reg's ear. "Listen, love. I won't let anything happen. I can handle these backward guards, should we meet them. Look how we handled the Grande Chancellor—"

The front door opening and slamming cut Querry's explanation short. He jumped guiltily away from his lover out of habit and turned toward the sound. What he saw—who he saw—in the doorway nearly stopped his heart.

The round, wide brim of the man's hat couldn't hide his face or his long, strawberry-blond hair. Querry rushed forward, grabbed him by the forearm, and dragged him across the hall and through a door to a small alcove lined in books. He pushed the hat away, and the leather cord fell over the man's throat before Querry pushed him against the wall.

"Happy to see me, monsieur?" Jean-Andre said with a lazy grin.

Querry recalled the Belvaisian spy, mercenary—he didn't know what to call the man—from the events in Halcyon. He'd wanted to sell Frolic's book and its secrets to the highest bidder. He'd tried to recruit Querry as a fellow... information broker? Querry had never really known what Jean-Andre wanted from him, only that he'd inexplicably disappeared after they'd destroyed the Grande Chancellor and his clock tower.

"What are you doing here?" Querry hissed, pinning the other man to the wall by pressing his forearm against Jean-Andre's throat.

"Let me speak, mon ami, and I'll tell you. I don't understand your hostility given the amount of times I saved your sorry skin back in Halcyon. I never said I wouldn't tell you what you want to know."

"Talk." Querry released him but kept his hand near his pistol. "Why are you here?"

"It is quite simple. The Empress of Belvais would find it very beneficial if the slave revolts weakened, or even destroyed, the government here. At that point, she could take over this very lucrative farmland. If she cannot claim it as a colony, she can at least grant these plantations to her loyal nobles. As you know, monsieur, your Anglicans like the sugar in their tea."

"So—what? You're here to help the rebels succeed?"

"A simplistic assessment, but correct, I suppose," Jean-Andre said. "You always were clever, Querrilous."

"Too clever to believe this can be a coincidence. What are you really doing here?"

"I've told you. I am here to weaken the government so the Empress can move in. As of late, I have been helping arrange shipments of weapons. That said, I'm still very interested in the knowledge you hold about clockworks. Many people would pay dearly for your Frolic's book...."

"Out of the question. Bother with him, and I'll kill you."

Jean-Andre laughed. "Will you, Monsieur Knotte? You think it would be so easy?"

"I don't trust you," Querry said.

"You'd be a fool if you did. And I do not ally myself with fools. Now, let us go before the others question what we're up to. You surely do not want your precious Reginald and Frolic to get the wrong idea, *non*?"

"Don't think you'll manipulate us," Querry warned as Jean-Andre walked back into the hall.

"Come with me," Jean-Andre said. "I will show you where you can rest."

Reluctantly, and with Reg and Frolic staring at him with curiosity and concern, Querry followed the suspicious Belvaisian out of the meeting hall. He certainly planned to have more words with Jean-Andre later, and find out what the man really intended.

CHAPTER 15

EVERYONE USED the following week to prepare for the delivery of the guns. Frolic spent his time in the makeshift workshop provided to him and Cornelia. It was little more than a slanted, wood-shingled roof above a patch of moist dirt, but it served their purposes. It contained a forge, anvil, and metal workbench, and what tools they couldn't find they made. Both of them knew they'd need carts to transport the weapons and the baron's supplies afterward. To that end, they worked to modify the vehicles they'd made after the airship crash. They needed to redesign the wheels, make them more adaptable to the uneven terrain they'd be traversing. It required very creative manipulation of the springs between the axles and the shafts. They also thought it prudent to attach weapons to each of the vehicles, in case they encountered savages, beasts, or imperial guards.

The humidity of the jungle made Frolic's hair go wild, his curls spiraling out in every direction, winding into tighter corkscrews than ever. He slid out from beneath one of the carts, stood, and pushed his unruly locks out of his eyes. One ringlet remained stained black by the sea monster's ichor, and Frolic wondered if it would ever return to its original pigment. With all the work needing done, though, he scarcely had time to waste a second worrying about it. He swiped the twisted locks off his forehead once again and was surprised when Cornelia approached him with a scrap of cloth. "What?" he asked as she folded the square in half.

"Hold still," she instructed as she tied the fabric about his head before slipping it down around his neck and pulling it back up. The cloth pulled his hair back out of his face. "There." She stood back and admired her handiwork. "How's that?"

Frolic checked his reflection in a shiny bit of metal. Corny had fashioned him a headband similar to those some of the sailors had worn on the ship. "Great." Frolic beamed, flashing his friend a thankful smile and returning to the task at hand. They worked in the comfortable silence that had become their routine, asking for assistance when they needed it but mostly tinkering diligently. Frolic rarely noticed the passage of time when he and Cornelia really got down to serious mechanics.

"That's lunch, lovey," Corny announced, dropping her large wrench. Frolic's bird fluttered down from the rafters and landed on her shoulder. "I'm wasting away to nothing here. I'll be back in an hour or so."

"Where are you going?" Frolic asked, as the two of them usually enjoyed their midday meal together.

Corny colored. "I—er, I'm having lunch with Jack Owens. He asked me, and I said all right. I hope you don't mind. It's just—couldn't see no harm in it—"

Frolic grinned and squeezed her shoulder. "You fancy him!"

"No! Well, I don't know. He's in good shape, and quite a supporter of clockwork weapons…."

"Corny, it's fine. Don't be nervous. You're a fantastic person, so don't pretend to be anything you're not."

She kissed him on the top of his head. "Thanks, Frolic. Bugger, I'm a little excited. Feel like I might throw up, really."

"You'll be fine," he said. "Have a wonderful time. I'm happy for you."

"Thanks, my friend," she whispered before leaving the workshop.

Frolic looked around at the tools and machines, wondering how he'd pass the hour. He decided to take a break too, hoping to find Querry and Reg at their meal as well.

He emerged into the midday sun. The bright light and heat didn't bother him. He could feel the temperature variations, but he couldn't sweat like most of the men he passed. Querry had taught him to adjust his wardrobe based on the discrepancies in the weather. He felt a smile stretch his lips as he remembered the time Querry had panicked when he'd seen Frolic in the middle of winter, stripped to his undershirt and sitting on the edge of the dock with his bare feet grazing the water.

His reminiscence was interrupted when he saw Tom Teezle with an armful of sacks hurrying toward one of the village homes. Multicolored smoke billowed from the chimney. Frolic found that very suspicious in the extreme heat. He trotted over to the faerie.

"Hello, Tom Teezle," he greeted as he fell into step with baron's valet. "Need any help?"

"Thanks to you, Frolic, but no. The human wizard wants these ingredients for his brew," Tom answered, not slowing his pace.

"Brew?"

"I've said too much," Teezle answered with a smirk.

"Aren't you bound to *not* say too much?" Frolic asked.

"Yes and no," Tom said.

"What does that mean?"

"I mustn't say too much, but I must be true to the baron's plans." Tom's smirk grew to a grin. Frolic only frowned, trying to work out the faerie's meaning. "I can't be deceptive if it will help the baron."

"So you can't lie in certain circumstances?" Frolic asked, making a leaping inference.

"No, indeed. If one asks the right questions," Teezle replied.

"That's interesting." Frolic chewed his lip, contemplating the new information. "So there are loopholes in the baron's agreements?"

"Most definitely."

"In ours?" Frolic asked with awe.

"I can't answer that." Teezle's smile remained firm. "That would be against the baron's best interests."

Frolic gasped. In not answering his question, Teezle had definitively answered his question. "There's a way out of our contracts," Frolic stated.

"I'm glad that's not a question." Tom snickered. "I'd have to deny it."

Frolic covered his mouth with his hand in surprise. Reg was right; faeries were terribly tricky. Tom managed to answer his questions without breaking his contract. Teezle was so clever.

"What are the bags for?" Frolic changed the subject, worried that pressing too hard would get Tom into trouble.

"Insurance," Teezle explained. "Want to watch?"

Frolic nodded enthusiastically, wondering what they could be planning. Teezle dashed to the hut that belched the rainbow smoke, and Frolic followed him inside.

The atmosphere in the little house was stifling. Starling hunched over a cauldron. Thick, spicy, and cloying steam emanated into the air. But underneath all that, Frolic smelled something else: the smell of death, of decay, like the smells of the factory workers cooking roadkill back in Halcyon. It made his gorge rise, but Frolic had nothing to vomit. Starling and Teezle conversed while the faerie flopped the sacks he'd been carrying down on a table near the baron.

The man, wearing nothing but dark trousers and covered in a sheen of sweat, rifled through the supplies, pulling out herbs, ingredients, and vials of viscous liquid. He mixed these things in without looking at Frolic or the faerie. "What's he doing here?" Starling asked.

"He offered to help me carry the supplies," Teezle answered with a shrug. The baron made a sound of dismissal and turned his attention back to the cauldron in the hearth. Apparently Frolic's presence wouldn't impact Starling's work. Frolic rolled to the balls of his feet and stretched his neck, trying to get a look at the contents bubbling over the fire. It was viscous and no color Frolic had ever seen in proper food. He pressed the back of his hand to his mouth and settled back on his heels.

"What is it?" Frolic asked Tom, who had drifted back to stand next to him.

"Protection brew. It should make us invisible to other Fair Folk for a bit," Teezle explained. "After we drink this, we shouldn't have to worry about giant, boar-headed men attacking us at every turn."

"We have to drink it?" Frolic asked, worry sneaking into his voice.

"Of course. How else would you suggest we get it into us?"

"I don't eat or drink. I don't need to."

"Oh." Teezle rubbed his chin in an oddly human gesture. "Well, that is a problem. You say you don't have to eat or drink. Have you ever tried?"

"I—" Frolic started to answer, but then he really thought about it. Had he never tried to eat? No. He'd tasted wine and some foods that Querry or Reg insisted he couldn't miss, but he'd never actually swallowed any of it. He related that to Teezle.

"Right, then let's see what'll happen." Teezle dug about in his waistcoat for a moment before producing a small, blue glass marble. "Here."

"What?" Frolic blurted.

"See if you can swallow this." Teezle held out the marble. Frolic regarded the shiny glass sphere for a moment before tentatively plucking it from the faerie's fingers. Frolic practiced swallowing while he studied the smooth, swirling surface.

"Go on," Teezle urged.

Frolic opened his mouth and plopped the marble on his tongue. He swallowed it. It was an odd sensation. He could feel the marble moving along through his throat and into whatever passed for his stomach.

Tom and Frolic both waited without breathing. Frolic wasn't sure what he expected to happen, but after a moment he took a breath and tilted his head questioningly. "That's it?" he asked Teezle.

"Don't lose that," Tom said with a smirk. "That's my favorite one." The two were about to share a laugh when the baron's voice barked, interrupting their moment.

"Teezle! Bring the Boar-man's heart. It's time for the words." Tom hustled to obey, retrieving a bundle from the table. When Teezle unwrapped it, Frolic saw a heart the size of a roast turkey. Tom took it reverently to the kettle where he eased it into the bubbling contents. The potion began to glow. "Words," the baron ordered once the heart had disappeared beneath the surface. Impossibly, the smell in the little hut grew worse.

Teezle and Starling joined hands above the kettle and started chanting words similar to those Frolic could hear in nature from time to time. Frolic's head swam a little in the heat and the stench. The words coalesced into something coherent: "Don't let them see us. We are the wind. Don't let them hear us. We are the silence. Don't let them smell us. We are the spirits. Don't let them sense us. We are the shadows." Then they started all over again.

Frolic wasn't sure how long the ritual took, but when they had finished, Starling dipped a ladle into the foul concoction and tipped the contents into his mouth, swallowing every drop. He closed his eyes, took a deep breath, and waited. A smile crept across his lips. "It worked," he declared. "Tom." He offered Teezle the ladle. Tom dipped and drank. Then he submerged the ladle a second time, transferring the contents to a thin, metal vial only half the size of his pinky finger. He corked the vessel and handed it to Frolic.

"What should I do with this?" Frolic asked, afraid he already knew the answer.

"Time to practice swallowing." Teezle nodded at the vial. Frolic didn't want that evil brew inside him, but at least he wouldn't have to taste it like everyone else. With a determined nod, he tipped his head back and pushed the vial into his throat, swallowing until it was well on its way inside. He opened his mouth to show the baron and Tom that it was gone. "Well done, Frolic." Teezle gave him a friendly pat on the back.

"You two," Starling said, retrieving a bottle of Tartan whiskey from the table. "Get that distributed to the rest of the men." He unscrewed the lid and took a swig right from the bottle, presumably to wash the taste of the boiled Boar-man's heart from his mouth. "Don't just stand there, go!" he barked. Frolic and Teezle scrambled to obey, grabbing a towel to hold the hot kettle and the ladle. They left the hut to find their companions.

They looked for their party members near the huts they'd been assigned by the chief. The mercenary brothers sat together, lounging after their noonday meal. Frolic grimaced, thinking about their bellies filled with food and the stink of the concoction he and Tom carried between them. To his surprise, the mercenaries drank the awful stuff without a word after Teezle explained its purpose.

Corny and Owens sat at a makeshift table around the corner. They, too, had finished their meal and were engaged in polite conversation. Corny blushed when Owens touched her hand, coaxing a smile from Frolic. The potion was presented and explained once more. Without ceremony, Owens grabbed the ladle and downed two scoopfuls of the stuff, then handed it to Corny. She stared at the ladle like it was a snake.

"Go on, Corny," Frolic encouraged. "It will keep you safe."

"Frolic, you know I don't go in for all this magic falderal." She eyed the kettle suspiciously.

"I know, Corny. But you also know it exists. I'm living proof."

"I can't argue with that," she conceded. "And it'll stop any more of those awful Boar-men?"

"That's the plan," Teezle answered. She looked at the three men gathered around her, sighed, and dipped the ladle in the potion. Then Corny pinched her nose and drank the contents of her ladle. The taste still made her cough and splutter. Owens grabbed her hand and patted her back until she recovered. Frolic asked if they'd seen Querry and Reg, and they pointed him to a small area on the edge of the village where the two men sat in the shade of a tree.

Frolic waved as he approached his two best friends in the world, and Reg returned the wave with a smile. "Where have you been hiding?" Querry asked, standing to embrace Frolic, who happily accepted the affection.

"I helped Tom with some bundles and then kind of got distracted," Frolic answered before explaining once more about the protection potion. Reg listened intently, though he periodically cast wary glances at the kettle. Querry only nodded, one eyebrow raised as Frolic finished.

"Good enough for me," Querry stated, ladling a healthy portion from the kettle.

Reg grabbed his hand before it could reach his lips. "Wait. How do we know it's not poison or something?"

"Starling needs us alive, Reggie," Querry answered. "Besides, you heard what Frolic said. All the others drank it, and they're fine."

"Well, yes. I suppose," Reg said thoughtfully, releasing Querry's arm. Querry sucked down the potion and replaced the ladle in the kettle.

"Your turn," he told Reg with a big grin. Reg chuckled nervously, reaching for the ladle. He stirred the remaining potion a couple of times apprehensively. "Come on, Reg. We've eaten worse. Remember the workhouse gruel?"

"Indeed. Vile stuff, that." Reg scooped up a bit of the potion and raised it, sniffing it. He winced horribly, sticking out his tongue.

"Best if you don't do that," Teezle advised.

"Fair point," Reg choked out. In an effort to help, Frolic reached out and pinched Reg's nose closed, mimicking what he'd seen Corny do. "Thanks." Reg's voice came out nasally. He squeezed his eyes shut and drank the potion. "Blagh!" he exclaimed once he'd finished it off. "You're... right," he said through gags. "Better than... the workhouse gruel." The small group laughed at that while Teezle retreated with the tiny amount of remaining potion. Frolic watched him go as Reg and Querry fell back into easy conversation. All of them sat back down on the grass, and Querry and Reg returned to the simple lunch spread out on a strip of cloth between them.

Reg drank a few healthy gulps of water. "I don't feel any different," he said, resting his hand over his belly. "What was in that stuff, anyway?"

Frolic grimaced as he recalled the stench inside the hut. "You probably don't want me to tell you."

Querry finished chewing a piece of melon and set down the rind. "Well, whatever it is, if it keeps the faeries from knowing our every move, I think it's brilliant. It's just a matter of walking through the jungle now, isn't it?"

"I don't think we should let our guard down," Reg warned. "We still have the guns to deliver, and if I understand correctly, that potion won't protect us from armed men."

"You worry too much, love." Querry stroked Reg's cheek with the back of his hand, but Reg flinched away and caught Querry's wrist.

"You don't worry enough, Querry. We're facing real and serious danger. It isn't a game."

"You really think I can't elude a couple of backwater guards—"

"Querry!"

"Please don't fight," Frolic pleaded.

Both of them looked down in shame. "I'm sorry," Reg said in a small voice. "I just think we need to stay alert. We shouldn't be overconfident."

"Reg, I'm good at what I do. You know I am. But I'll take any precaution you want. I just don't think this will be a big deal."

Reg made an exasperated noise and shook his head. Frolic didn't know what to say. He agreed with being cautious, but he also felt Querry knew his work, and the delivery wouldn't be as difficult as Reg thought. He actually thought it might be fun, and he certainly supported the cause. The idea of helping people, of having a worthy purpose, appealed to him.

"I'm just so afraid your luck's going to run out eventually. I can't stand thinking about something happening to either of you. I can't bear the thought of losing you."

Frolic heard so much genuine fear in Reg's voice that he reached out for him without worrying about who might be watching. He threw his arm around Reg's back, pulled him close, and pressed the side of his face to Reg's shoulder. "Please don't worry, Reggie. We'll be so careful, I promise. Me and Corny are working on several useful things to help us along the way. You'll get a chance to put on that armor I made you. Remember how lovely your legs looked in that leather?"

Querry chuckled and winked at Frolic. "I remember how tight it was on your sweet little ass."

Reg gasped, but it quickly turned into a low laugh, and he gave Frolic a quick kiss on the forehead. Querry's eyes twinkled as he watched them, his lips twisting into a suggestive grin Frolic knew well. It made his heart burn a little warmer and a pleasant little shiver tumble down his back. He snuggled closer to Reg as Querry slid his hand over Frolic's knee and up his thigh.

Before he spoke, Querry wet his lips with his tongue, making them glisten and causing Frolic to squirm as his trousers grew tight.

"We ought to spend some time together before we get back to work." Querry's gaze darted between Reg and Frolic's faces. "What do you say?"

"Honestly, love. Where would we go? We share a room with four other men. There isn't even a lock on the door."

"Tonight, then. We'll sneak out of here and hide in the jungle."

Frolic didn't have to see Reg's face to know Reg smirked and rolled his eyes. "It takes half a dozen men to open those gates."

Querry shrugged. "Won't be a problem. We'll just grapple up the wall and down the other side. I could use a bit of exercise anyway. Then we'll do our thing and scale the wall again. Easy."

"Oh, that sounds lovely," Frolic said sincerely.

Reg punched Querry playfully in the shoulder. "For a moment there, I wasn't entirely sure you were joking."

"Neither was I," Querry said with a wide grin.

"You mean, we aren't really going?" Frolic asked, disappointed.

Laughter burst from Querry and Reg until they could scarcely breathe. Frolic soon joined them, even though he didn't really understand the humor in it. It felt good to laugh, to see his friends happy and free of worry for a moment.

As soon as he calmed down enough to speak, Frolic said, "We *are* going, though, right?"

They broke into a fresh fit of laughter, and the last of the tension between them evaporated. Frolic held his sides and collapsed in the soft grass with the top of his head against Reggie's thigh and his cheek only inches from Querry's hip. He put one of his hands on each of their legs and watched a few puffy clouds creep across a sky so blue it almost looked unnatural. Despite the baron's potion, he still felt the wind and the trees whispering to him, telling him to abandon their quest, to be content and just enjoy the sun on his face. At the moment, he wanted nothing more than to agree. He considered sharing his perceptions with his partners, but he suspected it would shatter the peace and contentment they enjoyed. He was beginning to understand how human moods fluctuated, so he decided to just enjoy the proximity of his partners as they picked at the remains of their meal. Frolic liked listening to Querry and Reg chew and swallow, liked watching their jaws and throats move as they ate. It made him impatient to taste their lips.

They passed a quarter of an hour in easy silence, just enjoying each other's company. Though it was hot and sticky, a refreshing breeze rustled the broad leaves of the trees and ruffled their hair. Frolic felt perfect as he observed his lovers finishing their lunch. He never wanted to leave his spot beneath the tree.

The sound of heavy boots interrupted Frolic's peace, and he turned his head to see the leader of the quilombo, Abiya, approaching them with a chubby infant on his hip and a little girl in tow. The big man stopped a few feet from them with a gentle smile on his face.

Reg and Querry skidded away from Frolic, and it made him sad. He trusted their reasoning, though, and sat up, putting his weight on his palms behind him. He didn't trust himself to know the right things to say, so he stayed quiet and waited.

Reg, always the diplomat, smiled at the chieftain and said, "This is a beautiful country."

"I thank you for that," Abiya said with a nod. "To me, it is the most beautiful country in the world, but surely very different from your chilly Anglica, *non*?"

"Did Jean-Andre teach you Anglican, then?" Querry asked.

"*Oui*, he has been a valued friend," Abiya said. "Is that a problem?"

"Of course not," Querry muttered.

"What can we do for you, sir?" Reg asked.

Frolic propped himself up on his elbows and looked at the little girl peeking out from behind her father's knee. When he smiled, she ducked behind Abiya's leg, but she soon emerged with a coquettish grin. Frolic met her fascinated gaze. Her hair looked a little like his, but a bit frizzier, the curls not so defined. Humans were always less perfect, but it made them so much more intriguing. As Querry and Reg talked with Abiya about the delivery,

Frolic studied the little girl, amazed by her beauty and wondering what she might be thinking as she regarded him.

"I want you to know how much I appreciate what you're doing for us," Abiya said. Querry got to his feet to shake the other man's hand.

The little girl pointed at Frolic's left eye and giggled. He touched his brow bone and eyelid, expecting to find something amiss. His actions only amused her more, and she daringly reached out and captured the end of one of his ringlets. He held his breath as she pulled it completely straight, released it, and let it bounce back into shape with a laugh. She spoke a few words Frolic didn't understand at first. As he listened to her, though, he gradually made sense of her language and could respond.

"Your hair's a funny color," she said.

"Is it?"

"Like an old person's hair. But you ain't old."

"I'm over a hundred," Frolic said.

"I don't believe that. My Gran is only seventy-four. How come you got gold eyes?"

"I don't know."

"My pa always says I have me mum's eyes. Do you have your mum's eyes?"

"No."

"You must take after someone," she said.

"Maybe, but I don't know who," Frolic said. "I wish I did."

"I got a little brother," the child said with a wide grin, pointing to the baby Abiya held. "You got a brother?"

"I want to have one, someday soon," Frolic replied.

"Well, you should tell your mum," she said, seeming very pleased with herself as she planted her small hands on her hips. "She's got to make you one."

"Oh, I think I can make one myself," Frolic said. "As long as my friend helps me."

She laughed. "You got no idea how it works."

"Maybe," Frolic said, not sure how to counter her logic.

"You're pretty, like a doll," she said, fondling his hair again.

Frolic found it offended him, though he didn't blame the child, so he endured her clumsy groping until her father pulled her away. Since when had being considered a doll bothered him? Before, he'd liked it when Querry called him a doll, which he only did in their most private moments.

"I really want to thank you for all you're risking on our behalf," Abiya said, pulling his son and daughter near. "It makes me sick that this is necessary."

"Me too," Querry said, and Reg nodded.

"Thank you," Abiya said again. "I hope you don't feel coerced."

"I'm happy to do it," Frolic hurried to say.

"Thank you. The Fair Folk have been good to us." Abiya kissed Frolic's knuckles as he bowed. It made Frolic feel almost sick; he didn't want adulation, didn't feel he deserved it.

"Faerie—" The cute little girl hid behind her father as she pointed at Frolic.

"No—"

"Faerie, faerie," the girl sang.

"I'm not a damned faerie," Frolic shouted, standing, turning his back on them all, and swatting tree branches aside to enter the village's square. Querry and Reg hurried to follow him, reaching for his shoulders and asking him what was wrong.

Frolic didn't face them and kept walking because he didn't know what to say. He didn't know why it upset him to be called a faerie. He had nothing against faeries, and readily admitted part of him was fey. But he wasn't a faerie. Why couldn't people just see him as normal, the same as anyone else?

He turned to face his friends. "I'm sorry, Querry, Reg. I have no reason to be angry with you. I'm not angry, I just… I just need to go back to the workshop now, where I belong. I'll see you both later tonight."

Though they protested, Frolic hurried away, and eventually they stopped following. He hated leaving them hurt and confused, but he needed to be alone. He planned to work without stopping until the carts were ready and then beg Corny to help him get started on a companion. He pulled the metal feather amulet from inside his shirt and ran his finger along the edge, remembering the clockwork angels he'd been designed to command. What had his creator planned for him in the event of their destruction? Had he planned anything at all, or only intended Frolic to serve the purpose for which he'd been built? Had he imagined any other future for Frolic, anywhere he could belong?

It didn't matter. Since Frolic would never know what his maker intended, he'd build a world where he wasn't the only one of his kind, a world where he'd never have to be alone again.

CHAPTER 16

REG STOOD far off from the others as they loaded dozens of rifles and even some explosives in the four carts Frolic and Corny had built so adeptly from scrap. A fifth cart would carry the coal to fuel the others for the remainder of their journey. The sun hadn't risen, and the others worked by the light of several dozen torches affixed to the walls.

A young girl tugged at the cuff of Reg's sleeve and held out a basket full of native fruit and small, round loaves of bread. Reg muttered his thanks but waved it away. He felt much too sick to eat anything. Despite scouring Querry and Frolic's contract for twelve hours a day over the last week, he hadn't managed to find a way out of it. Now the men he loved would walk into one dangerous situation after another, and Reg could do little to protect them. How would they ever make it home now? Reg had one opportunity to save them all, and he'd failed. Now, he didn't even feel like he could face them. He felt like he didn't deserve to because Querry had watched out for him since they'd met as young boys, and he couldn't reciprocate.

The first fuzzy strip of pink light appeared above the sharp edge of the barricade just as the men of the quilombo finished loading and concealing the weapons. One by one, the engines fired up, spewing coal smoke and steam into the lightening sky. It felt unreal, more like a dream, as Reg walked toward the procession. Not for the first time, he felt it couldn't be happening, that he'd wake up nestled between his lovers with the sound of the Thalacean tide luring him back into unconsciousness. But of course, he knew it wouldn't happen, so he checked the antique pistols hanging from their leather holsters beside his hips. Frolic and Querry had augmented them, and Reg vowed to use them to defend his friends. It was time to be a man and face reality, instead of hoping for a miracle.

Everyone seemed to agree that Querry should lead the party, and he took his place at the front of the line with Lord Starling and Tom as the back gates creaked slowly open. Frolic and Corny made some last minute adjustments to the machinery, and they prepared to set out. They'd only made it a few hundred yards when the carts skidded to a halt. Reg, who'd been trailing along behind everyone else, lost in his thoughts, hurried forward to see what caused the delay.

Backlit by the morning light, Querry stood facing Jean-Andre with Frolic just behind him. The Belvaisian stood with his arms crossed, his posture relaxed, and a smirk on his face. Querry, in contrast, looked ready to explode with his hand waiting on the hilt of his sword.

"No one said anything about him coming along," Querry said, clearly fighting hard to keep from shouting.

"I am more qualified than anyone here to lead. I have been working with these people for months, and I know my way through the jungle." Jean-Andre sounded slightly amused. "What's your problem with me, anyway, Monsieur Knotte? I daresay you'd be dead if not for me. I remember when I found you naked in that Halcyon alleyway, half-covered by the snow—"

"Shut your mouth," Querry roared, lunging at the other man. Frolic barely managed to restrain him. "I don't need anything from you!"

Jean-Andre winked and thrust one hip up. Reg had to admit it made a seductive show. "I think you protest too much, mon ami."

"Fuck you," Querry said.

"I've always imagined it the other way around," Jean-Andre said.

"You son of a whore!"

The Belvaisian chuckled. "Well, we have that in common, Querrilous."

Reg didn't know what to do. He wanted to draw his blade, call Jean-Andre out, and defend his lover's honor. If Querry had been a woman, he wouldn't have hesitated. But he couldn't acknowledge their relationship, and Querry might be insulted if Reg implied he needed shielding, so he held his tongue as outrage coursed through his veins.

Frolic, who didn't know any better, hurried to stand in front of Querry. "Don't you dare threaten my friend! I'll take care of him. We'll take care of each other. We don't need you."

"Oh, go away, little machine." Jean-Andre flicked his fingers at Frolic like he was an annoying ball of dust.

"That's it." Querry rushed past Frolic, toward Jean-Andre, but the baron stepped deftly between them.

"Both of you are wasting my time," Starling said. "That's unacceptable. Both of you are useful to me at the moment, so *both of you* will focus on the task at hand. Is that understood?"

"He's a pompous ass." Querry stabbed a finger toward Jean-Andre.

"Pardon me, my lord, but I am not in any way beholden to you or your cause," Jean-Andre reminded the baron. "I don't have to cater to you as these others must. My only concern is securing the liberty of these people."

"Nonetheless, if you want to accompany me, you'll obey me," Starling said. "If that's not acceptable to you, stay behind. I won't deal with this distraction. I'm leaving."

With that, the baron waved his hands to direct the carts forward, and they followed him out of the gates and down the steep slope of the hill, into the jungle. Frolic grasped Querry's shoulders and said something Reg couldn't hear above the noise of the engines. Querry shook his head, pinched Frolic's chin, and fell into step beside the carts. Reg hesitated until he resumed his position at the flank, desiring distance from everything. He remained there for several hours as they descended into the tropical forest. The carts easily adjusted to the bumpy, winding trails between the ancient trees.

They stopped around midday to have a quick meal of roast goat, bread, and fresh fruit. After less than half an hour, they set out again. Reg stayed toward the back of the party, hoping to be left alone, but eventually Jean-Andre circled back to walk beside him.

"Reginald, *non*? That is a fine name. And you seem much more refined than these others. I assume you had a proper upbringing."

"I certainly did," Reg responded, recalling the hazy memories of his mother and father, his real mother and father, and not the wealthy couple who'd adopted him in the hope of marrying their way into the aristocracy.

"Good, good. May I speak frankly?"

"Go on," Reg told Jean-Andre. The two of them fell even further behind the others.

"You care a great deal about those men." Jean-Andre indicated Querry and Frolic with a jut of his chin. "Do not worry; I understand about men caring for each other. Loving each other. You want them to be safe."

"Of course I do," Reg allowed.

"I can make them safe, free them from this ridiculous agreement," Jean-Andre said.

"Oh really?"

"*Oui*. How badly do you want it?"

"Say what you mean, sir." Reg was through playing with the Belvaisian.

"Very well, then. I can do what you have been unable to accomplish. I can release your... friends... from their contract with the Anglican lord. For good."

"How?"

Jean-Andre laughed. "How do you think?"

"Dear God," Reg whispered, realizing what the other man implied.

"Too much for you, ami? I worried it might be."

"It isn't that," Reg said, nervous even discussing it. He'd killed for Querry and Frolic before, and he'd do it again. He just knew it wouldn't come for free. "What do you want in return?"

"Your friend Frolic's book," Jean-Andre said.

"Out of the question. It isn't mine to give."

"But you know better than them," Jean-Andre said. "They are impetuous, while you use reason. Get me that book, which your companion already knows by heart, and I will put an end to Lord Gavindale Starling. You'll all be free to leave. You can save them."

"No," Reg said. "Not like this."

"Then how will you keep those you love from harm?"

"I don't know," Reg admitted. "Not like this."

Jean-Andre's face betrayed no emotion. "My offer stands. Let me know if you reconsider. I think we will all die if you do not." With that, Jean-Andre walked quickly toward Tom and the baron.

Reg watched him go, wondering if he'd made the right decision. Was he simply too fragile to save Querry and Frolic? Jean-Andre presented a simple solution to the problem. If Reg agreed, they could all go home. But he'd spend the rest of his life knowing a man, maybe not a completely innocent one but not one who deserved it, was dead because of him. Frolic wouldn't willingly relinquish his book, and Querry would certainly take Frolic's side. They might never forgive Reg for taking it.

Reg tried to assure himself good sense and not weakness had made up his mind.

NOT LONG after they stopped for lunch, thick black clouds rolled in to cover the brilliant blue of the sky. Only minutes after they appeared, the storm broke open, dousing the jungle in a heavy downpour. Querry hurried to help the others pull the sheet metal coverings over the cart beds so the guns and explosives would stay dry. By the time they'd finished, Querry's clothing, including his protective leather waistcoat and heavy boots, dripped as if he'd just emerged from a lake. The water was warm as tears, and it intensified the cloying scents of jungle flowers and decaying leaf litter. The narrow trails they traveled turned to slippery mud, slowing their progress and making everyone irritable and uncomfortable, with the exception of Frolic, who stared with obvious fascination at the unusual vegetation, bright birds, and even occasional small monkeys they passed. But then, the warm water and the thick, heavy mist it conjured wouldn't annoy the clockwork boy the way it did the humans.

Querry looked back at Reg, trudging along several feet behind everyone else, wiping his foggy spectacles on his sleeve every few minutes. He knew Reg felt like he'd somehow let them down by failing to find a way out of their contract, but he hadn't predicted Reg's melancholy would last so long. Querry stepped off the trail, into the thick, dripping undergrowth, and waited for his friend to catch up. Then he fell into step beside Reg. They walked in silence for several minutes while Querry considered how to start the conversation. He abandoned his original intention of making some joke to cheer his friend, knowing what had to be said.

Querry took a deep breath and caught Reg's wrist. Both of them paused on the trail, and Querry took Reg's other hand and guided him around so they faced each other in the decreasing rain. Reg's blond hair sparkled in the weak sun finally breaking through the clouds. Querry reached up and gently removed his glasses. Even Reg's thick eyelashes glittered. Though Querry wanted nothing more in that moment than to tell Reg how beautiful he was, instead he said, "I'm sorry. I'm sorry any of us are here. But I need to say that it's my fault we are. Mine, not yours. I'd rather have you cross with me than feeling responsible. I made a mistake going to Starling's villa. You did nothing wrong. You're here with us when you didn't have to be. If I seem too confident, it's just because I know what the three of us can do together. Still, I should have listened to you from the beginning. From now on, I'm going to start. You're much cleverer than I am."

"Finally realized that, have you?" Reg smiled, and the lines of tension on his forehead and around his hazel eyes smoothed. "Look, we're here now, and we're not going anywhere anytime soon. There's no sense in getting cross with each other. We need to watch out for each other, now more than ever. What do you think of Jean-Andre?"

"He's a conceited prick. Why?"

"I don't understand what he's after. He claims he helped you back in Halcyon, and he may have. But why? Why is he here now? What does he stand to gain?"

"We shouldn't trust him," Querry said. "He'd do anything for a paycheck. I think he's worse than Owens and his lot. At least they admit what they are. I'll keep an eye on him, don't worry."

Reg's lips parted, as if he might say something more, but instead, he turned to look at the carts, almost a quarter of a mile ahead of them now. "I suppose we had best catch up. We should watch Jean-Andre around Frolic."

"Why do you say that, Reg?"

Reg looked away. "No reason in particular. Frolic is just susceptible to deception, and Jean-Andre is a master of it. There's no telling what he might try."

"Agreed. Let's catch up to them." Then, since the others were too far up the road to see, he gave Reg a quick peck at the corner of his mouth. Reg rewarded him by coloring across his cheeks and the bridge of his nose. "Thanks for putting up with my nonsense," Querry said.

"It isn't always easy," Reg said in a gravelly voice. "You'll have to make it up to me somehow."

"That's a promise, love. Let's get going."

The rain tapered to a light drizzle and finally ceased around sunset. The broad, wet leaves of the jungle trees looked metallic, reminding Querry of the faux, clockwork jungle his mentor, Dink, had built to house his mechanical menagerie. With a stab, Querry wondered how the old tinkerer, who'd been the closest thing to a father Querry'd ever known, fared back in Halcyon. Because of Dink, Querry had grown into a scavenger and a thief when he could easily have turned out much worse. Any moral compass and sense of honor he possessed he owed to that kind man. He suddenly missed him fiercely.

To take his mind off his unexpected homesickness, Querry sought out Lord Starling to see why their procession had suddenly stopped. Along the way, he noticed Frolic talking to a grinning Cornelia, raising his hand and pointing at his elbow to illustrate whatever he said to her. Reg was showing his augmented pistols to Jack Owens. The older mercenary nodded with approval as he looked down the sights of one of Reg's guns.

Querry found the baron standing a little removed from the rest of the company with Tom Teezle and Jean-Andre. They all turned at the sound of his approach, but continued talking in low voices as he joined them.

"We're within five miles or so of the slave camp," Jean-Andre said. "They may very well be expecting us. I think at this time it would be prudent to send scouts ahead. I know this land well, and so I will volunteer to go. I would like to take Monsieur Teezle with me. You can sense men, guards, can you not?"

"In most cases," Tom said, his expression and posture guarded. "If it's what my lord wishes, of course."

"I'm not used to doing without him," Starling said.

Jean-Andre bowed his head. "Of course."

"I could go with you," Querry offered, eager for some time alone to question Jean-Andre about his motives.

"Thank you, but no."

"Why not?" Querry asked. "What's wrong with me?"

"I'll take a few of my friends from the quilombo," Jean-Andre responded with a dismissive shrug. "They're more familiar with the area."

"A good plan," the baron agreed, and Jean-Andre bent at the waist before setting off to assemble his team. Then Starling turned to Querry with one of his dark brows arched. "Enlighten me. How are you acquainted with that man, Querrilous?"

Querry raked his soggy curls back as he considered how much to divulge. He didn't trust Starling, but he trusted Jean-Andre less, and decided maybe the baron needed to know why. Though he scarcely knew where to begin, he asked, "How much do you know about what happened back in Halcyon?"

"A bit," Starling said. "I daresay every magic-user for hundreds of miles knew when the Grande Chancellor fired up that clock tower. It interrupted the flow of the world's magic, and I felt it. Tom filled me in on the rest. I also know you, your friends, and a small group of ruffians managed to put a stop to it."

"Well, we had loads of help. Normally I'd cite my extraordinary skill"—Querry flashed Starling a smile—"but the fact is, plenty of people had a hand in it. Jean-Andre was one of them. He claimed he'd been watching out for me for weeks before I'd met him, and maybe he had. I don't know. Anyway, he offered me money for… certain information about Frolic. He wanted to sell it. He also offered me a job, as a spy, like him. Obtaining and selling information. Listen, mate. I'd appreciate it if you didn't say anything about this to Reg or Frolic. I never told them."

Starling surprised Querry with his shocked expression. "Really? That's interesting."

Shame welled up inside Querry. "I should have said something, but there was so much going on at the time, and I never considered accepting, anyway…. I'd like them to hear it from me."

"I respect that," Starling said. "It's not my place to say anything, and I won't. On my honor as a gentleman. More importantly, based on what you've said, I can only assume we're dealing with an opportunist, rather than a selfless defender of liberty. Typical. The race of men never ceases to disappoint me. Now I wish I'd sent Tom with him after all."

"It's hardly too late," the fey said. "Or do you forget I'm not hampered by human limitations? Sir," he hurried to add sarcastically.

Starling surprised Querry yet again when he turned to Tom and patted him on the shoulder with genuine affection. "I know you won't believe it, but I truly do appreciate you."

"I'm sure you do," Tom said with a sneer before vanishing into thin air.

Since both of them had dealt with the Fair Folk before, neither Querry nor Starling flinched at Tom's disappearance. Starling draped his arm over Querry's shoulder and led him back toward the others, saying, "I appreciate your honesty with me tonight, Querry. I know you don't trust me. I know you don't even like me, so I am truly grateful."

Though he kept quiet, Querry decided he disliked the baron a little less than before. "What do you want me to do? How can I help?"

Starling beamed at him with an expression Querry had seen on Dink's face when Querry had returned with a particularly rare bit of salvage or when Querry'd exceeded the tinkerer's expectations. "We should get moving. If there's something coming, you'll be the first to notice. I'd like you to stay with me, near the front of the line."

It wasn't lost on Querry that Starling had asked instead of commanding. The aristocrat appeared a little nervous, possibly because of the absence of his fey steward. He seemed to look to Querry to fill the void, and Querry didn't resent it.

Still, he said, "I need Reg and Frolic with me. No matter what, their safety comes first."

"Absolutely," Starling said, and the two of them moved to take their places.

Querry knew they were in for a long night. He checked his weapons and gear, prepared to use them soon.

Chapter 17

W ITH HIS senses so heightened in anticipation of trouble, Querry noticed every one of the countless noises of the jungle. All around him, he detected life: in the branches above, moving through the undergrowth, and stalking between the massive trunks of the strange, twisted trees. Some of the animals sounded large and lethal, while others made noises unlike anything Querry had ever imagined. Even the drone of the insects sounded alien. Querry sensed creatures, hungry, dangerous creatures, waiting just beyond the light their lanterns and torches cast.

Every muscle in Querry's body tensed, ready to react. The strain exhausted him, and his muscles ached as they proceeded slowly into the eerie forest, but every time he looked over his shoulder at Reg and Frolic, he renewed his determination to keep them from harm at any cost.

It hardly surprised Querry when, half an hour into their journey, Jean-Andre and the three former slaves he'd taken with him came crashing through the brush. They skidded to a halt in the mud before the baron.

"Be ready," Querry said to his friends, and Reg and Frolic drew their weapons.

"Where is Tom?" Starling barked.

Jean-Andre clutched his ribs and caught his breath before speaking. "He... he stayed behind to try to confuse the guards while we warned you. He is in no danger."

"Of course not." The baron paced in front of the carts, his arcane energy warping the air and making Querry's teeth wiggle. "Just tell me what we're looking at."

"A regiment of imperial guards," Jean-Andre said. "A dozen of them, accompanied by hired men from the plantation. From what I overheard, they have been searching the road between the camp and the quilombo for weeks.

They are expecting this delivery, and they plan to stop it. They outnumber us, and they're armed."

"The weapons have to make it through," one of the former slaves yelled, and the others loudly agreed. "Nothing else matters."

"They're coming," Jean-Andre warned. "What do we do?"

Querry turned to face the rest of the procession and held up his arms. "Drag the carts into the jungle. Hide them. Starling, can you do anything to make them less evident? A spell?"

"Of course." The baron hurried to trace arcane symbols in the thick air as the others pulled the carts off the road. Soon, the transports shimmered, looking translucent, almost invisible unless Querry caught them from the corner of his eye.

Querry pointed to Cornelia and the mercenaries. "Cover them if you have to. Keep it quiet. Don't be hasty. I'll lure them off you."

"Querry, no!" Reg protested.

"Let me come with you," Frolic pleaded.

"No." Querry slid the new goggles he and Frolic had designed over his eyes and turned the knob to the night-vision lenses. The forest clarified in bright green with gray shadows. He blinked to adjust his eyes. These were nearly as good as the ensorcelled goggles he'd lost in the airship crash.

"Querry—" Frolic sounded distraught.

"Please listen to me, beauty. Stay here. Trust me. Get the carts off the road. Now! Reggie, Frolic, look out for each other. God, just stay safe no matter what."

As he hurried onto the path, Querry detected the sound of galloping horses in the distance. It sounded like an army, but it didn't matter. He'd make sure it never reached the others. Clutching the hilt of his sword, ready to draw it, he sprinted up the trail. He had to hold them off long enough for the others to hide.

"Let's make this convincing, Querry," Starling said.

Querry started, not having heard Starling following him. "What do you suggest?"

"Show me what you've got, you filthy highwayman!" Starling shouted, just as the dozen men on horseback reached them.

Querry drew his blade and met Starling's with a resounding clang.

"Don't worry. I won't leave you to bear the brunt of this," the baron said. "Just make it look good enough for the others to get hidden."

"Right then. Let's see what you can do. Old man," Querry added with a grin.

"Old man?" the baron crooned. "The capriciousness of youth shall be undone," Starling stated with a smirk.

They dueled in earnest, the baron impressing Querry with his skill, as the guards approached. Querry had to suppress a smile as the men and horses sloshed toward them through the mud. The baron and the thief matched each other blow for blow until one of the riders called for them to desist.

Both Querry and Starling huffed, dragging in air after their serious match, as the guards looked down at them.

"I'm afraid you'll both have to come with us," the leader said in Anglican, but with a heavy accent.

Querry looked at Starling, and felt ecstatic when the aristocrat winked at him. "Like hell," Querry said, pointing his sword at the throat of the man in front of him. "Bring it on, then!"

The guards guided their mounts to circle Querry and Starling. Querry readied his sword in one hand and his pistol in the other, while Starling literally hummed with magical energy. Both of them backed away before the guards could close them in. Before long, the pair stood with their backs to the jungle, ready to run into the trees at the first opportunity. Querry didn't know how they'd accomplish it with a dozen rifles trained on them and the rough-looking men from the plantation drawing pistols and machetes of their own. He didn't know the extent of the baron's magical prowess. Could he stop bullets somehow? Querry certainly hoped so.

"Don't be a fool," the man leading the guards said to Starling. "We have you surrounded. You cannot hope to escape."

"You have no right to detain me," Starling snarled, clearly outraged. "On what charges do you impede me, anyway?"

"On the charges of treason and espionage." The man spat on the ground. "We have known for some time that the Belvaisian crown has been working to destroy our empire from within, sending weapons and supplies to arm our own slaves against us. And now it seems the Anglican queen has become our enemy as well."

"I am no agent of the queen!" Starling said. "I'm here on a scientific excursion, and I demand you stand out of my way."

The guard captain, or whatever rank he held, ignored the baron and jutted his chin toward Querry. "Who is this man?"

Querry chuckled. "I was just trying to rob him." He decided it was safer to be considered a thief than a spy at the moment.

"I find that unlikely. Two Anglicans? Take them into custody."

"I will warn you one last time to stand down," Starling said in a low, serious voice.

Predictably, the guards only chuckled as they started to close in. The men on foot edged around the legs of the horses, moving so close Querry could smell their rancid sweat. He noted with horror and disgust that some of them were almost as dark as the men, women, and children back at the quilombo. If they hunted their own people for profit, what would they do to him and the baron?

"We need to level the field, and soon," Querry said quietly to Starling.

Starling nodded once without looking at Querry and raised his hands, holding his arms out straight and stiff in front of his chest. A flash of white light erupted from his palms. Querry's night-vision goggles intensified the brilliance a hundred fold, scorching his eyes and tearing a ragged curse from his throat. He couldn't see a thing as he sailed backward through the air, knocked off his feet by the blast. He landed hard among thick leaves and fallen branches, the impact stealing his breath. As he struggled to draw in air, he pushed the goggles into his hair and blinked hard. The burning white had receded, leaving only inky darkness in its place, and not the darkness of the night. No stars shined above Querry, and no moonlight broke through the leaves to create variations in the shadows. Everything was an unbroken sheet of black.

Panic welled in Querry's chest as he groped desperately around to get some sense of his surroundings. All around him, horses screamed and beat the ground with their hooves. Men shouted, steel clanged, and shots rang out. He smelled sulfurous smoke over the rich scent of the forest floor. Querry rolled to his belly and pushed himself up on his hands and knees, continuing to feel around in the leaf litter. Finally his gloved hand connected with something warm, hard, and solid. He clutched his pistol as he felt out his path with his other hand. When he found the trunk of a tree, he used it to pull himself to his feet. He tried to make out Starling's voice amidst the cacophony and chaos all around him, but he couldn't locate the baron. Completely disoriented, he had no idea of his position or whether he faced toward or away from the fighting. He took a few tentative steps, his empty hand stretched out in front of him.

Someone grabbed Querry's lapels and pulled him forward, almost making him trip over something on the ground.

"Starling?" he choked.

An angry voice responded in a language Querry couldn't understand. Letting his instincts take over, he swung out with his pistol and connected with flesh. His attacker grunted and swore. Querry stumbled back a few steps, aimed in the direction of the sound, and fired. The thump he heard a few seconds later told him he'd hit his target, but he had no way of knowing how many more men waited in the darkness. He could be surrounded. He swung his arms wildly, his gun clutched tight in his fist.

"Drop your weapon!" a man yelled somewhere off to Querry's left.

Querry pointed his pistol in the direction of the voice and fired, but this time he missed. Footsteps swished through the leaves, and then someone hit Querry hard in the lower back, sending him to his knees. Querry threw his elbow back behind his head and succeeded in hitting his assailant in the groin. He hurried to his feet and backed away, his gun trained on his best estimate of the man's position. He hoped they didn't know he couldn't see, so he yelled, "Drop your weapons!"

A cruel laugh answered him, and he took a few more steps back until he collided with a large tree. At least no one could flank him. He moved his gun slowly in a semi-circle in front of him as he listened hard for anything that might alert him to his enemy's movement. At the telltale sound of a sword unsheathed, he dodged to the side, but not in time. A heavy blade connected with his ribs, but his leather waistcoat and the metal plates lining it took the worst of the blow. Querry squeezed off another shot but missed again. The sound of boots against the moist ground surrounded him as at least three or four men ran toward him.

"Keep him alive for questioning," one of them commanded.

Querry flailed his arms. "Just keep back," he said. "I'm warning you."

"You are hardly in any position to threaten us," another man said. He punched Querry in the diaphragm, making him double over, and pulled Querry's pistol from his hand. Two other men grabbed his arms, straining his shoulder sockets painfully.

Querry thrashed and swore as they dragged him away, but it was no use. He felt the warm, oily ring of a gun barrel pressed against his temple, and he let himself be guided. Soon he smelled horses and felt the terrain even out beneath his boots. His captors pulled his arms out in front of him and bound his wrists with coarse rope that would have likely torn his skin apart if not for his gloves.

They patted him down and removed his lock picks, grapple, and dagger. At least they didn't find the spare set of picks he kept concealed in the hollow heel of his boot.

A sharp tug almost pulled Querry off his feet. He regained his balance and hurried to catch up with the horse or whatever they'd tethered him to. It was the most awkward and uncomfortable situation he'd ever found himself in, trudging through absolute oblivion without even the use of his arms for balance. Somehow, he managed to adapt to it after a while, and he barely stumbled as they dragged him along.

The men conversed in their language, sounding very pleased with themselves. Querry could tell there were fewer of them now, as well as fewer horses. Starling's spell had likely scared some of the animals off. Somehow, Querry knew the baron had survived as well. He couldn't say how, but he still felt the magical contract binding him to Starling. It hadn't dissolved, and for the first time, Querry took that as a good sign.

Querry estimated close to two hours passed before they finally stopped. His calves and feet hurt by then, and his arms were so sore from being wrenched out in front of him that they trembled. His fingers had gone numb because of the rope, but at least his vision had started to return. He managed to make out blobs of grays and patches of light. The soft swishing on either side of him told him they walked across a field of some kind. The sound of all the animals and birds of the forest disappeared. Off in the distance, he smelled cooking fires and the savory scent of roasting meat.

They led him past a huge expanse of creamy white, and Querry realized it must be the manor house and that they'd come to the plantation. They continued around behind it and stopped at a stable long enough to hand their horses off to some slaves. Though his world still looked blurry, Querry thought he saw one of the guards untie his rope from the saddle before dismounting. He finally caught sight of Starling, tethered in a similar fashion to himself. Most of the soldiers remained in the barn, but one led both Querry and Starling by their ropes while two others kept rifles trained on them.

After walking down a small hill and across a footbridge over a narrow stream, Querry saw a low, square, stone building surrounded by a metal fence. It had a single, metal door and no windows. Querry had escaped from enough prisons to recognize one when he saw it. What he didn't understand was why a plantation needed a prison at all. Still, it hardly mattered. With the picks hidden in his boot, he didn't plan on staying long.

Inside, it reeked of rust, mold, human sweat, excrement, and blood. Querry gagged as the guards dragged him and Starling down the narrow corridor with cages on either side. Querry heard and smelled people inside them, but with his vision still impaired, he couldn't make them out. A guard opened a cell door and shoved Querry and Starling inside.

"No chances," said one of the men, pointing at his prisoners with his rifle. "Take their gear."

Before they untied him, two of the guards removed Querry's goggles, his gloves, waistcoat, and even his boots. They shoved him into the filthy straw covering the concrete floor.

"What about the other one, sir? A wizard like this doesn't need weapons or equipment to make trouble for us."

"Give me your rifle."

Querry scrambled to his feet and hurried to stand between the guard leader and the baron. Why would they keep Starling alive so long just to kill him now? "What do you think you're doing? This man is an Anglican noble. A baron! You can't just shoot him in the head."

"You are no longer in Anglica, you little cutpurse. Out of the way."

"No. I won't let you do this."

The leader said a few words in their language to one of his men, who nodded, grabbed Querry by the hair, and slammed Querry's chest against the stone wall of the cell. The other guard held his gun to Querry's head.

With his eyes screwed shut and his legs turning to porridge, Querry waited for the gun to discharge. Instead, he heard a sickly crack and a thud. When the guards released him, he turned and found Starling sprawled on his back, a nasty bump on his forehead and his eyes rolled back in his head. The men hadn't bothered to remove any of the baron's clothes or equipment.

"If he can't think or concentrate, he can't cast," the leader said. "We'll figure out another way to subdue him for interrogation." With that, the three of them left the cell and locked the door behind them.

It was as hot as a brick oven in the cell and lit only by a few smoking torches at irregular intervals along the walls. His vision hadn't quite recovered, which made it difficult for Querry to assess Starling's condition when he crouched down beside him. Clearly he'd been knocked unconscious, but his breathing sounded regular. Querry gingerly touched the big goose egg above Starling's eyebrow. It felt hot and throbbing. Querry wished he had a bit of ice or even a cool rag to press against it. Since he didn't, he lifted Starling's head into his lap.

Half an hour or so later, the baron groaned and started to come around. Starling winced as he touched his forehead. "That," he muttered, "is bloody sore. Ah, damn it. Would you help me sit up, Querry?"

Querry grasped the baron by the armpits and helped him lean against the wall. Starling's eyes fluttered, and he dropped his chin against his chest. A moment later, he jerked his head back up.

"Perhaps you should lie back down," Querry suggested. "Try to get a bit of sleep."

Starling laughed. "That's exactly what I mustn't do with a head injury like this. On the contrary, I have to keep myself awake somehow. Please, Querry. Don't let me fall asleep. If I do, I may not wake up."

"Is it true what they said?" Querry asked. "That you can't cast any spells?"

"Casting spells requires a great deal of concentration. Right now, it's taking all of mine to string words into coherent sentences."

Querry swore. "I was hoping you'd be able to get us out of here."

"Isn't that more your specialty than mine?"

"Usually," Querry conceded, "but these backwater guards weren't as clueless as I'd assumed. They took my boots, where I hide my emergency picks. If they hadn't, we'd be out of here already. I still might manage, but it'll take longer."

"Well, in that case…." Starling reached inside his waistcoat, pulled out an engraved silver flask, opened the lid, and took a swig. Then he handed it to Querry. "Gin."

Querry sighed with delight and drank. He held it in his mouth a few seconds before swallowing slowly, feeling the gin move in a warm little trail to his stomach. "You know, there are plenty of things I don't miss about Halcyon, but I have missed this. How do you get it in Thalacea?"

"Tom gets it for me. Unlike you and me, he can't be prevented from going back whenever he likes. Or whenever *I* like."

"Two titles are a lot to give up just to practice magic," Querry said. "Couldn't you have just kept it secret?"

Starling laughed. "A lot more than my use of magic got me exiled from Anglica, Querry."

"Oh?" Querry took another swig of gin.

"I reached a point in my life where I simply didn't care anymore," Starling said. His eyes went unfocused as he lost himself to something inside his head. He drank more gin and began to hum to himself.

To focus the baron's attention and keep him awake and talking, Querry asked, "What exactly did you do?"

"You know, I lost everything I cared about. Everything seemed so meaningless. I saw little to life beyond the pursuit of pleasure. So I pursued pleasure. With anyone who asked me for it. Married women. Visiting princesses. Artists, circus performers, scientists, and gypsies. I kept it no secret, because I didn't care. I didn't think anything could hurt me anymore. I think the queen's nephew was the last straw, though. And behind a bush during a royal garden party, at that."

Querry was a little shocked but mostly impressed. "I have to say, well done."

"I thought you might feel that way. After all, you seem to keep both your partners quite happy."

"I suppose I do," Querry said. "Damn. I miss them, you know. After only a few hours even. They're both very capable, but I worry when I'm not there to look after them."

"I hope you never lose them."

"Why would you say that?" Querry asked. "Did you lose someone?"

"It was a long time ago." Starling fished in his trouser pocket and pulled out a locket. He teared up a little as he looked at the photo inside.

"Your wife?"

"No. I have never been married."

Querry was torn. He had to keep Starling awake, but he didn't know how much to push him. He felt sure Starling had already told him more than he would if he hadn't been injured.

"I've had hundreds of lovers, Querry. Maybe a thousand. I've lost track of them over the years. But I've only ever been in love one time. I was sixteen years old. My father had just died, leaving me his titles. He also left me with a sort of freedom I'd never known before. He'd been the proper one, and he'd ruled the family like a tyrant. My mother was Belvaisian, a free spirit and a romantic. I'm much more like her, I think. Anyway, she almost encouraged me take lovers. Not long after, I met a farm boy named David and fell in love with him to the depths of my soul. I would have given up my estate and moved into his hovel if he'd asked me. I believe that's something you can understand."

Querry nodded. "What happened?"

"They found coal, bauxite ore, and copper deposits near his family's land and opened up mines and processing factories. Before long, the poison they spewed polluted the fine, old spring David's family used to water their crops. David got sick. I spent a fortune on doctors and even tried to use magic, but he wasted away. His hair and teeth fell out, and he couldn't keep food down. Sores covered his body, and he could hardly breathe. When David died at twenty, he looked like a ninety-year-old man. For a long time after I lost him, I didn't care about anything. I was finished with this world and didn't even care if I lived or died. I saw no hope for humanity, no remedy for our cruelty and avarice. Then I found the first mention of the magical energy source in an old book. 'The primal source, the beginning', it claimed. Make no mistake, Querry. I'm weary of this life. I don't expect to find happiness in it. But if I can leave humanity with a clean source of power, I will be honored to die attempting it. Can you understand a little?"

"A little," Querry conceded. "But if you despise people so much, why sacrifice yourself to help them?"

"Because no one deserves to die like my David did. Why can't anyone see? We, as a race, must embrace magic, not filthy industry! How can the world be so blind? Exiling sorcerers while the very air they breathe grows toxic? How does that make sense? I hate those disgusting machines, and I'll destroy them all if I can."

"I'm not sure I agree with that," Querry said, thinking of Frolic. "I think some sort of balance can be reached. Don't you?"

"No. If I find this wellspring, people will have all the energy they need. There will be no use for machines."

"Maybe, but can you imagine how much people will fight to control it? It might be more of a curse than a blessing."

"I can't hope to change human nature, Querry."

"You make it sound as though there isn't any chance of a better future."

"Not as long as people are willing to sacrifice each other for wealth and power. Not when material possessions are more important to them than human lives. Do you honestly think a time will come when they don't?"

"No," Querry whispered. He'd fought exploitation all his life. "I don't suppose that's ever likely to happen."

"Consider your own experience," the baron stated as if he spoke to Querry's thoughts. "Children utilized as nothing more than cogs in the machines of greed. That's industrialization, and that's what we have to look forward to."

They sat in demoralized silence for many minutes, both of them keeping their thoughts to themselves. Querry felt himself sinking into despair. Was there truly no hope for the world, and if not, why should he keep fighting? Then he remembered his lovers, his beautiful Reg and Frolic, and the thought renewed his determination. He would fight for them until he could no longer lift a finger.

"Right. Time to get out of this stinking pit, then. How's your head, majesty?"

"You little shit," Starling said with teasing affection. "Would it absolutely kill you to call me sir?"

"Only ever called one person that in my life," Querry said, standing to inspect the lock on their cell.

"And you found him worthy of it?"

Querry took a moment to remember his faerie patron fondly. "Yeah, he was. Say, do you have anything sharp or pointed about you?" He looked at Starling in the low light with almost perfectly restored vision. His gaze fell on the long pin with the pearl and sapphire tip through the aristocrat's wide, paisley tie. "I'll just have this," he said, sliding it out of the silk.

"Be careful with it, lad. It's a family heirloom."

Querry laughed. "I'll keep that in mind." Then he reached through the rusty, iron bars and set to work on the outdated mechanism standing between them and their freedom. He almost had it open when something exploded outside. Another explosion followed seconds later, shaking the ground, and the ensuing fires scented the night air with thick smoke.

Starling got to his feet, looking at least fairly steady and lucid. "Now is no time to slow down, Querry."

"Right." Querry eased the tiepin back into the lock. "Can you use magic yet? You have my back, or what?"

"I certainly do," Starling said. "These peons have made a grave error in underestimating us. Let's go."

Querry sprung the lock, slid Starling's jeweled pin through his own cravat, and pushed the door open. The thief and the baron hurried out of their cell, and men shouting and gunfire sounded beyond the walls of the filthy little prison.

CHAPTER 18

OVER AN hour passed with no word from Querry or Lord Starling. Reg grew restless, thinking the worst. Finally Jean-Andre announced they were safe to deliver the weapons. They fired up the carts and proceeded down the trail. After about three miles or so, they abandoned the well-trod paths and descended into the jungle. The carts bounced down the hills until they stood outside a ring of firelight. Half a dozen armed men hurried forward. Reg and the others held up their hands, and Jean-Andre spoke with their leader.

The men in the camp seemed to relax. They hurried toward the carts to unload the guns and explosives, hooting at the sight of them. While Reg was glad to help these people win their freedom, his real concern was for Querry. He didn't trust Lord Starling to look out for his friend's best interests. Obviously, the baron cared about little beyond his own goals. Reg wished for a second he'd accepted Jean-Andre's offer. If anything happened to Querry, he'd personally see Starling paid dearly for it.

A light touch on his elbow made Reg turn around. Frolic fondled the metal feather he wore around his neck and chewed his lower lip. "It's been an awfully long time since Querry left, Reggie. I think we should go look for him."

"I agree, but where will we even begin?"

All around them, the former slaves yelled to each other and passed out guns. They clearly didn't plan to wait for morning to free the rest of their people. A group of around fifty men gathered, and Jean-Andre stepped onto a wooden crate to address them.

"Here is what we must do, my friends. We must get weapons into the hands of the people on that plantation before we announce our presence. We must bolster our numbers before we face our enemies. This will require a great deal of finesse, as they may be expecting us. I will take two or three others, alert the slaves to our plan, arm them, and give the rest of you a signal to cover our escape. We should expect heavy resistance. They will not show us mercy."

Jean-Andre motioned Jack Owens over. "You're a soldier, *non*? You have led men in combat before?"

"Yes, sir, I have."

"I would ask you to lead these men, if you would, while I sneak the guns to the other slaves."

"Sure thing, mate."

Cornelia stepped forward. "I'm with you, Jack. I want to fight too."

The mercenary looked skeptical for only a moment before nodding. Then he, the brothers, Corny, and most of the other men moved a little deeper into the camp to plan their strategy.

"Reginald," Jean-Andre called. "I'd like you to come with me."

Reg and Frolic walked over to him. "Why me?" Reg asked.

Jean-Andre smiled, and it wasn't lost on Reg that he was a very nice-looking man. "I remember what a crack shot you are from back in Halcyon. Can I count on your help?"

"I suppose, but what I really need is to find Querry," Reg said. "He should have been back by now."

"I'll see to rescuing your friend and Lord Starling," Tom said, appearing suddenly after hours of absence.

"What do you mean 'rescuing'?" Reg asked, more alarmed by the word than the fey's unexpected presence.

"They were captured by the men sent looking for you. They're being held at the plantation. I can only assume the baron is injured, or he would have escaped by now. Something must be stopping him from using his magic."

"Well, I'm coming with you." Reg quickly checked his guns and the armor Frolic had crafted. The leather made him sweat in the jungle heat, but he trusted it to protect him. He didn't understand how any building on a simple farm could hold his master thief lover. He knew about the emergency picks Querry kept in his boot. If he hadn't used them to free himself, he likely couldn't for some reason. "What are we waiting for? Let's get going!"

The fey held up his graceful hand. "It is essential to my patron's goals that the guns make it into the hands of the humans on the plantation. Therefore, you must accompany Jean-Andre and see they do. This is in the best interests of my patron, so I must insist. I'll take Frolic with me, and we'll have no trouble, I promise you."

Reg wanted to protest. He didn't trust the faerie any more than Jean-Andre. Likely both of them had some ulterior motive, and with both his partners in danger, Reg had no time for it. "I'm going to get Querry, and Frolic's coming with me. I don't care what the rest of you do." He caught Frolic's hand as he turned to leave.

Tom blocked his way, a hard edge on his pretty, surreal features. He pressed his palm against Reg's chest, the warning clear in his jewel-like eyes. "If you do that, Reginald, this is what will happen. Most of these men will be captured or killed, and those remaining here in the camp won't give us our supplies as part of the bargain. It might take us weeks or months to get what we need before continuing. Lord Starling will not be dissuaded. He *will* continue on with this mission, no matter what he has to do. Do you really want to stay here longer than we have to? Do you really want to see these men die if they don't have to?"

Reg really couldn't argue with him. If accompanying Jean-Andre would really save as many innocent lives as Tom suggested, how could he refuse? "I just don't like splitting us up. Querry, Frolic, and I work best together."

"It's necessary. Your friends are capable men. Have some faith in them," Tom said. "Now, go quickly." He seized Frolic by the elbow and whisked him out of the camp, not even giving Reg a chance to embrace him or tell him to be careful. He could do nothing but trust in Frolic's ample skills. He just couldn't feel as confident with Frolic's ability to make decisions, especially lately. Sometimes Frolic didn't seem to value his own safety. He'd grown reckless, at times worse than Querry. Reg wondered if it was due to Tom Teezle's influence.

Jean-Andre didn't give Reg long to worry. He thrust two heavy, canvas sacks full of rifles into Reg's arms. Reg put the straps across his chest, surprised at how heavy and noisy the contents seemed. Then he followed Jean-Andre and two other men, all of whom carried similar loads, into the jungle. They picked their way slowly through the thick undergrowth, trying their best to stay quiet. Reg perspired until his clothing clung to him and his cheeks burned. By the time they reached the vast fields of sugar cane, he walked bent nearly in half beneath the weight of the guns.

Reg paused to mop his forehead with his sleeve, looking out over the miles and miles of tall stalks swaying in the light breeze. Beyond them, an exorbitant, neoclassical mansion with rows of white columns stood on a hill overlooking it all. Reg thought he saw some barns and storage sheds beyond it, but Jean-Andre led them in the opposite direction, toward a collection of tiny hovels and cabins. No light came from within any of the small buildings, and the small settlement stood as quiet as a cemetery.

Jean-Andre held up a hand to indicate they should wait. He leaned into Reg's hair and whispered: "Get your pistols out, mon ami. Patrols will be coming up the road. Watch for them, and do what you must."

Though he didn't look forward to it, Reg nodded his understanding and set his burden down. Feeling much lighter, he crept back to the road and crouched behind a clump of trees. Behind him, Jean-Andre knocked softly on one of the cabin doors and spoke in hushed tones with the man who opened it. Before long, guns were distributed, and people began gathering in the shadows between the shoddy buildings. Reg glanced over his shoulder, and his heart dropped into his boots when he saw not only strong men, but children and even women holding infants. None of them bothered with any possessions. Still, Jean-Andre appeared confident of his plan and quickly guided the women and children to the center of the armed men.

All of them moved quickly back onto the dirt path bisecting the field. Reg followed, staying at the back of the group and watching the road over his shoulder. Before they'd made it even half the distance back to the forest trails, he noticed a pair of men on horseback about a quarter mile from their position, riding down the hill from the manor house.

"We've got company," he said.

"Everyone off the road," Jean-Andre ordered, pointing into the cane field.

For such a large group, they quietly and efficiently hid among the stalks. The men knelt down, guns braced against their shoulders, while the women and children waited behind them. Jean-Andre, an intricately engraved, gold-tone pistol with an especially long barrel and an ivory handle in his hand, crouched down next to Reg.

"They will shoot on sight," he told Reg.

"What are you saying?"

"Best if they don't see us." Jean-Andre pulled back the hammer on his gun, and the click echoed in the silence.

Reg swallowed the bitter acid rising in his throat. He supposed these slavers deserved it, but it didn't sit well with him. As the men rode into range, turning their heads to scan the fields, he decided he'd worry about his conscience later. There were children cowering behind him, and they didn't have a Querry to protect them like he had. Reg remembered being young, helpless, and afraid as he got one of the men in his sights and squeezed the trigger. He hit his target in the center of the forehead, and the man flew out of his saddle and backward over his horse's haunches. The frightened animal reared, whinnied, and ran off. It was time for Reg to be the protector.

The guard's companion swore loudly and looked back and forth, clearly trying to determine what direction the shot had come from. Just as he opened his mouth to call for help or alert more men, Jean-Andre's pistol discharged only a few feet from Reg's ear. His bullet tore through the guard's throat with a spectacular fount of blood. He turned and winked at Reg, much more comfortable than Reg with taking life. "I suppose we're tied for now," he said with a grin. "I bet I'll beat your score before the night is over, though. What do you say the loser buys a bottle of wine?"

"And where are we going to get a bottle of wine out here?" Reg snapped, irritated by the Belvaisian's flippancy.

Then, from somewhere near the manor house, a bell began ringing. Jean-Andre got to his feet and called out, "There's no sense in hiding anymore. They know we're here. We must get back into the forest."

They stood and ran, weapons at the ready, keeping the women and children protected at the center of the group. Reg estimated only about half a mile stood between them and the blessed cover of the jungle trees. The guards might pursue them into the forest, but they'd be able to split up and confuse them. At least they'd have something to hide behind, and hopefully they'd find reinforcements waiting.

Jean-Andre shouted encouragements, pushing them hard. Reg's heart pounded with fear and exertion, and sweat flew from his hair. They'd almost made it when men and horses poured in from an intersecting path, blocking their way. Not long after, another group of guards appeared at their flank, boxing them in. Without a word of warning, one of the guards fired into the group. A man off to Reg's left collapsed in the dirt less than five feet away.

Reg looked down at his face. He couldn't have been more than fifteen or sixteen years old.

Without wasting a second to consider the moral implications, Reg shot the guard in the chest. Then he bent, retrieved his fallen comrade's rifle, and cast about for someone to wield it. A dark, young woman stood with her hand out. "Can you use this?" he asked. Her black eyes went wide with fright, but she nodded confidently. He thrust the weapon into her arms, and she raised it to her shoulder.

"Get down!" Reg yelled as the guards returned fire from both directions. The former slaves dropped and covered their heads, but at least a few wouldn't be getting back up. Time seemed to slow down as Reg dove sideways into the sugar cane. The guards on the horses and the thugs on the ground seemed sluggish, and he picked them off one by one, ducking their bullets easily. His party and the runaways scattered among the stalks, but the guards chased them down and slaughtered them. Over the sounds of men screaming and women crying, Reg heard the sound of more horses approaching.

A bullet severed a cane stalk only inches above Reg's head, and he dropped to his knees and shielded his face with his forearms as leaves rained down on him. On his hands and knees, he crawled away from the onslaught. When he emerged from the field again, he took the opportunity to shoot a guard who stood with his back to him. Something exploded somewhere in the distance, and the fields caught fire. As the guards rode by, they threw glass lamps full of oil into the stalks. Reg realized with horror that they'd destroy their crops to flush the runaways out. He got to his feet and looked for a mark, but he could barely distinguish his allies from his enemies amidst the thick smoke, flames, and running, screaming people.

Reg felt pressure against his back, and it comforted him a little. He'd seen Querry and Frolic assume such a stance so no one could sneak up on them. Jean-Andre chuckled and said, "Perhaps I think too highly of myself. You're at least six ahead of me now. So, what do you drink?"

A laugh of mixed relief and exasperation escaped Reg. "In that case, I do quite enjoy a Chateau La Belle Reve, and 1857 was a very good year."

Jean-Andre groaned. "I had no idea you were so refined. I'd better pick up my pace. Or start saving my gold."

"Just what's our plan here?" Reg asked, the moment of levity over.

Jean-Andre also grew serious as he looked out over the burning fields. "We have to fight our way to the tree line. Our people know to make for the jungle. If any of them are to survive, we have to help them get there."

"Let's go," Reg said in agreement. Still back to back, their pistols stretched out in front of them, they stepped sideways onto the path. Ahead of them, only a few hundred yards from the forest, a large group of former slaves fought hard against the guards. Now and then, a few of them managed to escape into the trees, but many others fell, injured or worse. The smoke, movement, and the way the group mingled and packed together made it impossible for Reg to take a shot.

"Damn it! I wish we could get higher. Above the smoke!" he yelled. Looking around, he didn't see any vantage point they could reach. With reinforcements coming from the manor house, he didn't see how they could prevail unless they did something drastic.

A loud crash came from the jungle, behind the guards. Reg didn't think he'd ever seen anything more beautiful than Jack Owens's blood-streaked face as he barreled out of the forest followed by nearly fifty armed men.

"Get your asses into the jungle!" he shouted, even as he plunged his combat knife into the base of a guard's skull. The former slaves hurried to obey him, trampling their enemies as Owens and the other mercenaries and fighters cut the guards down.

"What kept you?" Reg shouted.

"Met some opposition," Owens said, licking his bloody lips.

"I could kiss you," Reg said as the fresh fighters quickly turned the tide, and more and more of their people escaped. "Truly."

"Don't recommend you try it, lad," Owens said, slashing out with his blade.

"Fair enough," Reg called, lifting his pistol again to help cover their retreat.

FROLIC BARELY knew what was happening as Tom Teezle held his hand and pulled him through the burning fields toward the huge white house on the hill. Men screamed, ran, fought, and died around them, and Tom simply strolled through it like he walked in a park on a spring day. A quartet of soldiers with rifles jogged toward them, and Frolic caught Tom's elbow and tried to drag him into the field.

Tom jerked his arm out of Frolic's grasp and shot him a cross look. "What do you think you're doing, Frolic?"

"Trying to hide us, so we don't get shot?"

"Ridiculous. Keep hold of my hand."

Though baffled, Frolic did as the fey said. He liked the feeling of Tom's magic coursing down his arm and into his body, making his inner parts hum and wiggle, so he kept Tom's fingers, almost as small and slender as his own, clutched tight in his palm.

Tom walked boldly up to an especially nasty-looking man in nothing but his undershirt and a pair of torn trousers. Frolic flinched at the blood dripping from the man's machete, but the faerie seemed unfazed. Tom stopped in front of the man and stood with the tip of his pointed nose only inches from the man's stained shirt.

He gave Frolic a full-toothed grin that made him look slightly deranged and anything but human. "What's wrong you big, stinking donkey?" Tom taunted. "As blind as the rest of your kind, aren't you?"

The man completely ignored him, and Frolic began to understand.

Tom wasn't through toying with the thug. He reached up and ran his long finger along the edge of the man's ear. The man swatted at it as if an insect troubled him, and Tom giggled. Tom tickled the man's neck on the opposite side, and he scratched at it, looking back and forth suspiciously. Tom howled as though he'd never had so much fun before.

"Go on, Frolic!"

Gingerly, Frolic poked the man in his round belly. He started and jumped back. Tom laughed with approval. Frolic had to admit it was kind of funny, and he chuckled before he dug his knuckle into the man's rib, right where he sometimes tickled Reg. This time, the man shouted and flinched. Frolic laughed harder, and Tom sounded positively insane in his glee. The faerie grabbed a thick clump of the man's greasy hair and yanked it out. The ensuing cry of pain dowsed Frolic's mirth, but Tom kept laughing as the man turned and ran.

"Get back here, you oaf!" When Tom waved his hand, a shelf of rock jutted from the ground and caught the fleeing man in the knees. He landed hard on his chest, and Tom sprinted to catch up with him, dragging Frolic along.

Tom jabbed his toe into the man's fleshy cheek, and the man whimpered and covered his head with his arms.

"Tom, stop it," Frolic said, trying to tug him away.

"Why?" The faerie sounded genuinely confused.

"Well, we shouldn't be doing this. We're supposed to be rescuing Querry and Lord Starling."

Tom heaved a great sigh. "Very well." He made a chopping motion with his free hand, and the man on the ground tore in half from the top of his head to his tailbone.

Frolic covered his face to escape the sickening smell, glad the darkness spared him the sight of the awful stuff spilling out of the cleaved-open body. He wanted to say something to Tom, but the fey had already started sprinting toward the big house, and Frolic hurried to keep up. Tom's speed surprised him, since Frolic could run far faster than even Querry. Bullets whizzed over their heads, and fires raged behind them, but after what he'd just seen, Frolic didn't fear any of it. He feared Tom a little bit, but he also needed his help, since Tom knew where to find Querry.

They made it to the house in no time and hurried around behind it, past some large, plain, rectangular buildings and toward a small stone structure set apart from the others. Two men stood watch outside the single, metal door.

"There," Tom said, jutting his chin at what could only be a jail of some sort. "Let me get rid of those men."

"No," Frolic said. "They can't see us. Let's just sneak past them."

"Allowing them to live will put your friend in danger. I won't be able to shield all four of us after we get them out of there, and I'm sworn to protect the human wizard first."

"Do you have to kill them?" Frolic really didn't want to witness a repeat of what Tom had done in the field.

"You are a very strange creature," Tom said. He waved his hand at the two guards, and a moment later a pair of small, hairy monkeys ran screeching for the nearest tree. "Happy?"

"No, I don't think so," Frolic said, wondering if the two men retained their human minds or reverted to the instincts of beasts. He didn't know which would be worse, and he would remember to ask Tom about it when they had more time.

"Just get the door open," the fey said, pointing. "The iron in the steel weakens my magic, and I shudder to think what will happen to the people inside if I blast a hole through the wall."

"Right." Frolic took his picks from a pocket hidden in his waistcoat, knelt down, and started to work. Tom draped his hand over Frolic's shoulder to keep Frolic inside his spell. The lock, while old and rusty, contained only a simple mechanism, and Frolic had it open in minutes. Querry had taught him well.

Tom disengaged from his contact with Frolic as they went inside. He would be bound to protect Lord Starling now. Still, he patted Frolic's back when Frolic doubled over and held his sides at the horrible stench.

"Who would treat other people this way?" Frolic managed to gag out.

Tom shrugged. "I don't understand these creatures any better than you do."

"Let's get out of here." Frolic's eyesight adjusted to the low light, and he found Querry, Starling, and a group of practically nude and emaciated men and women near the back of the prison. Both Querry and the baron worked to open the rest of the cells, using the tietack and magic respectively. Frolic gave Querry a meaningful look and hurried to help them, horrified at the condition of the people inside the cages. All of them looked skeletal, and many had injuries that reeked of infection. A few of them were even missing some of their fingers and toes. Others, covered in bruises or lacerations, had clearly been beaten or flogged.

As soon as he opened the last cell, Frolic ran for the door. He had to get away from the stench and echoes of human misery in this awful place.

"Beauty, wait," Querry said, his voice raw and strained, though Frolic didn't think he was hurt, at least not physically. He sounded ready to cry, and it frightened Frolic. "These people are very weak, and many of them are hurt. I don't know how we'll get them through the fighting. I... just don't know what to do."

"We can't leave them here!"

"No, I know," Querry said. "I just don't think they—or any of us—will make it through."

Frantic, Frolic turned to Tom, scooped up both of his hands, and looked deep into his eyes. "Tom, I know you said you couldn't... but please. Please. Is there anything you can do?"

"With my lord's help, perhaps. But what about you? What will you give me in return?"

"Frolic—" Querry warned, slipping his waistcoat back on and stretching his newly retrieved gloves over his hands.

Frolic ignored Querry. He couldn't tear his attention from the frightened people looking at them with such guarded hope. They were suffering, and if left behind, they would die. Frolic couldn't live out the rest of his days knowing he'd had a chance to save them. "What will you have of me, Tom Teezle?"

"What I need from you, Frolic, is extremely valuable. You carry it always with you but can never hold it in your hand. Is that acceptable?"

"Um." Frolic glanced questioningly at Querry. "But what *is* that?"

"That is for you to decide," Tom answered with a smirk. "Once it is given, it can never be taken back."

"This is a bad idea," Querry said. "Believe me, I know."

"It doesn't sound bad at all," Frolic said. "Besides, we need to save these people somehow. This is going to haunt me forever. I can't leave them behind. Tom, if I agree, will you save them?"

"I agree to try. I'll weave the strongest illusion around us I can. If my lord lends me a hand, we might even succeed. But first, do you swear to give me what I ask when I need it?"

"I swear."

Querry groaned and shook his head as Tom pulled Frolic close and gave him a quick, brisk peck on the lips to seal their bargain. Frolic found it lovely, like a breath of cool, flower-scented, evening air on a hot night. For a few seconds, he completely forgot the stench and despair surrounding him, and it seemed even more profound when Tom withdrew his lips.

"Just remember, faerie, you're forbidden to work against my interests," Starling said, removing his cufflinks and pushing up his sleeves. "Now, let's do the magic. I can't see the last of this place too soon."

"Don't worry about me," Frolic said. "Don't waste the magic keeping me safe. Worry about these people. I can make it back to camp on my own."

"Like hell you will," Querry said. "But I agree. They won't find me and Frolic if we don't want to be found."

"Like they didn't find us?" Starling said.

"Majesty, we *wanted* to be found. And I still could have gotten us out of there if some jackass hadn't blinded me with a spell. Just go. We'll be fine."

It surprised Frolic a little when Starling grasped Querry by the shoulder and looked at him affectionately. "Querry, I will consider it a breach of contract if you allow yourself to be injured."

"Been injured enough for one night," Querry said. "Frolic, let's go. We may have some fighting to do."

Frolic drew his blade and smiled at the familiar hum. After what he'd seen here, he couldn't wait to give these horrible men a taste of his enchanted sword.

CHAPTER 19

BY THE time they found and reached the camp, both Querry and Frolic were muddy, damp, and spattered with blood. Querry was drenched in sweat beneath his clothing and armor, but he'd enjoyed himself with Frolic. They'd once again proved an almost unstoppable force, and they'd taught those filthy slavers a lesson they wouldn't soon forget. To Querry, these men were really no different than the bastards who'd locked him and Reggie in the workhouse. He still smiled as he remembered how they'd made sure the guards and thugs wouldn't exploit anyone else. Frolic squealed with delight as he'd vanquished them. Hearing him did things to Querry's body that still hadn't subsided. Querry had never seen Frolic enjoy battle like that before.

Querry's blood still sang with excitement, and his senses remained acute as they entered the ring of torchlight. Coming back from a successful excursion always aroused Querry, and tonight had left him hard and ravenous. Despite the heat, gooseflesh erupted over Querry's arms when the people in the camp stood and cheered as he and Frolic stepped into the circle of crude tents. He knew he grinned like a boy as he stopped and basked in their gratitude. Hell, he probably looked as awestruck and delighted as his beautiful Frolic. Querry had always taken pride in his skills, known he was exceptional at what he did, but it seldom earned him the accolades of others.

The crowd parted, and one of the slaves they'd freed from the prison limped forward. The young man had lost his right foot from the ankle down, and supported himself on a crude crutch. With about twenty or thirty pounds on him, he'd be quite handsome. Tears streamed down the young man's face as he smiled, clearly unable to speak. He grasped Querry's face in both hands and kissed Querry on the forehead. Then he threw his arms around Querry's neck and wept into his hair. With his emotions running so high, Querry returned his embrace and even choked back a few sobs. He couldn't remember ever feeling so good. His talents had truly helped people, and for once, they appreciated it.

Everyone clapped again, and more of the newly freed prisoners came forward to thank Querry and Frolic. After a while it became a little overwhelming, and Querry and Frolic retreated to the shadows beyond the fire. Before long the former slaves broke off to speak among themselves and tend to their wounded. Starling, Tom, Owens, Corny, and one of the leaders of the revolt sat crossed-legged on the ground across from Querry and Frolic.

"They will pursue you," the leader of the rebels said to the baron. "They won't just dismiss a blow like this. However, word of what you have done for us will spread to the other quilombos. We are grateful, and we'll do what we can to assist you. Your party is heading north?"

"Northwest," Starling clarified.

The other man nodded. "You'll find some of our camps along the way, and we'll provide you with what we can."

"I appreciate it," Starling said.

Querry couldn't pay attention as they continued to speak and plan. He couldn't keep his hands off Frolic, out of his curls or away from his slim arms and thighs. He knew he shouldn't be groping Frolic in full view of others, and he held back as much as he could, but the innocent, encouraging smiles Frolic gave him didn't make it easy. Damn, he could just imagine those perfect, rosebud lips pressed against his, stretched thin over his cock—

Querry shifted, his erection painful in his tight, leather pants. "Beauty, let's get out of here," he breathed, unable to mask the desperate lust in his voice.

"Where's Reggie?" Frolic asked.

Scanning around, Querry finally found his old friend sitting on a mossy log next to Jean-Andre. The two of them passed a bottle of wine back and forth, laughing and smiling easily as they conversed. Querry couldn't see Reg's eyes, only the firelight reflecting off his spectacles. As he watched, Jean-Andre cupped Reg's knee and leaned in to whisper in Reg's ear. Reg took a deep pull from the wine bottle.

"I'll just get him," Querry said to Frolic. "Meet us in the woods." Seeing Reg with the Belvaisian spy sent Querry's blood boiling. Jean-Andre's hand on Reg almost compelled Querry to lethal violence. He hurried past the fire to grab Reg by his lapels and haul him to his feet. "I need you, right now."

Reg looked startled but not unhappy. Querry didn't know how Jean-Andre responded, because he didn't care enough to look down. The flush on Reg's cheeks, the way he licked his parted lips, commanded all Querry's attention. It took all his willpower not to toss Reg on the ground and take him in front of everyone. Instead, he dragged him outside the light of the bonfire, into the rich, heavy shadows of the jungle. As soon as he felt confident the others couldn't see them, he slammed Reg against the trunk of a tree and forced his tongue into Reg's mouth.

"What are you doing with that Belvaisian, you little tart?" Querry panted against Reg's cheek. "You fancy him?"

"Have you seen him?" Reg responded. "I'm not blind, love. Or dead. Go on, then. Make me forget he even exists."

Querry literally rose to the challenge. He grasped the edges of Reg's armored waistcoat and pulled it open. Then he popped the buttons of Reg's shirt to expose his lovely, lean chest and torso. Working with the sailors had put a good amount of trim muscle on Reg's body. Querry ran his hands over the delightful sinew, savoring Reg's hard muscles beneath his hot, damp skin. He watched Reg heaving with desire as his head rolled back against the tree, his skin pale in the darkness.

"Fuck, you're so beautiful," Querry said as he moved his lips down Reg's waist, dragging them over the trail of sparse hair on Reg's belly and enjoying the texture. Reg thrust his groin toward Querry's chin, and Querry started on his trouser flap. "I love you, Reggie."

"Show me," Reg said, pushing his trousers to his knees and freeing his erection. He thumbed his foreskin back to show Querry his plump, wine-dark cockhead. Querry didn't wait a moment before wrapping his lips around it and delighting in the strong flavor of Reg's sweat and precome. It made Querry's cock even harder as he lapped at Reg's slit. Reg dug his fingers into Querry's hair and groaned. "More, Querry."

Querry chuckled, a little surprised. Reg wasn't usually so assertive. He usually liked Querry to take charge, but Querry didn't mind switching. Digging his nails into Reg's hips, he slid his mouth very slowly up Reg's shaft, drawing it out, teasing Reg, and making him moan. He pressed his tongue to the belly of Reg's cock, enjoying the texture of the veins and ridges. Reg smelled of sweat and blood, and it drove Querry crazy. He felt his own fluids leaking out as he tasted Reg's. Querry continued his slow descent on Reg's erection until he let the tip slide into his throat, and Reg's blond curls tickled the end of his nose.

"Querry," Reg said, as soft as the breeze. "Look at me. Let me see your eyes."

Querry opened his eyes and tilted his head back slightly, just enough to see Reg looking down on him. Even in the scant, flickering light of the distant bonfire, Querry saw all the love and desire Reg held for him in the curve of his swollen lips and the way his lids drooped over his sparkling, hazel eyes. Reg pushed Querry's fringe off his forehead and never broke eye contact as Querry slid his mouth over Reg's flesh.

"My dear love. How could I ever want anyone else? Your mouth is amazing. Oh God. I must reek."

Reluctantly, Querry let Reg's erection fall from between his lips to answer him. "I don't care. You smell like adventure and fighting and justice. It's fucking brilliant." Querry seized the base of Reg's cock and drew it back into his mouth, sucking hard on the head and swiping his tongue over the tip to harvest the first few drops of Reg's seed. He let his eyes close again as he cupped Reg's soft, full sac and sped up the motion of his lips.

A soft, slurping sound made Querry look up again. Frolic stood next to Reg, kissing Reg enthusiastically as he circled Reg's nipple with his finger. Querry watched their jaws moving and their lips growing plump and slick. Frolic reached down and tangled his fingers in Querry's curls right over top of Reg's. Frolic's erection strained against the fabric of his trousers. Querry rubbed it a few times with the heel of his hand before he deftly unbuttoned the flap. He caught Frolic's stiff cock as it sprung out and ran his palm up the velvety flesh.

It took only a few strokes before Frolic cried out with release. Querry hoped the others wouldn't hear him over the celebration going on in the camp, but he honestly couldn't worry. He loved the sweet sounds Frolic made, loved knowing how much pleasure he gave Frolic. Reg clearly enjoyed it too; his cock jerked in Querry's mouth. Querry growled with hunger and ground his tongue against the delicious groove beneath Reg's cockhead. He twisted Frolic's erection in his fist and gave Frolic a second climax as Reg shot into his mouth. Querry didn't let up, and soon had Reg and Frolic trembling, whimpering, and clinging to each other just to stay on their feet. Both of them clamped their eyes shut, and they rested their foreheads against each other. Querry thought they were the two most beautiful men in the world, especially in the throes of bliss, and they were both his. He loved that he could make them fall apart with ecstasy.

Finally, reluctantly, Querry moved away from them. Though he didn't want to stop touching them for even a second, he had to get out of his leather gear before he passed out in the jungle heat. As he undressed, Reg and Frolic kissed lazily and rubbed their cocks together, their postures drooping with satisfaction. Reg reached up and untied the ribbon over Frolic's collar.

"I'm going to fuck you so hard," Querry said in a husky voice.

They pulled away from each other and looked at him. Reg grinned in an adorable, almost shy way, and Frolic looked rapacious with his big, gold eyes glowing like a cat's.

"Me?" Reg asked.

"Do you want it?" The night air felt good on Querry's flushed skin as he reached out for them, wrapping his arms around their waists to draw them close. Reg was delightfully damp with sweat, while Frolic felt like cool satin in comparison. Both of them smelled of gunpowder and blood, with the strong aroma of Reg's arousal making the mix even more intoxicating. Querry almost couldn't think as his cock slid against their bodies. His muscles clenched, and he worried he'd spill across them just from their scents and the textures of their skin.

"Fuck yes, I want it." Reg licked the sweat from the side of Querry's neck and nipped his earlobe.

"I want it too, Querry," Frolic said. "So much. I'm out of my mind with it. I think it was the fighting. Our victory."

"Yeah," Reg breathed, surprising Querry a little. "I feel so alive. My blood's on fire. Damn it, Querry. I want you to give it to me hard."

Their words, and the desperation in their tones, made Querry's cock leak. "Tell me," he panted, moving his hands down their backs to cup their soft, slim asses. "Tell me how much you want my cock. Do you love it?"

"I love it when you get so turned on you don't worry about hurting me," Reg said. "Not that you ever do hurt me, except in the good way. I just love it when you can't hold back."

"Oh fuck, Reggie. It's your fault if I can't control myself. Yours and my beauty's."

"Don't then," Reg muttered, "just take me." He turned away and knelt down on the forest floor, his elbows on the ground and his sweet little ass hoisted proudly in the air and spread open in offering.

Querry knew Reg loved that position, because it let Querry thrust so deep into him. Then he had a horrible realization. "Damn. I don't have anything with me. I don't want to hurt you, not for real."

"I have it." Frolic reached in his waistcoat pocket and withdrew the little chemist's tin full of oily lotion.

"You little harlot," Querry said, smiling. "You've been carrying it with you?"

Frolic nodded. "Ever since you suggested grappling over the wall. I miss touching the two of you. I need to do it."

"Well done," Querry said, reaching for the ointment.

Frolic didn't relinquish it. Instead, he knelt down behind Reg and peppered Reg's back with light kisses. Reg shivered pleasantly beneath him.

"Oh, beauty," Reg panted.

"I like it when you call me that," Frolic said, opening the tin and digging his fingers into the thick, clear liniment. He spread it liberally over Reg's cleft and then wriggled a finger into Reg's opening. Reg gasped at the penetration even as he pushed back against Frolic's hand. Frolic slid a second finger inside him and pushed it in to the knuckle. "Is that it, Reggie? Your special place?"

"Ah. Yeah, that's it. Oh God, Frolic."

Querry stood watching Frolic's pale, graceful fingers disappear into Reg, and he couldn't believe how much it excited him. Reg circled his hips and moaned wantonly with enjoyment. It occurred to Querry that Frolic had never expressed any desire to penetrate either of them, but he sure seemed to delight in it. So did Reggie. It gave Querry an idea.

"Beauty, do you want to make love to Reg?"

Querry had expected Frolic to react with uncertainty, to maybe need some convincing, but he leaned down and kissed Reg's tailbone before saying, "Yes, very much. Do you want me, Reggie?"

"Oh yes, my love."

Querry watched intently as Frolic guided himself to Reg's hole and pushed gently inside. "I've never felt anything like this," Frolic gasped. "Oh, Reggie. I... do you...." Frolic collapsed across Reg's back and clutched his ribs, trembling and moaning as he climaxed. Slowly he came back to himself and began thrusting into Reg with his forehead still pressed between Reg's shoulder blades.

"Bloody hell, you're beautiful," Querry whispered, watching them move awkwardly against each other at first before finding a rhythm. Their muscles strained with their exertion, and a sheen of sweat covered Reg, while Frolic looked pearlescent in the darkness. Querry retrieved the tin Frolic had dropped in his fascination with Reg, and moved around behind Frolic.

"Querry, let me suck your cock," Reg demanded as he clawed at the forest floor. "Please. I miss the taste of your come. I want it so much."

"Oh, my love." Querry ran his hand over Frolic's satiny backside before he stood. He hurried to move in front of Reg, knelt down, and touched Reggie's beautiful face. He traced circles over Reg's full lips before grasping his cock at the base and steering it between them. Just as Reg wanted, Querry let himself go, thrusting into Reg's warm, tight throat. Reg accepted him with barely a gag as his tongue flicked at the base of Querry's dick. Querry threw his head back, grasped Reg's hair, and fought not to explode too soon. Querry and Frolic thrust into Reg, and Reg pressed back and forth against them. Querry's knees sank into the mud as he forgot everything besides his lovers.

He leaned over to kiss Frolic as he pushed into Reg's throat. He just couldn't hold back anymore. The sight of Frolic and Reg making love, the sight of the three of them pulling and thrusting against each other, muttering each other's names, and declaring their love, pushed Querry over the edge. His whole body tensed and then relaxed as he came down Reggie's throat. He fell over Reg's back and nipped at his salty skin. The top of Frolic's head touched Querry's as he, too, draped his body over Reg's as he lost himself to yet another orgasm. With one hand, Querry clasped the back of Frolic's neck, and with the other, he clutched Reg's mud-coated hand. Frolic reached down to bring Reg to completion with his fist. The three of them shook hard with the intensity of their lovemaking, their love. When he could avoid it no longer, Querry collapsed into the leaves.

The exertion of the fighting coupled with their bout of lovemaking caught up with Querry. He rolled to his back in the cool, wet soil and drew both Reg and Frolic onto his chest, crossing his arms over their backs. He fell asleep to the sound of them conversing softly, stopping now and then to kiss.

TERROR STRUCK Querry as a hand on his shoulder shook him awake, and he realized Reg and Frolic still lay sprawled across him. He instinctively reached for a nonexistent weapon at his naked hip. Slowly, his eyes focused on his undressed lovers, smeared with mud and reeking of sex. Even though he feared being discovered, Querry couldn't help but smile at how pleasing they looked with their dirty limbs, swollen lips, heavy-lidded eyes, and disheveled hair. He knew getting hard beneath them was the absolute worst thing he could do, yet he couldn't help it.

The Baron Starling shot Querry a smug smile. "Good morning, Querry. I thought your performance last night earned you a lie in. I also thought I might be wise to awaken you myself. It seems I wasn't wrong. Believe me, I understand, but you must be more careful."

Querry relaxed, more grateful to Starling than he could express. He thanked the baron, but it felt insufficient.

"Yes, yes." Starling flicked his hand in front of his face in his annoying way, as if he waved away an unpleasant odor. "I also brought you this." He set down a bucket of water, a bar of bright yellow soap, and a washing cloth. "I suggest you use them quickly and join the rest of us at the camp. We're just about to set off."

Without waiting for a response, Starling turned and gave them some privacy.

Querry felt Reg release the breath he'd been holding. "We can't be so careless again. This was stupid."

"It was wonderful," Querry said, his tone dreamy with the memory of their lovely evening. "To hell and the devil with what anyone else thinks. I don't regret it."

"I truly can't understand what we did wrong," Frolic said as he stood and stretched his lithe arms over his head. "We haven't hurt anyone."

"It's not that simple," Reg said as he plunged the rag into the water and scrubbed the dried remainder of their passion from his body. "We were careless, and we can't be again. Tell him, Querry."

"He's right," Querry admitted.

"But why?" Frolic persisted. "I thought humans celebrated love. Look how they adore weddings. Why are we different?"

Querry balked. Never before had Frolic referred to humans as a separate race, called them "they." Frolic thought of himself as something apart from Querry and Reg, and Querry didn't feel any more comfortable with it than he did with the other recent changes in Frolic. Without a word, he took the cloth from Frolic and cleaned himself as best as he could before retrieving his clothes from the forest floor and getting dressed.

"The fey don't see any problem with people taking pleasure together," Frolic, now washed and dressed, persevered. "Why should we bow to the opinions of these others?"

As much as he agreed, Querry didn't know what to say. Reg also remained silent as they walked up the hill toward the camp.

"Why do we have to pretend we don't love each other?" Frolic asked again.

"It's just the way it is." Querry knew he offered a weak, sorry response to an honest question, but he didn't know what else to say. He was no philosopher.

"Why do we accept the way it is?" Frolic asked. "Why just agree to this… this absurdity?"

"We must for now," Reg said in a soothing voice as the three of them entered the crude encampment.

"I think this is ludicrous," Frolic whispered as they stepped into the circle of tents.

Querry worried as the others emerged to meet them. He'd never seen Frolic so angry and indignant. He realized his worst fears as Tom Teezle came forward and kissed Frolic full on the mouth in front of everyone gathered there. Frolic, instead of pulling away, kissed him back before daring all of them, with his angry gaze, to object. Then the two of them clasped hands and went to sit in the dirt around the central fire. Querry glanced at Reg and found Reg equally conflicted. They sat together across the fire from Frolic and Tom. Thankfully, most of the other men thought Frolic a fey like Tom. The Fair Folk had assisted them, and they knew faerie ways differed from their own, so they did little more than mumble and whisper at the display. It still irritated Querry. He'd told Frolic many times to be discreet.

Starling stepped to the center of the group and waited for the former slaves to cease applauding. Querry expected him to make some sort of flowery speech, to thank the others for the supplies and encourage his men. Instead, Starling indicated a line of five carts with a swipe of his hand. "Thanks to these good people, we're well equipped and ready to set out. Finally. I'd like those of you accompanying me to be ready to leave within the hour. Tom, with me." Then he turned and left.

Querry, Reg, and Frolic readied their things and placed what they couldn't carry on one of the four carts. The fifth held only the coal they'd need for fuel. Then Querry and Reg gratefully accepted the roast meat and strong coffee the former slaves offered. Querry knew they'd be subsisting on dried and preserved food until they completed their mission, so he savored the fresh fare.

Soon they all gathered around the carts: Corny and the three mercenaries, a trio of men from the quilombo, and a small young man in a crisp white shirt and wide-brimmed hat. Querry hadn't seen him before and wondered at the wisdom at taking such a young man into danger. The boy, while dark, wasn't one of the former slaves. His straight, smooth hair was pulled into a braid that trailed down his back. To Querry's surprise, Jean-Andre also waited with the others. When the Belvaisian grinned and winked at Reg, Querry balled his fists until his nails broke his skin. Frolic, who normally wore every emotion on his face, stood with a blank expression, watching Starling and Tom at the head of the procession.

Querry found himself in a foul mood as they slowly descended into the jungle, the carts maneuvering the narrow, winding trails admirably. Thinking about Jean-Andre and Reg and Frolic and Tom made him angrier and angrier. He couldn't believe Tom had actually kissed Frolic, and Jean-Andre's intentions were obvious. Still, he trusted his partners and knew he shouldn't be jealous, but he couldn't help his frustration as he began to sweat in the hot, heavy air. Since he had no desire to speak with any of them, not even his lovers, Querry fell into step with the young man in the hat.

"Hello," he said. What's your name?"

The boy turned and smiled at Querry. "It's Manuela, friend. Who are you?"

The name, and the sound of the voice, made Querry realize the mistake he'd made. "You're a woman," he said with surprise.

"Is that a problem?" she asked.

"Not at all. I'm just surprised. I'm Querrilous Knotte, by the way. Querry." He took the hand she offered and shook it. "What's your job in all this?"

"Guide," she said. "My people lived near your destination, though you'll be going farther than any white man has ever ventured. Still, I can speak the languages of many of the tribes we'll encounter. Hopefully, I can convince them to help us find our way when we move beyond the parts of the jungle I'm familiar with. What about you? What do you do?"

Querry wondered how to answer. "I work for Baron Starling. I'm an expert in... infiltration."

Manuela laughed. "A thief, then?"

"Well, when you put it that way, it sounds so common," he teased, flashing her what he knew was a charming grin. "I'm very good at what I do."

"Well, I don't have anything a white man would value, so I guess I have nothing to worry about."

"Even if you did, you'd have nothing to fear from me. I've only ever stolen from those who deserved it."

"And who deserves it, Querry?"

He shrugged. "Old, fat, rich, entitled pigs who don't care anything about the people who work their asses off while they line their pockets. Bastards like the ones back at that plantation."

She giggled. How had Querry ever mistaken her for a man? "You are like the Anglican story. Like your Robin of the Greenwood, no?"

"Except that I keep what I take," Querry said. "I just don't take it from people who need or deserve what they have."

"I think we'll get along fine," Manuela said. "My people didn't hold to the standards of the colonists."

He wondered if she referred to his profession or to Reg and Frolic or the relationship between the three of them.

"We didn't care much what anyone did, so long as they pulled their weight and didn't hurt anyone. It was easy to pull your weight. The forests provided everything. We hunted and cooked for two days, and spent the next six or seven at our leisure. Most of your people don't appreciate that. They want only to hoard wealth, which was hard for us to understand. We valued the enjoyment of life, the time to savor it, over possessions. You probably wouldn't have liked it, though. There was nothing to steal that we wouldn't have happily shared with you for free."

"You talk of your people as though in the past," Querry noted. "What happened to them?"

"Cholera," she said. "The Portalegrese missionaries thought they were doing us such a favor, saving us from our backward ways, but they brought the disease that killed all but a handful of my people. I loved the life they took. I miss it. I hate wearing all these clothes. Really, what's the point of them?"

Querry wondered what Manuela would think if presented with what a proper Anglican lady wore. He said, "I'm sorry about your people, and I appreciate having your knowledge."

Manuela shielded her eyes from the sun with her hand and looked out across the wide valley they'd just discovered. She nodded and said, "Where we're going, you're going to need it, and then some. I don't look forward to this, and I only hope we'll survive."

CHAPTER 20

FROLIC COULDN'T believe the beauty of the jungle they passed through. After a few days, they moved beyond even the most rural of colonial settlements and farms. Nothing but wild, rugged majesty surrounded them. There were no trails here, not even the most basic, and it slowed their progress considerably, but Frolic didn't mind. He spent the hours observing flora and creatures unlike anything he'd imagined: bright gold and emerald serpents as wide as his thigh, orange and scarlet frogs, and monkeys resembling small, hairy, human men. Some had black hair, others bright red, but Frolic sensed the intelligence behind their eyes as they watched his party from the trees. He also noticed graceful cats of various sizes, some spotted to mimic the sunlight and shade filtering through the trees and others as black as night. Frolic missed the two small cats he and Querry had left behind with Dink, and wondered if he could entice one of these wild beasts to accompany him.

Frolic perceived layer upon layer of life, beings existing in harmony, just as they should. No silly rules governed them. They wanted only to survive, to find enough to eat and flourish in this glorious paradise. The attitude the humans showed toward his love for Querry and Reg seemed even more appalling as Frolic thought about it. He didn't like the way it made him feel to contemplate their judgments, the anger it stirred in him, so he soothed himself by returning his attention to the gorgeous flowers and bright birds.

After a few more days travel, the small group stopped at what their guide, Manuela, said would be the last quilombo before they passed into exclusively native lands. The men living in the tiny settlement of only about two dozen huts had heard of the party's exploits on their peoples' behalf, and they welcomed them for a fine meal of roasted meat and fresh fruit. Since he didn't eat, Frolic didn't feel like he could participate in the merriment. Even Tom smiled as he nibbled at a slice of melon, but there was nothing for Frolic to enjoy, so he simply waited for the feast to conclude and the others to load a few last-minute supplies onto the carts. By early afternoon, they set off once again.

Lord Starling, determined to make up for the time he'd lost, pushed them hard, not stopping to make camp until hours after dark. Frolic could have easily continued, but the humans groaned with relief as they pitched their simple tents and lit small fires. As soon as they'd finished, they collapsed on the forest floor. Once again, they reveled in eating and rest, things Frolic didn't need.

After growing restless watching the others enjoy their dinner and a few tin cups of rum, Frolic got up and wandered to Corny's tent, which was twice the size of the others and had open sides to allow her to enhance and repair their equipment if needed. Frolic hoped she might need some help, and he knew he could talk to her. The white canvas roof glowed as he approached, giving him hope for a few hours of tinkering and respite from his concerns.

As soon as he entered the tent, Corny threw a sheet over whatever she had on the collapsible workbench. Jack Owens sat in the corner on a wooden crate. Both of them went from easy, relaxed conversation to stiffened surprise when Frolic entered.

"Hello, lovey." Corny hurried to clasp his hands and kiss him on the cheek, even as her gaze traveled suspiciously back to the work surface.

What could she be hiding from him? Frolic had a suspicion she was working on a magic absorbing device, despite his arguments against it. He'd told her of the tragedy such a device had caused back in Halcyon, and how he and his partners had destroyed it even though it meant sacrificing the clockwork angels he thought of as his brothers. It hurt that she didn't trust his wisdom. After all, he'd seen the consequences of such a vile machine, and she hadn't.

"Hello, Corny. What's that you're working on? Do you need any help?"

She stammered. She never stuttered when talking to him, yet—"Er, nothing. That is, nothing important. Just passing the time, yeah? A side project, nothing important."

Frolic pulled away from her grasp. "I think I understand. I just wanted to stop by and see if you've given any thought to our special job." He glanced at his book sitting beneath an open toolbox on a makeshift shelf. He'd never trusted anyone but Querry, Reg, and Dink with the secret knowledge he held, and Corny used it to prop up her equipment. Offended, he hurried over, snatched it up, and clutched it to his chest.

Corny looked over at Jack as if to ask advice on how to answer. Something passed between them, and the mercenary left the tent so Frolic and Corny could be alone.

"Look, Frolic. Everything about your construction is extremely complex. I think I might be able to do it, in a proper shop with the right equipment. Out here... I just don't know. I don't even know if my goggles can magnify the tiny gears to the degree we'll need. But there's a bigger issue."

"What?" Frolic asked. "I can see the gears without any problem. I just need some help. Why can't we proceed?"

"The materials," Corny answered. "Just to make the skeleton, we need a great deal of gold. From what I've read, it's heavy, but it resists tarnish, which is essential. I don't know how you'll ever find enough gold."

"I'll get the gold," Frolic said. "When I do, are you still willing to help me?"

"I promised I would."

"Thanks," he muttered, knowing by the way Corny glanced at the tent flap that she would rather spend her time with Jack Owens. "Good evening, then, Cornelia."

She stumbled over some pitiful excuses, but Frolic wasn't the fool everyone assumed. He knew when he wasn't wanted, so he hurried away from her pavilion, back into the camp. Most everyone had gone to bed, so he made his way toward the tent he shared with Querry and Reg. When he entered, he found them drowsing on the ground in separate bedrolls. A lantern burned low on a small barrel; probably it gave just enough light for the humans to see. Querry and Reg lifted their heads and blinked at Frolic's entrance.

"Beauty," Querry said in a voice rough with sleep. He indicated a third pile of blankets, a few feet removed from his own. "Get some rest."

"I don't want rest," Frolic said. "Do either of you want to spend some time with me? Show me you love me?"

Reg rubbed his eyes. "We love you, Frolic. We just can't risk being as careless as we were before."

"Not even after all this time?" Frolic asked, frustrated.

"It's not a good idea," Querry agreed. "Just sleep for tonight."

"I don't feel like it," Frolic said, turning his back on them and leaving the tent. Outside, he waited a few minutes to see if either of them might ask him back, but they didn't. He felt alone in a way he hadn't experienced since his solitary decades in the doll maker's basement. He glanced around for Tom, but couldn't locate him either visually or through the hum of the magic the faerie trailed. Frolic just wanted to be with someone, to not be all by himself, but no one was available or willing. He stood on the outside, neither human nor fey. Reaching inside his shirt, he fondled the metal feather he wore as a necklace and remembered the beautiful, clockwork angels his father had created. Why did his mind always return to them? Had they been intended to keep him company? Surely Frolic's father wouldn't have left him so alone. But the angels had been destroyed, so where did that leave him? Frolic knew he was the last of his kind. Not even Querry and Reg could comprehend it. No one did.

Frolic wandered away from the orange light of the camp, deeper and deeper into the jungle. He listened to the song of the insects, night birds, and nocturnal creatures he couldn't identify. He sensed the forest cats stalking just beyond the scope of his sight and hearing, but they posed no danger to him, as he wasn't made of meat. The sky told him another storm waited on the horizon, and the plants expressed their desire for life-giving water. They demonstrated a lovely, symbiotic relationship Frolic couldn't help but envy. Their language now made more sense to him than the empty words of the people he traveled with.

As he delved deeper and deeper into the jungle, Frolic began to sense other presences watching him. He saw them when he looked up into the tree branches: tiny, human-like creatures with fluid bodies and large heads. Made of shadow, they morphed easily into different forms as they followed Frolic. They moved like liquid, translucent and sparkling as they stretched and contracted to progress along the branches. Their luminous, star-bright eyes never left Frolic. Frolic felt their fascination as he watched them from the corners of his eyes, creeping along, curious to know more about him, but shy and maybe afraid. They felt Other, but not like the fey. They were much simpler and more pure—old, but without the deception and trickery the Fair Folk so adored.

Frolic stopped and closed his eyes, letting his perception reach out to the novel creatures. He felt only their desire to protect the jungle and its inhabitants. He let them know they had nothing to fear from him, and he was interested in friendship. In response, the shadow-creatures made a few eerie, hooting noises. Though not exactly a language, Frolic understood the intent behind the sounds: the unusual beings accepted him as one of their kind, a creature of magic. Slowly, they crept closer, some to the ends of the branches and others through the thick brush until they stood only a few feet from Frolic, canting their heads at odd angles and blinking their eyes.

Moving cautiously, afraid to startle the creatures, Frolic sat down on the forest floor and drew his knees up against his chest. Gradually, fascination replaced apprehension, and the magical beings drew nearer. As they passed through the stripes of shadow cast by the thick leaves above them, they melted into the darkness, disappearing until they emerged into a scrap of moonlight. Frolic could tell by their movement that they contained nothing hard or sharp, like the bones and joints humans possessed or his mechanical reproductions. They flowed like water, growing taller or squatter on a whim. Some were translucent, while others seemed more solid, but like everything about them, it morphed and changed.

Even so, they provided Frolic with companionship, and he sat with them in amiable silence for many hours before returning to the camp.

REG'S RESTLESS night had left him groggy and cranky. He'd woken probably a dozen times and reached for Querry and Frolic only to find Frolic gone. He hadn't slept without Frolic for almost a year, and found he couldn't relax with Frolic absent. Today, the jungle felt even hotter, the damp air that much more oppressive. An early morning rain had wet the leaf litter, and Reg sank almost to his ankles as he trudged along, mopping the sweat from his face and the mist from his spectacles. He felt like he could barely breathe beneath his leather armor, but after some of the creatures he'd seen stalking through the jungle, he didn't dare take it off.

Reg stared into the shadows the thick vegetation cast, recalling the panther Jack Owens had chased off a few days ago, and its teeth, as long and thick as his finger. He remembered the strange things he heard at night, sometimes right outside the tent, and suppressed a shudder.

Up ahead, Jean-Andre took his turn dozing in the back of one of the carts with his wide-brimmed, wool hat over his face to keep the flies away. Reg couldn't help enjoying the Belvaisian's company. Jean-Andre possessed wit and charm, as well as knowledge of wine, music, and literature. Reg quickly looked away when he noticed Querry, near the front with their guide, glaring back at him. Truly, he couldn't understand Querry's deep-seated hatred of Jean-Andre.

Reg glanced around for Frolic and finally found him a dozen feet behind everyone else, staring distractedly into the trees. He hadn't said much to either of them, or even Corny, who he seemed to like so well, all day. Reg knew he was still upset about the previous night, and he couldn't stand to see Frolic so miserable, so he slowed his pace and waited for Frolic to catch up.

When Frolic reached him, Reg smiled and patted him on the shoulder, but Frolic hadn't quite mastered the human art of false expression. His lower lip jutted out in a peak, and he blinked his thick, white lashes in clear confusion. Reg couldn't help but hope Frolic never needed to learn deceit.

"Hello, Reggie," Frolic said. "Have you seen Tom Teezle?"

"Actually no. I haven't seen him or the baron all day. Why?"

"I want to talk to him about something."

"What?" Reg asked, still not comfortable with Frolic and Tom's sudden friendship. "Frolic, you need to be very careful around him."

Frolic sighed. "I don't want to hear this again."

"I'm sorry, beauty," Reg muttered. He hadn't meant to imply Frolic was stupid. "It's the fey I don't trust, not you, love."

"I just want to talk to him."

"Will I do instead?" Reg asked, running his hand down Frolic's back, a little surprised to find his shirt crisp and dry, even though he knew Frolic didn't sweat.

"I'm always happy to be with you, Reg. I miss it."

"So do I. I miss it so much, I'd actually rather not talk, if you don't mind."

Frolic's eyes went wide, and a genuine smile lit his face, increasing his beauty. He seized Reg's hand, dragged Reg a few hundred yards into the jungle, and leaned against a tree, grasping Reg by the hips and pulling their bellies together. Frolic slid his palms up Reg's waist, chest, and neck before cupping Reg's face and staring at him with so much lust and adoration in his eyes that it made Reg's breath falter and color rise to his cheeks and ears. Reg folded his spectacles and slipped them into his waistcoat pocket before leaning in to Frolic's lips.

"We don't have long," he said against them.

"Don't need long," Frolic said, his breath heating Reg's face.

As they kissed, Reg wriggled his hand into Frolic's trousers and ran the heel down Frolic's length. When he reached the base, he cupped Frolic's balls and gave them a soft tug and squeeze. Frolic moaned into Reg's mouth and circled his hips. Reg reached behind Frolic's compact little sac and pressed against the strip of flesh between it and Frolic's opening. Frolic's knees buckled, and he clung to Reg's bracers just to stay on his feet as he shook almost violently with his climax. Reg thought the sweet little cries Frolic uttered made the risk worthwhile. He moved his hand back up Frolic's shaft and jerked his tip with short, quick strokes, giving him a second orgasm in less than a minute.

Frolic threw his head back and yelled Reg's name to the sky. Afraid someone from their party might hear, Reg pressed his finger across Frolic's lips, smoothed his curls with his unoccupied hand, and whispered in his ear. "Hush, love. You have to be quiet."

Frolic sucked Reg's finger into his mouth and took deep, shaky breaths through his nose as he rode out the crest of his pleasure. Gradually, Frolic returned to his senses and relaxed against Reg, releasing his finger to give Reg a lingering peck at the center of his mouth. "Thank you. I know you only did this as a favor to me."

"And what's wrong with that?" Reg pulled away to adjust Frolic's clothing, tucking his shirttails back into his trousers. "I love you, and I want to see you happy."

"But what about you?" Frolic's gaze stopped on Reg's obvious erection. "You didn't get anything out of it."

"That's not true." Reg reached up and pinned an errant curl behind Frolic's small ear. "I enjoy giving you pleasure, listening to the little noises you make. Touching you. Besides, I make a mess, and you don't. Come on, now. We should catch up to the others before we're missed."

Looking much happier than he had before, Frolic followed Reg out of the jungle, and the two of them sprinted after the others, following the trail of coal-smoke and steam. Soon they crested a hill and looked down into a wide valley, probably miles across. The way down was steep and strewn with large, sharp rocks. The carts descended slowly, but before long, metal screeched, and a great puff of black smoke rose into the sky.

"Frolic! There you are!" Corny called, waving her hands in the air and already donning her thick goggles. "I could use a little help down here, mate."

Frolic looked over, and Reg nodded. Frolic rose to his tiptoes and leaned over as if to kiss Reg, but then he seemed to remember he shouldn't, frowned a little, and picked his way carefully over the loose gravel toward the others.

Reg stood at the cusp of the ravine as Corny hauled a toolbox from another vehicle, flipped the lid open, and handed Frolic a wrench. She pointed at something Reg couldn't see beyond the people gathered around, and Frolic slid beneath the cart.

A rustling off to his left caught Reg's attention, and he pulled his pistol, expecting some sort of predatory beast to emerge from the undergrowth. Instead, he saw Lord Starling dragging an obviously outraged Tom Teezle by the wrist. Reg quickly ducked behind a large rock as they passed in front of him. They dipped behind a tall, bushy tree covered in clusters of dark red fruit. Though Reg didn't know what compelled him or how he found the courage, he crouched down and made his way from bush to bush until he could watch them through the dark, glossy fronds of another species of tree. He hoped he might glean something he could use against Starling to get his friends out of their agreement. He also thought he might learn something about Tom's association with Frolic. Careful not to snap so much as a twig and practically holding his breath, he listened hard to discern their soft voices over the noise of the jungle.

Starling released Tom so roughly the faerie stumbled a few steps before regaining his balance. Tom rubbed his wrist with his teeth bared and his eyes little more than slits. Reg curled his shoulders forward and dared to sink a little lower. Fey were violent and irrational on the best of days, and Tom looked murderously angry at the moment.

The baron didn't seem concerned. "Come now, Tom. You know this is necessary."

"It's an absolute insult," the faerie snarled. "You should hope I'm never in the position to avenge it."

Starling looked older and more tired than ever as he sighed. "I have nothing left to hope for, fey. As you well know. This expedition is all I live for now."

"Preposterous human. Go curl up and die if you long for it so desperately. Honestly, I've never seen any creature work so hard at being miserable."

"It's no work. Misery comes to the people of this world as easily as breath. It's our one, constant companion from the cradle to the grave. I don't suppose it's something your kind can understand." Starling fished around in his jacket pocket until he withdrew something Reg couldn't quite see. He only knew it caught and reflected the light, like a crystal or perhaps a piece of polished metal.

"Not even I would wish upon you what will happen when the lord of the Palace of Tears finds out you stole from him," Tom said in a low, threatening voice.

"Yes, yes. So you've said." Starling sounded almost bored as he reached for Tom's arm and gently pushed the sleeve up. Reg easily recognized the next item the baron produced from his coat: a small, sharp dagger.

Tom let out a high-pitched cry as Starling made a small cut across the top of his forearm. The sound of genuine pain made Reg cringe. As the fey spewed angry words in his language, Starling caught a few drops of his blood on what looked like a shard of bluish glass. When he held the jagged object above his head, it glowed with a silvery light, which increased and decreased. It shined brightest when he held it in the direction of the valley.

"As I thought," Starling said. "We'll have to cross the valley after all, and probably the hills beyond."

Tom only glared, holding his arm and looking absolutely feral and deadly.

"Come, Tom. We have the information we require. Let's see if we can assist the others and get this party moving again. There's still a very long way to go."

Reg couldn't believe what he'd just seen. Against his better judgment, his heart softened for Tom Teezle. Maybe if he stole the baron's bauble he could save Tom from further injury and bring the expedition to a halt at the same time. Unfortunately, he didn't possess the skill to pull it off. Querry did, though. Querry could pluck it straight from Starling's pocket while Starling stood watching. Reg wondered whether to share what he'd witnessed with his partners. It would only strengthen Frolic's resolve to free Tom at any cost, and Frolic already acted impulsively around the fey. As for Querry, once Reg told him about the crystal, he might not be able to talk Querry out of going after it, even if it violated Querry's contract. Querry would see it as a challenge, a chance to prove how clever he was, and then nothing would stop him. Reg decided to keep his knowledge to himself for the moment, though the silence felt deceptive, and he'd never lied to Querry or Frolic before.

Before he returned to the others, Reg gathered some fruit from the nearby tree, just in case he had to explain his absence.

Chapter 21

Though it only spanned ten miles or so, it took the party almost a week to traverse the valley, due to the damage to the carts, the thick undergrowth, and the daily rainstorms. Querry had never seen such rampant vegetation: trees as wide as a barn, hairy vines thicker than his waist, and bright flowers the size of dinner plates. Fruit dangled from the branches like holiday ornaments. Everything competed for space. Brush and mushrooms grew from the black soil gathered in the indentations of the tree roots. Some of the leaves were even broad enough to support small oases of life.

The bizarre, beautiful environment enthralled Querry for a day or two, and then he grew restless. It was hotter than the devil's ass, and the bugs were terrible. Querry recalled a vibrating, serrated blade Dink had once made for him as a weapon, and with the assistance of Corny and Frolic, he modified the design to help them cut a swath through the jungle. After that, though, he found little to keep himself occupied.

In the evenings, Reg often sat by the fire with Jean-Andre, the Belvaisian producing bottles of fine wine as if by magic. Frolic usually made his way to Corny's tent, hoping for work, but the tinkerer often spurned him in favor of that smug bastard, Owens. If he couldn't find Tom Teezle, Frolic simply spent his nights wandering in the woods. Left with little else to do, Querry sat beneath Starling's canopy, drinking gin and trading stories of their various conquests with the baron.

"And Frolic, completely appalled by the chef's barbarity, reached into the boiling water and pulled the lobster out!" Querry finished his story.

Starling laughed, a jovial bark. "The heat didn't bother him?"

"Not as much as the cries of the lobster, apparently," Querry answered. "We kept it for nearly a week until Frolic was satisfied it would survive, and then we released it back into the ocean."

"And what did the people at the inn have to say?" the baron asked, still amused.

"We paid for it, didn't we? It was ours to eat—" Querry paused. "—or to keep in a tub of saltwater and name Nigel until we set the little bugger free!" Starling and Querry toasted with their tin cups of gin.

"It must be exasperating," Starling stated before he sipped his drink.

"At first," Querry agreed. "But I wouldn't trade him for the world." Querry contemplated his gin, then took a sip. He caught Starling's gaze over the rim of the cup. "It may seem silly to you, but many of the points Frolic makes are difficult to argue with. He's a much better person than most humans."

"And what about your Reginald? He's such a mother hen. Does it not test your nerves, a man like you, who can clearly take care of himself?"

"No," Querry said softly. "No, I love it. It makes me feel like someone cares about me. I never had that, before I met them, and I treasure it. I'm not a good man, majesty, but I'm better because of them."

Starling considered that statement. "I'll drink to that." He raised his cup, and Querry dutifully bumped his own into it before they both drank the fiery, piney liquid.

What's happening to us? Querry worried as he shared stories of Reg and Frolic. Before, the three of them had cherished every second they could spend together. Now they barely spoke. It was tearing Querry apart. Usually he simply decided what he wanted and had it. He just wasn't used to anything as subtle as this. Querry had to admit, his lovers, by their disinterest, had accomplished something nothing in the world had done so far: not the workhouse, not the authorities, the faeries, nor even the bloody Grande Chancellor of Anglica—they'd kicked his ass and almost defeated him.

Almost.

Querry held hope as they finally left the sweltering little valley, telling himself boredom and discomfort took their toll on all of them. They reached the crest of a hill where the cool air circulated around them. As they continued along the top of the ridge, Querry slipped off his armored vest and loosened his tie. Though they said nothing, Reg and Frolic joined him as they traveled high above the jungle, looking down on a vast expanse of glistening emerald. It seemed to stretch into eternity.

Starling stopped a few times, getting his bearings by some unknown means, but they finally found a path west with Manuela's help.

Frolic clasped a hand over his mouth, and Reg gasped as they stepped from the jungle shadows. At first, Querry thought he looked down at half a dozen trees covered in scarlet blossoms. But as soon as they disturbed the branches, probably a hundred vibrant birds rose into the sky. Querry felt like a boy again as he laughed out loud. Reg clasped his hand, and Frolic twirled around, catching some of the red, violet, and turquoise feathers as they spiraled down.

"This is the most beautiful place I've ever seen," Frolic said, clutching the feathers to his chest.

Reg, lost for words, only shook his head, pushed his spectacles up, and dabbed at his eyes.

"I'm so glad we're all seeing this together," Querry said in a voice soft with awe. "I never want to forget this moment." He caught their hands and held them tight as the three of them looked down on the gorgeous vista. Querry didn't care if anyone saw. To hell with them.

Beyond the miles of verdant, sloping jungle, a wide river with deep, cursive bends reflected the bright blue sky. On the other edge, the forest stretched as far as he could see. "Isn't it exhilarating?" Querry asked. "Setting foot where no man has ever been before? Somewhere completely uncharted?"

Manuela elbowed Querry playfully in the ribs as she walked by. "You mean to say no *white* man has been here before, Querry. There have been people living beneath these trees since before they made their way to your little island. Be careful, now. I'm not sure what to expect. I've never been this far into the jungle."

"We should stay together no matter what," Reg suggested. "Look out for each other."

"Yes, Reggie," Frolic said, giving Querry's hand a small squeeze.

"Right, then," Querry said, feeling like his world now spun securely on its axis once again instead of hurtling haphazardly through a void. He rarely lapsed into silly sentimentality, but Querry said, "If I have you two with me, I feel like I can do anything." As soon as the words left his mouth, he felt foolish and flushed.

"I feel the same," Reg said, surprising Querry. "Let's get this done. I want to go home and sleep for a week after this. Oh, and Querry, you can bring me my meals in bed."

A tremor moved through Querry's loins. "I'll give you a right feast in bed, love."

"I bet you will." Reg licked his lips.

Frolic groaned. "I won't be able to walk properly soon if you two keep on talking like that. I do miss… privacy. So much."

Reg grew serious out of nowhere. "When we make camp tonight, I need to speak with both of you."

"Just speak?" Querry asked, trying to salvage the flirtatious mood he'd missed so much over the last week.

"Querry, love, I really need to get some things off my chest."

"Of course," Querry hurried to say. "Anything you need."

"Let's go," Frolic said, and the three of them made their way down the mountainside.

Querry sensed an eerie presence among the trees, foreign and unpredictable, but not necessarily malign. He screwed his eyes shut and felt around for the faerie sight his gentleman had given him. He found it more easily than before and let it slip into place, just as he might slide his goggles over his eyes. When he saw the hundreds of strange little beings running along beside them, or sprouting wings from their fluid bodies and soaring next to their faces, he barely stifled a shriek.

WITH THE modifications Frolic and Cornelia had made to the carts, the expedition reached the river basin by sunset. Reg stayed close to his partners, unnerved by the peculiar silence of the jungle. He'd become used to the strata of noises, and their absence felt odd and wrong as they moved toward the water's edge.

Manuela made her way to the front of the group, with the two mercenaries, Istvan and Attila, close behind her. The brothers didn't say much, but they seemed quite capable, Reg thought. Their hands on their guns looked quite steady.

The rest of them stayed a few dozen feet away. Reg had no idea what they worried over, and the uncertainty made his heart pound and his hands travel instinctively to his pistols. He couldn't see a thing beneath the canopy, not even his fingers on his guns. Still, he felt Querry and Frolic at his shoulders and didn't panic.

Manuela led them along the river's edge, through the dense mist rising from the water and spilling out between the trees. Yet again, sweat soaked

Reg's shirt, but he'd almost become used to it. Strange how his body had adapted to heat that made Thalacea seem like a Tartan autumn.

The party wound their way along the deep curves of the massive river until Manuela held up a hand to stop them. Everyone froze. As he readied his own weapon, Reg heard the people behind him drawing their guns and clicking the levers. Jack Owens and the mercenaries crouched in the brush. Querry pressed his back against a tree, his clockwork pistol ready, and his goggles penetrating the gloom. Frolic's mystic sword sang as he unsheathed it. Tom Teezle and Lord Starling exchanged a few whispered words, and not long after, Reg felt their magic warping the night all around him, raising the fine hair on his arms and the back of his neck. To Reg's bewilderment, Frolic held his arm out as if he expected a bird to land on his wrist. Frolic's golden eyes burned tunnels in the darkness.

Reg felt sure they were in for a fight, and he was glad to see Jean-Andre nestled behind a shrub not far off, his strange pistol in his hand. The two of them made eye contact and smiled, their little contest resumed. Reg wished he felt his companion's amusement instead of the cold dread in his belly.

All around them, men covered in nothing but body paint and beaded necklaces broke from the cover of the trees. At least two hundred natives surrounded the small party, their bows and reed blowguns trained on the outsiders. Despite his companions' superior technology, Reg knew they couldn't prevail against such numbers. He hurried to the tree Querry crouched behind, ready to make a stand next to his oldest and dearest friend. Frolic watched them from across the path as if he understood. Reg blew him a kiss. If they were about to die, what did it matter?

Manuela barked a trio of crisp words into the night. No man in Starling's expedition lowered his weapon, though the native girl stood completely unprotected and exposed. She continued to talk, and soon lured the indigenous warriors from beneath the canopy.

Reg, along with everyone else, took aim at the stark-naked men as soon as they appeared. Starling's team all held their fire while their guide struggled to communicate with the natives. They seemed to understand some of what Manuela said, but not all of it. Even so, the two parties managed to make some progress and eventually reached an understanding.

"Stand down," Manuela called. "These are peaceful people. If we don't threaten them, we have nothing to fear. They don't understand war as you would bring it to them."

"Tell them we do not bring war," Starling called out. The magic in the air fizzled out.

Ashamed, Reg holstered his gun and stood up. Gradually, the others followed suit, Querry and Frolic right away and the mercenaries hesitating but acquiescing. After an excruciating quarter of an hour, their entire party stood unarmed, facing the lithe, naked warriors. Manuela exchanged a few more words with their leader before motioning them down a narrow footpath.

They arrived in the native village to a hero's welcome Reg didn't feel they deserved. Women and children, in the same state of undress as the warriors, emerged from stick huts roofed with something like reeds or straw. They unabashedly approached the newcomers and touched their hair, clothing, weapons, and carts. Even in the scant light of their fires, Reg saw they were beautiful people with straight, dark hair, full lips, large, expressive eyes, and nimble, muscular bodies. Frolic and Tom drew more of their interest than the others, and a group of young women led the clockwork boy and the fey to the central fire and urged them to sit on the ground in front of it. Soon a procession of people carried baskets of berries, fruit, and roasted meat to their honored guests. Tom picked at the fruit, while Frolic just looked perplexed. Cornelia's red hair also garnered wonder from the villagers. They stood on their tiptoes to touch it, making the tinkerer blush and shy away.

After speaking more with some of the warriors, Manuela approached them and said, "The tribal elders wish to speak with our leaders. Starling, since there are seven of them, you should choose six others to accompany you. Who would you like to bring, besides me?"

"Querry is my first choice, and his friend, I suppose. Jack Owens, Cornelia, and my servant."

It surprised Reg Starling didn't include Jean-Andre, but if the Belvaisian felt slighted, he didn't show it. Instead, he pushed his wide-brimmed hat off and let it hang down his back by a string around his neck. He wandered away and batted his eyes flirtatiously at the lovely young men and women who came forward to marvel at his red-gold hair and sapphire eyes. He stood still, almost encouraging their fondling.

"Will Frolic be all right on his own?" Reg asked.

"What do you think?" Manuela extended her chin toward the fire, where Frolic sat surrounded by youths and children eager to pet his hair or offer him gifts. Already fruit and flowers filled his lap, and dozens of rows of small, bright beads hung from his neck. Frolic returned the friendly smiles he received, and managed to say a few words in the native language, much to the delight of the villagers. "Come, now. We shouldn't keep them waiting. And Anglican"—she addressed Starling—"a small display of magic will go a long way toward earning these peoples' respect. They'll think of you as one of the spirits they revere."

The baron nodded, and all of them approached a hut no different from the others. Reg thought it might be larger or somehow grander, but it looked identical to the rest. Inside, they faced a group of older natives: four men and three women. Feathers, shells, and beads adorned their bare bodies. Black lines, like cat's whiskers, streaked their cheeks and foreheads. Starling and the rest sat cross-legged on the bare earth as their hosts did. Manuela said what Reg presumed were a few words of introduction, indicating each of them in turn with her hand. Though these people hadn't threatened them, Reg couldn't relax yet, as they all looked so stern.

"Tell them I am a great sorcerer," Starling said. Then he opened his hand, and a green dragon straight from a storybook materialized. It flapped its wings, rose into the air, and performed some graceful loops and dives before dissipating with a puff of emerald smoke and a shower of champagne-colored rose petals.

Tom rolled his eyes, but the elders looked impressed.

"They want to know what you wish of them," Manuela said.

"Ask them if there are any hostile elements in the area," Owens said.

She relayed his concerns, and responded with: "Absolutely not. They say nothing exists beyond the spirit land past their hunting grounds."

"Can they provide us with a guide to the edge of their lands?" Starling asked.

"They can spare a few hunters."

"Give them my thanks," the baron said.

Manuela did, and then said, "They say you are honored guests, as companions of the spirits. I think they mean your Tom and Frolic. They invite you to stay the night, share their food, and join them for a very special ceremony tomorrow evening. After that, they'd be interested in trading, and will spare what supplies they can before you set off."

"Tell me, girl," Starling said. "Why do you say 'you' instead of 'us'? Do you not plan on accompanying me any farther?"

Manuela shook her head. "These wise elders warn that dire peril lies beyond the spirit land. No one passes beyond its borders. Besides, I want to stay here with them. They remind me of my own people. I know this way of life can't last. Eventually the colonists and missionaries will come, and they'll either kill these people and their customs off or convince them they're inferior. I just want to live as I did before for as long as I can, before this entire, beautiful world disappears forever. I know it is inevitable."

Reg hung his head, shamed and wounded by her words. He wondered if the destruction of this culture was as inescapable as Manuela believed. Unfortunately, he suspected it was, and it saddened him.

Querry cleared his throat, interrupting Reg's thoughts. "Um, beg your pardon, elders. But how can there be nothing beyond the spirit lands and also dire peril?"

"Quite right," Reg agreed. "And what are the spirit lands?"

Manuela spoke to the central elder. "The spirit lands lie within a dense forest. Beyond that there is nothing. Beyond that there is dire peril." The old man added something. "I think he's saying certain death."

"Well, that clears everything up." Reg rolled his eyes, exasperated.

"Can you ask him to explain?" Starling spoke to Manuela. She relayed Starling's question, and the old man scratched a diagram of concentric lines in the dirt. As he pointed to the different areas, Manuela translated.

"The hunting grounds," she said as he pointed to the innermost area. Then he pointed to the next. "The spirit land." The next band. "Nothing." He opened his hand as he described the last area. "Certain death," Manuela finished. The old man crossed his arms and raised his chin. They all took the hint; the conversation was over.

Everyone within the hut stood, and when the Anglicans extended their hands to what Manuela called the Panther People, the natives grasped them. Reg just couldn't get used to their nudity, but he bet they felt more comfortable in the jungle heat than he did in his layers of leather and linen. Still, he couldn't imagine prancing about with his bits and pieces on display, but these people didn't hold to his values, and he knew he had no right to judge them.

"So there's just a band of nothing out there?" Querry whispered to Reg, who shrugged silently in response. He had no idea what the old man could mean.

Reg and his comrades pitched their tents and accepted the food and fresh water the Panther People offered. Reg had never encountered people so generous and friendly. Everyone he saw offered him a smile, and they seemed genuinely happy to share. Amazingly, they expected nothing in return. As he snuggled into his bedroll beside Querry, Reg felt safe for the first time in weeks. He propped himself up on his elbow and kissed Querry before settling in. A few minutes later, Frolic entered the tent with strands of beads rattling as he walked, braids in his hair, and an earring made from the feathers he'd collected earlier that day. He looked pleased and kissed Reg and Querry on their foreheads before going, without complaint, to his blankets. As he put out the light, Reg felt good, though he couldn't help but worry something horrible waited just around the next bend. In his experience, it always did. Happiness never lasted.

THEY SPENT the next day at ease, doing little but lounging in the cool shade as the Panther People prepared for their feast. The natives carried all manner of creatures into the encampment: monkeys, birds, lizards, snakes, porpoises and fish from the river, and creatures Reg couldn't identify. The women and children skinned and prepared the meat and set it to roasting on spits above the fires or in the coals beneath. Others brought baskets of melons, berries, root vegetables, and the red-skinned fruit Reg had picked before descending into the basin. It tasted very much like strawberries.

Reg, Querry, Owens, and many of the others bathed in the river, the threats of carnivorous fish paling before their desire to be clean of layers of sweat and grime. Like the natives, each of them stripped to nothing, even Cornelia. After a few awkward moments, they all forgot their differences and enjoyed a leisurely swim. Jack Owens stayed close to Corny, and at least once, Reg saw him embrace her in the water and kiss her. Reg swam to Querry, treading water near the center of the river, and ran his hands over Querry's chilled flesh. They kissed and let their bodies graze beneath the surface of the river. Querry's sparse, wet hair tickled Reg's chest and belly.

"This is a paradise," Reg said. "I could stay here forever."

"Thinking of going native?" Querry teased, fondling Reg's nipple as he churned his feet to stay afloat.

"It's tempting. These people are truly without avarice. They care about each other, and even us. Seeing them, I realize how useless all things I left behind in Halcyon really are. I don't need any of that rubbish to be happy. I just need food, a place to sleep, you, and Frolic. We'd be free to love each other here."

Querry kissed along Reg's stubble-coated jawline. "I'd get bored. It's *too* perfect."

"Why do you need conflict, love? I don't understand."

"Just do," Querry said in his usual way. He took Reg's hard dick in his fist and stroked it.

Reg reciprocated, and in minutes they'd satisfied each other. The broad, oily, green river swept away all evidence of their tryst, and they swam slowly to the shore. When they reached the muddy bank, Reg and Querry stretched out nude in the sun, just as the natives did. The warmth and light wind felt divine against Reg's bare body, and his lack of modesty surprised him.

"I would stay," he said softly, wistfully. "I love this. We're safe and well provided for. I like the honesty of that. No one gives a damn if we touch each other. I think I could be happy here."

In response, Querry simply stroked Reg's stretched waist, tickling him and making him giggle and jerk. "We can't."

"I know. But I can dream."

They did just that, drowsing in the warmth for the rest of the afternoon, slipping in and out of sleep and talking, kissing, and caressing in between. Reg felt like he spent an afternoon in heaven, free from worry of any kind, completely relaxed. No matter what happened next, he'd always hold this gorgeous day close to his heart as maybe the happiest he'd ever been. If only Frolic had been with him, it would have been perfect. When the sun started to sink behind the western hills, they roused themselves, dressed, and returned to camp.

The Panther People handed Reg and Querry flowers and draped beads around their necks. They guided Reg and Querry to the center of their settlement, where piles of meat, vegetables, and fruit waited on large leaves. Frolic joined them as they sat and ate. Reg was famished, and found the food fresh and delectable, despite the burnt skin on the meat.

After the feast, the women and children retired to their huts. Even Corny and Manuela withdrew for some mysterious, female ritual. The native men stoked the central fire, adding deadfall timber, as night fell over the forest. Some of them brought out drums while others danced around the bright blaze, looking to Reg like black silhouettes against the orange light. They moved with grace and speed, performing amazing acrobatics before the bonfire. Some of them juggled torches to the steady rhythm of the drums.

Reg, pleased to be a spectator, reached to his sides to hold Querry and Frolic's hands.

After an hour of appreciating the prowess of the dancers, a native man with a bowl and a dagger stood before them. He said a few words, but Reg had no idea of his intentions.

"He wants us to take part in the ritual," Frolic said. "It's quite an honor."

"I'll do it," Querry offered, with his usual haste and lack of forethought. "How?"

"He just needs to make a small cut on your arm," Frolic explained. "Then he'll pour the essence of the jungle frogs into your blood. It will lead you to the spirits."

"All right." Querry freed his cufflink and rolled up his sleeve.

"I am honored to be invited." Baron Starling also exposed his naked flesh, holding his arm stiff and proud before the native man.

Reg, though reluctant, also bunched his shirt around his elbow. He wouldn't cower from experiences the others accepted. He wanted as much in common with his partners as he could get. Still, he couldn't suppress a shiver of anxiety as he recalled something Manuela had said. "Aren't those frogs poisonous?"

Frolic relayed Reg's concerns to the native man, nodded at his answer, then said, "Not in such a small amount. He says it will help you see and understand the Other world. But you can still say no, Reg. He says not everyone is ready to know."

"No, I'll do it. I've always wondered what it is you and Querry see that I don't."

The nude, native man dipped his finger into a clay bowl. He drew three lines across each of Reg's cheeks with his fingers. Then he painted Reg's eyes with the bright clay. Next, he made a small incision near Reg's wrist that Reg hardly felt. The liquid he poured over the wound, though, burned like acid when it hit Reg's blood. Heat flooded his veins. Reg looked over as the man repeated the ritual. In the black, white, and red face-paint, Querry and Starling resembled the lethal panthers the tribe revered, while Frolic looked more like a kitten with his wide eyes and rouge-stained nose. Tom had declined to take any part in the ceremony, and Jean-Andre had conveniently made himself scarce.

The feeling that washed over Reg about a quarter of an hour later had nothing in common with the warm, relaxed, giddy feeling he experienced after a couple bottles of wine. It had the heat in common; sweat dripped from Reg's chin and into his eyes. No matter how many times he swept his damp fringe out of his face, it just fell again, heavy and wet, across his eyes. He soon abandoned his foggy spectacles and put them in his waistcoat pocket. When he saw Querry and Starling strip to nothing but their trousers, he followed suit, leaving his waistcoat and shirt in a heap on the ground and his bracers hanging around the outsides of his thighs. He even took his boots and socks off and dug his bare toes into the loam.

The fire the natives danced around grew blurred, the flames spiraling impossibly high into the night. They snaked into the sky as if alive, their flickering tips shifting from gaslight blue, to bright lilac, to the intense pink of a jungle dawn. Reg watched them, mesmerized, as his heart beat to the rhythm of the drums. A strange energy coursed through him, and he wanted to move. He *had* to move. Almost as if they lived separately from the rest of him, his arms stretched out to his sides and mimicked the serpentine motions of the flames, each of them leaving bright orange trails in its wake. His feet and legs squirmed, carving trenches in the dark soil. He circled his groin. Reg realized how aroused he'd suddenly become, and his nipples and cock stuck out, but it didn't seem important.

His location also seemed insignificant, like he inhabited a world of shifting shadow and prismatic flame somewhere beyond the bounds of reality. As Reg contemplated it and realized he couldn't banish his confusion, he started to grow scared. Panic sped his heart. He didn't know where he was or how he'd find his way back. His limbs felt weak and shaky; he couldn't trust them. Everything looked alien, and he feared he'd be trapped forever in the hellish realm. Reg found it hard to breathe as he looked frantically about for anything familiar. Just as debilitating terror threatened to reduce him to a curled-up mass on the forest floor, Querry and Frolic appeared to save him, each of them grabbing one of his arms and hauling him to his feet. With Querry leading and Frolic skipping behind him, they led Reg round and round the fire, and the delight he found in dancing made him forget about his dread.

After he'd been adopted by a wealthy couple, Reg had taken lessons to learn to dance properly. His parents wanted nothing more than to marry him off to a low-ranking noblewoman and thus worm their way into the aristocracy. Reg completely disregarded the reserved techniques he'd been taught as he gamboled around the fire between his lovers, tossing his head from side to side, flailing his arms and legs, leaping into the air, and spinning around until the stars above him smeared to silver streaks.

What felt like hours later, or maybe only a few minutes, Reg stumbled to the edge of the firelight to catch his breath. Querry, Frolic, and the native dancers seemed to glide around the blaze without their feet grazing the ground. They looked ethereal, just like the spirits the Panther People said he'd see. As he watched them, he noticed half a dozen great, black cats stalking the perimeter, and he instinctively reached for the pistols he'd discarded earlier along with his clothes. Then, to his relief, he realized he saw only shadows of panthers, echoes, some primal, otherworldly form of the mighty predators. Perhaps because of the strange elixir singing in his blood, Reg knew the creatures posed his friends no threat, so he looked away from them, into the trees. He almost fell to his knees when he saw the hundreds of small, black, human-like creatures tilting their bodies to impossible angles to look down on the dancers. Seeing them and knowing they'd been watching all along sent an uncanny shiver through Reg, even as he knew they might be apathetic, but they weren't aspersive.

Reg spent a few minutes watching the bizarre beings before he realized he desperately needed water. His tongue stuck to the roof of his mouth, and his throat felt plastered shut. Looking at the black and orange smudges the jungle had become, he wandered in the direction he thought the river laid. He swatted broad leaves out of his face as he staggered through the trees. In no time, he knew he was hopelessly lost, and he had no idea what he'd do. He felt like the only man inside hundreds of acres of forest. Where were Querry and Frolic? He needed them to give him direction. Then Reg noticed the weirdly proportioned little spirits standing before him, canting their heads toward a footpath in the undergrowth. When they walked or flew in its direction, Reg followed without a second thought.

The shadowy spirits led him to the river even though he'd been going in the completely wrong direction. Reg dropped to his knees and cupped his hands to drink. After he'd slaked his thirst, he flopped down on his back and closed his eyes, just as he had earlier that day. Contentment flooded over him as he listened to the rush of the river and the song of the nocturnal creatures. Reg rolled to his side and reached out to caress Querry. Querry's skin felt cold beneath his fingers, and he opened his eyes. Querry lay moon-white against the dark bank, his bluish lips parted and his open eyes milky. An array of bullet wounds marred his chest and belly, oozing rancid blood, dark against the pallor of his skin. Querry turned to face Reg, and when he spoke, black ichor sprayed from his lips.

"Reggie, why did you let me do it? I always listened to you. You should have stopped me. You gave up on me when I needed you most."

Reg clapped a hand over his mouth to stifle a sob as he turned away. On his other side, he found Frolic's wide, yellow eyes staring back at him. Frolic pushed himself up on his elbows with a screech of metal. From his waist down, nothing remained but the stump of a golden spinal cord twitching erratically. Heaps of metal shards and bent and broken gears surrounded it. Frolic still tried to pull himself closer to Reg with his hands. Reg couldn't help but recoil.

"You lied to us, Reggie. We trusted you, and you kept secrets from us. How could you do this to me? I wish someone else had found me. I never had a chance with you."

Reg tripped over his feet to stand and ran from what he knew were horrible, drug-induced apparitions. But did that make what they said less true? In no state to ponder it, Reg just put distance between himself and the horrific sights. Somewhere along the beach, Reg caught his ankle on a downed tree and tripped, sprawling on his chest. Dark mud filled his mouth, and he sputtered to spit it out. As he gasped for air, feeling drowned, Querry and Frolic materialized before him, Querry, pale and covered in gore, and Frolic's severed form floating above the ground. Instead of saying anything, they scowled and pointed their fingers at Reg. Reg curled in on himself and yanked at his hair, screaming until he lost his voice.

"I tried to tell you. I will. I know it isn't too late," he told them. "I won't let this happen. This isn't real!"

"We needed you."

"Shut up! Go away! You aren't real. You aren't real."

"Wait and see, Reggie. You're going to lose us. You can't keep anybody."

"No…."

"If you love us, you won't come back. But you're too afraid to be on your own. You're a coward."

Reg folded into a tighter ball and cried and trembled. He hoped he'd die, but either way, he never planned to leave this spot. The taste of death and decay was strong in the back of his throat. His partners were better off without him. They could defend themselves; he'd always been an unnecessary addition. He was the one who needed them to protect him.

A warm hand shook Reg's shoulder, and he looked up to see Tom Teezle frowning down at him. Reg swiped at his teary eyes to get a clear view of the fey in his smart, three-piece green suit. Irrationally, it occurred to Reg that Tom's suit didn't get dirty. It looked as fresh, crisp, and clean as the first time Reg had laid eyes on the faerie. It almost made him laugh. Almost. Tom regarded Reg with pity and disgust as he knelt down and pushed his fingertip between Reg's brows. As soon as he withdrew his hand, Reg felt completely lucid and a bit foolish. He wondered what could have possibly motivated Teezle to give him aid, but he welcomed it. At least Tom had freed him from the nightmare, taken it away somehow.

"Get back to camp, human," the faerie said. "Your friends are waiting for you. Honestly, I don't know why, but they want you back, so get moving. Do you need me to show you the way?"

"No, I can make it." Back in his right mind, Reg easily discerned the trail leading to the soft glow of the camp. To his astonishment, it waited only a few hundred yards away. He easily found his way to their tent and squealed with joy when he saw Querry and Frolic sleeping inside, half-naked, with their foreheads pressed together and their arms wound around each other's waists like vines around tree branches. Reg wondered if he should take his place beside them, if he deserved it. He told himself the frog venom had made him conjure the horrible visions, and that his partners loved him. A doubt remained at the back of his mind, and maybe it always would, but he needed to feel loved and included so badly. He snuggled up behind Frolic, kissed Frolic's shoulder, smoothed Querry's damp curls out of his eyes, and pulled the scratchy blanket over himself. Reg vowed, no matter what he might have meant to these men before, he'd be worthy of their love. To start off, he'd share all the secrets he'd been keeping, no matter what it cost him. The decision unburdened Reg's conscience and allowed him to drift to sleep.

CHAPTER 22

AS THEY made their way through the jungle, a troupe of malleable, black creatures followed Frolic, running along at his heels or drifting through the canopy above him. One of them seemed especially fond of him and spent much of the day perched on his shoulder. It made Frolic feel good to have a constant companion. When he reached up to stroke his new friend, it rubbed its face against his knuckles like a cat and fluttered its bat-like wings. Frolic didn't know if these beings had names, but he decided to call his Whisper, at least in his mind.

Since the Panther warriors guiding them knew the forest well, the party made excellent progress over the next week and a half. Frolic couldn't believe the extent of what the natives called their hunting grounds; the territory had to span twice the area from southern Anglica to the tip of Tartan, maybe more. Yet, it comprised only a fraction of the miraculous wilderness.

During the day, they traveled with relative ease, making only minor alterations to the carts. Their provisions ran low, but the warriors kept them well supplied with fresh meat. Frolic was glad he didn't have to eat the flesh of the monkeys because, especially when skinned, they looked just like tiny men. At night they ate, made camp, and slept until dawn. Corny continued to keep her work secret from Frolic, covering it up as soon as he came near. He knew she worked on a magic-absorbing device, and he regretted it had ruined the friendship between them.

Eventually, they reached a point where the Panther People would go no farther.

"Is there nothing I can offer them to convince them to continue?" Starling pleaded, desperation plain in his tone.

Frolic translated. Then, shaking his head, he told the baron, "No. You possess nothing they desire. In fact, they're begging us not to go on. They say no one who passes beyond this point is ever seen again. The forest swallows them up. They say it belongs to the spirits, and we mustn't desecrate it. I think we should seriously think about what they say. According to these men, it's been this way for a hundred generations. They're truly worried about us."

Frolic didn't add that the small spirits flitting around him gave him the same warning: to turn back, to avoid this cursed place, or pay the price. He didn't like the idea of Querry and Reg venturing somewhere so dangerous. He hoped he could make Starling understand. "Baron Starling, please reconsider."

Ignoring him, Starling grabbed Tom Teezle by the wrist and dragged him beyond what he probably thought was earshot. He hadn't accounted for Frolic's sensitive hearing, though. Frolic easily eavesdropped on everything they whispered to each other.

"Tom, is this just foolish superstition?"

"Not at all. I sense something beyond dreadful in these woods."

"That could be a good thing," Starling responded. "This much opposition must be guarding something worthwhile."

"Or it could be this place is just ancient and forsaken," the fey said nonchalantly. "There are many such places in this world. You can't dispute that."

"But can we succeed?"

"I'm not sure," Tom said. "I have no intention of sacrificing myself to this excursion."

"You will do as I say," Starling reminded him.

"Oh, always," Tom replied sarcastically.

Starling turned to the rest of his group. "We will continue. No native legend will stand in the way of our mission. Remember what we'll be bringing to mankind if, no, *when* we prevail. We don't need a guide, either. I can use my arts to find our way. Prepare to move on after the midday meal."

Predictably, Reg rushed forth. "You're out of your mind! I won't allow this."

"And what will you do to stop me?" Starling lifted his chin and crossed his arms over his chest. "Honestly, I have no desire to waste more of my time with this useless argument. As I have said many times before, you're more than welcome to stay behind. In fact, you have my blessing. I have no use for you."

Both Querry and Jean-Andre hurried to stand at Reg's shoulders. When they finished staring each other down, Jean-Andre said, "This sounds like a suicide mission, monsieur. See reason."

"I never asked for your counsel either, Belvaisian! Don't think I don't know why you're really here."

"Oh, and why is that?" Jean-Andre curled his lip and narrowed his eyes.

Starling never got a chance to answer, because Querry stepped in front of Reg and said, "I'll go with you, majesty. Let Reg and Frolic go. You know I have the skill to get you there. Nobody else needs to risk their lives. Please."

The baron's mouth hung open, probably because very few people ever heard Querry ask humbly for anything, let alone plead. As a thief, he usually just took what he wanted.

"I'm on a job," Owens said. "I'll finish it. Always do. Professional ethics." Istvan and Attila nodded their assent.

"I want to see it," Corny said. "What sort of adventure is this if we turn back as soon as we face the unknown?"

"I have to go," Querry said, though Frolic thought he saw a spark of excitement in his partner's gleaming blue eyes. Querry adored a challenge.

"I'm not leaving you," Reg said, grasping Querry's shoulder. "Unless you actually think I'm useless to you, don't argue. If you don't feel you need me, tell me, and I'll go."

"You even have to ask me that?" Querry said. "I just want you to be safe."

"I don't want to be safe on my own, worrying. I want to fight beside you."

"So do I," Frolic quickly said. He couldn't imagine being left alone, even if Starling conceded. Being alone frightened him more than being destroyed.

"Then we're in agreement," Starling said. "Good. Take your refreshment quickly, if you please."

One of the Panther hunters, a beautiful young man with six lines tattooed across each of his cheeks and large, coral shells stretching his earlobes, hurried forward to clasp Frolic's hands. The concern in his dark eyes couldn't be misinterpreted. "Spirit-walker, you must not go into this part of the forest. Please. There's no sense in it, anyway. Even if you reach the edge of the cursed wood, you'll only find yourself at the Edge of the World. You'll be able to go no farther. Come back with me, and you'll have a fine feast every night. We'd be honored to have you watching over our tribe."

"I'm afraid I can't." Frolic, moved by this virtual stranger's concern for him, kissed the young man's smooth cheek. "I must go on, to whatever awaits us."

"At least let us try to protect you."

"How?" Frolic asked.

"Wait here." The young hunter returned to his kinsmen and spoke briefly with them, before all of them disappeared among the trees. *Edge of the world?* Frolic thought. *Manuela misinterpreted that as "nothing."* Soon, they returned with bundles of roots and leaves that they set about roasting over a small fire, adding water and chunks of animal fat to the mixture. By the time the others had finished their afternoon meal, the Panther People were ready with their concoction.

"Just what is this?" Reg asked. "Another foul brew for us to choke back? I can hardly wait."

Frolic voiced Reg's concern a little more diplomatically to the natives, and gave Reg their explanation. "They wish to make sacred marks upon our skin, to repel evil and protect us from our enemies. It isn't something they'd normally offer to someone outside their tribe. They're terribly concerned about us."

"These marks are permanent, then?" Reg asked with obvious reluctance.

Frolic nodded. "I don't think it will work on me, though. My skin is much too tough."

"I'll do it," Querry said, already rolling up his sleeve.

The native man shook his head and pointed at Querry's eyes.

"My face? Seriously? Well... all right, I suppose...."

"Querry, are you sure?" Reg protested.

"What? Afraid it'll lose me my seat in the House of Ancient Nobility?" Querry asked with the grin and wink that could convince the queen herself to dance in a tutu and striped corset.

Reg rolled his eyes. "I'm not doing it. I have to believe I might still have a life to go back to when this is over. Maybe a respectable means of employment at some point."

"You're beautiful already," Querry said to him, his expression soft and full of love. "I wouldn't want you changed. Will you still love me if I do this?"

Jack Owens cleared his throat theatrically, but Corny elbowed him in the ribs.

Reg, flushed and sweating, wiped his spectacles on his sleeve. "Yes. Yes, always."

At that, Querry lay down on the forest floor, and one of the Panther warriors knelt beside him with a small, ink-filled shell and a sharp stick in his hands.

"Bloody hell!" Querry cried as the native man pierced the skin beside his eye with the sharpened end of the twig. "Fuck, that hurts."

Frolic hurried to kneel next to Querry and clutch his hand. Reg sat next to him and cast a worried glance at Querry, then at Frolic. At this proximity, Frolic saw that the native warrior worked with a hollow, reed-like instrument. He dipped it into the ink then drove the pointed end beneath Querry's skin. Now and then, he stopped to wipe Querry's blood away with the handkerchief Reg proffered. Querry lay with his eyes screwed shut until the native man, through Frolic, admonished him against wrinkling his skin. Soon, curiosity compelled the others to stand in a crescent and look down on Querry's ordeal. When he became aware of their scrutiny, Querry let his features go slack and blank, though he squeezed Frolic's hand almost hard enough to hurt.

Finally, the native man dabbed the last splatters of dark pigment from Querry's skin, and Querry sat up. At the outer corners of each of his brows, two tiny lines curled up toward his hairline. Another, thicker line, less than an inch long, stretched down from the peak at the center of his dark tresses. Two more very small, understated strokes slanted ever so slightly up from the outer corners of his eyes. Though so subtle no one would notice the markings unless they came close and looked hard, they gave Querry a slight resemblance to a panther, a predator who not only belonged within, but ruled the jungle. Frolic hoped the simple design might help the beasts and spirits see Querry as something to fear and avoid. According to the hunters, it had worked for them since before anyone could remember.

As Reg gingerly touched the markings with the tip of his finger, leaning close and donning his spectacles to examine them, the native man looked up at the others, his brows raised.

Frolic understood. "He wants to know if anybody else wants it done."

They all looked at each other, as if each of them waited to see what the others would do. Corny stepped forward. "I will."

She received some pigment around her eyes that made them look slanted and cat-like, while Starling got three lines below his lip, over the center of his chin, and Jack Owens got a pair of whisker-like lines extending about an inch from his sideburns on each cheek. The four of them took a few minutes to admire each other's new adornments, talking of the pain. Frolic thought maybe it brought them a little closer together to have shared a common experience. All of them seemed more comfortable with each other.

They shared a quick, last lunch with the Panther People, and then the hunters turned to leave. Frolic hugged them and clasped their hands before watching them disappear into the jungle. He'd miss them. In many ways, he thought himself much like them: they spoke and behaved honestly, with no knowledge of the complex nuances of Anglican social interaction. One never had to wonder what they really meant when they communicated. Whisper, on Frolic's shoulder, let out a long, mournful note, as if he sensed Frolic's regret. Frolic leaned his head against Whisper and reached up to stroke his doughy leg. The creature's wings fluttered softly.

Less than an hour after they set out, the forest changed dramatically. All sounds of birds singing, insects chirping, monkeys howling, and creatures moving through the branches faded and died. After becoming so used to the myriad reminders of life, Frolic found the silence eerie. It had always been gloomy beneath the thick growth of the jungle, but it grew almost as dark as twilight. Not a single shaft of sun broke through, and no breeze rustled the thick vines and broad leaves. It felt like being suspended in a perpetual dusk, and no matter how far they ventured, it didn't change. Along with the little creatures he'd met before, Frolic sensed other beings. Now and then he caught a glimpse of them flitting past: the size of men but made from shadow like the smaller creatures.

Frolic, who'd felt ill at ease and stayed close to Reg and Querry, broke away to catch up with Tom Teezle. "You see them. I know you do."

Tom chuckled. "That wasn't a question, so I don't need to give you a false answer."

"What are they? Not fey, I can tell that much."

"No," Tom agreed. "If I had to guess, I'd say they're the spirits of humans who perished here over the centuries, now bound to protect this place. There's a powerful enchantment over this land, unlike anything I've ever felt.

It's old and complex, and I believe it's trapped them here. The same could happen to the rest of these humans if they're unlucky enough to die beneath the veil of the curse."

"Are they dangerous?"

"Most certainly," the fey said. "They'll be bloodthirsty and mad after being tethered here so long when they should have moved on. I must admit, this is magic beyond even my understanding. I can tell you with absolute certainty we aren't welcome here."

"Well, how can we protect ourselves?" Frolic asked.

Tom stopped on the narrow trail, ignoring the others, who had to steer the carts up an embankment to avoid him and Frolic, who faced one another. "To me, ribbons are the most wonderful things in the world. Here."

He took a strip of blue-black silk from a trouser pocket, pinched a lock of Frolic's hair at the tip, and wrapped the fabric around a clump of it before tying it off at the end. Frolic reached up and touched it, rattling the beads, feathers, and braids the native children had given him. For some reason, they'd been fascinated with his hair.

"Thank you, Tom Teezle. I actually do feel better. How can I keep Querry and Reg safe?"

"You can't." The faerie turned away from him to rejoin the baron, who led the procession.

Frolic hurried back to his friends. No matter what Tom claimed, Frolic planned to protect them somehow.

When they stopped to camp for the night, Frolic saw Starling sprinkling something around the perimeter of the tents. Faint magic wafted from the shimmering trail it left, but Frolic still felt apprehensive as he entered the small tent he shared with Reg and Querry. Enchantment whizzed and hummed all around, not with the focused intent of a spell, but chaotically. Frolic sensed the spirit-panthers and deceased warriors stalking just beyond the baron's boundary. He felt their hunger and desire to kill, as well as a protectiveness he understood well.

"We don't belong here," he whispered.

"That much is obvious," Reg said. "Even to me. Querry, Frolic, tell me. What's out there?"

Frolic looked to Querry, wondering how much to say. He never knew how much to keep to himself, so he waited for Querry to explain it.

With a deep sigh, Querry combed his hair out of his face with his fingers. It, along with Reg's hair, had grown several inches since they'd left Thalacea. The ends brushed their collarbones. Frolic liked running his hands through Reg's soft, straight tresses and Querry's loose, black waves. With Querry's sun-darkened skin, Frolic thought his lover could almost pass for one of the natives, and even Reg's skin had deepened to a lovely, freckle-dusted, golden brown. Only Frolic remained a rose-tinted porcelain, and he always would. No matter what he lived through or where he went, his experiences would never change him, never show on his face as they did on his friends.

After a few silent minutes, Querry composed himself enough to speak. "I only catch glimpses of the Other World. I can't see it all the time, but I can feel it, somewhere down at the base of my spine. We've been surrounded by... something ever since we reached the Panther Peoples' valley. I don't know what they are, but they're not fey. At least not fey like we have back home. Sometimes I see them out of the corner of my eye."

"They're not evil," Frolic hurried to say, watching his little Whisper tilt its head at the few, functional items in the tent. It flapped its wings and flicked its newly materialized, cat-like tail. "I can say for certain they don't mean us any harm. But there are others. Tom says they are the spirits of humans who died here, now doomed to keep others away from this place. We shouldn't be here. It feels horribly wrong to me."

"We have no choice," Querry said.

At that, Reg slumped his shoulders, slipped his spectacles off, and rubbed his temples and tired-looking eyes. "Actually, we do."

"What do you mean?" Querry asked. "Did you find a way out of the contract?"

"No, it's... something else. I should have told you before. I don't know why I didn't. Jean-Andre offered to... to get Starling out of our way."

"Fuck me," Querry whispered. "Not for free, I'm sure."

"No."

Frolic didn't understand, and said so.

"Jean-Andre offered to kill Lord Starling," Reg explained gently, curling his fingers around Frolic's wrist and looking deep into his eyes.

"Kill?" Frolic barely whispered, his voice no louder than the brush of his clothing as he shifted uncomfortably.

"And what did he want in return?" Querry demanded.

"Querry, I don't know why you hate him as you do—"

"What did he want, Reggie?"

"Frolic's book."

"Fuck me." Querry slammed the side of his fist into the ground. "I should have known."

"Known how?" Reg asked, his eyes narrowing.

Frolic turned his attention to his book, sitting on top of a crate in the corner. He couldn't lose it. Not only did it potentially hold secrets from his creator as to his purpose, it would also help him fashion himself a companion. Without it, he'd find himself alone. Almost as if reading his mind, Whisper fluttered over to the large, leather-bound tome and curled up on top of it. Frolic looked back at Querry, who fidgeted with his belts and the pouches dangling from them, clearly anxious.

"Querry?" Reg persisted.

"Back in Halcyon, just before we took on the Grande Chancellor, Jean-Andre tried to get me to give him the book. He offered me a lot of money for it. He also offered me a sort of job, finding out and selling secrets. That's why I don't trust him. It's too much of a coincidence that he's even here. And what's more, he just abandoned his so-called job for the empress. Does that seem right to you?"

"How come you never told us?" Reg sounded hurt.

"Because I never even considered accepting," Querry said. "We had so much else going on, it just seemed like the least of our worries. After that, I guess I put it out of my mind. I never meant to keep anything from you, I swear it. Reggie, I know Jean-Andre can be charming. Just don't let your guard down."

"I could say the same to you about your newest mate, the *esteemed* Baron Starling."

"Oh?" Querry arched his brows. "If nothing else, his majesty's been honest about his intentions."

"No, he hasn't." The chilly edge to Reg's tone made Frolic shiver, and he moved closer to his friends, leaning against Reg's shoulder and stretching his feet into Querry's lap.

As Reg explained what he'd witnessed regarding Starling, Tom, and the strange talisman, Querry unbuckled Frolic's boots, slipped his stockings off, and kneaded the soles of Frolic's feet with his thumbs. As nice as it felt, Querry's caresses couldn't banish the horror spreading through Frolic at Reg's account. He bolted up from reclining against Reg.

"We have to save Tom! We must work harder than ever to set him free! No matter what."

Reg rubbed his back. "Ah, beauty. I knew you'd feel that way. That's why I was afraid to say anything. I worried you'd put yourself in danger on his behalf."

"I am tied to him now," Frolic said softly.

"What?" Reg asked, the color draining from his face.

"I made a deal with him. To save the slaves on that plantation."

Reg dropped his head into his hands. "God, no. What did you promise him?"

"Something I carry inside but can't hold in my hands. Don't be angry, Reggie. I had to do it. All those people would have died otherwise. I couldn't bear to see them suffering."

Reg hissed out a breath through his clenched teeth. "At least there are no more secrets between us. Are there?"

"No," Querry said. "I'm sorry there ever were. I'm sorry they drove us apart, even a little. Never again. Let's promise. We must trust each other, not the Belvaisian or the fey. Will you swear it?"

"Or the baron," Reg added.

"Right." Querry nodded. "From now on, we tell each other everything, no matter what."

Frolic nodded enthusiastically.

"None of us has ever had any family," Reg said thoughtfully, almost to himself. "Until now."

All of them joined hands as an unspoken oath passed between them. As Frolic looked into his partners' eyes and saw his love and devotion reflected back, much of his doubt and isolation faded, at least for the moment. He might be the last of his kind, but he knew he had a place where he belonged: here, with these men who loved him and would protect him. Frolic grinned, and he felt so happy he would have certainly cried if he'd been able. However, he still felt perplexed about giving voice to his thoughts.

"So," Frolic said, "I should say whatever is on my mind? Because sometimes you tell me not to. How will I know the difference?"

"Beauty, when it's just us alone, feel free to say anything you like," Querry told him, and Reg nodded in agreement.

"Then there's one other thing you should know." Frolic explained about Whisper, tilting his head to the small creature sleeping on top of his book. "He chose me. I feel like he's looking out for me, for us. Please don't be afraid of him."

"I think I see him," Querry said, squinting into the darkened corner and smirking. "Just a shadowy outline, but he's adorable. A bit like a kitten, isn't he?"

"If he wants to keep you safe, I have no issue with him," Reg said. "But I wish I could see him too."

"He's winking at you," Frolic said, leaning in and running the tip of his nose up Reggie's cheek. The way Reggie shuddered made Frolic respond in kind, and before long, they pressed their lips together as Querry moved his hands up their backs and into their hair. Then Querry put out the light, and the three of them consummated the vows they'd made to one another in the most wonderful ways.

Chapter 23

In spite of everything, Reg couldn't stop smiling as they trudged through the dark, malleable forest. His most private places felt tender and hot, a result of his passionate union with Querry and Frolic the night before. Their promises to be honest with each other and protect one another had enflamed Reg's desire for them as nothing had in quite some time. Now, they walked together, with Reg between Querry and Frolic, and every time Reg looked over and found one of them watching him, he flushed and grinned. He felt like a thirteen-year-old boy, but he liked it.

Reg's warm mood almost allowed him to ignore his surroundings, but not quite. Once again, they traveled almost in darkness, as the thick jungle canopy blotted out the sun. The spongy ground smelled of rust and decay, almost of blood. Unnaturally thick trees, covered in bizarre bumps and whorls, rose higher into the sky than any Anglican cathedral tower. Shadows moved and flitted in Reg's peripheral vision, though there was no light to cast them. Despite the stifling heat and humidity, Reg shivered.

Starling, with his grotesque compass, led their procession slowly. Reg's stomach lurched each time he caught a glimpse of the bluish shard. The trails between the trees shifted and changed, both behind them and ahead, as if the forest toyed with them and made them lost on purpose. Still, the baron made progress, though a few times he led them to the edge of a ravine, an impassable mass of brush, or a sinkhole full of the treacherous mud the Panther warriors had insisted they avoid.

Somehow they gained ground, though Reg estimated they cleared only about ten miles a day over the following week. Though he sensed danger all around them, no actual threat appeared. Reg waited out the daylight hours, eager for camp. Their frank discussion had reignited Querry, Frolic, and his own passion for each other, and they made good use of their evenings.

On their eighth day after parting from the Panther People, they entered a patch of woods even more bizarre than the rest. The trees twisted into impossible formations, and interwoven branches blocked their way. Jack Owens, Querry, and the mercenaries cut them down with the rotating blades Querry had designed, but they grew back, trapping the small group within a tiny clearing. The dark spirits Reg had seen at the edges of his vision appeared, surrounding them. They closed in, nothing more than desiccated corpses, skeletons wrapped in pitch-black skin. In a sick negative reflection of the Panther People, the things wore white lines around their eyes and across their cheeks. Reg pulled his pistol and hit one of the abominations square in the chest, but the bullet moved through it as if through a shadow. Frolic, with his enchanted blade, managed to overcome one of the monstrosities, causing it to dissolve into the darkness when he sliced its neck. Frolic turned to face the next creature, but there were too many. He'd never be able to vanquish them alone.

Tom Teezle held his hands out and spread his long fingers, speaking a few commanding words that made the spirits retreat from him. Baron Starling conjured a golden, glowing shield around his hand, but the creatures continued to advance. Only Tom and Frolic managed to give them pause, and against the dozens spilling out of the forest shadow, they wouldn't be enough to save the others.

With a great war-cry, Cornelia emerged from the back of the group, her gas-powered torch in hand, the heavy tank shoved down the back of her leather vest. She waved the bluish flame in wide arcs, driving the creatures back. The others gathered behind her as she cut a swath through the dark beings. Even after they finally dispersed, she led the way with her torch glowing brightly in front of her. Baron Starling stood at her side, pointing them in the proper direction.

They traveled in such a manner all through the night, and through the next day, afraid to pause for a second. The horrid spirits followed them, waiting just beyond the firelight, biding their time. Eventually, though, the fuel in Corny's tank ran out, and the flame sputtered and died.

"Well, bugger," she said, smacking the nozzle of her torch with the heel of her hand. "I'm all out."

"We need fire," Jack Owens said. "Use the lamp oil." He ripped his shirt from his body and shredded it into strips. Then he found a thick branch on the ground, and wrapped the remnants around it. Attila poured some fuel over his torch and set it alight. He and his brother constructed similar torches, giving one to Querry and one to Cornelia. The rest of them stayed, along with the carts, within the ring of light, moving quickly toward an unknown destination. They raced with time, knowing the last of the oil would soon run out.

Reg huffed with exhaustion, his legs aching, as they approached the first patch of sunlight they'd seen in over a week. The dark spirits still surrounded them, just waiting for a gap in their defenses. Those on the outside waved their torches to drive them back, but one by one, the fires burned out, the fuel exhausted. Though he knew it might not do much good, Reg drew his gun and stood shoulder to shoulder with Frolic.

"We've got to hold them off," Reg panted.

"We will." Frolic's magical blade cut golden crescents through the gloom.

As the torches reduced to embers, the party finally broke through the trees. Starling blasted gouts of flame behind him, making the creatures hiss and letting the others put a few hundred yards between themselves and the dank jungle. When he depleted his magic, though, dozens more creatures burst from beneath the trees. Their numbers seemed endless.

Tom elbowed his way to the front of the group and looked quickly from side to side. His eyes widened, and he motioned for the others to follow him down a steep embankment. The cart holding most of their food toppled over and rolled down the hill. Reg retrieved a few sacks of fruit and dried meat, slinging them over his shoulders as he sidestepped jutting roots and leapt over fallen branches. About a quarter mile ahead, a small stream, probably a tributary of the larger river, tumbled downhill between some large, moss-coated rocks.

"Most spirits can't cross running water!" the fey yelled over his shoulder, avoiding the obstacles with much more grace than the rest of them.

"What about the carts?" Corny called.

Starling, at the rear of the group, managed a few more spurts of flame, buying them a little more distance from the abominations. "Take what you can carry! Leave the rest!"

When they reached the water, they obeyed the baron, salvaging as much equipment as they could. Then they scrabbled over the rounded stones and plunged into the water. Istvan and Attila waded in, holding crates of guns above their heads as the water reached their chests. Reg didn't see Corny until he looked over his shoulder and found her hauling a wooden box as long as she was tall from the back of a cart. Though Jack Owens helped her, their load seemed very heavy. Reg could guess as to the contents: the magic-negating device Frolic opposed so vehemently.

"For the love of God, leave it!" he called, even as he spun around to assist them.

"No," Corny said. "I won't. Not under any circumstances." With Reg and Jack's help, they pulled the crate from the bed of the cart, and it landed heavily on the ground.

"You'll never get it across the river. You're going to die if you don't leave it and run." Reg tugged at the tinkerer's sleeve as she heaved a huge spool of metal wire as thick as her wrist from the cart. It likely weighed as much or more than she did, but she looped the end through a brass handle on the crate, secured it, and hoisted the rest of the spool onto her shoulder. Then, slowly, she pulled her precious creation toward the water's edge, with the spirits close on their heels. Jack Owens shouted as one of them swiped at the back of his leg, opening a quartet of deep gashes across his hamstring.

"We'll never make it," Reg pleaded. Querry and Frolic called to him from the other side of the stream, and he knew without a doubt they'd come back for him soon if he didn't hurry. He couldn't let that happen. "Corny, please."

In response, she set her jaw in a hard, determined line and picked up speed, actually managing to jog while dragging the cumbersome cargo. Though her strength amazed Reg, the creatures had almost caught up with them. One of them grabbed for Reg's hair, and he barely dodged it. His spectacles fell from his nose, and he crushed them with his boot as he stumbled to regain his balance. Holding his antique pistol by the barrel, he swung the handle wildly, though it did little good. Finally, they reached the rocks lining the bank. Corny knelt behind the crate and fought to push it over the top of the huge stone. Dozens of creatures closed in, surrounding them.

A desperate idea formed in Reg's mind, and he turned to Jack Owens. "Give me your lighter, and help her get that bloody thing into the water."

The older mercenary merely nodded once and did as Reg said. Reg fished inside his waistcoat and found his flask. He turned toward the twisted spirits and took a healthy pull as he flicked Owens' brass lighter. Then he lifted the flame to his lips and spit. The expensive single-malt caught, and for a moment Reg saw nothing but a blurry ball of fire. He smelled scorched hair as it singed his fringe and eyebrows. The heat stung his face, but when it faded, he'd driven the creatures back almost a dozen feet. He lifted the flask to his mouth again.

As soon as Reg heard the loud splash he hoped meant they'd got the crate into the water, he threw his flask and the lighter at the creatures' feet, scrabbled over the rocks, and dove into the stream. The water soothed his tender face as he sank below the tepid, oily surface. Reg kicked and pumped his arms, swimming underwater for several strokes before resurfacing.

Reg took a deep breath and pushed his wet, tangled hair out of his face. Safe now, he swam slowly to the center of the stream before stopping to look around. The water, at its deepest, reached almost to his chin. Without the aid of his spectacles, the creatures they'd just fled looked like black smears as they stood just beyond the rocks. On the opposite bank, everyone, with the exception of Corny and Jack Owens, who toiled to haul her cargo across the water, busily checked the supplies and equipment they'd managed to save.

When Reg came ashore, he set down the satchels of food, peeled off his leather vest and trousers, and hung them on a branch to dry. Then he removed his dripping shirt and tie. The jungle had taught him health and comfort trumped modesty, but he still couldn't bring himself to strip off his pants. Querry and Frolic, similarly undressed, ran to embrace him. Reg clung to them, trembling, ready to cry. Funny, but he'd been lucid and alert as he'd faced the creatures, but now, safe in his lovers' arms, he barely held himself together.

Frolic scowled when Corny and Jack Owens finally made it ashore with their massive spool of metal rope. They started pulling the crate toward the bank. "You shouldn't have helped her, Reggie," Frolic whispered into his hair.

"I had to, beauty. She'd have died to protect it."

Frolic broke away from them and shot Corny a glare. He turned his back on them, wandered over to Reg's garments, took one of Reg's pistols from its holster, and sat on a flat stone to start taking it apart. A little farther down the beach, Jean-Andre, Istvan, and Attila attended to their own weapons. Reg couldn't help but let his gaze linger a few extra seconds on Jean-Andre's practically naked body and shiny, red hair.

Jack Owens slapped one of his big hands over Reg's shoulder. "That was good thinking back there, mate," he said.

"Thanks," Reg said, realizing that, from the seasoned mercenary, this was high praise indeed.

Looking back across the river, Reg wondered what would happen to them now. They couldn't go back the way they'd come, and they'd been forced to leave many of their supplies, food included, behind with the carts. They'd have to push onward, but into what? If those angry spirits protected Starling's precious wellspring at this distance, what would they encounter when they drew nearer?

"We'll get through it," Querry said and clasped Reg's hand, as if he read Reg's mind. "We just have to stay together and look out for each other, just like we promised."

"I just pray it will be enough," Reg said.

CHAPTER 24

REG'S CONCERNS about what they might face as they drew closer to the magical power source proved unfounded, because after three days' travel, they could go no farther.

All ten of them stood side by side, awed into absolute silence. Querry could scarcely breathe as he looked into a ravine that seemed to extend to the very center of the world. The wide, lazy river at the bottom looked like nothing more than a thin, silver thread. The walls rising above it were smooth, sheer, gray stone. To Querry, they looked impossible to scale; there were no protrusions or indentations to hold onto. The distance across the crevasse was probably less than a quarter of a mile, but the depth to the river and jungle below was probably four times more. The opposite bank lay a few dozen feet lower than the one all of them stood on. The early morning sunlight against the sheets of shimmering mist cast shifting streaks of light on the rock face.

"This is the band of nothing," Querry stated. "Now it makes sense."

"We can't go any farther," Reg said, his whisper a mélange of worry and wonder. "We can't get across, and we can't go back the way we came. What are we going to do now?"

"This will not stop me," Starling said in a clear, commanding voice.

"Will you use magic?" Frolic asked, his eyes wide and reflecting the strong sun.

"No skill of mine can get us across," the baron said.

"What about Tom?" Frolic asked.

"I could easily get myself anywhere I want. The rest of you are on your own."

Querry didn't know if he believed the fey. After all, his gentleman had transported both of them halfway around the world in less than a second. Maybe Tom just wasn't as powerful. More likely, he wasn't willing.

"This is what the Panther People warned us about," Frolic said, a trace of hopelessness creeping into his tone. "This is the Edge of the World."

Tom's gaze snapped in Frolic's direction. He looked ravenous all of a sudden. "What did you say?"

"Before the hunters left us, they told me nothing waited between their territory and certain death but the Edge of the World."

"Do you hear that, my lord?" Tom asked with a sneer.

"It is no matter. This will not stand in my way, not when I'm this close. I'll entertain suggestions. In the absence of any, we walk south until we encounter some way to cross."

"Walk?" Jean-Andre swept his hand along the chasm, which extended to the limits of Querry's vision in both directions.

Querry, never one to give up easily, recalled the spool of wire Corny and Owens used to drag their cargo. He looked over at the tinkerer and asked, "Could we fashion some sort of a grapple strong enough to reach the other side and hold to the stone?"

She shrugged. "Sure, we could. If I had any of my equipment or any materials to work with. Maybe… maybe there is a way, though."

"Out with it, girl," Starling said.

Corny turned, walked back to her crate, knelt down, and caressed the wooden edge with reverence. "This is the finest thing I ever made," she said softly. "But I'd hoped for more time to work on them."

Frolic pushed past Querry to stand over her, his hands on his hips. "Corny, no."

"Ah, Frolic…." She flipped the lid open, and all of them gathered around to see what the case held.

Inside, cradled by layers of wool felt, was a set of gold and brass wings, folded tightly together. The sun glinted off the intricately carved feathers. Even without examining them more closely, Querry saw how small and elaborate the gears at their joints were. He'd never seen anything like them; not even the creatures Frolic constructed could compare. Querry didn't even think his old mentor, Dink, could have made them. *Well, maybe Dink*, he decided.

Frolic covered his mouth with both hands and took a step back. Corny looked up at him, and their gazes locked. No one else dared even shuffle his feet.

"They're for you," Corny said with a crack in her voice and an obvious stammer. "You... you were always talking about those angels, and... and you seemed so fascinated with birds and flying... I'm sorry I kept them secret. I wanted them to be a surprise."

The group parted to allow Frolic to approach his friend. He reached down, took her hands, and pulled her up into a powerful embrace. She returned the hug, lifting Frolic off his feet. "You're my best mate," she said. "Best I ever had."

"Me too," Frolic said, his voice trembling with emotion. Querry knew if he'd been able, he'd be crying right along with Corny.

"This is all very moving," Starling said, not unkindly. "But how will it help all of us cross the ravine? Frolic can't exactly carry us over."

"No," Corny said, bouncing on the balls of her feet and grinning. "But he can carry the spool of steel cord across and secure it. The rest of us can loop a piece of metal over top and slide right down."

Reg came forward and stood between Corny and Frolic, his arms spread protectively. "Corny, I don't mean any disrespect, but you said yourself you wished you had more time. The last time you said that, our airship crashed and almost killed us all. These are marvelous, amazing even, but they haven't been tested. For all you know, they won't work, and Frolic will plummet to the bottom of that abyss. This course of action is just too rash."

"We don't seem to have much choice," Starling said.

Reg whirled around and stabbed his finger at the baron's face. "You do it, then!"

"I'll do it," Querry offered. He remembered the sensation of swinging between the rooftops of Halcyon from his grapple; he remembered the view of the city from Dink's airship, how free he'd felt above the greed, cruelty, and desperation. To actually fly.... He couldn't imagine anything more wonderful than to have wings of his own to spread, to truly *fly*.

"Afraid not, mate," Corny said. "They're for Frolic. They'll only work on him. And if you're worried, we can test them out beforehand. I don't want anything happening to Frolic. But I'm telling you, they'll work. They're based largely on the concepts I learned from Frolic's creator, from the book."

She lifted them from their crate like a holy relic and carefully unfolded them. They were massive: probably a dozen feet or more from tip to tip. "Frolic, come try them on."

Without a word, he stepped forward and held his arms outstretched while Corny removed his waistcoat. She fastened a series of leather buckles over his chest. Then she produced two clockwork gauntlets, sliding them onto his arms. The gauntlets trailed wires and pistons that attached behind his shoulders, connecting them to the magnificent wings with a sequence of complex gears. A series of dials and levers lined the palms of the gauntlets. Frolic's fingers went to the controls almost out of instinct.

"They're so light," Frolic said. "Tell me how they work."

"Everything's hollow," Corny told him. "And they work on some of the same principles as my little bird. As you. See here"—she pointed to a rounded, roughly triangular glass vial affixed to the leather over Frolic's heart—"this collects the moisture from the air, just like you do when you breathe in. Only the wings use a sort of series of reverse fans to draw the air into these tubes." She ran her finger along the piping artfully running into the skeleton, joints, and feathers.

"I've been experimenting with ways to amplify the heat of the jungle and the heat produced by your heart. This little gadget absorbs the sun and heat of the forest and stores it within. It's lined with mirrors to intensify the effect. You're always saying how you don't want anything you make relying on fuel. Anyway, the steam will force hot air into the channels within the 'bones'. It should give you the extra lift to get you in the air and keep you up. It will insure that you and the wings stay light enough to remain aloft. Here. Let me show you how to operate them."

"I think I can figure it out." Frolic had always possessed an innate understanding of clockwork and machinery. After fiddling with the knobs and dials for only a few minutes, he unfurled the wings to their complete, glorious span. Then he flapped them in front of him, and they lifted him off the ground and carried him back several feet. He continued to experiment, testing the amazing range of motion the fully articulated wings provided. No one standing even ten feet from him would have any clue they weren't completely organic, they moved so smoothly.

It took only half an hour or so before Frolic took complete control of the wings and moved as though he'd been born with them. He flapped them three times, rose a dozen feet into the air, glided over, and touched down lightly on top of a rock high above the others. Everyone cheered, and Corny swiped moisture from her cheeks with the back of her hand.

Querry had never had any time for religion, but as he looked up at his perfect beauty with his sparkling, silver curls and the bright sun glinting off his outstretched wings, he felt uncharacteristically choked up. Frolic was just so beautiful in every way, just... perfection. He truly looked like an angel who'd just descended from heaven, not that Querry would ever utter such a silly statement out loud. He might whisper it to Frolic, though, later, when they were alone. Frolic would like hearing it.

Reg stepped up beside Querry and braided their fingers together. Everyone else focused their attention on Frolic, so they didn't notice. "He's amazing," Reg whispered, shading his eyes with his other hand. "Almost supernatural. Sometimes I can't even believe he's real, let alone that he's ours."

"Yeah," Querry said in a soft sigh.

"Are you sure he'll be all right?"

Querry nodded, a small part of him envious, still wishing he'd be the one to soar across the ravine. "Cornelia's a true genius. I had no idea. And Frolic's taken to those wings like he's never been without them."

"Our Prince of Angels," Reg said, a little bitterly, probably recalling the destruction of the clock tower, the angels, and the many ill effects the whole mess had left on Frolic. Both of them felt partially responsible for what had happened and how he'd changed as a result of their decisions. They didn't discuss it often, but Querry knew well both of them dredged it up from time to time. He could tell by the wistful way Reg sometimes looked at Frolic.

Querry squeezed his hand as Frolic glided over their heads and landed near the edge of the ravine.

"I think I'm ready to go," Frolic announced, smiling with a trace of the innocence and wonder he'd once expressed so freely and often.

Reg let go of Querry's hand and turned to Corny. "That steel wire won't make him too heavy, will it?"

She shook her head, looking confident, almost smug. "I didn't cut corners, mate. Those wings could lift a horse."

"Oh, Corny!" Frolic squealed with delight. "Could we make a winged horse? Wouldn't that be lovely?"

She chuckled. "Talk to me when we get back to the real world, where there are tools, and furnaces, and proper workshops."

"I will," Frolic said as she handed him the heavy spool of rope. He tucked it under one elbow as if it weighted nothing and put his delicate fingers on the steering mechanisms.

"Wait," Jack Owens said. "We have to anchor it to something sturdy on our end. I don't fancy the idea of it coming loose when I'm hanging over the middle of that forsaken pit. Let's wedge it under one of these big rocks."

He motioned to his men. "Help me shift this."

Together with Corny, Reg, and Querry, the three mercenaries managed to lift the massive boulder. Frolic placed a good few feet of the steel cord beneath it before they set it back down.

"Will it hold?" Reg asked.

Owens slapped Reg on the back. "If it don't, lad, you won't be worried over it for long."

"How very reassuring," Reg replied.

"Step aside," Starling said. "I'll make sure it doesn't come loose." Kneeling, he held his palms a few inches above the wire. Flames, as white-hot as those from Corny's welding torch, shot from his hands with a loud whoosh. Beneath the magical fire, the rock melted and bubbled, melding stone and steel into the ground. "Give it a few minutes to solidify before you set off."

Frolic nodded and went to wait at the edge of the chasm, his wings unfurled and practically trembling with anticipation. Querry couldn't blame him at all.

As the rest of them waited, Jean-Andre approached Cornelia, scooped up her hand, and kissed her knuckles. "An absolutely ingenious creation, my lady. I would be honored if you'd tell me more about how they were made."

Corny blushed but didn't pull away. In a heartbeat, Jack Owens stood beside her, his muscles tense and bulging like an attack dog straining against his chain.

"I... er, I don't know. Trade secrets, and all. You understand. Besides, they'll only ever work on Frolic, so there's no need to make more. They need the heat from his heart to function properly."

"I'm merely interested in the theory," Jean-Andre continued, rubbing his thumb across the back of her hand. "And perhaps some conversation with such a brilliant young woman."

"The lady said no," Owens growled through clenched teeth. He stepped forward until he stood chest to chest with Jean-Andre.

The Belvaisian merely offered the much larger man a lazy smile, fluttered his eyelashes, and dropped Corny's hand. He shrugged, as if none of it mattered. "I am never one to argue with a lady's prerogative, monsieur."

Querry felt suddenly nervous and wondered what Frolic had done with his book. Then he saw the leather satchel draped across Frolic's shoulder, his prized tome next to his hip, as always.

"One more thing," Tom Teezle said. He wriggled his long, slender fingers beneath the cuff of his shirtsleeve and pulled out a length of shimmering, silver and gold brocade ribbon. He tied it to the end of one of Frolic's wings, where it fluttered in the slight breeze. Then he kissed Frolic lightly on the lips. "For luck."

All of them ran to the edge of the gorge as Frolic took off. Querry's heartbeat shook his entire body, and Reg clutched Querry's arm so hard it would surely bruise as they watched Frolic fumble and lose a few feet of altitude before flapping his wings and catching a current of air.

"READY?" FROLIC said softly to Whisper as he pushed off the edge of the cliff with his feet and beat down with his wings. The little creature made a pleasant sound somewhere between a cat's meow and a dove's coo as it followed him. Frolic dropped a few feet before he managed to clear the rocks and extend his wings fully. The powerful propellers let him glide along with almost no effort, while the hot air kept him afloat as if he weighed nothing.

Frolic had never experienced such exuberant bliss as he did riding the air currents, listening to the voice of the wind, and angling his body as he sailed along a mile or more above the forest floor. His happiness built inside until it burst forth in a high-pitched laugh. He'd never even imagined such sensations as he enjoyed as the breeze rushed over him, caressing his skin and making his curls bounce and flap around his face. He had never felt so free, so unencumbered by the heavy, ugly things of the human world. He even managed to forget about everything that had plagued him since the events in Halcyon. Nothing mattered to him but the warmth of the sun on his back, the contrasting coolness of the breeze, the way he began to sense the movement of the air around him, and the feeling that he could just keep going, go anywhere, with absolutely no rules or restrictions. He felt as warm, light, and buoyant as the vapors filling his wings as he glided along, with Whisper weaving through the sky beside him playfully, sometimes dipping and flying in circles around Frolic.

Too soon, Frolic reached the other side of the ravine. He sailed over the tops of the trees until he found one almost as wide as a barn. Then, with Whisper gliding along beside him, he circled the trunk six times, wrapping the wire around it and pulling so tightly the line embedded in the bark. He dropped the spool and flew back through the trees, testing his wings in close quarters and quickly learning how to angle and fold them to avoid branches and vines. Whisper played with him, weaving through the woods, hiding, and springing out when Frolic soared past him. Then he flew ahead, hovered in the air until Frolic almost reached him, and darted away again.

At the edge of the canyon, Frolic dove, pressed his wings almost parallel to his body, and dropped several dozen feet before spreading them out and catching a current of wind. He could go much faster without the spool, and without the worry of staying in a straight line so he wouldn't tangle the rope. The wind rushed loudly past his ears as he descended almost to the river. He smelled the water as he glided above it, watching his bird-like shadow on the rippling, greenish surface beneath him. He traversed a mile or more in only a few minutes before turning sharply and beating his wings to climb back to the edge of the cliff. Just for fun, he twisted his belly to the sky and glided along on his back, with Whisper doing his best imitation. Together, they attempted a few more flips and flashy maneuvers.

It all came so naturally to Frolic. He didn't even have to think about the controls; the gauntlets, and the wings, felt no different from any other part of his body, although he'd already had a few ideas to improve the steering mechanisms. He wondered if maybe his creator had planned this for him all along. Maybe he'd given him the knowledge, the instinct, and just hadn't gotten around to constructing the wings. Frolic felt like he was meant to have them, and he decided, when he built himself a companion, he'd fashion another set just like them. He could only imagine how much fun flying would be with a friend along.

Though he could have happily spent the rest of the day in the air, Frolic knew he had to get back to the others. Everyone ran toward him as soon as he touched down. Whisper perched on his shoulder and twisted his head to the side, as if perplexed by the humans. Querry reached Frolic first and caught his hands. "Beauty! How was it? What was it like?"

"More amazing than I can even express."

"I was worried," Reg said, stroking Frolic's hair, "but I think maybe you should fly more often. I haven't seen you this happy in a long time. I want to see more of it."

"Oh, Reggie, it was like a beautiful dream."

"Controls worked all right, then?" Corny asked. "Not too touchy, are they?"

Frolic shook his head. "I didn't even have to think about them. The wings felt like part of my body. Thank you for doing this for me, Corny. You don't know how much it means."

"I wanted to," she said. "But take care of them. I don't ever plan on making another set."

"But maybe one more set." Frolic caught her gaze and tried to communicate his meaning through his expression.

She nodded slowly, understanding. "Maybe one."

"Thank you. It's safe for all of you to cross now. I made sure of it. I'll meet you on the other side." Frolic hurried away, as much to escape Querry and Reg's confused frowns as to get back into the air. He'd tell them his intentions, as they'd promised each other, but later.

CHAPTER 25

QUERRY MADE sliding across the wire look easy, as did Starling, Jean-Andre, Istvan, Attila, and even Corny. Tom Teezle found his own way across the gorge, and soon Reg stood alone with Jack Owens. Looking down into the chasm made Reg feel like he'd be sick, and he jammed his hands in his trouser pockets so Owens wouldn't see how hard they shook. He had no strength in them; under no circumstances could he grip the tiny, metal bar, let alone support his weight across the gulley. His muscles felt no sturdier than watery gruel, but he didn't want the mercenary to see his fear, his weakness. He felt so ashamed; all the others had crossed the ravine without a problem.

Reg expected Owens to mock or insult him, but when he faced Reg, his dark, lined face displayed compassion and understanding. "Listen, lad. You faced those monsters back there like a warrior. You never even flinched. You can do this too."

"I can't." Reg's legs trembled; he felt like he'd collapse. He'd never make it.

"You just gonna leave your mates behind, then? Let them go on without you? You feel all right about that?"

"No, but—"

Owens pressed the metal bar into Reg's hands. "Now, just hold on tight, tuck your legs up next to your belly, and close your eyes. It'll all be over in a minute."

Before Reg could protest, Jack gave him a hard shove between the shoulder blades. The ground fell away beneath his feet, and he pulled his knees up as he'd been instructed. He plummeted forward, air whipping past him. He tried to ignore everything but his grip on the iron bar. He just had to hold on a little bit longer. Nothing else mattered but keeping his grip on that piece of metal. Then he made the mistake of opening his eyes for a split second.

The river whizzed by beneath his boots. He could picture, in horrible, vivid detail, tumbling into that void. He had to hold on, but his palms sweated and started to slip from the bar. His arms and legs shook so hard he knew he'd fall off. His hands slid until only his fingers remained curled around the iron. He closed his eyes again; he didn't want to witness his fall. For a second, he thought Querry could still save him. Or maybe Frolic. Maybe Frolic would fly over at the last minute and pluck him from the sky. In his logical mind, though, he knew they couldn't save him.

Just as Reg's cramped, shaking fingers fell from the bar, a set of strong, lean arms closed around his waist and pulled him the last few inches to the edge of the cliff. He threw his arms around Querry and buried his face against Querry's neck. Querry helped him stumble a few feet, to where Frolic sat beneath a tree, his wings folded behind him like a bird resting on a twig. When Querry released him, Reg crumpled at Frolic's side and dropped his cheek to Frolic's shoulder. Frolic squeezed Reg's hand, and his terror dissipated much faster than he'd expected. In only a few minutes, it felt like a bad dream, and Reg was embarrassed by his panic.

"Glad that's over," he said, forcing a laugh. The knowing looks his friends gave him told him they'd never mention the incident again, and he couldn't begin to express his gratitude.

Jack Owens came over to them and offered Reg a canteen of water. "Well done, lad."

All of them silently agreed just to relax for a few moments, and they found shady patches to recline. Reg had almost dozed off when he heard Istvan calling from somewhere deeper in the jungle.

"Sir," he yelled in his heavy accent. "Sir, you have to see this."

Owens, who'd been sleeping on his back next to Corny, had his gun in his hand before he reached his feet. Jean-Andre pulled his pistol just as quickly and sprinted into the trees, his hat flapping behind him. Starling wreathed his hand in a glove of flame and called for Tom to follow him. The faerie, with a secret smile on his lips, followed at his own, leisurely pace.

Querry groaned and rubbed his forehead with the knuckles of the hand holding his pistols. "Fuck me. How much more can happen to us?"

"Did you think we were going on a holiday?" Reg grabbed Querry's elbow and helped his groggy friend to his feet. "What fun would it be to just lie on a beach all day? That doesn't make an interesting story to tell in the pub."

"Prick," Querry teased. "Let's go."

Frolic hurried to stand in front of them. "This isn't a joke. Something strange is happening, and we need to be very careful." He clutched something Reg couldn't see, presumably his little pet, tight against his chest.

Reg expected anything but what he saw within the round clearing. A dozen tables draped in crisp, white cloths waited beneath a porcelain tea service. Tiered platters overflowing with tiny snacks and sandwiches sat at their centers, next to crystal vases full of flowers, and not exotic jungle flowers, but good, Anglican, summer blossoms: pink roses, sweet peas, hydrangeas, snapdragons, foxglove, and honeysuckles. The fragrances recalled to Reg his afternoons after being adopted by the Whitneys. He'd spent many of them at garden parties such as this. White candles sparkled within crystal lamps, and cloth lanterns hung from the tree branches, just like they had at the manor house.

At the sight of the food, the mercenaries cried out with joy and ran toward the nearest table.

"Don't eat or drink anything, you dunces!" Querry yelled. "Where do you think all this came from?"

"Listen to him," Starling cautioned.

The three mercenaries stopped a few feet from a tray of what looked like egg salad, cucumber, and watercress sandwiches, looking like little boys who'd had their hands slapped reaching into a tin of biscuits. Reg couldn't blame them. After weeks of nothing but fruit and the bland, charred meat of whatever they could kill, he'd have traded his fortune for a buttered scone. For a cup of tea, he thought he'd sacrifice a limb. Not surprisingly, his gaze fell on a tray of buttered scones and a steaming cup of tea he would have sworn wasn't there a moment ago. A little silver dish of sugar cubes and a pitcher of fresh cream sat next to it. He didn't reach for it, because he also knew the fey, the spirits, or whoever had laid this feast would know to tempt him with his heart's desire. Who knew if the mercenaries or the others even witnessed the same things he did. Maybe the brothers inhaled the savory aroma of a pot of their native goulash, or the delicious paprika chicken Reg had sampled while visiting their country. Querry likely saw a plate of greasy chips with vinegar, a slab of battered fish, and a big bottle of gin.

Reg edged close to Frolic, who would be able to see through the glamour. "What's going on here, beauty? What do your eyes see?"

Before Frolic could answer, Reg heard a voice that made his bones feel like they melted and dripped out of his body. He grabbed Frolic's elbow and froze.

"Now, now, Mr. Knotte. And you, Baron Starling, Viscount of the End of Dreams. There's no need to be rude to my guests."

Reg turned slowly, dreading who he knew he'd see. The faerie gentleman who'd hired Querry for so many ridiculous jobs, no doubt with some unfathomable agenda of his own, stood holding a flute of pale, sparkling wine. He wore a suit of emerald velvet with long tails, paisley lining, and a floral-printed cravat. His shining golden hair spilled over his shoulders, almost to his waist, and his bright green eyes looked as wild and unpredictable as Reg remembered.

"Sir?" Querry said, hurrying to stand before his former patron. "What are you doing here?"

There was something between them, or there had been, Reg knew. He saw it in their posture, the way their eyes met, and their lips twitched up when they regarded one another. Though annoyed, he trusted Querry. Whatever Querry had allowed in the past wouldn't recur, he felt sure. Still, he didn't like it.

"Well, Querrilous, I'm here to celebrate a very special occasion. Please, join me in a toast." Crystal glasses of pale, effervescent wine materialized in everyone's hands. "To my son." The gentleman raised his glass, and the others, either ensorcelled or just afraid, mirrored his actions.

Reg's arm jerked up almost involuntarily, spilling wine over his lapels. He scowled at the dark splotches on the leather.

Querry clapped the powerful and terrifying fey on the shoulder, as if they'd been friends for many years. Reg supposed, in a way, they had. "Oh, sir! That's wonderful and... a bit unexpected. Where is the little fellow?"

"Querry, you misunderstand." The wizard Kristof, the gentleman's partner, stepped from beneath the shadow of a tree, puffing on his pipe.

Reg was glad to see Kristof in his simple, antiquated clothing, with his long, auburn hair loose around his shoulders. The gentle young sorcerer seemed able to influence the gentleman's unpredictable and often violent moods. If needed, he'd protect the others from his lover's wrath.

"Misunderstand how?" Querry asked. By now, the others had gathered in a crescent around him to listen and observe.

Reg still clung to Frolic's shirt. He couldn't deny his fear and even hatred of Querry's "gentleman." He'd been witness to the events the fey had set in motion in Halcyon, whether he'd intended to or not. The gentleman seemed to have an instinct to incite chaos. He was the last thing they needed on their already ill-fated excursion.

"What is it I don't understand?" Querry repeated.

"My son is already here," the gentleman said with a proud smile. He elbowed Reg aside to put his arm over Frolic's shoulders. "The son resulting from my union with the one love of my endless existence." When he looked fondly at Kristof, he seemed almost human.

"What?" Querry asked.

But Reg understood. When the faerie gentleman and his wizard lover had repaired Frolic's heart, they'd needed elemental fire, fever dreams, and oaths spoken during love. So, they'd used as a spell component the very words they'd spoken to each other in the heat of passion. Their oaths not only helped to keep Frolic's heart eternally warm, but apparently they gave the gentleman some sort of delusional claim over Frolic.

"Exactly one year ago today, the love between Kristof and myself brought Frolic into the living world. Our desire for one another heated his veins and roused him from the edge of death. He is our son, a product of our love, the same as any child. We wish to celebrate his birthday."

"It's not his birthday," Reg growled under his breath, unsure what inspired him to verbally disagree with the crazy fey.

"What's that, *Reginald*?" the gentleman asked with a sneer.

Reg puffed up and straightened to his full height. He was angry. Irrationally so. "I said, it's not Frolic's birthday." Querry reached a warning hand out, but Reg shrugged it off. He noticed Kristof slip up behind the gentleman. "We don't know Frolic's birthday. None of us. Not even Frolic."

"That is true, sir," Frolic added innocently. Poor Frolic was totally unaware he witnessed some complex and unspoken power struggle. "Only my creator knows the day I was born."

The gentleman heaved a theatrical sigh and pinched the bridge of his nose. "The things I suffer in the name of family," he said with exaggerated persecution.

"Reg, what are you doing?" Querry whispered while the gentleman appeared to swoon.

"He has no claim to Frolic," Reg answered without whispering. "I'm sick of being a slave to his whims."

"He helped us once before." Querry continued to whisper. "He could help us again." Reg stood firm, his chin thrust out. "We wouldn't even have Frolic if it wasn't for him."

That hit home. Reg deflated a little. Querry was right. Despite the fey's insanely unpredictable nature, he was a being of immense power, and he might be able to get them out of this godforsaken jungle sooner. He looked at Frolic. The clockwork boy looked back, his golden eyes wide and an earnest expression on his smooth, porcelain skin.

"I'm sorry," Reg stated without really feeling sorry.

"Now he's sorry!" the gentleman exclaimed and motioned grandly at Reg. Then he dropped his head to Frolic's shoulder and wept dramatically. Frolic looked around at his traveling companions for some advice as to how to handle the faerie sobbing on his shoulder. Reg rolled his eyes. Querry bit his lip. Cornelia shrugged. Frolic reached behind the gentleman and patted him gently. When the fey finally recovered, a placating smile had appeared on his pale lips. "Fine, Reginald. No," he stated, before Reg could open his mouth. "What would you have me celebrate?"

"I don't know. I mean, really it was more of a rebirth than a birth, wasn't it?" Reg suggested.

"Are you honestly suggesting we call my son's most special day a *re*birthday?" The gentleman clucked, disgusted, before Reg could respond. "No, Reginald. That's just silly. We're not doing that." The faerie struck a grand pose and announced, "Please join me in celebrating my son's *birthday*!"

The faerie gentleman waved his hand, and a grand, seven-tiered cake decorated in frosted, golden roses appeared. Almost a hundred candles flickered along the layers. Reg doubted the queen herself received such a display on her birthday, but he mistrusted it. He mistrusted everything to do with this so-called gentleman. He wondered how he'd warn Frolic to beware of the deception without upsetting the faerie again.

"I want to make my son happy," the gentleman continued. "What father wishes for more?"

Kristof colored, though he didn't seem opposed to his partner's reasoning. "There is a little something of both of us in you, Frolic. I'm proud to be part of the person you've become. Proud to be a sort of parent to you."

A few minutes of awkward silence ensued, during which Frolic gradually moved behind Reg. Reg was only too happy to shield him, to keep him from this corruption.

"Well, what are you waiting for? Come, sit. Celebrate!" The gentleman motioned to the tables where all manner of creatures had suddenly appeared. Some of them looked similar to the gentleman, almost human but for strange attributes like horns, pointed ears, or eyes seemingly too big for their faces. Others were definitely not human. Reg saw a tree sitting across from an overlarge hedgehog in Edwardian finery with fine silver pince-nez perched on his twitching nose. The gentleman didn't wait for his guests; he strode to a table at the head of the celebration, exchanging pleasantries with the strange creatures as he passed them: two men with long white beards and pointed red hats, and a woman clothed only in leaves with an odd, green cast to her skin. He shook hands with a donkey-headed man and kissed the hand of a woman who had flames where her hair should be.

"It's all right," Kristof assured them. Reg jumped a little when the wizard touched his shoulder. "The food is safe, and we have no intention of harming anyone. We truly just want to celebrate the amazing life of our Frolic." Reg rankled at the term "our Frolic," but he didn't protest. Starling and Tom Teezle walked over to his trio and the wizard. "You're welcome here as well, Viscount."

"Thank you." Starling inclined his head. "I think we could all use a proper meal, Mr.—?"

"I am Kristof," the other wizard answered, offering a hand to Starling.

Starling extended his hand slowly. "Kristof?" Starling gripped his hand and shook it. "The wizard Kristof?"

"That's right," Kristof said, nodding. He released Starling's hand, and Reg was surprised that their tormentor stood staring at the hand that had recently been in Kristof's embrace. The other wizard turned to Starling's servant. "Are you still calling yourself Merrifont?" Kristof asked.

"Tom Teezle."

"Then I suppose you're welcome too, Mr. *Teezle*." Kristof accented the faerie's last name.

Reg frowned. He couldn't fathom the intricacies of fey society or how all the little lies and oddities fit together. The wizard walked off. Starling gave the rest of his company permission to join the party, though he warned them against accepting gifts from, giving thanks to, or touching any of the fey guests. The men eagerly obeyed, while Cornelia walked over to Frolic, grabbing his hands. She looked frantic.

"Frolic, what is all this? I don't like it. Not one bit." Her words spilled forth in a rush. Sweat shined on her forehead. Reg realized this clearing wasn't hot like the rest of the jungle. It was actually quite pleasant, like an Anglican spring afternoon. "It's all terribly magic-y and strange. I don't understand any of it, and I feel ill."

"Calm down, Corny. It's really going to be fine." He pulled a handkerchief from his pocket and kindly mopped her brow. "These two men are old friends. They saved my life. We're just going to have dinner and be on our way." He smiled at her, and she relaxed slightly. Reg almost believed Frolic's words; the clockwork boy's tone was so sincere. "Hungry?" he asked Corny.

"Always," she said, relief in her tone.

"Go on, then. Join Jack. It looks like he's having a little trouble with that rabbit fellow in the tuxedo jacket." Frolic pointed toward the large man. He appeared to be determinedly explaining something to the disinterested rabbit waiter.

"Oh, for heaven's sake." Corny rolled her eyes and dashed over to the man, taking his arm and speaking politely to the rabbit.

"Well, I suppose we might as well have a bite to eat," Querry said, a little too nonchalantly for Reg's taste. He reached out and grabbed Querry before he could get too far. "What?" Querry asked, turning back.

"Are you serious about this?" Reg asked.

"You heard Kristof. It's safe. And we're starving." He had a point.

"Come on, Reggie," Frolic said, taking Reg's other arm. "Let's enjoy the break while it lasts."

Unable to think of any valid arguments, Reg allowed his lovers to steer him to the gentleman's table.

While they ate, the gentleman instructed some of the local wildlife in the proper handling of musical instruments, and the monkeys played a jaunty tune for the revelers. Starling and Kristof conversed enthusiastically, and it seemed as though everyone breathed a collective sigh of relief for a few hours. Even Corny had relaxed and was busy repairing the hedgehog gentleman's watch. She'd managed to find something she understood in all this madness. Reg wished he could say the same. He still glanced at the faerie gentleman suspiciously from time to time. Querry spoke to the gentleman about the state of things in Halcyon. The gentleman kept trying to change the subject to marbles, shoes, various cheeses, and epic battles he'd fought centuries ago, although it seemed to amuse Querry rather than frustrate him.

Some of the faerie beings moved the tables apart so they could dance to the monkey music. Reg was shocked when the mercenary brothers joined them. He worried for a moment, having heard the stories about men being led astray by fey dancers, but then he noticed Starling clapping and laughing at them. Surely, if they were in real danger, Starling would have put a stop to it. Then his gaze fell on something slightly more worrisome. Tom Teezle sat in his chair, arms folded with a scowl plastered across his face. The faerie hadn't touched his meal.

Frolic had wandered off to speak with some of the partygoers. They stood in a circle as if watching something, periodically chuckling and applauding. Reg assumed they observed Frolic's new pet. He wished he could see the creature. That, along with everything else, made him feel a bit isolated in the middle of all the chaos. He searched the crowd and saw Jean-Andre sitting at a table alone. He decided to join the Belvaisian.

"Hello, Reg," Jean-Andre greeted him as he approached. "Enjoying this little soiree?"

"Eh," Reg grunted. "The food was acceptable, but the company leaves a bit to be desired."

Jean-Andre laughed. "You seem to be the only one who thinks so, mon ami."

"I've long thought I was the only one among us with any sense," Reg stated dryly. That earned another hearty laugh from Jean-Andre. Before they could continue their conversation, their host stood at his table and called for the attention of the guests, clinking his salad fork against his flute. "I'd better join them," Reg said as the rest of his friends returned to the head table.

Jean-Andre nodded. "A pity, but I understand."

Reg, feeling heat crawl up the sides of his neck at Jean-Andre's suggestive smile, walked after the others.

"I'm glad that you've all decided to join us for this birthday." The gentleman paused, throwing a dark look in Reg's direction. "That's right, *birthday* celebration. As the evening draws to a close, I'd like you to join me in wishing my dear son a happy birthday!"

The gathered guests all cried out in unison, "Happy Birthday, Frolic!" and toasted the birthday boy.

"Excellent," the gentleman announced. "And now, my guests, please stay and enjoy the food and the music as long as you wish. It's time for Kristof, Frolic, and I to bid you farewell." The faerie guests applauded, but the humans gasped as one. There were scattered mutterings of disbelief.

"What do you mean by that, sir?" Starling demanded.

"Oh. Didn't I mention we were taking Frolic along?" The gentleman studied his nails, disinterested in the baron's protests.

"You can't take Frolic," Reg shouted.

"I can do what I like."

"Darling," Kristof said, standing. "We discussed this. You can't just take Frolic away from his friends if he doesn't wish to go."

"Why not?" the faerie asked with a pout.

"Frolic has a right to choose his own destiny," Kristof answered. It was obvious in his tone that this wasn't a new argument.

"He isn't yours to take," Querry argued, standing as well. Reg was glad his lover challenged the faerie for once. "He isn't anyone's. He belongs to himself."

"Not to mention, he's under contract to me at the moment," Starling stated angrily. Reg found himself oddly grateful for the cursed bargain for once.

"Is he now?" the gentleman asked, clearly unconvinced. "We do not break our contracts, as I'm sure you know, but I'm sure we can reach some sort of an arrangement, Viscount."

"It doesn't matter." Reg joined the argument. "You're not taking him."

"And what makes you think you can tell me what to do, Reginald?" The gentleman spat the words like venom, his eyes flashing dangerously.

"Don't I get a say in all this?" Frolic interrupted in a small voice.

Reg pressed his balled fist to his lips. Damn. "Of course you do, beauty."

"We're sorry, Frolic," Querry added. "You tell him what you want to do."

Frolic stood and faced the gentleman. "I appreciate everything that you've done. No one's ever thrown me a birthday party before. It's been lovely. Really, it has. Where would you take me, anyway?"

The gentleman beamed at Frolic's praise and the possibilities in his question. "I'll take you anywhere you want to go, in this world or any other. I can show you things unlike you've ever imagined. Marvels and miracles. Doesn't that sound like a lovely time?"

"I don't know...."

"You belong with me and Kristof," the gentleman persisted. "We should raise you as fathers. I have always desired a son above anything. You need us to teach you who you are and what you can do. Like all good parents, we'll help you understand and grow into your potential."

"I am very confused about many things," Frolic admitted.

Reg froze. He'd never contemplated Frolic wanting to go with Kristof and the gentleman. If Frolic wanted to go, Reg knew he had no more right to force him to stay than the gentleman had to take him. Querry had spoken truly: Frolic was free to choose for himself. Reg couldn't breathe as he waited for the conversation to continue.

"Can you tell me why I am the way I am?" Frolic asked.

"Of course," the gentleman said. "Come with me, and I can tell you everything you need to know."

"I am very intrigued. And grateful. But I can't go with you. I have a job to finish first. And I have people who are counting on me." A cloud passed behind the faerie gentleman's eyes, and thunder rumbled in the distant sky. Frolic sensed the dangerous turn in the faerie's mood. "I'm sure it would be quite enjoyable to join you. And I certainly hope to see you again."

Frolic's attempts to appease the gentleman were only making him angrier. "Sir, um. Father, it's been a pleasure, but we have to be on our way."

That got him, Reg thought. *Well done, Frolic.* The gentleman thrust his lip out once again, pouting, and Reg was confident Frolic managed to change the creature's mind.

"That's unacceptable!" The gentleman stamped his foot, and Reg felt the ground beneath him tremble. Everything in the jungle seemed to grow still and quiet in the wake of the faerie's rage.

"Love," Kristof said softly, stroking the gentleman's elbow. "You promised we wouldn't force him. We have to let them go for now."

"Well, at least have some cake first," the gentleman offered peevishly.

"I wish I could," Frolic answered. "But I don't eat, Father."

"Impossible!" The gentleman threw up his hands. He turned on his heel and disappeared.

"Happy birthday, Frolic," Kristof said, approaching Frolic with open arms. "Be well and watch out for each other," he said as they embraced. "Here. I'd like you to have this. It's just a little something I made, a locket that will show you whatever you most want to see when you open it." He draped the delicate chain around Frolic's neck and bid the others a polite farewell, just before his faerie companion reappeared to collect him. Before departing, he thrust a small box wrapped in shimmering, leaf-like, green paper and topped with a gold bow at a perplexed Frolic. When they disappeared, the rest of the party disappeared with them. Starling's group was once again alone in the jungle.

Frolic opened his gift, handed the gilded ribbon to Tom, and held up what looked like a pair of golden pruning shears. After staring at them for many moments, Frolic shook his head and slipped them into a pocket.

"Damn it!" Reg barked and stomped his foot. "We didn't ask your grandstanding associate to help us get away from this wretched place."

"Um, Reg—" Querry tugged on Reg's sleeve. "I think he did."

Reg looked at Querry. His blue eyes were wide with shock, and it took a fair bit to shock Querry. Reg followed his deep blue gaze, sure he wore an identical expression of astonishment. What he saw just through the trees was unlike anything he'd ever seen before.

A great stone structure stretched toward the sky above the jungle. "I'll be damned," Reg breathed.

CHAPTER 26

QUERRY DIDN'T know much about architecture or antiquities, but the structure in front of them looked more than ancient. Giant stones worn with weather and age formed the sloping outer walls. It was obvious that men didn't come to this place; the jungle had descended, and moss and vines covered the structure with patches where small trees and bushes had found purchase. Atop it all, like a crown of nature, grew an enormous tree, with a trunk that filled the entire roof of the structure. *Temple*, Querry thought. *Damn.* He could feel it, the reverence that had gone into building this monolith. It was a monument to something he couldn't even fathom.

As the party approached the ancient structure, Querry shaded his eyes as his gaze traveled up the stepped walls. It occurred to Querry that the tree wasn't indigenous to the jungle. It looked more like something one would find in an Anglican hunting forest. It wasn't quite a willow tree. Trees weren't really Querry's area of expertise. Reg would probably be able to name it. The branches reached out over the sanctuary, and they moved into the shade of its leaves.

People spoke. Starling. Jean-Andre. They discussed how to get in. Querry barely registered it as he finally realized the true scope of this sacred place. They approached it almost at one of the corners. He looked along the wall, searching for the opposite corner and couldn't see it. If he couldn't see it, how long would it take to reach? A day? More? For a reason he wouldn't have been able to explain to anyone else, he walked up and placed his hand on the stone. A thrill ran up his arm. Power. He could feel it. He leaned in, pressing his sun-stung skin to the stone. Despite sitting in the middle of a tropical jungle, the stone was cool. Because of magic or the shade from the tree above, Querry didn't know.

"Amazing." Frolic's voice startled Querry. He hadn't realized he'd closed his eyes. "Isn't it?"

"I can feel the magic in it," Querry whispered. He wasn't sure why he whispered, but he didn't want the others to hear him.

"It's impossible not to," Frolic agreed. "Can you hear its voice?"

Querry listened as hard as he could. He tried to translate the feeling of his eyes slipping into faerie sight to his hearing. For a brief moment, he heard something. It was almost like weeping, but then it was gone. "Not really," he told Frolic.

"That's all right. It's upset. Lonely. It feels the way I did while I waited in that cellar. No one comes here anymore. They're too afraid. Even the faeries. That's why we haven't seen any." Frolic whispered too. "The gentleman found us."

Why hadn't Querry realized it? "Our potions have worn off." It wasn't a guess.

"Your bodies probably processed and excreted it."

"That makes sense." Their faces still pressed against the stone, Querry looked deep into Frolic's beautiful golden eyes. He wanted nothing more than to lavish his lover's mouth in kisses, but now wasn't the time. He forced his mind to turn to more practical matters. "Can you tell if there's a way in?" Querry asked.

"No. Nothing so specific." Frolic reached over and grasped Querry's hand.

"Are you two quite finished huggin' the ruins?" Jack Owens's gruff voice called from around the corner. Querry pushed back from the stone, suddenly feeling very silly. Frolic followed. "Good. We've got to find a way into this thing."

Around the corner, Starling, Reg, and Jean-Andre discussed their plan of attack. Jack Owens stepped to the center, ready to instruct the others. Deftly Querry slipped around the bigger man and scratched a square in the ground at their feet. "The best way to do this is for half of us to go this way and half of us to go that way."

"Do you really think we should split up?" Cornelia asked apprehensively. "What about strength in numbers?"

"Each of these walls may be a day's walk or more. If we don't want to wander around for a week, we need to split up," Querry told her firmly. She nodded in response.

"How will the group that finds the entrance signal to the other?" Jack Owens asked gruffly.

"Look at the size of this temple. There's no way to get word between the groups," Querry answered and snorted. Tom Teezle appeared as though he wanted to say something, thought better of it, and remained silent. "The team that finds the entrance will just have to wait for the other group to reach them."

"That's our plan?" Owens sneered.

"You have a better one?" Querry challenged. Owens opened his mouth to argue but apparently didn't have a better plan and just remained silent. "Good."

"Can't Tom move between teams?" Reg asked.

"Yes," the baron answered.

"I'm not sure I can," Tom contradicted. "This place is strange. If I travel, it may not have the results I intend. Best if I don't test it."

"Fine. What are the teams?" Starling asked.

"Reg and Frolic are with me. The rest you can settle on your own," Querry responded.

"I will go with them," the baron said. "Owens, you take Tom Teezle and the rest. Is that acceptable to everyone?"

"Suits me," Owens grumbled. Cornelia seemed torn between wanting to stick with Owens and not wanting to let Frolic out of her sight. Ultimately she begged her clockwork friend to promise to stay safe, and she remained with the mercenaries.

"I would like to join you as well, Monsieur Baron," Jean-Andre stated. "If you don't mind."

"Not at all," Starling answered. "Let's not dawdle." With his declaration, Starling stalked away, presumably to make preparations while instructing Tom Teezle how to behave in his absence. Owens gathered his men and their group and disappeared around the corner of the temple.

"How do we get in once we find the entrance?" Reg asked. "I presume we won't be permitted to just walk in."

"No, I shouldn't think so," Jean-Andre agreed.

"Let me handle that," Starling interrupted. "Come, let's be on our way." Without looking back, the baron marched off along the wall of the temple. Jean-Andre followed.

"Are we ready, my loves?" Frolic asked. He didn't wait for their answer, just walked off, dragging the crate containing his wings.

"Why didn't we get Frolic to fly around and look for the entrance?" Reg asked.

"The rest of us would need to walk to the entrance still," Querry explained. "And what would happen if there's some sort of trap and he crashed? He'd have no way to contact us. Plus there's the magic that Tom mentioned. We don't know what effect it will have."

"That's a fair point." They walked side by side as they joined the rest of their party.

After a few hours, the conversation tapered off, and the trip became increasingly tedious. There was nothing of note anywhere on the face of the temple, no windows, no architectural accents, and definitely no entrances. Frolic took the lead quickly, not tiring like his human companions.

Evening arrived early in the shade of the canopy of the giant tree, but Starling pushed them until all the light was sapped from the jungle, and it was impossible for them to see anything. "Can we stop for a rest at least?" Querry finally asked. "We can't see anything in this light anyway. It would really be a kick in the ass if we passed the entrance because we couldn't see it in the dark."

"I can conjure a light for us to see by," Starling answered. When the wizard cast the spell and the light erupted in the palm of his hand, the glow it cast on his face revealed the manic obsession driving him. "Press on."

"Starling." Querry's tone took on a smooth, calming tone. "You're exhausted. We all are. We'll rest for a few hours and continue on. We want to find the entrance as much as you do."

Starling closed his eyes and took a deep, steadying breath. "Of course you're right, Querry. We're so close now. I can almost taste it." He released the light, and it floated near his shoulder. Then he walked up to the wall and laid his hands flat against the stone. "I can feel it throbbing with magic."

Querry hid a smirk as he and Reg shared an amused glance at the baron's choice of words. Exhaustion had left them both as giddy as boys. "It's been here for who knows how long. I'm sure it will wait for us to have a bit of a lie down," Querry said, offering the baron a canteen. Starling surrendered and accepted the canteen, taking a long drink.

They all rested with their backs against the stone of the temple. The spongy moss actually made for a comfortable seat, and it wasn't long before

Querry's eyelids grew heavy. His head snapped up just before he dozed off. Next to him, Starling dropped his head to Querry's shoulder and snored lightly, his flask in his hand. No sound came from Jean-Andre. Querry reached out for Reg's hand, and his old, dear friend shifted, but his breathing remained rhythmic and relaxed. Querry fought another wave of sleep washing over him, successfully resisting it once more.

"Go ahead, Querry," Frolic whispered.

"I'm fine, beauty," he said, a sleepy smile lounging on his lips.

"You're exhausted. Rest. I'll watch over you."

Querry wanted to. Desperately. "Thanks, Frolic." He heard Frolic respond, but the next time his eyes closed, he fell fast asleep.

Frolic roused them when the first light of dawn penetrated the jungle, and with little delay, they resumed their search for a way into the temple. They had little gear or provisions to worry over, after all. It proved to be as fruitless as the previous day's search. They trudged on and on with no end in sight until midday when they finally found the corner at the other end of the temple wall, having traversed one full side of the structure.

They rested for only a few moments. It seemed more and more like they weren't going to find the entrance. But Querry knew there had to be some way in. He always found the way in. No one would build a temple that was impossible to enter. Would they? He groaned inwardly. Faeries might. If that was who built this place. Faeries didn't usually build things, though.

"I hope the others are having better luck," Reg groused. "This is beginning to seem hopeless."

"On the bright side, if we pass another corner, we know they've stopped because they've found the entrance," Jean-Andre offered.

"Or they're dead," Starling said. While it might be the truth, Querry didn't think it was particularly helpful given their situation. The rest of the day passed in relative silence as they continued to trace the perimeter of the temple.

There seemed to be some silent understanding that they would press on until they reached the next corner because no one suggested they stop, and even though Querry knew they all had to be as exhausted as himself, no one complained.

It wasn't until Lord Starling collapsed that they finally paused. Starling was fine, but when Querry sat down he knew he wouldn't be getting back up. Looking around at his fellow travelers, he knew they felt the same. Jean-

Andre was already lying sprawled on his back. Reg leaned against the stone wall with his head lolling. Only Frolic remained standing. They had rested just long enough that Querry began to doze. He was disturbed when Starling, bracing himself against the temple, got to his feet.

"What are you doing?" Querry demanded.

"We've got to be nearing the next corner. We should forge ahead," Starling responded. Querry understood his determination, the victorious thrill of accomplishing something everyone said you couldn't. But if Starling didn't stop for at least a while, he'd kill himself. The baron's stubbornness was frustrating, and Querry wondered if he sometimes seemed as delusional and pigheaded.

"No, Baron. You must rest," Frolic said, putting a hand on Starling's shoulder.

"You don't understand. I have to do this," Starling argued. "I must."

"Starling, don't be mad. You're not a young man," Reg said.

"My age doesn't matter. This is my life's work." Starling still tried to resist Frolic, but Querry knew his lover was much stronger.

"I have an idea," Frolic offered. "Are you able to conjure one of those magic lights for me?"

"Of course. Why do you ask?" Starling wasn't resisting anymore, his curiosity getting the better of him.

"Cast a light for me, and I'll push on to the next corner. I don't need it to see, but if we are as close as you think, you'll be able to keep an eye on me by watching the light. I'm not tired, and I won't get tired, so I'll walk to the corner, and if I don't see the rest of our party, I'll come right back."

"That's too dangerous, Frolic," Reg warned. "We have no idea what's out there."

"No. I'll be fine. I have my sword, and I'm much more resilient than a human. If there are faeries about, I'm the only one they won't be able to detect."

"He has a point," Querry agreed. Frolic could take care of himself, and he didn't have far to go.

"Querry! How can you say that?"

"Reg," Frolic interrupted. "It's a good plan. You don't have to worry. You'll be able to see the light."

"I won't try to talk you out of it," Reg answered with a scowl. "But I still don't like it."

"It is a good plan," Starling agreed and conjured Frolic a light.

Frolic hugged Querry and Reg, whispering, "Don't worry. Have faith," in Reg's ear. He straightened, waved a good-bye, and walked off into the night. The glowing orb floating by his shoulder cast enough light that for a while they could see Frolic's silhouette growing smaller as he ventured deeper into the strange, shifting shadows. Then it was just a small, blue ball bobbing in the darkness. As soon as Frolic's form blurred and melded into the night, Querry regretted letting him go alone. It took everything he had not to run after the pale, azure pinprick in the distance.

ONCE FROLIC got far enough away from the others that he could no longer hear their nervous whispers and hushed debates, Whisper, who'd fluttered off when they'd stopped to rest, drifted down from the branches and landed lightly on Frolic's shoulder. Frolic reached up to pet him, glad for the company. Whisper wrapped his tail around Frolic's wrist and made a soft, rattling sound.

"I know you're scared," Frolic said softly. He didn't know if the little creature could comprehend language, but he sensed Whisper at least understood the sentiment, and Frolic liked talking to Whisper when no one else was around, because he didn't have to worry about how much to say and how much to keep to himself.

"I'm scared too, Whisper. I'd never want Querry and Reggie to know how much. They'd only worry. But something is very wrong here. Every living thing is crying out for us to go. Querry was right about the magic here, but it doesn't feel like a wellspring of energy. I don't know what it is, but I feel it coming up from the ground, into my feet and into my body. It makes my bones feel cold and brittle. It doesn't matter, though, because I have to find it. Querry and Reg can't go home until I do. Do you understand, Whisper?"

Whisper cooed softly, a regretful and sympathetic sound.

"Maybe I should have gone with my father. I wonder if I made the right decision. He could have helped me, and I'm sure I could have asked him to get my friends to safety. I just can't stand the thought of being without Querry and Reg."

Frolic had nearly approached the corner, and he still saw nothing but the shadows cast where thin strands of moonlight penetrated the thick foliage. He heard nothing but the rustle of the leaves, not even an insect or a nocturnal bird. Taking a few steps back from the unbroken monotony of the smooth wall, he looked up into the branches of the great tree towering hundreds of feet above him. Hundreds of small, glittering specks looked down at him, and Frolic knew they were eyes. He couldn't imagine what sort of beings they belonged to, but they didn't feel anything like Whisper. They didn't feel malevolent; they were just watching, and Frolic got the sense they had been for a very long time. Their presence did nothing to help him find the temple's entrance or the rest of his party.

Frolic sighed and dropped his face into his palms. He felt like he'd girdled this fortress a dozen times, and maybe he had. It all looked the same, right down to the vines covering the stones and the dense brush along the perimeter. "Whisper, what am I going to do?"

The little creature nestled his head into Frolic's hair and made a low, mournful howl, echoing the despair Frolic felt. Then he flapped his wings and lifted off Frolic's shoulder, touching down on a little knoll a few feet away. He sat on his haunches and canted his head. When Frolic hesitated, Whisper motioned him forward in a disturbingly human gesture. Reluctantly, feeling like he'd tumbled into a dream, Frolic approached him. The canopy above them shifted, casting Whisper in a shaft of silvery light. Frolic crouched, resting an elbow on his knee as he tried to discern what Whisper wanted to show him. After peeling back some of the thick groundcover, he noticed a smooth, gray stone inscribed with some oddly familiar, swirling markings.

Frolic brushed away the remainder of the vines and moss so he could see the entire slab. If he let his eyes relax and unfocus, he found he understood the writing. The longer he stared at it, the less he noticed the jungle. He felt like he existed alone in a dark void with nothing but the shard of rock. Before he realized he was speaking, Frolic mumbled, "The way inside lies above, between heaven and earth, the struggle to the key will yield the fruit of knowledge. Knowledge must be absorbed, and the door will open."

For an immeasurable amount of time, Frolic sat staring at the stone with Whisper curled in his lap. Then, from somewhere far away, he heard someone calling his name. Gradually, the shapes of the trees and leaves around him grew crisp and solid again. When he looked over his shoulder, he saw the rest of his group rounding the corner of the temple, Corny and Jack brandishing odd, glowing sticks and leading the others. Corny called out to him, relief plain in her tone. Before they reached him, Frolic dug his nails beneath the piece of rock and dislodged it from the earth. A human surely would have broken his nails, and maybe his fingers freeing it, but Frolic easily dug it loose. It was just the size of the little book of poetry Reg had carried back in Halcyon, and Frolic slid it into his waistcoat pocket.

Corny rushed forth and lifted Frolic to his feet, burying her face in his neck. "Oh, thank heavens you're all right. I was so worried I'd never see you again."

Frolic pulled away from her and kissed her brow. "Everything is fine now, Corny. The others are just a bit farther back. I know what to do now. It'll all soon be over."

"Will it?" she asked, still encircling his waist. "As much as I want to see the world, this place is too strange. I would be happy to get away from here."

"You will," Frolic said. "I know just what to do."

"How?" she asked with a hint of suspicion.

Instead of answering, Frolic pulled away from her and turned to head back to Querry and Reg. She continued to assail him with questions, but he responded with his own questions, wondering how she'd fashioned the glow-sticks. She explained about the phosphorescent mold they had found on their journey around the temple. He stretched his arm out for Whisper to perch upon and hurried back to his lovers, eager to bring their ordeal to an end now that he knew how.

CHAPTER 27

IT TOOK only about a half an hour for Frolic to reach the rest of his group. He found Querry and Reg standing on the path hand in hand, waiting for him with worried expressions. To Frolic's surprise, Reg kissed him on the mouth, and Querry practically collapsed against him as they embraced. A few feet away, Jean-Andre slept on the ground with his hat over his face, while Starling huddled against the stone wall with his knees tucked almost to his chest, deep in slumber. Frolic hated to disturb his rest, but he knew the baron would want to hear what he had to say, so he cleared his throat and waited for Starling to drag himself from unconsciousness.

Starling sat up stiffly and rubbed his eyes with his fists. When he noticed Frolic had returned, he said, in a scratchy voice, "What have you found?"

"A great many things," Frolic responded. "The rest of our people, and our way inside the temple."

That roused the baron to full alertness, and he got to his feet. "You can get in?"

"I think so."

"How?" Querry asked.

"I need to find something in the tree," Frolic said, pointing upward. "Some source of knowledge we can absorb. I'll need my wings." He looked longingly at the crate containing them, eager to fly again.

"How do you know this?" Starling asked, alert and authoritative already.

Frolic wasn't intimidated by the baron's tone. "I found this," he said, pulling the stone from his pocket. "It says what we need is halfway up the tree, the tree of knowledge."

"How can you read this?" Starling barked. "You're making it up."

"He's not." Tom Teezle stepped up beside the baron. He took the slab of rock from Frolic and studied it for a few seconds. "This is a very ancient form of our language. Even to me, the meaning is obscure. But I can understand the underlying sentiment. The fruit of the tree is the way to the temple."

"I can get that fruit," Frolic said. "Can't we get this over with? The people I love are unhappy here."

The Baron Starling stared down at his folded hands. "Can this really be the way?"

"I'm sure of it," Frolic said. Without waiting for the baron's response, he went to the crate, opened it, and took out his wings. Then he slipped them on as easily and comfortably as a worn glove. He adjusted them and flapped them. They already felt natural, a part of him. He wondered how he'd ever lived without them.

"I'm under contract to you," Frolic said, trying to bargain in the way of the humans and the fey. "Will you have me retrieve the key to opening this temple? If not, you must release us, because we can go no further. Do you want me to go?"

Starling looked at Tom, who nodded.

"Very well," the baron said. Querry and Reg hurried to Frolic's side, nervous expressions on their faces

"Wait," Reg pleaded. "What if there are traps or the magic effects your wings? Querry, you said it might not be safe."

"There's no way to be sure," Querry responded to Reg's concerns. "Reg is right, beauty. This could go horribly wrong."

Frolic just smiled and clasped their hands. "I can do this. You must trust me. It'll all be over soon," he told them, "and then we can go home. Or find another one. Please don't argue. Just give me a kiss for luck."

Neither of them hesitated to press their lips to the corners of Frolic's mouth despite their reservations. He closed his eyes and just enjoyed the closeness, forgetting about everything else until they pulled away. Querry stroked his face and offered him an encouraging smile.

"Please be careful," Reg said, pressing his forehead against Frolic's. "I love you very much."

As he flapped his wings and ascended, Frolic felt an unfamiliar twinge, a sinking sensation in his belly. He hadn't been completely honest with Querry and Reg. He'd told them he would only be plucking a piece of fruit, but he'd neglected to mention the hundreds of creatures sitting in the branches. He didn't want to tell them he'd be in danger and leave them anxious, but deceiving them made him feel just awful.

Whisper stayed close to Frolic as he glided in circles around the tree, moving higher and closer with each loop. He stayed far enough away not to rustle the long, thin, silvery leaves of the drooping branches. Eventually he reached a proximity from which he could see the creatures crouched on the branches. They were clearly fey, but a sort he'd never seen before. Only about the height of a young child, they were extremely thin with twig-like limbs and thick, gray skin with a slight sheen similar to the bark of the tree. Some of them held sticks sharpened into spears or tridents, but all of them had dagger-like claws. Instead of hair, leaves and branches sprouted from their heads and even grew from the points of their exceptionally long ears. Unlike most fey, they possessed little beauty in their long noses, pointed chins, and the beady, shining eyes that darted anywhere Frolic accidentally disturbed a leaf.

Frolic stayed back as he searched for the fruit. He circled around and around, but he didn't see anything but the thick leaves and their guardians. Many of the creatures, growing suspicious, got to their feet and hoisted their weapons. A few times, Frolic felt sure they'd seen him or heard the whir of his wings as he soared past. Whisper clearly didn't like the tree faeries, and he stayed well away from them, off to Frolic's right.

Frolic angled his wings down and shot up into the sky, flying all the way to the very pinnacle of the great tree. As he hovered above it, his friends looked like tiny specks moving across the forest floor. The other trees around him looked like dollhouse miniatures, and even the temple walls seemed more like an average building, the ruins of some human citadel back in Anglica. Frolic still didn't see anything resembling fruit. Looking down, he saw nothing but a wavering sea of gray and green, parting now and then to show him the glittering eyes of the creatures searching the sky for whatever disturbed their sacred duty.

Frolic finally saw a faint glint of moonlight off something shiny and yellowish about halfway down the tree, close to the trunk. His throat swelled, making it hard for him to swallow, as he realized he'd have to enter the branches and move among the creatures to retrieve it. Tom's assurances the fey couldn't see him did little to assuage his nerves, but he knew he had no choice. He drew his wings close to his body and dropped half the height of the tree.

At the end of a branch the size of a small bridge, Frolic saw the melon-like fruit dangling. He'd have to pass twenty or more of the faerie sentinels in order to pick it. Steeling his resolve, swearing a silent oath not to fail his friends, he lit down on the end of the branch, barely jiggling it. Though terrified, Whisper landed on his shoulder and clutched his hair. A few of the creatures turned toward them, and Frolic froze as they sniffed the air. He waited many minutes for them to lose interest before he took his first tentative step toward the heart of the great tree. He folded his wings at his back so they wouldn't brush the hanging leaves.

Frolic made it a few feet before he encountered the first of the wardens. It sat on its haunches, its eyes darting back and forth. Frolic held his breath as he stepped carefully around it, passing so close the satchel containing his book grazed the leaves growing from its head. The creature turned its head in Frolic's direction, but it couldn't see him. On his tiptoes, Frolic made his way past half a dozen more of the small, nasty-looking fey.

The fruit hung only perhaps ten feet away. It was the size of Frolic's head, but oval and elongated, with shiny, golden skin dotted with orange and scarlet. Beneath it sat eight of the creatures, shoulder to shoulder, spears pointed out. Many more waited in the branches above. Frolic inched a little closer, until the creatures' pointed noses were mere inches from his knees. Whisper made a soft, frightened sound, and all the creatures turned toward them, staring hard at where Frolic stood, afraid to even breathe. He hesitated, hoping the things might lose interest, but they didn't. Knowing he had to take his chance, he stretched his waist and reached out until he had the fruit in both hands. He tugged, expecting it to come free from the branch, but it stayed connected. His efforts rustled the leaves and drew more of the protectors from nearby branches. They opened their mouths, revealing rows of sharp, yellowed teeth, hissed, and either swiped their claws or thrust their spears where they'd seen movement in the leaves.

Frolic pulled harder on the fruit, but it wouldn't budge. By now, the creatures had discerned his location and stabbed at him with their weapons. He struggled to swallow his cries as they pierced his skin, causing much more pain than their size would indicate. Even as they dropped from above, landing on Frolic's shoulders, tearing at his hair and scratching his skin, he kept a firm grip on the fruit and wrenched at it with all his considerable strength. Whisper squealed as one of the fey got hold of his tail. Frolic kicked at the creatures swarming the branch, sending some into the leaves below. More and more of them appeared, clawing at Frolic's trousers, climbing up the fabric, and trying to pull him down. As small as they were, Frolic knew if they piled on top of him in their great numbers, he wouldn't escape.

Something occurred to Frolic, and he couldn't believe he hadn't thought of it before. As he kicked wildly to free his legs, he reached into his pocket for the birthday gift the gentleman, his father, had given him: the golden shears. They easily severed the stem, and the fruit dropped into Frolic's hand. He hurried to tuck it between his elbow and his body. Then he used the shears to stab at a creature attacking Whisper and lifted Whisper to his shoulder. Whisper cowered in a ball as Frolic swiped his shears in front of him as he ran for the end of the branch. Even when he dove into the air, some of the creatures held tight to his clothing. Frolic pitched from side to side, twirled in the air, and shook his limbs until he dislodged them. Then he glided down to the base of the temple and his friends.

As soon as he landed, Frolic fell to his knees, his wings spread out behind him. He swallowed great breaths of air as he tried to calm down. Everyone stood in a circle around him, and Querry put his hand on Frolic's shoulder. Reg knelt down in front of him and pinched Frolic's chin, inclining Frolic's face until their eyes met.

Reg gasped. "Oh my God!"

Frolic reached up and felt the torn skin over his cheek. Pain shot across his face as he fingered the ragged edges of his flesh and the warm, smooth metal beneath it. As much as it hurt, it worried him more for the others, especially Querry and Reg, to see him like this, to see such a strong reminder of how different he was. Worried he'd disgust them, he tried to look away, but Reg held him firmly.

Querry clasped Frolic's hand, stretched his arm out, and pushed his shirtsleeve up. Querry cursed when he saw the cuts and punctures. Frolic just wanted to hide. He didn't want them to think of him as a machine.

"Somebody, do something," Reg said, looking up at the confused faces around them.

"I can't," Corny said in a trembling voice, ready to cry. "Frolic's skin, according to the book, is mostly magical."

"Majesty, Tom, please help him," Querry said. "You can help him, can't you?"

"It should be easy enough," the fey said, crouching down. "The enchantment has just come unwoven. Were you attacked by magic?"

"There were creatures in the trees," Frolic answered, not meeting Tom's emerald gaze. "Please fix me, Tom. I'm hideous."

"I'll help," Starling offered.

"I have no need of your power," Tom snapped, brushing the baron away with a flick of his wrist. He ran just the tips of his fingers over the wounds on Frolic's face, infusing Frolic with a warm, soothing flow of magic. The pain ebbed away in seconds, and when Frolic felt his skin again, he found it smooth and flawless.

Tom proceeded to close the other tears in Frolic's skin one by one. By the time he finished, the enchantment left Frolic feeling relaxed and a little euphoric. Giggling to himself, his skin sensitive and tingling, Frolic leaned back against Querry's chest, reaching up to enjoy the unique texture of the stubble along Querry's jaw. It felt scratchy against Frolic's palm, and it made him imagine how it might feel elsewhere on his body.

Reg sat beside him, toying with the ribbon, beads, feathers, and other things Frolic had collected to weave into his curls. Tremors of pleasure shot down Frolic's neck as Reg traced the edge of his ear. He groaned, getting hard, suddenly very desperate for some time alone with the men he loved.

"Are you feeling better, Frolic?" Starling asked in a compassionate tone with just a dash of impatience.

"I feel wonderful," Frolic said dreamily, watching enrapt as Reg licked his lips.

"I'm glad to hear it, and I certainly appreciate your bravery. Please, if you would be so kind, tell us how we should proceed."

Frolic sat up slowly, feeling a little dizzy from the magic coursing through him. He'd all but forgotten about the fruit he'd fought so hard to acquire. It laid abandoned a few feet from his leg. He reached over and picked it up.

"That's it, then?" Corny seemed incredulous. "That's how we get inside? A melon? What do we do with it?"

"Eat it," Frolic answered.

"Don't like that idea," she said.

"I ain't doing it," Owens said, crossing his arms. "I didn't sign up for this. We have no idea what it is. It could kill us."

"It's the only way," Frolic said.

"Give it here," Querry said. "I'll eat it. Anything to get us the hell out of this place."

"Querry, that's very foolish," Reg said. "Jack's right. It very well might be poison."

"One way to find out." Querry smacked the melon on a nearby rock and split the rind in half. The inside was bright red and liquid, reminiscent of blood and flesh. Without hesitation, ignoring Reg's vehement protests and pleas, Querry scooped up some of the pulp with his fingers, shoveled it into his mouth, chewed, and swallowed. "Bitter," he said, wrinkling his nose, "and a little hot. A little like a cross between peppers, lemons, elderberries, and wine. My tongue's a little numb, but I don't feel…. Oh, damn."

"What is it?" Reg asked, worried.

With wide eyes, Querry looked up into the tree and pointed at the malicious creatures watching them. "Bloody hell, look at that."

The others waited a few minutes, and when Querry didn't vomit, convulse, or fall down dead, Starling, Reg, and even Corny ate a generous portion of the fruit. All of them looked around with amazement.

"My God," Reg whispered. "Frolic, is this what it's like for you? You see this all the time?"

Frolic nodded. "Maybe, but I bet you see more. Do you see a way in? Do you know which way we need to go?"

"I… I think I do," Starling said, shielding his eyes as if it was a bright morning instead of the dead of night. "There's a sort of faint, glowing trail here on the ground…."

"I see it too," Reg said. "This is the way, I'm sure of it."

"Let's get this done," Querry said. "Not a bloody minute too soon."

Since he couldn't eat, Frolic didn't see the pathway, and he didn't see the glowing door the others claimed they'd found on the monotonous surface of the stone. Jack and the other mercenaries stood well back, whispering among themselves.

"Well, we found it," Querry said, flattening his palms on the doorway Frolic couldn't see. "Now how the hell do we open it?"

"Leave that to me," Starling said with a frown. "Tom…."

"No."

"Curse it, you must obey me." The baron grabbed the fey by the sleeve and pulled him over, stretching his arm out and bunching the fabric to expose his golden-brown skin.

"Just what do you think you're doing?" Reg stepped forward, his hand on one of his pistols, and stood chest to chest with Starling.

Instead of the insults Frolic expected, Starling sighed and shook his head. "This pains me too. But it is necessary. Only fey may enter this place. It is unpleasant, but I promise it won't do any permanent harm. Please, I must ask you to defer to my knowledge of these matters."

Without waiting for Reg to acquiesce, Starling drew a dagger and dragged it across the inside of Tom's arm. The faerie let out a bone-chilling cry of pain as his blood splattered the ground and splashed against the stones along the base of the temple. Those who'd eaten the fruit gasped, and though Frolic couldn't see what occurred, he felt the air around him shift and shimmer. Everything jiggled like gelatin, and a rush of cool, grass-scented wind washed over them.

"At last," Starling said.

Tom Teezle yanked his arm away from the baron and pressed his hand to his oozing wound. "That is the last time you'll touch me, human. Mark my words."

"Tom, I am sorry. If I knew any other way—"

Tom held up his hand. "Save your hollow words, sorcerer. They mean nothing to me, and they'll do nothing to save you. As soon as I like, I'll be done with you, so you'd do well to proceed while I'm inclined to remain."

Without another word, Starling stepped inside what Frolic saw as a dark splotch on the stone and disappeared. Querry took Reg and Frolic's hands and, with a stiff spine and a guarded posture, led them inside the ancient, ensorcelled temple.

Chapter 28

THE THIEF'S instinct, as Querry had always thought of his uncanny ability to sense wealth and treasure, told him something precious waited within these labyrinthine corridors. His goggles allowed him to see quite well as the group traversed the narrow, winding halls, so he stayed with Frolic at the flank of the party, while Starling, with his bluish orb, led them along with a sulking and reluctant Tom Teezle. Corny, Jack, Istvan, and Attila stayed between them, while Reg and Jean-Andre, pistols ready, guarded the sides.

The glass-smooth stone they walked across sloped downward so gradually Querry barely noticed their descent into the earth. He thought it wise to keep some record of the way they'd come, so he used his dagger to make small marks on the walls at regular intervals. Everything looked the same. Much to Querry's confusion, Frolic was determined to find gold. To Querry's further astonishment, he managed to locate several hidden alcoves, small rooms off the main tunnel, containing piles of gold nuggets. Querry didn't understand Frolic's sudden appreciation of wealth, as Frolic had always valued strange things like sea glass and feathers above actual money, but he certainly didn't argue as he filled his pockets and pouches with all he could carry. There was more than enough for all of them to share, and everyone but Tom and Starling loaded up. Before long, the crate that had carried Frolic's wings was nearly full of raw gold. If they got out of this, they'd live like kings.

It was impossible to keep track of time in the perpetual gloom, and Querry had no idea how long they'd been below ground when the corridors opened up to a large, round room. Starling held up a hand to pause the group, and Querry moved to the front. His skills would allow him to detect any kind of traps or obstacles. The baron directed his glowing ball to the center of the chamber, and it illuminated a large space with a ceiling so high it remained in shadow. Querry took a few steps into the room, his breath echoing in the vastness. He did a quick scan, checking the walls for levers and the floor for any irregular tiles that might indicate a pressure plate. He squinted into the gloom, looking for anything that might drop down upon them, but he found nothing. Not for the first time, he wondered what the Fair Folk had intended when building this place, because he now felt sure they had.

Querry was just about to tell the others to proceed, that he'd found nothing amiss, when he saw a group of people, eight of them, standing at the opposite end of the chamber.

"Get ready," he told the others as he drew his sword and pistol.

REG READIED himself for a fight. The eight people in their party stood facing eight enemies. Without his spectacles, and at such a distance, Reg couldn't make out many details, but something about their opponents seemed oddly familiar. Both he and Jean-Andre raised their guns and took aim at one of their adversaries. Miraculously, both of them missed. The others stepped into the icy light, and Reg's insides knotted up, his fist trembling around the handle of his gun. They faced exact replicas of themselves; the imitation Querry and Frolic were so perfect Reg couldn't bring himself to attack them. Instead, he set his sights on the Baron Starling, who he reasoned would be the most dangerous. He fired, but the faux-Starling dodged and avoided his bullet. Reg turned, aiming at Tom Teezle. Before he could squeeze the trigger, his opposite approached him, blocking his shot.

The other Reg wore a fine, fawn-colored suit, with long tails and a matching waistcoat. A gold and green, paisley cravat held by a pearl pin encircled his neck, and gold-rimmed spectacles shot the real Reg's reflection back at him. A tan bowler hat sat atop neatly trimmed, blond locks. When Reg raised his firearm and his doppelgänger did the same, it felt surreal, as if he looked in a mirror. Reg resisted the disconcerting sensation and fired. Just as he would in its situation, the copy dropped and covered its head. As soon as it recovered, it braced its wrists against its knee and aimed at Reg.

Reg desperately sought cover, and found a shelf of stone protruding from the wall. He dove behind it just as his opposite fired. Bullets ricocheted off stone, and smoke and the smell of sulfur filled the air. Reg peeked around the edge and saw his copy scanning around for him. He turned and pressed his back to the rock, trying to steady his erratic breathing. He just had to hide, keep himself safe, until Querry, Frolic, or Jean-Andre destroyed the other Reg.

More bullets pinged off the stone. Reg risked a look beyond his cover. All of the others fought with their opposites, Frolic crossing swords with his doppelgänger, Querry trading blows with his copy, Jean-Andre firing on the other Belvaisian, and Starling exchanging volleys of magical energy with his replica. The other Reg pushed his spectacles up the bridge of his nose and grinned madly as he approached. The light on the glass obscured his eyes. Still, Reg crouched, waiting for one of his friends to save him as they always did.

Above the din of the others fighting, Reg heard his nemesis approach, his fancy, custom-made, wing-tip shoes clicking on the stone. Reg still thought Querry would rescue him, and he worked his body into the corner. Still the other Reg drew nearer. Reg knew Querry would save him; Querry always saved him; he had since they'd been boys.

The shadow of the other Reg stretched long before it as it approached the corner where Reg cowered. Reg now knew no one would save him. In that moment, he realized how much he'd always relied on Querry to protect him. Though he'd fought beside his friends, somewhere in the back of his mind, he'd always depended upon Querry to ultimately face the threats. He could take care of himself, but he'd still always expected Querry to come to his rescue. He'd always placed his fate in Querry's hands, but he couldn't do it any longer. He had to face this threat himself, alone. It was his greatest fear, but he had only himself to rely on.

Reg peeked past the stone wall and saw his copy walking leisurely toward him. He knew he was on his own, not because Querry didn't treasure him, but because Querry trusted in Reg's abilities. Reg, determined to prove him right, looked down his sights at his replica's belly. Querry believed in him. So did Frolic. He wasn't a damsel waiting to be saved. No. He could take care of himself. Reg squeezed the trigger, and his bullet tore through his mirror image, dissolving it into a column of smoke.

Reg collapsed, his ass smacking the smooth stone. He wanted to help his friends, but he knew they had to face themselves and their weaknesses as he had. He wondered if they could accomplish it. Still, he mopped the sweat from his brow with his sleeve and reloaded his guns. Maybe for once, he'd be the one winning the day.

FROLIC FACED an exact duplicate of himself, except that the other clockwork boy lacked the embellishments to its hair Frolic had acquired traveling through the jungle, and of course it didn't have the resplendent, golden wings sprouting from its back. It wore garments like Frolic had when Querry had found him in the doll maker's cellar: a lacey shirt, short, velveteen trousers, hose, and little blue shoes with bows on top. Frolic hated the sight of it looking so obviously like a doll and nothing else. Its expression was vapid: a dull smile and wide, empty eyes. To Frolic, it personified everything he detested about himself, and he drew his sword to destroy it.

Frolic thrust his weapon toward the doll's heart, but with remarkable speed, it reached up and grabbed his blade. Its insipid grin never faltered as it snapped the enchanted sword in half with a twist of its wrist. Frolic stared in horror at his beloved sword. The doll used his distraction to draw back and hit him in the face. It felt like getting smacked with a metal bar, and Frolic heard a clang inside his skull as he flew backward and landed on the floor. Before he could get back to his feet, his duplicate jumped and straddled him, grabbing the sides of his hair and smacking the back of his head against the stone. Frolic's vision grew fuzzy, and he stabbed desperately at his enemy with the remains of his weapon. The sword tore through the other Frolic's skin, but its metal skeleton prevented any real damage.

Reg called out to Frolic, his voice sounding garbled and far away. A shot rang out, striking the imitation Frolic in the shoulder. The bullet pinged off the doppelgänger's gold bone, once again inflicting little injury, but managing to knock the pretender back. Frolic used the few seconds Reg had bought him to reverse their positions, hurrying to push his duplicate to its back and hold his blade to its throat.

Unfazed, the pretty doll backhanded Frolic in the cheek, sending him slumping on his side. It arched its back and got to its feet in a seamless motion. Frolic rolled just in time to avoid the foot it aimed at his face. He grabbed for the duplicate's leg, hoping to throw it off balance, but it stepped out of reach and kicked him in the ribs, driving the air from his lungs. Coughing and gasping, Frolic struggled to sit up and scuttle away from his double, but before he could, it reached down, took hold of his throat, and lifted him off his feet.

Frolic couldn't breathe, and the lack of water vapor to produce steam made his gears move slowly. He found it increasingly difficult to move his limbs, as if the mechanisms inside him had rusted and couldn't turn. As Frolic twisted and clawed at the doll's arm in an attempt to free himself, it looked up at him with the same, serene smile. It was just too strong and too fast. It wasn't human, but a machine with far superior power and resilience. Then, just as he was about to lose consciousness, Frolic realized he had the same advantage. He didn't want to be different from Querry and Reg, but he was. He didn't like being metal and gears instead of flesh, but he was. If he wanted to save himself, he had to use the advantages he'd been given. With the last of his strength, Frolic drove his truncated sword into the other's wide, golden eye. It shattered and released a plume of steam. The imitation howled with pain and dropped Frolic to cover its ruined eye.

Frolic landed on his feet and staggered back a few steps, swallowing air until he recovered his normal range of motion. Then he grabbed his duplicate's corkscrew curls, held its head, and drove his fist into the side of its face over and over. He couldn't think of it, or himself, as human, he knew. Metal dented and caved in beneath Frolic's onslaught. The doll's beautiful face became misshapen and grotesque. When it tried to strike back, Frolic seized it just above its bicep and pulled, severing the joint with a loud pop and a grinding of gears. Its arm dangled uselessly beside it. Then, feeling like he moved through some horrific nightmare, Frolic drew back and plunged his hand into the other clockwork's chest, just beneath its metal sternum. He drove his arm up until his fist closed around a blistering hot, glass orb. Frolic squeezed, shattering the other doll's heart, destroying it the same way he'd once been killed. As soon as he did, it dissolved into a sheet of steam and dispersed.

All around Frolic, the others faced similar obstacles. Reg, Tom, the mercenaries, and Jack Owens seemed to have defeated their doubles, but Corny still struggled against a version of herself in a ridiculously elaborate, upholstered dress, and the baron battled another wizard with gouts of flame and flashes of colored light. As Frolic hurried to help them, he hoped none of them had seen what he'd had to do. He didn't want them to know what he, a machine, was really capable of inflicting.

THE SON of a bitch was fast, but Querry was fast, so why wouldn't he be? Querry was still the real thing, and he had no doubt he'd prevail over a cheap imitation. He couldn't help but admire the way his double moved with the grace and fluidity of a cat as it dived to avoid his bullet, tucked into a roll, and fired on him all at the same time.

Querry dodged to the left, his boots sliding across the smooth stone as if it were ice. As soon as he skidded to a stop, he crouched and aimed at his duplicate again. This time, the other Querry took a grapple from his belt, shot it into the darkness above them, and soared into the air with a delighted chuckle Querry knew well. Swearing, Querry peered into the gloom through his night vision lenses, searching the shadows until he found the other looking back at him through identical goggles. Querry wondered if he looked as smug as his doppelgänger when he grinned. Instead of thinking too much on it, he located the rope the other Querry clung to, looked down his sight, and fired. Querry had always been a decent enough shot, but he didn't have Reg's uncanny aim, so it surprised him a bit when his bullet severed the rope.

The other Querry landed lightly, barely raising a cloud of dust. He drew his sword, and Querry mirrored the action. Both of them ran to face each other, their boots making almost no sound against the stone floors. Their blades met with a resounding clang and the scrape of metal against metal. The duplicate attacked, and Querry parried. Querry attacked, and his copy dodged. They sparred back and forth, each of them landing a glancing blow here and there, but neither causing any real injury.

Querry started to sweat as the duel continued, neither of them getting the upper hand. Both of them slowed as their muscles started to fatigue. Querry heard the cacophony of magic, swordplay, and gunfire around him as the others fought their duplicates. He just wanted to dispatch this annoying copy of himself so he could make sure Reg and Frolic were all right. Even though he'd tired the bastard out, it continued to slash at him with an exact replica of his rapier. Querry blocked most of the attacks, sustaining only a few scratches, but he didn't manage to hurt the imitation, either. Damn it, why did he have to be so good?

Querry feigned to the left before swinging his fist at his double's ribs. Querry wouldn't have been fooled by such a trick, and it wasn't, either. It leapt back a few inches and avoided the blow. Querry cursed again and spit on the ground. How the hell could he best something as clever, quick, agile, and experienced as himself? It anticipated every ruse, parried every attack, and returned with every bit of Querry's speed. Worse yet, it was better equipped than Querry, having not lost most of its gear in the jungle. Even so, he saw his own frustration mirrored on its face.

Somewhere behind him, Frolic cried out, and a shot followed. Without even thinking about it, Querry spun to make sure his beauty wasn't hurt. He no sooner located Frolic, who stood with Reg and Jean-Andre, fighting the Belvaisian's double, when he felt a slash across his lower back. He heard the leather of his waistcoat tear, but the metal plates beneath it saved his skin from a similar wound. Twirling back around, Querry raised his sword just in time to block the other's blade, which it aimed directly at his throat. He still saw no end to their battle in the near future, so he kept fighting, trying desperately to think of something the other Querry wouldn't expect. And then it came to him. He would never, ever surrender.

So that's exactly what he did. "That's it! I give up. I'm finished." He threw down his sword and pistol. The other Querry looked at the discarded weapons with total confusion. That was when Querry kicked himself in the bollocks. He winced vicariously as his doppelgänger doubled over. "I can't believe I fell for that," Querry said and laughed at his other self.

The other Querry was straightening up once more, and the look on its face was pure murder. Querry stopped laughing abruptly under the intensity of that gaze.

"Querry, drop!" Starling yelled over the chaos of the battle.

Without a second thought, Querry fell to his knees and covered his head with his arms. A bright, bluish-green stream of magic sliced through the stale air just above his head, striking his adversary in the chest and knocking it to its back. Querry heard the sick, hollow thud of its skull against the stone. It lay stunned and twitching.

"Hurry and finish it off," Starling called.

In a shocked daze, Querry stumbled over and drove the point of his sword through his double's windpipe. It gurgled for a moment, spitting up blood, before disappearing with a puff of smoke. Breathing hard, Querry looked around the room. The others had defeated their doppelgängers, and aside from some minor scrapes and bruises, they looked unharmed. Reg and Frolic busily bandaged Jean-Andre's hand with some strips of fabric that had been Reg's right sleeve. Corny examined a gash on the side of Jack Owens's waist. Querry wandered over to the baron, who held a handkerchief to a burn on the side of his neck.

"Thanks for that," he said sheepishly, staring at his boots. "What gave you the idea?"

Starling snorted out a surprised laugh. "I simply waited for your duplicate to do something rash and stupid. How in the world did you not know to do the same?"

"I—what are you saying?"

Starling simply shook his head and clapped Querry on the shoulder before calling Tom over to tend to his wounds. He sat cross-legged on the floor while the glowering fey looked at the blisters on his neck. Querry sat down with Reg, Frolic, and Jean-Andre to take advantage of a little rest while the baron permitted it. He couldn't stop thinking about what Starling had said. Was he impulsive without even realizing it? Did everyone think he behaved like an ass, even his partners? If they did, maybe they were right. After all, the others had managed to defeat their doubles without help. Everyone but Querry. What had they seen that he hadn't? He'd spent his life in a world where he had to make split-second decisions, and it would prove a hard habit to break. His ability to think fast had saved his life plenty of times. Now, though, he kept mulling the details of the battle over and over, wondering what he'd missed, what he could have done differently.

None of them spoke as they sat patching up their wounds and sharing the remainder of their water and bits of dried meat and fruit. Querry wondered what his partners had experienced, what they didn't want to discuss. He didn't press them, though, because he didn't really want to talk either. As tired as he was, he was glad when Starling roused them to move on. Action he understood, and he needed a distraction from his thoughts. He found himself hoping he'd encounter something he could just kill, the good old-fashioned way.

CHAPTER 29

QUERRY FELT like he'd been walking for days, but it may have only been hours. He had no way to tell in the ever-present darkness. He only knew his thighs ached, his feet hurt, and his clothing and gear felt like they weighed a hundred pounds. All of them plodded along in almost complete silence. Only the sound of their feet, their breathing, and the scrape of Frolic dragging his crate cut through the tomb-like silence. To Querry, that was how he saw this place as they descended: a tomb. He saw no evidence of a life-giving fount of magical energy. This place felt beyond dead.

After Starling stumbled, fell to his knees, and couldn't stand again without Tom's assistance, he finally agreed to let them stop and rest. Querry found a rounded corner and collapsed, drawing Reg and Frolic's heads to his chest and wrapping his arms around them. To hell with what Owens or anyone else thought. What could they possibly do that would be worse than being stuck in this horrible place? He let the tension bleed out of his muscles as he raked his fingers through his lovers' hair. Reg's had grown past his shoulders, and he had to pin his fringe behind his ears to keep it out of his eyes. Querry liked running his fingers through it, and pondered if there was any way he might convince Reg to keep it long. He doubted it. Querry wondered if Frolic would keep the beads and feathers woven into his locks when they left this place. *If,* he reminded himself.

"I'm sorry," he said in a voice scratchy and thick from disuse, resting his cheek on the top of Reggie's head.

"For what?" Reg asked.

"For us even being here. For putting you two in danger. For just generally being an ass and not thinking things through."

Querry expected Reg to respond with some mild sarcasm, but he merely reached up and touched Querry's face. "We've been over this, love. Too many times."

"I'll make it up to you," Querry vowed. "I'll see we get out of this, no matter what it takes, and then I'll do something special for you two. We have all this gold. What should we do with it? Take a holiday? We can go anywhere in the world."

"I want to go home," Reg said in a broken whisper.

"We can't," Querry said, his heart shattering like glass. "That's my fault too."

"No, it's mine," Frolic said. "But it doesn't matter. What's done is done, and we can't change it. All we can do is keep living as best we can. Look how fortunate we are to be free and to be together. We almost weren't. We don't know how much time we have with each other, so we can't waste it on regret and wondering what might have been different."

Once again, Frolic, for all his lack of experience, proved the wisest of them. Querry and Reg sat silently contemplating the truth of his words.

"You two are all I need," Reg said. "I'm just feeling sentimental. Whatever has happened, no matter who's to blame, I love you more than ever. I suppose we should try to get some sleep."

Querry looked across the chamber they occupied to a small hallway thick with shadow. "How would you feel about sneaking off?"

Frolic giggled and cuddled closer to Querry, while Reg looked up at him with wide eyes and a wry smile tugging at his lips. "You're out of your mind. With everything going on, that's what you're thinking about? I guess I shouldn't be surprised. I know where you keep your brain by now, after all."

Querry leaned down and covered Reg's lips with his own. "Is that a no?"

Reg, already coloring, shook his head. "Not a no. I suppose there's nothing really happening just now, anyway."

Frolic kissed the back of Reg's hand, then Querry led them both to the mouth of the corridor.

"WE HAVE to be quiet," Reg panted as Querry tore his trouser flap open and gripped his erect cock greedily, possessively.

Querry made a grunt of acknowledgement before he sucked the skin of Reg's throat between his teeth and pushed Reg's foreskin back. He pressed Reg to the wall of the narrow corridor they occupied as he fondled Reg's fat, swollen cockhead and slick, leaking slit. Reg's sweat tasted divine, and so did Frolic's lips when Frolic caught Querry's long hair and turned his face to kiss him. Reg thrust into the tunnel Querry's fingers formed around his flesh, clawing at Querry's hair, while Frolic ground his erection against Querry's hip as he worked the buckles of Querry's leather waistcoat loose. Already the closeness, hot, damp air, and his arousal had Querry coated in perspiration. Querry pulled away from them just long enough to shrug off his armored vest.

Reg grasped Frolic by the hips and pulled him close, kissing him so hard their teeth scraped together. Frolic yanked Reg's shirttails free of his waistband and plunged his hands beneath Reg's linen and leather to knead the flesh of his chest. Reg cupped Frolic's ass and urged Frolic tighter against his belly and groin. Both of them circled their hips, rubbing their cocks together as they nipped and suckled each other's heated skin, their breath growing erratic.

Querry hurried out of his clothes and left them scattered over the floor. As much as he enjoyed watching Reg and Frolic together, at this rate, with the urgency and need they showed, they'd satisfy themselves before he ever got a chance to join in the fun. With a low moan, he gripped his erection at the base just as Frolic brushed Reg's shirt from his shoulders. Bloody hell, Reg had really toned up since coming to the jungle. His wiry muscles bulged and rippled as he wound his arms around Frolic. Querry had never imagined seeing Reg as he was now, with his long, sun-bleached hair, thick stubble, and taut, powerful body. Damn, he was beautiful, so strong and aggressively male, but still possessed of his gentle nature and quick wit. Frolic, of course, looked the same as ever as Reg peeled away his layers of clothing: flawlessly pale, perfectly proportioned, eternally adolescent, ideal in every way.

As soon as he got himself naked, Querry hurried to join his lovers. He pried them apart to take his place between them, pressing his palms to their ribs to push both of their backs against the wall. They joined hands as they stood side by side, allowing Querry to explore their bodies with his hands and mouth. He dropped to his knees, fondling Reg's full sac as he sucked Frolic's cock into his mouth. In minutes he brought Frolic to climax, and Frolic's knees knocked together as he gripped Querry's hair with one hand and reached for Reg with the other. As they kissed, Reg swallowed Frolic's cries of bliss. Querry turned his attention to Reg, hoping to show him the same pleasure, but his lovers had other ideas.

Reg and Frolic both turned and pressed their chests against the cool stone. They reached down and touched each other's erections, sliding their fingers up and down each other's hard flesh and turning their heads to kiss. Still on his knees, Querry burrowed his nose into Reg's cleft while he massaged the lithe crescent of Frolic's ass. Reg stepped to the side to open his legs, and Querry pressed his face between Reg's cheeks, his tongue seeking out and finding Reg's clenching, wrinkled rosette. As he ran the tip around the rim of Reg's opening, Querry imagined plunging deep inside him, feeling the familiar sensation of Reg's muscles hugging his cock. He wriggled his tongue inside Reg as his fingers found Frolic's opening and eased it open. Both of them moaned with need and muttered encouragements as they pushed back against Querry. When he could take no more, Querry got to his feet, ready to explode with the feelings these men inspired in him.

"I want to fuck you," he mumbled, staring down at both their asses arched forward in offering. "Both of you. Fuck, I wish I had two cocks."

Frolic looked over his shoulder and grinned at Querry, managing to look seductive, wanton, and innocent all at the same time. "I'm sure you'll manage, Querry."

Frolic licked his lips, making them glisten in the low light, his gaze met Querry's, and Querry was lost. He spit into his palm, rubbed the moisture over his throbbing, almost painful erection, and seized Frolic by the hips. He crossed his arms over Frolic's chest as he thrust into him, pushing past any resistance, desperate to be deep within him. Frolic cried out in a mélange of pain and pleasure as he spread his legs and leaned further forward, his back almost parallel to the floor. Reg pumped his cock and kissed his shoulder as Querry plowed into him, trying to be gentle but too aroused to control his frantic movements. Frolic cried out rhythmically with his release, his muscles clamping down on Querry's cock and his cheek pressed against the wall. Both Querry and Reg wound their arms around his waist to support him as he fell apart, once, and then again seconds later.

Frolic's flesh clung to Querry as he pulled out, as if reluctant to let him go. Querry missed his tight heat as soon as he left it, but he wanted his Reggie, his first love, the first man he'd ever been inside. He wanted his Reg to tremble with bliss and abandon from his touch, as he'd done years ago, before they were even grown men. Querry raked his nails lightly down Reg's sweaty back. He'd never tire of the feel of Reg's soft skin, now a rich, enticing bronze dotted with freckles. He bent to run his tongue up Reg's spine and savor the taste of his arousal.

"Reggie, fuck—"

"Please," Reg whispered, opening his thighs in invitation. As Frolic had, he looked over his shoulders with his eyes glazed and his lids heavy. His needy expression, full of lust and devotion, devastated Querry as Frolic's had.

Querry couldn't think or speak and only whimpered as he nodded. He sank back to his knees and ran his tongue along Reg's cleft to get him moist and ready. With his eyes closed, he listened to the sensuous sound of Frolic kissing, licking, and nipping along Reg's taut belly and up the sides of his waist. Reg giggled as Frolic grazed the ticklish spot above his hip. His laughter, and Frolic's resulting chuckle, made their bodies tremble delightfully. Querry mopped his chin with the back of his hand as he stood up. Reg bent at the waist, but Querry caught his hand and gently turned him around. He raked the overlong fringe out of Reggie's face and kissed him softly.

"God, Reggie, you're just as beautiful as the first day I saw you. I've loved you since then. I don't deserve either of you."

"Querry, that's not true," Frolic whispered.

Reg just told Querry to shut up, kissed him, wrapped his leg around Querry's waist, and guided Querry's cock to where he wanted it. Incredible heat and pressure surrounded Querry as Reg shuddered at the penetration. Querry seized his other thigh and lifted him off his feet, pressing into him and pushing his back against the wall.

"Oh, my love," Reg panted. "You... you're just the most alluring, passionate, incredible man... I... I can't tell you how I feel, you or Frolic. I'm so happy. So... good. I want more. I want this forever."

"Forever," Frolic said, pressing his lips to the corners of Querry and Reg's, all three of them kissing, opening their mouths and twining their tongues together.

Querry, reaching the limits of his endurance, lowered Reg to the floor, careful not to separate from his body. He paused in his movements, not quite ready to end their union, and just looked down at Reg's flushed, sparkling skin. "Beauty," Querry said, "there's still one thing we've never done together. I want to do everything with the two of you. Do you want that, Frolic?"

"I love touching you more than anything in the world," Frolic said.

"Then show me," Querry told him, taking his wrist and pulling him over. "Make love to me."

At first, Frolic gasped and hesitated, but then he smiled and knelt behind Querry. He held his hand to Querry's lips, and Querry sucked his fingers and lapped at his palm, getting it wet. Reg also planted damp kisses over Frolic's hand. When he removed it, Querry and Reg found each other's mouths.

Querry's spine stiffened as Frolic's fingers dipped into him, but Frolic deftly found his sweet spot, and Querry's apprehension drained away, replaced by intense pleasure. "Oh, beauty, that's perfect. Oh, Frolic, fuck. That's enough. I want you inside me. Let me share this with you."

Frolic haltingly penetrated Querry, clearly uncertain. It hurt; it had been a long time since Querry had been on this end of things and he would have paid half the gold he'd amassed for a tin of salve, but he struggled not to let on and add to Frolic's nerves. Reg gave a little squeal, and Querry realized he'd bitten down on Reggie's lip.

"It's all right, love," Reg whispered.

"Querry, move," Frolic said, resting his hands lightly on Querry's lower back. "Show me how you like it. Show me how fast and how deep you want me. I want it to be good for you."

"It's good," Querry said, circling his hips and setting the rhythm. "It's always good."

"Because we love each other?" Frolic asked in a throaty whisper.

"That's right, beauty," Reg said. "We're perfect together."

Querry saw a shadow block the firelight, but Reg and Frolic didn't seem to notice and kept moving and muttering endearments. Squinting into the gloom, Querry noticed a slight, graceful silhouette at the mouth of the hall. He knew by the glowing, green eyes that Tom Teezle watched them making love. At first he flinched, stunned and embarrassed, but just as the fey pressed his long finger to his mouth, signaling for Querry to stay quiet, Reg caught Querry's lips, and Frolic pushed deep into him. In seconds, Querry forgot about Tom. Let him watch. What did he care? Nothing mattered to Querry but his beautiful lovers and the amazing feelings they conjured in his body and heart.

Chapter 30

THOUGH THE gloomy half-light and monotonous stone walls remained the same, something felt different to Querry when he woke. He had no idea how long he'd slept after his quick tryst with his partners; it was impossible to tell without the cycle of day and night. Querry felt restless and eager to leave this dank pit. As much as he loved the night—to him it symbolized safety and freedom—the shadows here felt oppressive. The whole place felt like a prison he couldn't escape, and Querry hated it.

Something was about to happen; he felt it in his bones. He'd always possessed almost a sixth sense when it came to trouble. He felt it in the hairs on the back of his neck and the way his muscles tightened and twitched. The others were on edge as well: Frolic toyed with the beads and feathers in his hair, Reg flinched whenever someone spoke to him, and even Jean-Andre's amused apathy cracked, and he drew his pistol at shadows.

"Hold on," Jack Owens said after another several hours of plodding down corridors identical to those they'd traveled since entering the temple.

Everyone stopped walking, and Starling turned to face the mercenary, his brows lifted in curiosity.

The big man rubbed his forehead. "With all due respect, sir, we're getting nowhere fast. There ain't nothing here, and everybody knows it but you. We're out of food, almost out of ammunition, and almost out of water. Time to face facts, I say."

"Meaning what?" Starling asked.

"Meaning, it's time to admit we've lost, sir. A good soldier knows when to retreat."

"I am not giving up on this!" Starling's eyes widened, and he looked manic in the faltering light of his mystic lanterns.

"We are," Owens said. Istvan and Attila nodded. "We're leaving this godforsaken place. He turned to Corny and took her hand. "Come with us."

"But my friends—" Corny's eyes glittered as she stared at Frolic.

"Don't die down here, dove," Owens said in a voice so gentle Querry couldn't believe it came from the man he'd been traveling with all these weeks.

"I—but—"

"No," Frolic said. "It's all right, Corny. You should go with them. I want you to be safe."

"Frolic, are you sure? What will happen to you?" she asked, coming up to Frolic and gripping his shoulders.

"I don't know," he answered.

At that, she folded him in her arms and cried. Owens laid his hand on her back and said, "Listen. We'll wait outside the temple as long as we can. At least we can find fruit and collect rainwater."

"Go," Frolic said in a small voice.

Scrubbing her eyes with her fists, Corny nodded, kissed him on the cheek, and turned away to collect her gear. Without saying anything further, she and the three mercenaries began retracing their steps back through the twisting halls.

Starling stood stunned, mouth gaping, for a full minute. Then he ran to the mouth of the hall and called after the deserters. "Wait! Hold on, damn it! I'll pay you double! Triple! You can name your price! I'll pay you anything you want! Come back here. I demand it. You must obey me! You are still in my employ!"

Querry couldn't help feeling a little sorry for the poor, deluded fool. "They're not coming back, majesty."

"Damn it!" Starling punched the wall again and again, bloodying his knuckles until Querry caught his wrists and restrained him with some difficulty.

"You've got to get a hold of yourself," he told the baron.

"I—you're absolutely correct. I apologize. We'll press on without those cowards."

"I hardly think it's fair to call them cowards," Reg said, but without the hostility he usually aimed at Baron Starling. "They're only being practical. Sane."

"You are more than welcome to join them, Mr. Whitney!"

"Majesty," Querry warned, "I'll ask you to show Reg some respect. You bloody well know he deserves it. Look at all he's done for this mission even though he didn't have to."

"To hell with this nonsense," Reg spat, rightly irritated. "I think this is madness. Anything I've done has been for Querry and Frolic, nothing more."

"This is getting us nowhere," Jean-Andre said. In the heat of their debate, Querry had forgotten him. Now he wondered what the Belvaisian had to gain by staying and risking his life. Jean-Andre certainly didn't share the baron's idealism or zeal. Maybe he simply hoped to find more gold.

"The water is going to be a problem," Reg said.

"You should leave," Frolic said, his voice both insistent and full of fear. Querry had never heard him so afraid. "Let me go on alone. I don't need to eat or drink. Please, Baron Starling. Please let my friends go. I swear I'll find whatever you're looking for. Don't risk their lives, or your own."

Starling bunched his brows together as he regarded Frolic, considering. Querry didn't know if the baron had researched Frolic's history somehow, but he couldn't possibly know how much the thought of being alone, especially in a dank, underground chamber so like the cellar where he'd waited for nearly a century, terrified the clockwork boy. Querry did, and the depth of his lover's selfless bravery and devotion astounded him.

"Beauty," Querry said in a weak voice, "I'd sooner starve to death next to you than leave you here alone. I won't even think about it."

"Nor will I," Reg said. "Remember what we promised each other. I won't abandon you just because things are a little tenuous."

"But Reggie—"

Reg held up his hand to stop Frolic's arguments. "Forever, remember?"

THEY DIDN'T get much farther before the path became steep, even narrower, and jaggedly hewn instead of smooth and polished. As small as he was, Frolic's wings scraped against the walls even though he folded them close to his body. The others had to slouch and often turn sideways to navigate the close quarters. He continued, dragging the crate full of gold nuggets, toward a faint voice, a promise luring him on, a voice calling him instead of warning him away as everything else had. For the first time since entering the accursed temple, he felt a glimmer of hope waiting at the bottom of the tunnel.

"We should hurry," he said, his voice breaking hours of silence. "We're almost there. We're really going to make it."

"I agree," Starling said, smiling. Frolic didn't remember seeing him smile before, at least not with genuine happiness. Until now, his smiles had all been bitter mockeries of hope and joy, mockeries of himself. "The magic is strong. It's flowing up from below. We must move faster. We must get to the source." The baron cackled maniacally and ran as best he could bent almost in half. "I'm coming!"

Querry and Reg cast confused glances at one another before hurrying to follow, and Jean-Andre shook his head and pinched the bridge of his nose. Tom Teezle hesitated, hanging back until he and Frolic were alone in the tunnel. The fey's eyes burned with emerald fire as he looked deep into Frolic's eyes. When he touched Frolic's elbow, Frolic recoiled in alarm from both his rapacious expression and the power surging from him.

"It is time for you to fulfill your contract with me, Frolic."

"I won't do anything to hurt anyone," Frolic hurried to say. Right now, Tom really frightened him. "I never agreed to hurt anyone."

Tom stroked Frolic's cheek with the back of his hand and licked his lips. Frolic recognized the spark in his eyes: he saw it in his lovers' gazes when they wanted to touch him. That same desperation wafted from Tom, and Frolic wanted to run from him because it felt nothing like being with Querry and Reg.

"You swore an oath to me, and you must follow through. There are rules."

"What, then?" Frolic breathed.

Tom smiled, bearing his teeth. "Give me the deepest desire of your heart. Give me your blackest and most hidden secret, the one you've never even told to your lovers. The one you fear even to think about when you're alone. Give me that piece of yourself that no one has ever seen. Do not lie to me, or I'll know."

Frolic exhaled, profoundly relieved. He'd expected Tom to demand something horrible. In a way, it was liberating to give voice to the thoughts that had tormented him even before leaving Thalacea. His words came out in a rush, tumbling from his lips almost before forming in his mind. "I don't want to be different. I hate it. For a long time, I thought I wanted to be human like Querry and Reg. I wanted to be able to die when they did, so I wouldn't be alone. But now—I'm so ashamed to even think this way, but I don't want to be human anymore. Humans are so easy to break. I don't want to have to depend on food and water. I like being strong. I mean, I can fly. You, the fey, and me, we can do so many things they can't...."

"Say it. Give it to me."

"I wish I could make Querry and Reg like me."

"Frolic, tell me." Tom was panting and clutching the straps that held Frolic's wings to his back.

Frolic squeezed his eyes shut as tight as he could. He couldn't bear to look Tom in the eye as he said what he couldn't even admit to himself until now. "We're... I'm... more. I'm better than a human."

Tom threw his head back, laughed victoriously, and clapped his hands. Whisper howled with fright and buried his face in Frolic's hair. Frolic had no idea what had just happened, what Tom could possibly have gained from his confession, but a green glow outlined the fey, and he seemed taller and far more powerful. In fact, Tom seemed almost as much a force of nature as Frolic's father, the gentleman. What had changed in him all of a sudden?

Frolic never got a chance to ask, because Tom waved his hand, and they all stood in a rounded chamber with a raised dais in the center. The ceiling was so high Frolic couldn't see it, and from somewhere, a cold, blue light shone on the platform and the rough-cut, stone stairs spiraling around it. Tom hadn't been able to transport himself or others outside the temple. Whatever changed in him must have negated that limitation.

"Come," something atop the pulpit whispered. "Come to me. I've been waiting."

Starling, so ecstatic at the discovery of what could only be the wellspring, never noticed the drastic change in his servant. The baron punched the air and hooted in a very un-aristocratic way. "I knew I could do it! I knew everything inflicted on me meant something. There was a point to everything after all. A point!"

The baron, chuckling madly and smiling until he looked like he'd split his face in two, ran up to Jean-Andre and kissed him hard on the mouth. "Merci, monsieur," Starling said, spinning Jean-Andre around as if they waltzed. "Merci, mon ami. If only I were a younger man, I could show you such gratitude."

Jean-Andre, so much more relaxed and less susceptible to surprise than any human Frolic had ever met, just winked and said, "You seem in perfect health to me, monsieur."

Starling kissed him again before moving to stand in front of Reg. "Mr. Whitney. Reg. I sorely misjudged you, sir. You are brave, capable, and dedicated to your lovers. They are fortunate men indeed." He extended his hand, and Reg stared at it a moment before grasping it and shaking.

"Querrilous," Starling said, touching Querry's hair lightly and then cupping his cheek. His eyes misted, and a few tears spilled down his cheeks, though Frolic couldn't imagine why. "Querry."

"Majesty?" Querry asked, perplexed.

Starling blinked, shook his head, and kissed Querry softly on the top of his hair. Then he moved on to Frolic.

Frolic felt very self-conscious as Starling regarded him with red, watery eyes and a strange, almost sad smile. "Do you know that you're a marvel?"

Frolic shuffled his feet and looked at his worn and filthy boots. "I suppose."

"You are, dear Frolic. You're very special. A very special person. I'm glad I had the opportunity to meet you."

"Um, thank you. And likewise, Baron Starling." Frolic extended his hand, as was only polite. Instead of taking it, Starling wrapped his arms around Frolic and hugged him tight.

"Now then," the baron said, "let us all ascend those stairs together. After all, we would not be here if not for each other, so let us share in this great victory."

His triumphant mood spread, and everyone but Frolic and Tom Teezle clapped.

"Come," the voice whispered, like the distant sound of the waves crashing on the beach, or the wind rustling the high grass. Frolic felt an almost physical pull as he walked slowly up the stairs, ready to witness the magical fount the others had spoken of with such disbelief and awe. Finally he stepped onto the dais, eager to behold the wonder.

The sight waiting for him made Frolic cry out. He stumbled backward and almost plummeted from the platform. On a stone slab lay the naked and desiccated body of a tall faerie. A dozen long, iron spikes held it to the rock. Though little more than a skeleton wrapped in wrinkled, gray skin, it was alive. Frolic sensed the life force behind its sightless, milky eyes, and now and then it twitched slightly and a horrific, raspy sound escaped its leathery lips.

Jean-Andre covered his eyes with his arm and whimpered. "I 'ave... never seen something so... 'orrible." His native accent came forward with his distress.

Reg clutched his stomach and threw up over the edge of the platform. Then he buried his face against Querry's chest and sobbed. Querry held him, his face absent of both color and emotion.

"Kill it," Frolic choked out, not even sure he spoke aloud. It all felt like a horrible nightmare. "Querry... somebody put a stop to this."

"What is the meaning of this?" Starling demanded. "Teezle!"

"I am no longer yours to command, human," the fey said, as if oblivious to the misery of his kin. "If you wish something of me now, it will cost."

"I must understand," Starling said. "What is the price of that?"

"Everything," Tom said with a shrug.

"Very well. Explain this... this atrocity."

Frolic didn't think anything in the world could explain something so awful. If he had his sword, he would end this creature's misery, for he knew it had lasted a long, long time. His lonely years in the doll maker's cellar were the blink of an eye in comparison.

Tom Teezle, unmoved, knelt beside the other faerie's table. He ran his fingers over the swirling script engraved around the base. Then he gasped as he swore a strong oath in his language. "This... this is the first of my kind. Deposed by his son, him who we call Good Father, the Shining One. The tales of his defeat of this creature, his father, were thought to be mere legend, metaphor. They say the Good Father saved the races of fey and man by slaying his sire, who sought only to devour them. Not even my people believed these stories. Not even the oldest of the Fair Folk has ever seen the

Radiant One. If you fool mortals have any sense, you'll leave and forget you've ever seen this place. It is not meant to be known. We should have listened to everything warning us away. We shouldn't be here."

"But, but the source of all life, the great magic," Starling stammered.

"You ass!" Tom got to his feet and slapped the baron with the back of his hand. "You misunderstood those texts you stole from my people. This is the taker of life and of magic. Leave it."

Then the Baron Starling did something Frolic couldn't believe he could endure: he stood beside the twisted form of the first of the fey, put his palms against the stone on either side of its head, and looked down at its face. For a long time he neither moved nor spoke, but simply stared into those cloudy, yellowed, blind orbs.

"It's not only machines that steal life," Frolic said. "Magic is just as bad. Anything powerful can be evil in the hands of someone who wants to do harm."

Starling ignored him and continued to gaze into the awful creature's face.

"Majesty?" Querry sounded worried, which worried Frolic. Querry didn't panic over just anything. "Starling?"

The baron didn't respond, apparently transfixed by something Frolic couldn't comprehend. He dared to take two steps closer to the baron, fighting past his terror and disgust. When he nudged Starling's shoulder, the aristocrat didn't acknowledge him. Frolic shoved him harder. Starling stumbled to regain his balance, but he didn't look away from the withered faerie. Then Starling plunged his hand through the cracked, wizened skin and pulled out the creature's dehydrated heart. Everyone stood awestruck as he bit into it with a feral growl. A puff of rust-colored dust rose from the organ, but Baron Starling kept eating, determined to consume the fey's heart. Querry tried to wrench it away, but Starling swatted him in the face and knocked him down. Jean-Andre drew his unique pistol, but it flew from his hand and tumbled down the stairs with a gesture from the baron.

No matter what any of them attempted, Starling managed to consume the dried-up organ. Frolic and his mates winced at the disturbing dry, crunching sounds as Starling's teeth ground the desiccated flesh. Frolic might not be able to eat, but he could taste, and the imagined taste of that horrific organ was enough to make him wretch even though he couldn't vomit. Afterward, Starling faced them, his chest heaving and red-brown smears covering his face. Frolic wondered if the others saw the thin red line connecting the baron to the ancient faerie. If his sword hadn't been destroyed, Frolic knew he could have severed it. No one else controlled magic, though, except—

"Tom," Frolic yelled. "Stop this. Do something!"

"No." The faerie crossed his arms and sneered. "He has it coming. Thanks to you, Frolic, I am free of him. I'll watch him destroy himself and spit on his corpse." With that, Tom Teezle shimmered and disappeared.

Frolic had no time to contemplate the faerie's indifference, because Starling turned on them and raised his hands.

CHAPTER 31

THOUGH HE didn't understand what had happened to the baron, fear and survival instinct took over, and Reg raised one of his pistols and fired on the twisted and altered body of the aristocrat. Without conscious intent, knowing only that he had to stop whatever was happening, Reg squeezed his trigger until he depleted his ammunition, and kept squeezing even after he'd emptied the magazine. Jean-Andre raised his gun and followed suit.

Their bullets fell out of the air and pinged uselessly at Starling's feet. The baron flicked his fingers in their direction, a force struck them like a stone wall, and Reg and Jean-Andre flew from the dais. Reg landed on the stone floor a dozen feet below, the breath knocked from his lungs and sure he'd broken his spine. For a few minutes he couldn't move and stared at the shadows above him with wavering vision. Then a hand clasped his wrist and pulled him to his feet. Jean-Andre's lips moved, but all Reg heard was the rhythmic throb of his pulse in his head.

"Take a deep breath," Jean-Andre advised.

Reg did, and his sight and hearing clarified with the return of air to his lungs. Upon hitting the ground, his pistol had flown from his hand and slid somewhere into the shadows. He drew the other and ran for the steps, shouting over his shoulder to Jean-Andre. "What the hell is going on?"

"It would seem the Anglican lord mistranslated some of the texts. If I have to guess, I'd say the creature on the slab has gained control of him."

Reg felt like he'd been stabbed in the chest. "Which means—"

"*Oui.* Which means your Querrilous and Frolic are bound by contract not to harm him and what he has become. It is up to us."

They reached the foot of the steps and took them two at a time. Just before they reached the top of the platform, Reg caught Jean-Andre's elbow and pulled him down into a crouch. "What are we going to do?"

Jean-Andre regarded his pistol. "I have two shots left. You?"

"Five or six?" Reg did some quick calculations, but he really didn't know.

"Then I will try to draw the baron's attention. You must sneak around behind him, and make those shots count. Understand?"

Reg nodded, wishing he had his spectacles and could see properly. Jean-Andre's face looked blurred only inches from his own, but Reg didn't miss the other man's odd expression.

"Ah, Reginald. Forgive me, but I don't want to die without ever having done this." He grabbed Reg by the collar and pulled him into a passionate, open-mouthed kiss. Reg didn't know if fear or the battle-lust in his blood compelled him, but he kissed back for all he was worth. When they separated, Jean-Andre smoothed Reg's hair and gave him a quick peck on the bridge of his nose. Then he stood and strode to the center of the platform and faced the Baron Starling, or whatever he'd become.

Starling faced him. For a second, the strange, blue glow left his eyes. "Jean-Andre?"

"Baron Starling, you must fight this thing," the Belvaisian said in response.

Starling trembled and clawed at the sides of his head, tearing out clumps of hair. He fell to his knees and screamed until his voice broke.

"Come on, majesty," Querry encouraged.

When the baron went silent and got back on his feet, it was clear to all of them he'd lost the battle. His eyes burned with what Reg somehow knew was pure, arcane power, and magical energy swirled in the air around him. The voice that issued from him was as deep and resounding as thunder. It echoed through the massive chamber and shook the rocks. Just the sound made Reg want to curl in a ball and whimper, but he forced himself to crouch and creep slowly and carefully toward Starling's flank.

"What a disgusting feeling, inhabiting such a frail body," the voice said, looking at Starling's outstretched hands with contempt. Then the baron looked down at the slab. "Is this what has become of my form? Unacceptable." Starling touched the husk with a glowing hand, and it twitched and made a rattling noise. Its flesh grew just a little plumper, its skin less wrinkled, and bright, fresh blood oozed from the spears holding it to the stone.

Reg, ten feet behind the baron now, lifted his gun, lined it up with Starling's head, and pulled the trigger three times in quick succession. Just in time, Starling spun around and raised his hand. He not only stopped the bullets, but reversed their course and sent them back toward Reg. Reg had no time to react, and two of the bullets struck the metal reinforced plates of the vest Frolic had made him and bounced off almost harmlessly. The third grazed him just below his elbow. Despite the great pain and the sheet of blood coating his arm, Reg knew the bullet had done little real damage, so he bit his lips and pressed the heel of his hand against the wound.

Several things happened at once. Querry yelled Reg's name, drew his sword, and rushed Starling. He got within two feet of the baron before he crumpled, holding his stomach. As Querry forced himself to take another step, Jean-Andre fired on Starling. Starling raised his right arm, lifting Jean-Andre high into the air. When he lowered his arm, Jean-Andre smacked against the stone, knocked instantly unconscious. The baron magically lifted his limp body from the floor of the dais for another blow.

"Stop! You'll kill him!" Frolic stood between Starling and Jean-Andre, spreading his wings into a protective wall. "You don't have to hurt us. We aren't the ones who did this to you."

Starling canted his head to an almost unnatural angle and blinked his glowing eyes. "What in the name of the first stars are you? You are neither man nor fey. Has a new race of beings emerged while I've been a prisoner here? Has it been so long?" He took a few steps toward Frolic, and though Frolic looked terrified, he stood his ground.

"You are very powerful," the baron continued. "The magic within you is strong and complex. It will go a long way toward helping me restore myself."

Everyone stood still. "What do you mean?" Frolic asked in a quivering whisper.

Baron Starling traced around the edge of Frolic's face with the tip of his finger. He ran his hand down Frolic's throat before holding it over his heart. Starling exhaled with satisfaction, and his eyelids fluttered with bliss. If Reg really concentrated, he could see a faint, golden light moving from Frolic's chest, down Starling's arm, and across the gossamer thread tethering him to the ancient creature on the block. Frolic's golden eyes dimmed as the faerie fleshed out, looking healthier by the second. Frolic tried to fish for something in his pocket, but he seemed to have great difficulty lifting his arm and moving his fingers. His eyelids drooped, and his slight shoulders curled forward. His wings fell, the tips of the feathers scraping the ground.

Ignoring the blood trickling from his eyes and nose, Querry fought through the pain Starling's magical contract inflicted. He raised his blade and thrust it at the baron, but the agony was too much for him, and he collapsed, coughing up mouthfuls of frothy blood.

"Leave him alone!" Reg grabbed Starling by the shoulders and tried to pull him away from Frolic, but it was like trying to move the mountain itself. The baron never so much as flinched when Reg struck him in the side of the head. He seemed made of rock, cut from the floor of the temple itself. Reg threw himself at the baron, planning to tackle him. He had to stop him, no matter what it took. Just as Reg launched himself at Starling, Starling raised his unoccupied hand and swatted him away like a fly. Reg flew through the air and landed hard on his side. Disregarding what felt like at least a few cracked ribs, Reg hurried to stand. Astoundingly, Querry had pushed himself up on his hands and knees. He clutched Starling's trouser leg, trying to haul himself up. Frolic was almost gone.

"Reggie," the clockwork boy panted, struggling to draw breath, "my... birthday...." Then Frolic collapsed, unable to finish his statement.

Reg hurried to his prone body and touched his cool cheek. Frolic's eyes, while open, looked dull and dead. He wasn't quite gone, though: a glittering, golden stream of light twined up from his heart to the baron's hand. In a panic, Reg covered Frolic's chest with his palms, as if he could hold his essence in. The blood from Reg's wound splattered Frolic's waistcoat. What could he have meant by mentioning his birthday? Maybe he'd been delirious. With no other straw to grasp, Reg thought back to the odd little celebration, trying to recall anything that could save them. His gaze fell on the simple locket Kristof had given Frolic, twisted up in the chain of the clockwork angel's feather Frolic kept as a charm. He flipped it open. Kristof had said it would show whatever one most wanted to see, and Reg concentrated on seeing something, anything, that could save Frolic's life.

"This creature's magic will not be enough," Starling said. "I must seek out more."

Tears stung Reg's eyes as he stared into the swirling mutable depths of the locket. Slowly, a picture formed and clarified: an image of the pruning shears the gentleman had given Frolic at the party. Understanding, Reg reached into Frolic's pocket and seized them. He knew he'd only have one chance, but he couldn't wait any longer or he'd lose Frolic. He rose to his knees, lunged forward, and snipped the glittering thread binding Starling to the faerie.

THE EXCRUCIATING feeling of Querry's bones and organs going through a meat grinder ceased abruptly, and he lifted his head from the cool stone and tried to wipe the worst of the blood from his face. For the last few minutes, he had been able to perceive nothing but the pain, and he knew he'd come close to killing himself. Sitting up, still aching, he saw Reg dragging Frolic's limp body away from the baron with much difficulty. Frolic was heavy, but Reg was determined. Jean-Andre lay a few feet away, knocked out and bleeding from a gash across his forehead.

Starling looked around as if he had no idea what had just happened. Maybe he didn't. Then his gaze locked with Querry's, and he knelt to grab Querry by the shoulders. "Kill me, Querry."

"What?" Querry gasped.

"I feel it inside me, clawing its way back up, trying to take over. It's only a matter of time. You must kill me before it succeeds, or everyone here, maybe everyone in the world, is doomed."

"Majesty, I can't even hurt you! Just trying to get you off Frolic about did me in," Querry argued.

"Of course." Starling looked tired, defeated, and resigned. Querry had an irrational desire to embrace and comfort him. "Querrilous Knotte. Frolic. I hereby release you from your contracts. Any and all obligations between you and me are rendered null and void. Now, Querry, please. You know what needs to be done, and you must hurry." Starling pressed the hilt of Querry's sword into his hand.

"I don't want to." Querry knew he sounded silly and immature, but he meant it and couldn't think of a more eloquent way to say so. "I actually kind of like you, majesty."

The baron held Querry's cheeks in his hands and looked deep into Querry's eyes. "I have nothing left to live for now."

"That's not true," Querry started to say.

"This is no time for debate, Querry. You must listen to me. I have made a grievous error. I wanted to save the world, but my motivations don't matter now. I only ask that you don't let this world's destruction be my legacy instead. You must kill me, and then you must burn my body and this thing's heart along with it. Let me die knowing you're safe and that no one else has been hurt by my foolishness. Do it for your lovers if you cannot do it for me. I beg you, Querry. Don't let me become a monster. Can I count on you as I've come to do? One last time?"

With a bitter taste in his mouth and tears streaming down his cheeks, Querry nodded. He didn't know why this hurt so damn much, but it hurt like a bitch to lose Starling and the friendship they'd nurtured.

Starling swiped away Querry's tears with the back of his hand. "I never wanted to make you suffer. I regret that this is the only way. You must do this for me."

"Yes," Querry choked out. "Yes, sir."

The baron smiled at that and kissed Querry on the cheek. "Good boy. Here," Starling rasped as he slipped something from within his coat and into Querry's. "This is my spell book. It belongs to you now. Keep it safe." He barely finished his sentence when his eyes rolled back in his head, and he gurgled. "It's coming!"

Querry folded Baron Gavindale Starling in his arms and held him. Then he drew his dagger and drove it beneath the base of the baron's skull. Starling twitched only once before he fell still.

"No!" the creature on the slab growled as the baron's body lay limp in Querry's arms. Querry heard a strange sucking noise, followed by a papery footstep. It occurred to Querry that the thing must be freeing itself from the iron spikes just before the monster grabbed Querry and Starling's corpse and wrenched them apart. Querry grasped at Starling's body and screamed until he lost his voice.

"Do shut up," the creature said, tossing Querry across the room where he hit the wall of the chamber. Reg and Frolic scrambled to check on him. "There's still a bit of magic left in you," the ancient faerie observed before placing his mouth over the corpse's. The fey absorbed residual magical energy seeping out of Starling's body. Its skin became plumper and smoother even as Starling shriveled slightly, the color fading from his flesh.

"This has to stop," Frolic stood with grim determination.

Reg grabbed Frolic's arm. "You can't, Frolic. Think what happened last time it touched you. It will kill you, and your magic will make it even stronger."

"Reggie—" Frolic tried to protest, but Querry placed his hand on Frolic's arm as well and shook his head.

"You can't," Querry croaked. Frolic opened his mouth to argue, but his attention, along with Querry's and Reg's, was drawn to the sound of bones cracking. The creature broke into the baron's rib cage and reached in with a clawed hand, tearing out Starling's heart.

"I'll have this back," it said with a malicious grin. The ancient faerie's hair grew lusher, and its eyes sparkled with new life. It angled the stolen organ toward the hole the baron had made in its chest moments before. Tendrils like vines snaked out of that cavity and eagerly reached for the heart. Before they could properly grip it, Tom Teezle appeared out of thin air and slapped the organ out of the monster's grasp.

"Oh no you don't," he shouted before disappearing. He reappeared seconds later, catching the heart before it could hit the ground.

"No! I won't be undone!" the ancient fey cried and lunged at Teezle, but Tom disappeared again before the monster could lay hands on him. The creature roared with anger and frustration.

Tom reemerged behind Querry and his mates. "We have to make sure he doesn't get this," Tom explained. "Or me."

"Or Frolic," Reg added. "Tom, take him and the heart someplace safe. Querry and I will deal with this."

"Reggie, no," Frolic protested.

"This is not up for debate, Frolic! We can't allow him to gain any more power if we have any hope of defeating him! You're going with Tom!" Reg shouted, inviting no more arguments. Teezle didn't wait for an answer. He grabbed Frolic by his shirt and nodded.

"Not this time, *Tom!*" the heartless fey snarled and pointed at them.

"Blast," Tom spat.

"What?" Reg asked.

"I can't travel. He's done something. I'm trapped."

"We're trapped," Frolic clarified.

"Split up," Querry shouted, grabbing the heart and dashing away from his friends. "Divide his attention!" Reg, Frolic, and Tom didn't argue. They all scattered in different directions around the chamber. The ancient faerie took a few halting steps as if deciding who to pursue first.

"You think you're so clever, little human?" it asked as it tossed a spell toward Querry, knocking him off balance, and lunging for him as he fell.

"Reg!" Querry shouted and threw the heart. Reg caught the organ and continued running. The beast snarled and ran toward Reg. Before it reached Reg, he tossed the heart off to Frolic. The monster snatched at Frolic, but he flew up to the ceiling of the chamber with his metal wings.

"This is exceedingly tedious," the creature said as it aimed a spell at Frolic.

"We have to burn the heart!" Querry shouted. The monster turned on Querry, forgetting Frolic for the moment and grabbing Querry round the neck.

"Tom! Fire," Frolic shouted as he returned to the ground, tossing the heart to Teezle.

"Oh no you don't, Tommy!" The creature's hand whipped out, and the heart stopped in mid-air. "That's sorted. Now for you." The ancient fey tightened his grip. Frolic grabbed a piece of masonry and launched it at the monster, slamming into its skull. It dropped Querry and turned on Frolic, its eyes blazing with anger and magical energy. "You awful, little thing," it hissed, throwing a spell that lifted Frolic off his feet and sent him flying through the air. "I'll drain you and then I'll eat your little friends." The primordial creature advanced on Frolic, flexing its clawed fingers.

"Over my dead body!" Reg shouted and dashed at the creature, throwing his shoulder against it.

"If you prefer, I'll start with you," the monster said, recovering from Reg's attack. It reached for Reg as Frolic reached for the hovering heart. Sensing the treachery, the faerie hissed and pointed a finger at Starling's heart, beckoning it closer. The organ floated toward the faerie's outstretched hand. "I refuse to be undone by the likes of you."

Suddenly the faerie's outstretched hand fell, along with Starling's heart, to the stone floor. The creature shrieked as Jean-Andre stood, a sword in his uninjured hand and a smirk on his lips. "What are you waiting for, mon ami? Burn that damned thing."

Teezle aimed his hands at the heart and flames burst forth, setting the organ ablaze.

"I'm very tired of you, little faerie," the beast said, backhanding Jean-Andre and advancing on Teezle. "Perhaps I'll take your heart after I've taken your magic." It reached for Tom.

"No!" Frolic shouted. Reg dove at the monster, tackling it around the legs, dragging it to the floor. Without words, Querry and Jean-Andre followed his lead, leaping on the creature's arms and pinning it to the ground. "Now,

Tom! Now!" Frolic shouted. Teezle nodded and conjured flames, trying not to hit Frolic's friends.

The creature screamed, thrashed about, and tossed the humans from him. Tom increased the intensity of his blaze as the faerie stood. Its pained shrieks vibrated the chamber as it marched toward its attacker. Frolic stepped up behind the creature with Jean-Andre's sword in his hand. Frolic lopped off the first fey's head, and the shrieks stopped abruptly. Tom continued to focus his flames on the body until the he reduced their adversary to nothing more than ash and a scorch on the floor.

Querry crawled up the steps to Starling's abused corpse and pulled him onto his lap. Now that the danger had passed, the true impact of the baron's sacrifice inundated Querry's emotions, and the floodgates of his sorrow opened. He closed his eyes and wept over Starling's corpse. He could hear his friends moving around the chamber, but he couldn't see what they were doing, and he didn't care.

QUERRY DIDN'T know how long he cried before he felt a light touch on his shoulder. Looking up, he saw Reg, Frolic, and Jean-Andre standing in a circle around him. None of them said anything; there was no need. Querry sniffled and swallowed the lump in his throat. He supposed in some way they'd won, though this felt like anything but a victory.

For the first few hours, Querry carried Starling's body cradled in his arms like a sleeping child. He refused the others' offers of help. Eventually, though, his injured and exhausted body would no longer cooperate. The corpse was getting stiff and starting to smell bad, so Querry set it gently on the ground and stopped to rest for a few moments. He'd never been so thirsty in his life.

He shook his head and spoke for the first time in many hours. "What are we going to do without any water? It took us days and days to walk this far into the temple. We won't last the days it will take to make it out. What happened to Tom?"

No one had an answer. Querry leaned back against the wall and closed his eyes. For one of the only times in his life, he didn't know if he could keep fighting impossible odds. He was so tired, more completely drained in body and soul than he would have ever imagined possible.

Querry thought he must have fallen asleep and drifted into a dream. He felt warmth on his face and a breeze ruffling his hair. Birds sang somewhere above him, and leaves rattled softly. Querry opened his eyes to a small clearing covered in soft grass and edged with flowering bushes. He blinked, expecting it to fade away, but it didn't. Corny and the three mercenaries also looked perplexed. Baron Starling's body still lay a few feet from Querry's legs. His skin had gone gray, and seeing him summoned a fresh wave of grief in Querry. What he saw next inspired only rage.

Tom Teezle stood at the center of the glade with his arms crossed. "You son of a bitch," Querry snarled, advancing on the faerie. "You could have saved him!"

Tom shrugged. "I didn't want to. I did, however, save you, so show some gratitude." He made a sweeping gesture with his hand, indicating a break in the trees.

All of them approached the gap and looked out. A few miles away, a city sprawled at the bottom of a hill. Beyond it, hundreds of ships bobbed on the glimmering waves in the large harbor.

"The capital city of Morazan," Tom explained. "You will find many of your people there, and from there, you can secure travel if you wish."

"Where will you go?" Frolic asked.

"I must return to the Other Lands and tell my people of what happened here. We must devise a way to make sure it never happens again. Though I destroyed my ancestor's body, I doubt I truly vanquished him if even the Good Father couldn't accomplish it. My people must insure he isn't given the opportunity to return. The temple can never be discovered by another human."

"But I'm afraid that's impossible," Reg said. "The colonists here are clearing away more and more of the jungle to make room for plantations. It might take many years, but they'll reach it eventually, and it's human nature to be curious."

"We will make sure that doesn't happen," Tom said. "Now, farewell. Many of you I will not see again. Frolic, I wish to speak with you. I have something for you."

"I'm not sure I want anything from you," Frolic said even as he approached Tom.

"You will want this." Tom reached into the pocket of the new, green and gold striped trousers he wore and handed Frolic what looked like a ruby the size of his fist wrapped in a paisley handkerchief. Querry couldn't even imagine its value, and as he looked at it, he thought it seemed somehow familiar.

"I do need this," Frolic said in a voice soft with awe. "What do you ask in return?"

"Nothing," the fey said. "I want you to have it. I want to see what you'll do with it. I like you, Frolic. You entertain me. I'm hoping another of you will entertain me even more. Will you accept it?"

"Yes. Thank you, Merrifont."

"Be careful. It's extremely hot." The faerie handed Frolic the gem.

Querry understood. Tom Teezle, Merrifont, or whatever name the faerie now preferred, had made Frolic a heart. Querry remembered accompanying his gentleman on a quest for the components necessary to construct the eternally hot arcane miracle: fire flowers, the essence of an elemental salamander, fever dreams, and oaths spoken during love. He recalled Tom watching the three of them make love, but he wondered where the fey had found the rest of the ingredients, and more importantly, what Frolic planned to do with it.

Nearby, Jean-Andre practically drooled at the sight of the jewel. He moved to step closer, but Reg intercepted him and looked at Frolic. "What are you planning to do with that, beauty?"

"I thought to make another like me," Frolic said softly. "I don't want to be the only one anymore, and I'm afraid to be alone again when you and Querry... when you're gone."

"But... you'll have us for years and years," Reg countered in a wounded tone.

"But not forever," Frolic whispered, staring into the swirling depths of the glowing gem. "No matter what we say or what promises we make, it can never be forever."

Querry's eyes stung, and he scrubbed at the moisture on his cheeks while everyone stood in awkward silence around him. He'd had no idea Frolic had been concealing so much pain.

"I suppose that's it, then," Corny said. "We should make our way to the city. I want a real meal, a bath, and a bed for the night. I'll worry about the rest after that."

"Let's go," Owens agreed.

"There's something I have to do first," Querry said, looking at Lord Starling for probably the last time.

They spent the next few hours building a pyre from deadfall before placing the baron atop it and sending him to his final rest. Querry hoped Gavindale Starling would find peace at last. His tears flowed freely, and the others cried as well as they stood around the fire until nothing remained but a pile of ash and cinders. No one would ever know the baron rested here; no one would visit this nameless clearing and spend a few minutes remembering him. No monument would mark his grave or remind others that he'd lived at all. To Querry, that was one hell of a shame. He hoped maybe Reg might write something about Lord Starling in his memoirs. He hoped history might remember the baron as an idealist, a dreamer who fell just short, and not dismiss him as a failure.

Chapter 32

REG'S EASY assimilation to life in Morazan surprised him. Querry, with his knowledge of the darker elements of cities such as this, had quickly found a buyer for the gold they'd taken from the temple, although Frolic had insisted they not sell more gold than would comfortably sustain them for a while, wishing to keep most of the treasure intact as the future bones of the companion he'd create. They rented a lovely house not far from the beach, in a part of town full of cafes, open-air markets, bakeries, flower shops, playhouses, and best of all, bookstores. A trip to a local physician had confirmed what Reg already knew: he'd broken two ribs and cracked two others.

Today, weeks later, Reg spent the morning as he usually did, sitting at his desk in front of the window, looking out at the vibrant colors of the city and its people, and trying to pen the story of what he'd lived since leaving Thalacea before the details faded from his mind.

The local girl they'd hired to cook for them, Constantia, brought Reg a cup of the excellent local coffee along with some toast and bacon. He smiled as she set them down. A few hours later, Querry and Frolic returned from the market. Having money agreed with Querry. As they entered the sitting room, Reg wondered what exotic gift his lover had purchased for him this time. He set his pen and new spectacles down and rose from his leather chair to greet them, taking their hands and kissing each of them on the cheek. Reg felt relieved to see both of them in good spirits. The days since Starling's demise had left all of them shaken, and Frolic most of all.

"Look what I found," Querry said, handing Reg a small package wrapped in brown paper.

Reg unwrapped the parcel and found a twin of the faerie book Frolic had stolen from Starling's villa, the book that had been destroyed when the airship crashed. Reg smiled, kissed Querry again, and put the book on the shelf with the rest of his growing collection.

"You didn't forget we're meeting Corny for lunch today, did you, Reggie?" Frolic asked. His hair had returned to its usual silvery white, and he'd removed the braids and beads, though he kept Tom Teezle's dark gray ribbon wound around one of his curls, and he still wore the feather earring the Panther People had made for him.

"Of course not, beauty. Just let me splash some water on my face." Reg went to the washroom and wiped the ink splotches from his fingers. He brushed his freshly cut hair and put on a wide, brown tie, securing it with a gold pin he hoped Querry had *bought* for him.

They walked a few blocks in the direction of the coastline to a quaint eatery not far from the small, pink plaster house Corny and Jack Owens shared. They found the mercenary and the tinkerer already seated at a long, wooden table next to the smoky pit where a local man roasted meat and fish. Men in three-piece suits and women in white dresses, with parasols and bonnets, strolled by just as they would in Halcyon. Reg watched them, and it was hard to believe the primordial jungle and all its mysteries waited only a day away. Soon after, Jean-Andre, who'd been staying at an expensive hotel, arrived in a steam carriage. He still wore a cast and a sling on his right arm.

"Always good to see you, my friends," he said as he sat down. "If I may ask, what's the occasion?"

Corny poured them all wine. "Well, I'm afraid it's to say good-bye. Me and Jack are going back to Anglica tomorrow morning. We've talked a lot about it, and we're planning to open a small shop in south Halcyon, near where I grew up. Do repairs and whatnot."

"Settling down?" Reg asked Owens, a bit incredulous. Owens was a little too much like Querry. Reg worried he'd grow bored and crave danger and excitement after a while.

Owens nodded. "It's time. I ain't exactly a young man anymore. I figure I can retire with what I made off this job. To new beginnings." He raised his glass, and all of them drank, with the exception of Frolic, who looked utterly crushed.

Corny reached across the table and squeezed Frolic's hand. "Now, love. Don't be sad. You're welcome to come visit any time you like. And we can write to each other. I still plan to help you build yourself a friend."

Reg rankled at the idea of being replaced, even if he understood Frolic's motivation.

"I hope you'll be very happy, Corny," Frolic said, forcing a smile. "I'll miss you very much, and I hope you won't forget me."

"How will I forget the best mate I ever had?" she asked with a wink.

As they spent the next couple of hours discussing their plans for the future, Reg realized he and his partners hadn't yet had the important conversation themselves. He liked Morazan well enough and wouldn't mind staying. Would he finally be able to convince Querry to settle down and give up his criminal ways? What about Frolic and his new obsession with making himself a companion?

He considered what he'd say to them as they walked home. Frolic stopped at a stand and bought a bunch of bright pink lilies. "Do you miss Whisper?" Reg asked.

"I don't have to miss him. I was able to bind him to the heart that Tom made for me," Frolic answered as he fondled the velvety petals and looked out over the rooftops toward the sea. "He was a good friend to me, and I didn't want to lose him."

Reg barely concealed his shock. "How?" he breathed. "How did you manage it?"

"I don't know," Frolic answered. "I listened to the magic in my own heart, and it instructed me."

This new development made Reg very uncomfortable. "That's wonderful," Reg lied against his better judgment.

"We've had to leave so many," Frolic lamented. "I miss Baron Starling. I miss Dink and Lizard. Now Corny's leaving too. Is this how life will always be? People come into your life, become important to you, and then just go?"

Reg couldn't lie to him. "It used to seem that way to me too. Sometimes it still does."

"What do we do?" Frolic stopped in the street and looked at them, desperate for guidance and clearly hurting. He dipped his head to the side and nuzzled the invisible Whisper.

"We hold onto each other as tight as we can," Querry said. "We fight for each other, and we don't stop fighting, no matter what. Beauty, I'm not going anywhere."

Frolic nodded and resumed walking, but Reg could almost read his mind. He'd bet Frolic was thinking about how much longer he'd survive compared to Reg and Querry. Reg hated feeling like he'd let Frolic down by being mortal.

They arrived home to find a small boy waiting on their front steps. He held a large, official-looking envelope that seemed to contain a thick book. "Mr. Starling?" he asked, addressing Querry.

"No." Querry paled and took a step away from the young courier.

"But this is the address I was told. Are you sure you're not Querrilous Starling?"

"Let me see that." Querry took the package and stared hard at the fancy, looping script scrawled across it. Reg put his glasses on and looked over his shoulder. Nothing but a name was written on the thick, ivory paper: Querrilous Knotte-Starling.

Reg offered the boy a coin as Querry walked slowly inside the house without closing the door. He sat down cross-legged on the floor and tore the envelope open. Reg and Frolic stood a few feet away as Querry sorted through the stack of papers it contained. As he read, tears trickled down his face until he sobbed softly. Finally he looked up at Reg and said, "These can't be real, can they, Reggie? Please tell me this is some sort of sick joke."

"What do they say?" Reg asked cautiously.

Querry, gripped by a fresh bout of grief, just shook his head and scrubbed at his red eyes. Reg slid the stack of papers gently out of his hand and walked to the window where he had some light to examine. "Oh no," he whispered as soon as he saw the first line.

I, Gavindale Cesar Starling the Third, Baron of Greymont and Sele, also the Viscount du Marches, being of sound mind and body, do hereby will all my earthly possessions and titles to my son, Querrilous Knotte-Starling, upon the event of my death.

Reg read on and on through the endless caveats and clauses. Everything seemed authentic. He recognized the names of the solicitors Querry was to contact back in Halcyon. "This... appears to be in perfect order, Querry. Starling used some very clever legal trickery to allow you, an illegitimate, to inherit his titles, but he seems to have pulled it off. According to this, you are the next Baron Starling."

Querry stood and punched a hole in the yellow plaster wall. "Are you telling me I killed my father?"

"Querry, Starling had no family. You might not be related to him by blood. Maybe he just respected you and had no one else to inherit his fortune."

"Fuck!" Querry shouted, pressing his fists against his forehead as he paced back and forth. "How am I ever going to know? He did look a little like me. What if he was my father? Why wouldn't he tell me? Why would he do this to me? Frolic? Reg? Tell me!"

"I don't have the answers to give you," Reg said.

"Reg, I could have known my father." Querry sank back down to the floor and hugged his knees. "He was so much like me. He was, wasn't he? Reggie?"

Reg just shook his head. He could see parallels between his lover and the late Baron Starling: passion, determination, idealism, and a certain recklessness. There was a slight resemblance, especially in their coloring. Then again, it all seemed like an impossible coincidence that they'd both ended up in that tiny Thalacean port. Unless Starling had been watching Querry. If he had, how had he allowed Querry to suffer through the childhood he'd endured?

Querry stood and went down the hall to their bedroom. Reg and Frolic followed, both of them glancing at each other, each hoping the other might suggest a way to ease their friend's anguish. They stopped at the door as Querry collapsed on the bed and curled into a ball. He pulled a small, leather-bound book from inside his shirt and caressed the spine.

"Querry?" Frolic asked. "Is there anything I can do?"

"Not now, beauty. I think I'd like to be alone." He rolled away from them, clutching the book to his chest, and would say nothing else.

THE FOLLOWING evening, after dinner, while Reg, Querry, and Frolic sat on the veranda beyond their dining room, Reg heard a knock on the door. Querry flinched and said, "What now?"

"I'll go," Reg offered. He opened the door with a deep dread, but it dissipated when he saw it was only Jean-Andre, dressed in a beautiful, pale blue suit and holding a few bottles in a basket. Reg invited him inside, and they returned to the terrace just as the sun fell below jagged mountains to the west. Frolic lit the glass lamp and candles on the table.

"My friends, you will never believe what I've found." He brandished the dark glass bottles. "Absinthe. I did not know one could acquire it here, and I thought we might enjoy a glass or two together to celebrate your recent good fortune, Baron Starling."

Reg crossed his arms. "How could you have found out so soon?"

"People talk in this city the same as any other, if one knows where to listen."

Reg doubted it was so simple, but with all the conflict and tension in their household over the last day, he didn't want to argue with Jean-Andre. It hardly mattered how he'd found out, anyway.

"Shall we have a drink?" Jean-Andre asked again.

Querry's eyes looked dark, but he must have realized Jean-Andre meant no harm, so he nodded. "I think I might quite like that, actually. Let's go into the sitting room. I'll find some glasses."

Reg stoked the small fire in the hearth, and all of them settled into the comfortable chairs, with him and Jean-Andre sharing the small sofa. Querry lined three glasses up on the low, wooden table, and Jean-Andre poured the absinthe over the sugar cubes. "To the Baron of Greymont and Sele, Lord Querrilous Knotte-Starling."

"No," Querry said. "I don't want to drink to that."

"Very well, my friend," Jean-Andre said. "What would you prefer?"

Querry swirled his drink in his glass and stared at the milky green liquid, deep in thought. "How about to death? It's the only thing we can really depend on, isn't it? Everything else is just a distraction while we wait for it."

"Oh, Querry," Frolic whispered, rubbing his back.

"Let's forget the toast and just drink," Jean-Andre suggested.

"Good idea." Querry raised his glass and finished the absinthe in a few large gulps. "Mind if I serve myself?" he asked, reaching for the bottle again.

"Not at all," Jean-Andre said.

Querry slopped the greenish liquid into his glass, filling over half of it before adding the water. Reg sipped at his drink and winced. It was very strong, and it burned his throat and nostrils. The next sip he took wasn't as bad, though, and before he knew it, he'd finished his first glass. Jean-Andre slid it out of his hand and prepared him another.

"Would you like to try it, Frolic?" Jean-Andre asked.

Frolic looked uncertain, but Querry and Jean-Andre encouraged him until he finally agreed and took a tiny sip from Jean-Andre's glass. As soon as the intense liqueur hit his tongue, Frolic screwed his eyes shut and grimaced dramatically. He cast his glance from side to side, looking for somewhere to spit it out. Just as he was about to leap from his chair, Querry, who'd finished his fourth glass, grabbed Frolic by the shirt and pulled Frolic to his mouth. He kissed Frolic hard, his Adam's apple bobbing as he swallowed the liquid as it drained from Frolic's mouth. They continued kissing sloppily, wetting each other's lips and flashing their tongues.

"Mon dieu," Jean-Andre said under his breath, squirming on the sofa for reasons obvious to Reg.

When Reg looked over at the other man, his hair seemed much redder than it had before, bright, glowing orange like the seaside clouds at sunset. His tan, freckled skin glistened with a light sheen of sweat, and his blue eyes sparkled. He was beautiful in an almost fey-like way. Jean-Andre smiled, looking very satisfied, and raised his glass once again. Reg looked quickly away, back at Querry and Frolic who still kissed enthusiastically, moaning and slurping at each other's mouths. Jean-Andre brushed the outside of Reg's thigh with the back of his good hand and then cupped his knee.

"I don't mind you admiring me, Reginald. I like it, actually. Do you find me pleasing to look at?"

Reg didn't know what to say. He felt a little dizzy, like the walls and ceiling rotated slowly around him. He was suddenly terribly warm and thirsty. He squirmed out of his jacket and tossed it over the back of the sofa, followed by his tie. Then he removed his cufflinks, set them on the table, rolled his sleeves up around his elbows, and took a long pull from his drink, finishing it. Jean-Andre took his glass and prepared him another.

Still parched, Reg drank over half of it down. Everything looked soft and fuzzy in the firelight. Reg sank back into the sofa, and the upholstery ensconced him like a warm cloud. His body felt light and insubstantial even as his skin felt acute. He felt the air currents in the room moving over him, ruffling the sparse hair on his arms. Jean-Andre moved closer to him, their thighs pressing together. A sensation like an electric shock shot up Reg's leg.

Jean-Andre combed through Reg's hair with his fingers, the impression of his nails against Reg's scalp simply amazing.

Across from him, Frolic sat on Querry's lap with his slender legs hanging over the arm of the chair. His white shirt, open up the center, barely covered his shoulders, and Querry had removed his entirely. Querry held his glass to Frolic's lips, and Frolic took a sip of the absinthe before letting it flow from his mouth into Querry's. Querry moaned as he licked every vestige of the liqueur from his chin and lips. It occurred to Reg that maybe they shouldn't be doing that in front of a guest, especially when Querry reached up to fondle Frolic's nipple, but it didn't seem terribly important. Reg let his head fall back against the sofa. His body felt like liquid, like it could flow off the furniture and pool on the floor. The shadows dancing on the walls took the shape of little creatures like Frolic's Whisper. Reg closed his eyes, but that only made the room spin faster.

Something smelled like perfume. Reg lifted his head, wondering if he'd fallen asleep and for how long. He couldn't seem to focus his eyes, and perceived only smears of light and color. A hand cradled the back of his neck, and something warm, oily, and metallic pressed to his lips. He inhaled a small puff of the fragrant smoke and promptly coughed it back out. The rim of a glass touched his mouth, and he drank the proffered absinthe to soothe his raw throat. In a bleary haze, he saw Querry and Frolic, stripped to their trousers and seated on the floor in front of him, passing the long pipe back and forth. Reg wiggled his toes, wondering when he'd taken off his shoes and socks.

The pipe pressed to his mouth again, and he drew the sweet smoke into his lungs and held it there for a second before exhaling an impressive cloud. Then the moist brass was replaced by a set of even warmer lips. Reg opened his mouth as they slid against it. Their two sets of lips formed a tight seal before the other breathed out a plume of smoke, and Reg inhaled it. They stayed connected, exchanging breaths, until Reg felt like he'd pass out. Then the other mouth pulled away, and Reg's head lolled back, his eyes fluttering shut. He didn't think he'd ever felt so good, like he floated along on a warm breeze, his whole body tingling with pleasure.

He felt lips close over the cord of muscle running down his neck. He groaned; it felt so good. Other lips skimmed down the opposite side of his neck, and still more explored his face before meeting his mouth. For a fleeting second, Reg thought maybe that was too many pairs of lips, but he couldn't be concerned. Hands—it felt like dozens of them—roamed over Reg's body. His shirt was whisked away. Cool air caressed his flushed, damp skin. Teeth skimmed up over his ribs, making Reg tremble. He opened his eyes but saw only flashes of silver, copper, black, and skin, skin everywhere. He felt it moving against him, smelled it surrounding him, tasted it. He wanted more of it, and clutched at flesh and bone wherever it met his hands. Another chilly draft washed over his cock as his trouser flap opened. A hand closed around his stiff flesh. Two hands. God, it was good. Reg spread his legs and sank further into the sofa, just enjoying the sensations as lithe bodies moved over him....

REG WOKE, naked on the sofa, with his head throbbing and his throat feeling like a dried and twisted tube of ink. He staggered out to the kitchen and drank water straight from the pitcher. He didn't quite remember what had happened the previous evening, but he knew he hurt almost everywhere. The sun streaming through the kitchen window stung his eyes, so he hurried back down the hall, into the blessed shadows of their bedroom.

Querry and Frolic lay nude, tangled up in each other's limbs and the sheets they'd torn from the mattress. Reg flopped down beside Querry, and they all slept until late in the afternoon.

When he woke for the second time that day, Reg felt much more lucid, and with it came a feeling of horror. While he couldn't recall everything that had happened the night before, he remembered enough to be completely ashamed of his behavior.

Reg noted the bruises on Querry's neck and chest as Querry made coffee in the kitchen while Frolic toasted bread and fried eggs. "What did we do?" he asked.

"My memory's a little spotty," Querry said. "I had way too much to drink."

"Mine too," Frolic said. "That strange smoke made me feel really off."

"Jean-Andre was here," Reg said. "I'm pretty sure he stayed the night, or most of it. Enough, if you know what I mean. I'm sorry. I feel awful. How could we have let this happen?"

"What's the problem, Reggie?" Querry sat a cup of coffee down in front of him, and Reg couldn't decide if it smelled enticing or sickening. "Whatever happened, there's no harm done."

Reg rubbed his temples, still unable to completely process the implications. He wanted to rail against Querry's dismissal of what they'd done, but he hadn't complained at the time. Maybe he should just forget about it. Maybe Querry was right. After all, they hadn't hurt anyone, and nobody but the four of them knew about it.

"I think I'll do some tinkering," Frolic said. "I had some very bizarre dreams last night. They've given me some interesting ideas." He kissed Reg and Querry before leaving the kitchen for the unused, second bedroom where he worked.

Reg dipped the corner of his toast into the yoke of the perfect egg Frolic had cooked. He was seriously considering going back to bed until dinnertime. "Bloody hell, Querry, I feel terrible."

"Eat. It'll help."

Reg nodded and took another bite of his toast. The coffee helped his head, and he was actually starting to feel a little better when he heard Frolic scream. Both he and Querry bolted down the hall, knocking over their chairs in their haste.

Frolic stood with his fists balled and a little crease marring his perfect brow. At his feet, the leather satchel where he kept his book lay empty. "He took it. That... that... *hell cock* took my book!"

Under any other circumstances, Frolic's first attempt at cursing might have been humorous. Reg crumpled against the doorframe, his urge to be sick returning in full force.

"We'll get him, beauty," Querry said. "Both of you, get your gear. We have to find him before he can get too far. We can't let him sell your secrets."

Reg knew Querry was right, and he suddenly felt painfully sober. His hopes for a peaceful life where their biggest problem would be what to make for dinner each day faded along with the fog in his head. He'd chosen to love these men, to share his life with them, and that might mean never settling down. If this was their life, he'd embrace it. He'd accept it for everything it was. Damn it, he'd become pretty adept at kicking some ass when he had to.

"I'm with you," he told Querry and Frolic. "Now, and forever. Let's find that Belvaisian bastard and show him he crossed the wrong men."

"Thank you," Frolic said.

"No need, beauty," Querry told him. "I'm going to enjoy this."

Without saying anything more, the three of them donned their weapons and armored clothing. They packed their essentials and left yet another home behind, but it didn't hurt Reg so much this time. They weren't meant to settle anywhere; home was anywhere they were together. Life didn't always meet one's expectations. Sometimes it demanded more, pushed one to become better, sharper. As he looked at Querry and Frolic, Reg couldn't complain about what life had given him.

Now, it was time to fight to keep them.

AUGUST (GUS) LI is a creator of fantasy worlds. When not writing, he enjoys drawing, illustration, costuming and cosplay, and making things in general. He lives near Philadelphia with two cats and too many ball-jointed dolls. He loves to travel and is trying to see as much of the world as possible. Other hobbies include reading (of course), tattoos, and playing video games.

For more info, visit Books by Eon and Gus:
http://www.booksbyeonandgus.com

EON DE BEAUMONT is a versatile author, craftsmen, and raconteur. He has written a number of short stories, novellas, and novels, both solo and with his long-time writing partner and best friend, Augusta Li. Eon is an accomplished playwright and actor under an alternate identity. Above all Eon loves storytelling in all its myriad forms and sometimes has trouble sleeping for the abundance of ideas in his brain. Eon is alternately a mask maker, seamstress, doll maker, and amateur cook, as well. His passions include makeup, shoes, comics, movies, and the pursuit of an ever-higher gamer score. He's currently working on a number of projects in various states of completion including a manga, a pirate story, a thriller/horror script, and a young adult novel. Eon welcomes and encourages feedback and questions from his readers at mascaraboy13@hotmail.com, or through his Facebook or Gus and Eon's website: http://www.yaoimagic.com, and above all he hopes that his readers find enjoyment in his work.

BOOTS
FOR THE
GENTLEMAN

AUGUST LI AND
EON DE BEAUMONT

http://www.dreamspinnerpress.com

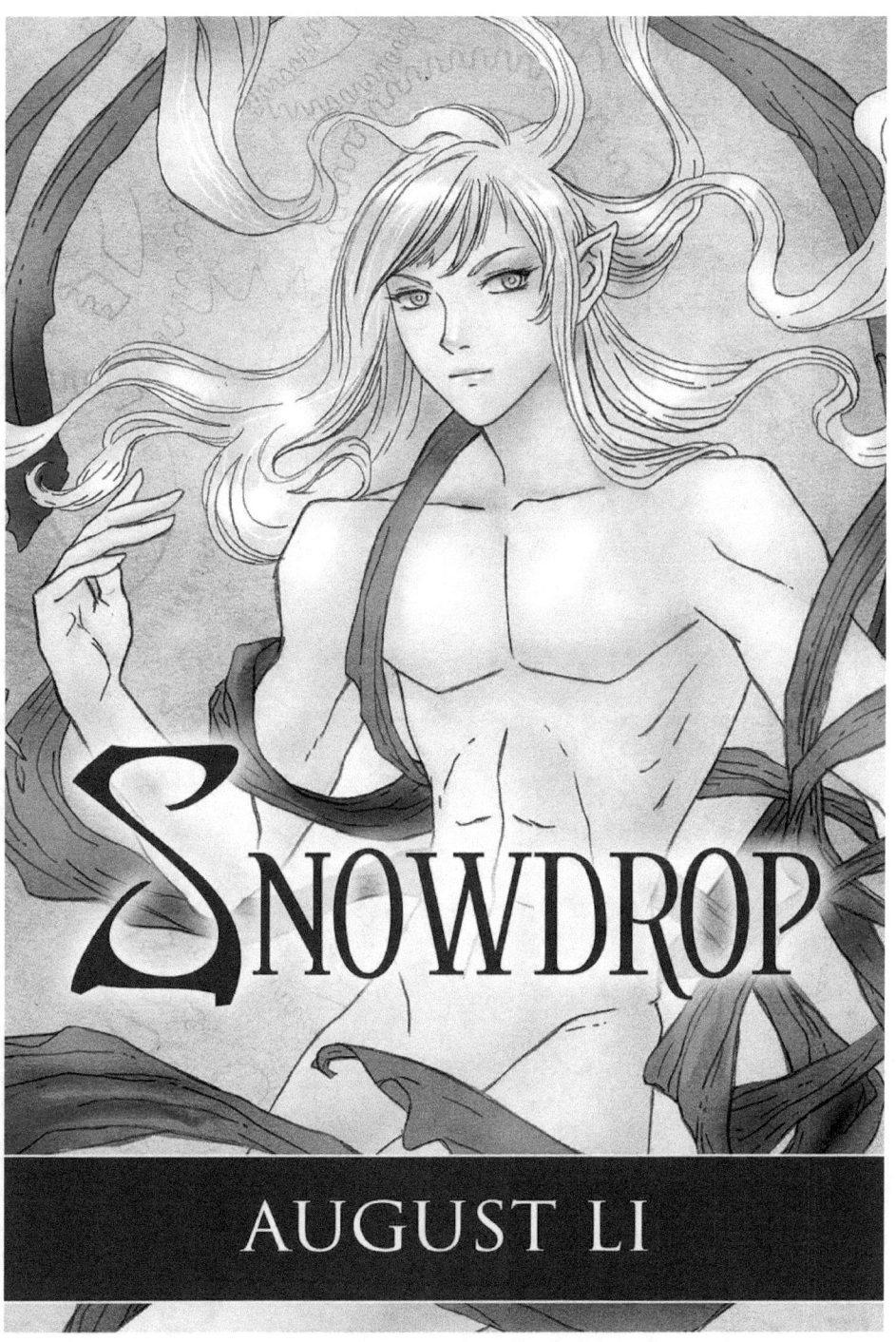

SNOWDROP

AUGUST LI

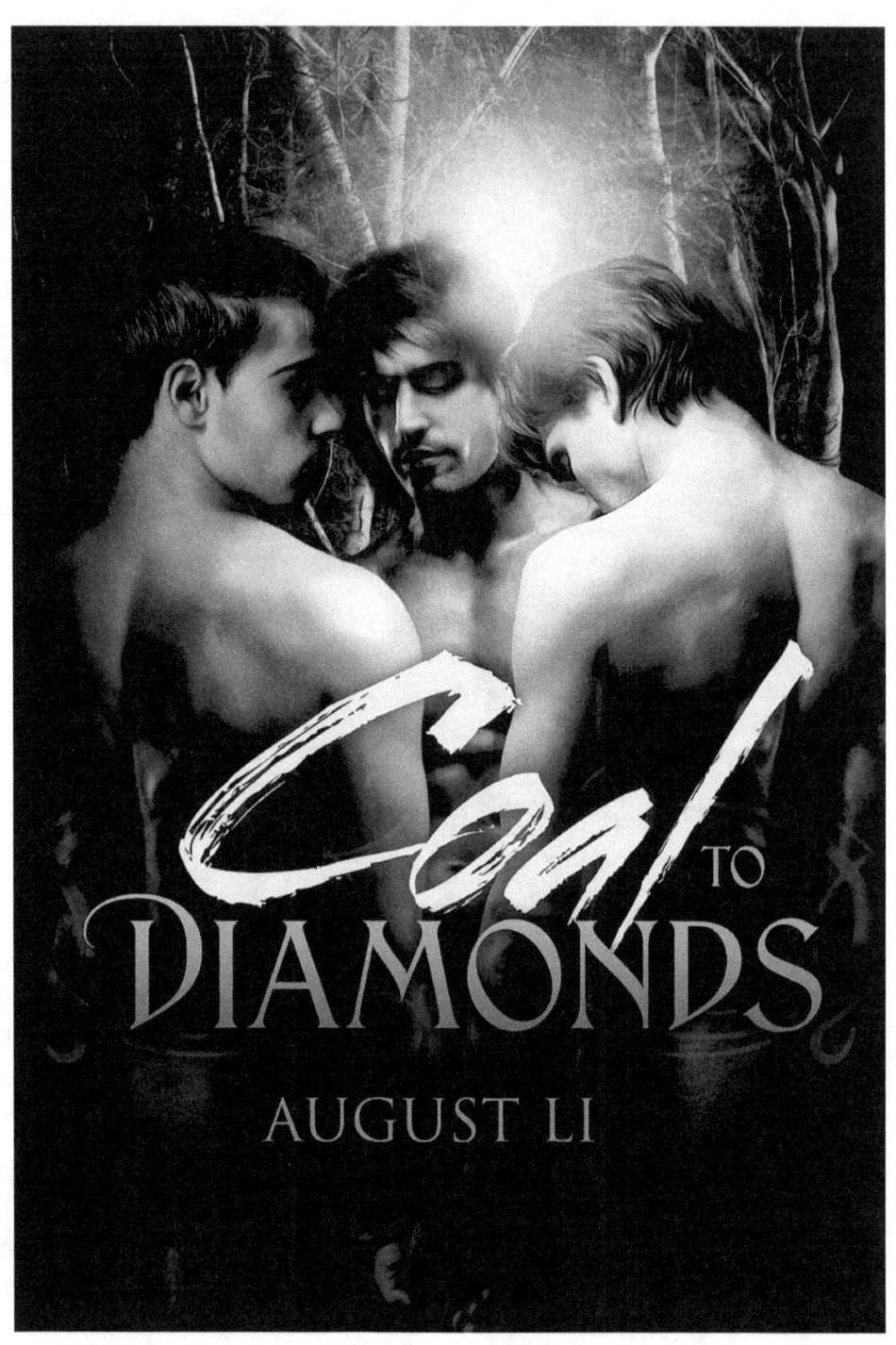

Coal TO DIAMONDS

AUGUST LI

http://www.dreamspinnerpress.com

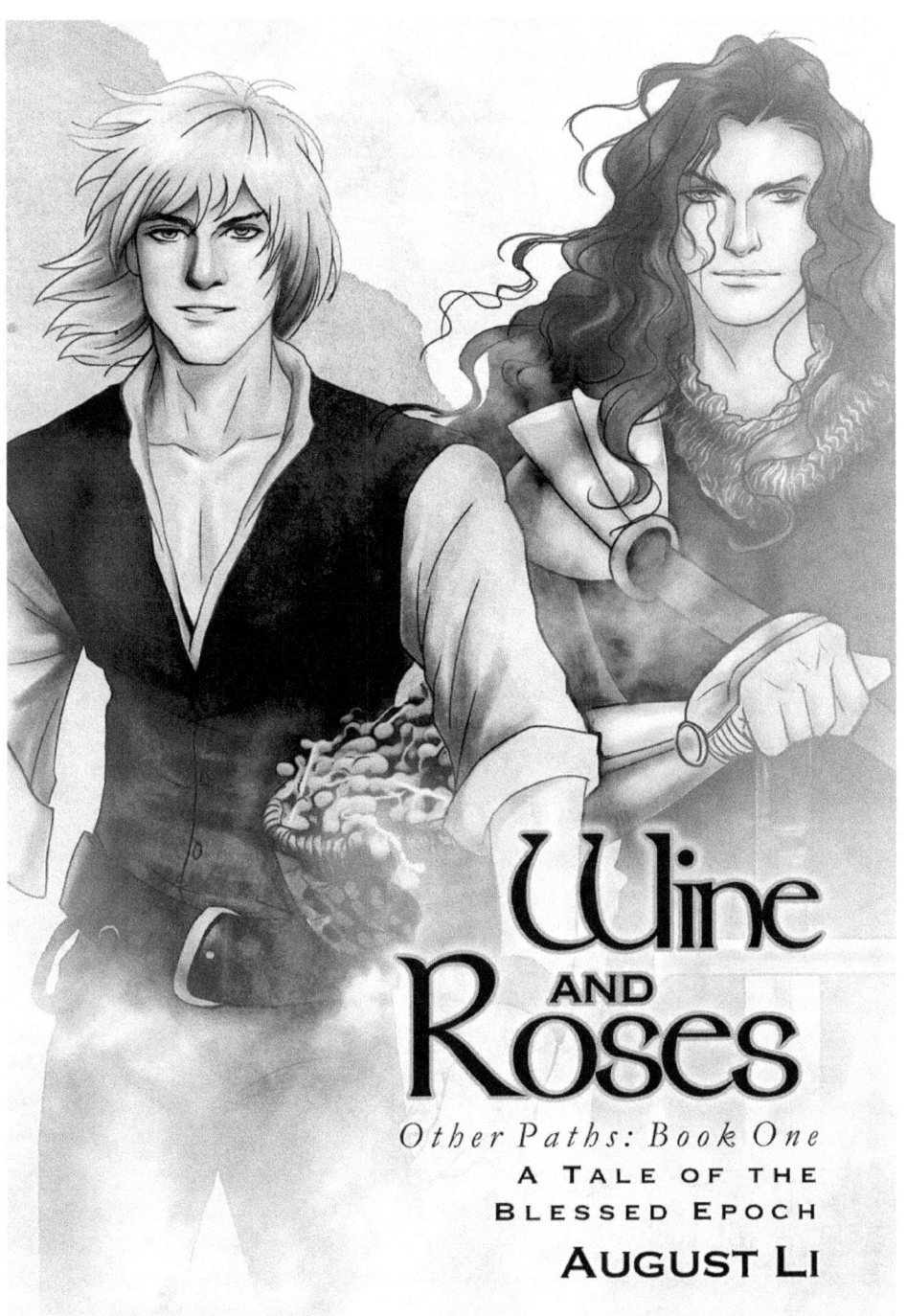

Wine
AND
Roses

Other Paths: Book One

A TALE OF THE
BLESSED EPOCH

AUGUST LI

http://www.dreamspinnerpress.com

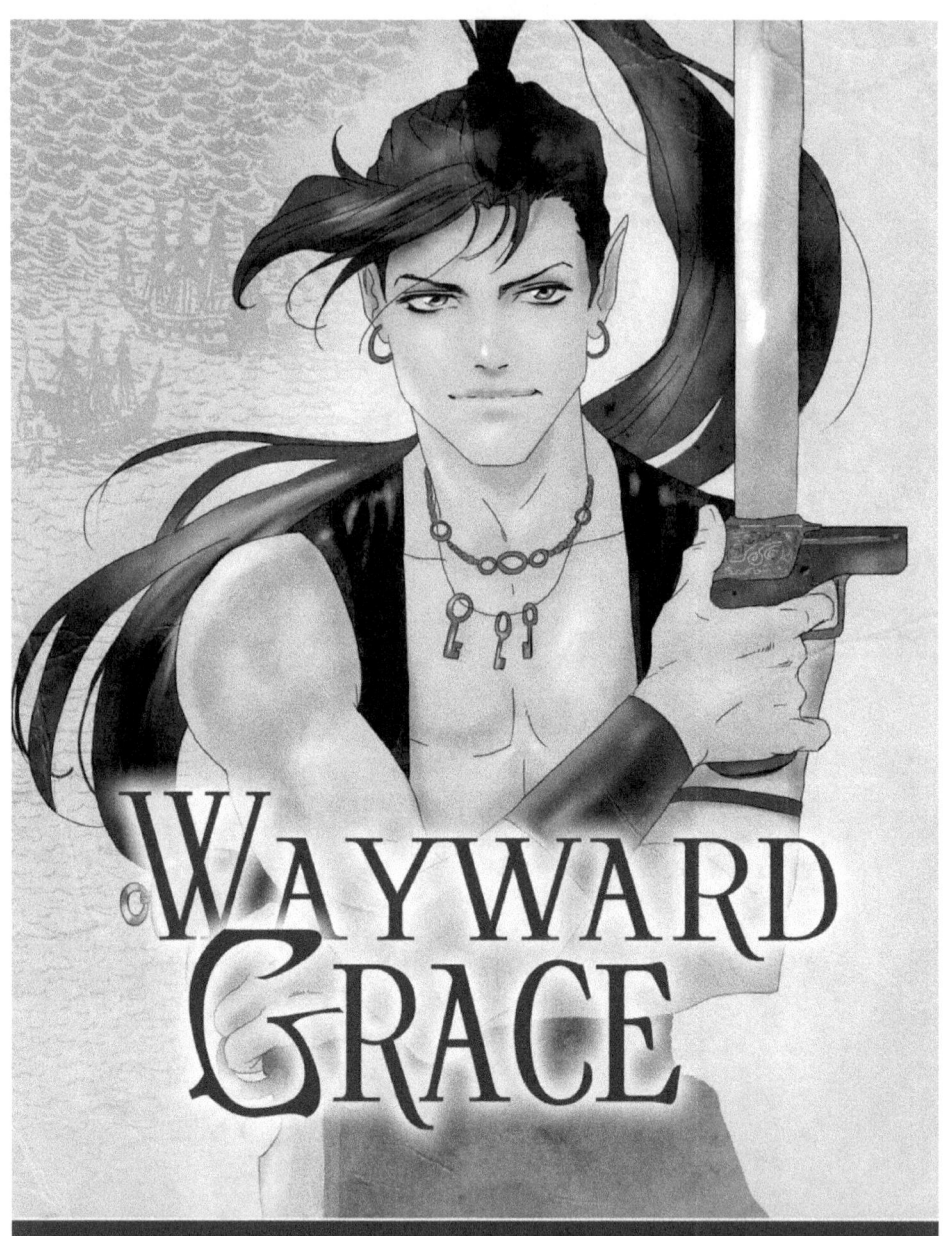

WAYWARD GRACE

EON DE BEAUMONT

http://www.dreamspinnerpress.com

EON DE BEAUMONT

RUM &
GINGER

ON
TINSEL
Wings

AUGUST LI

http://www.dreamspinnerpress.com

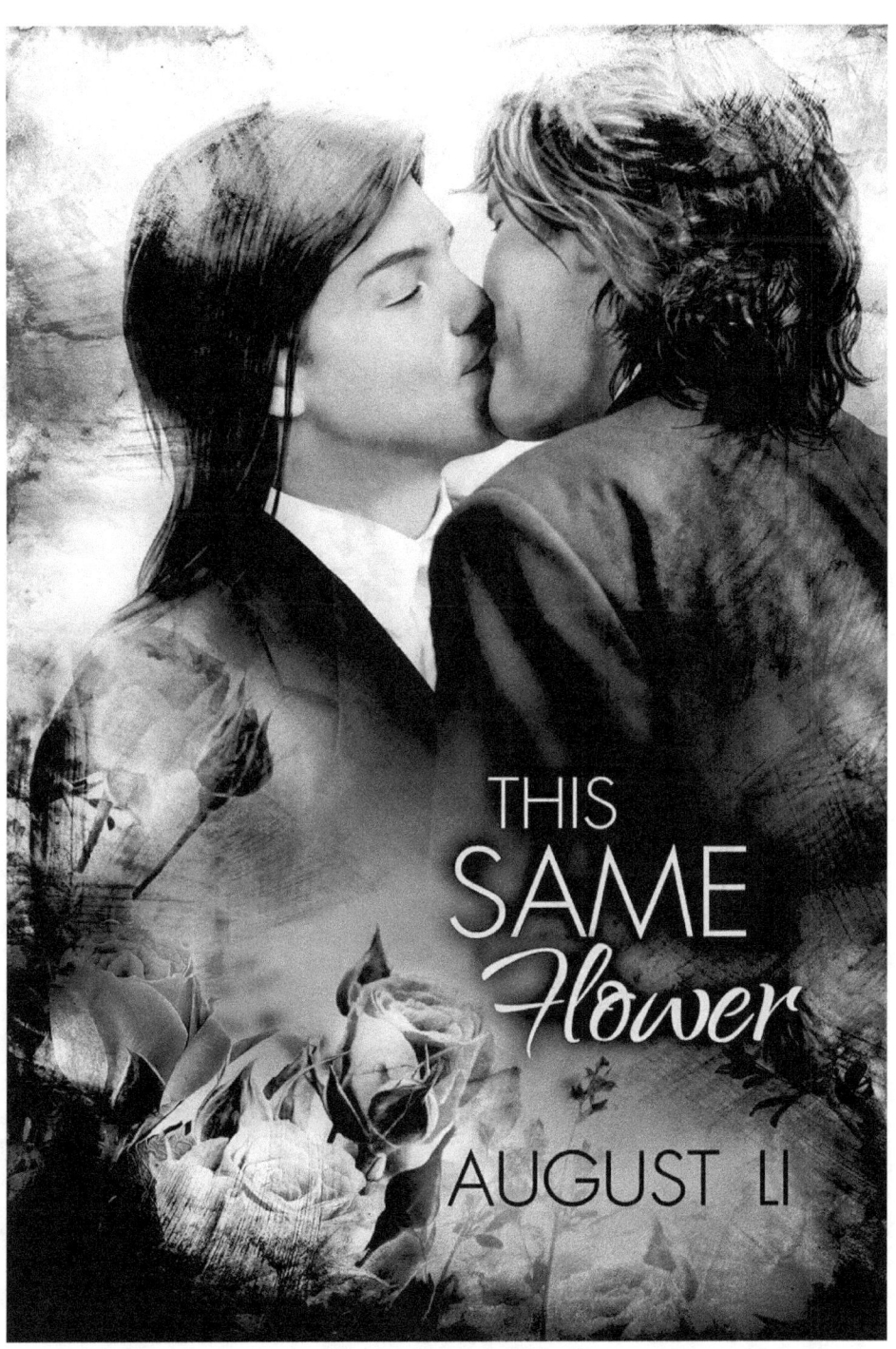

THIS
SAME
Flower

AUGUST LI

http://www.dreamspinnerpress.com

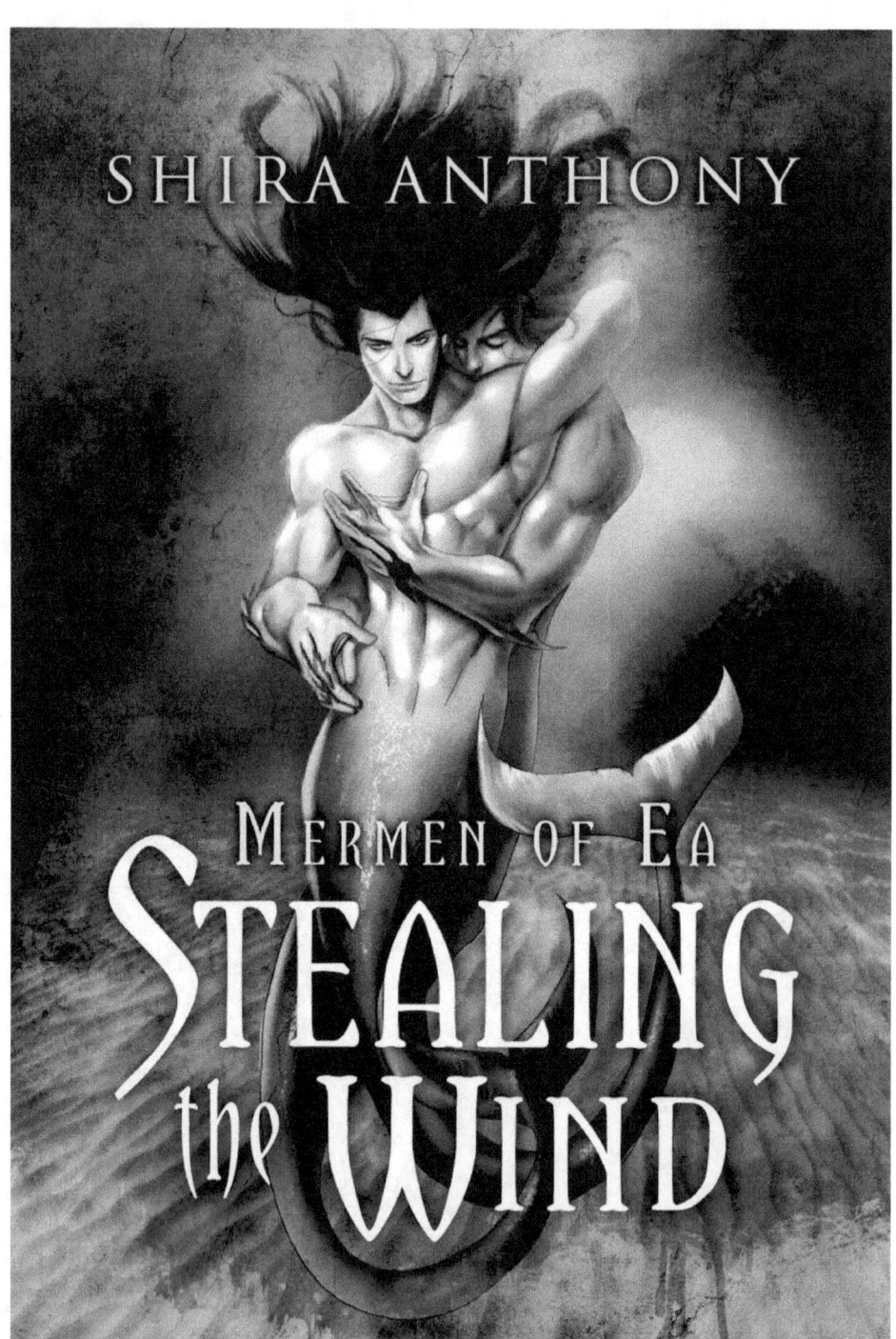

SHIRA ANTHONY

MERMEN OF EA

STEALING
the WIND

http://www.dreamspinnerpress.com

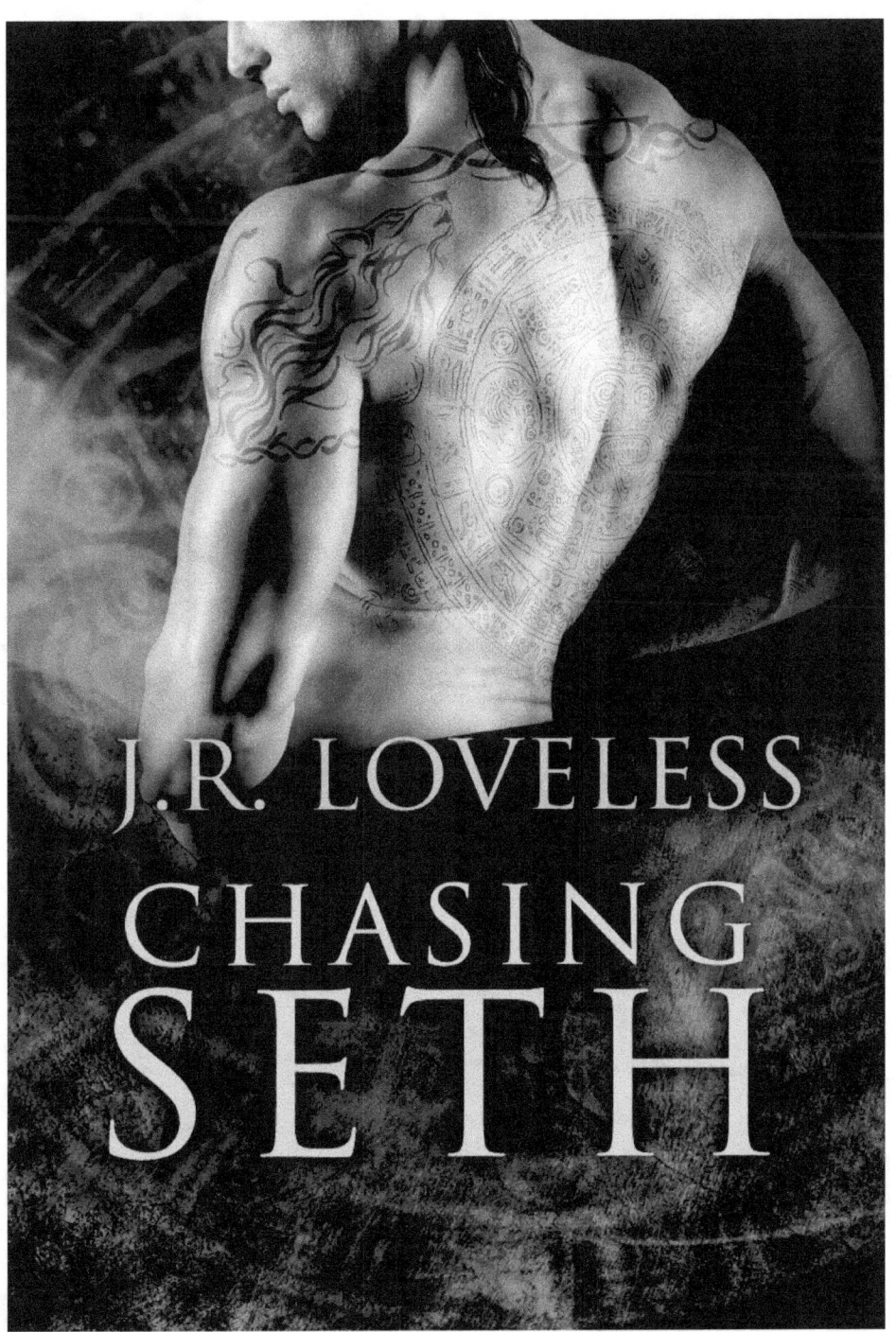

J.R. LOVELESS

CHASING
SETH

http://www.dreamspinnerpress.com

JoAnne Soper-Cook

The Eye of Heaven

http://www.dreamspinnerpress.com

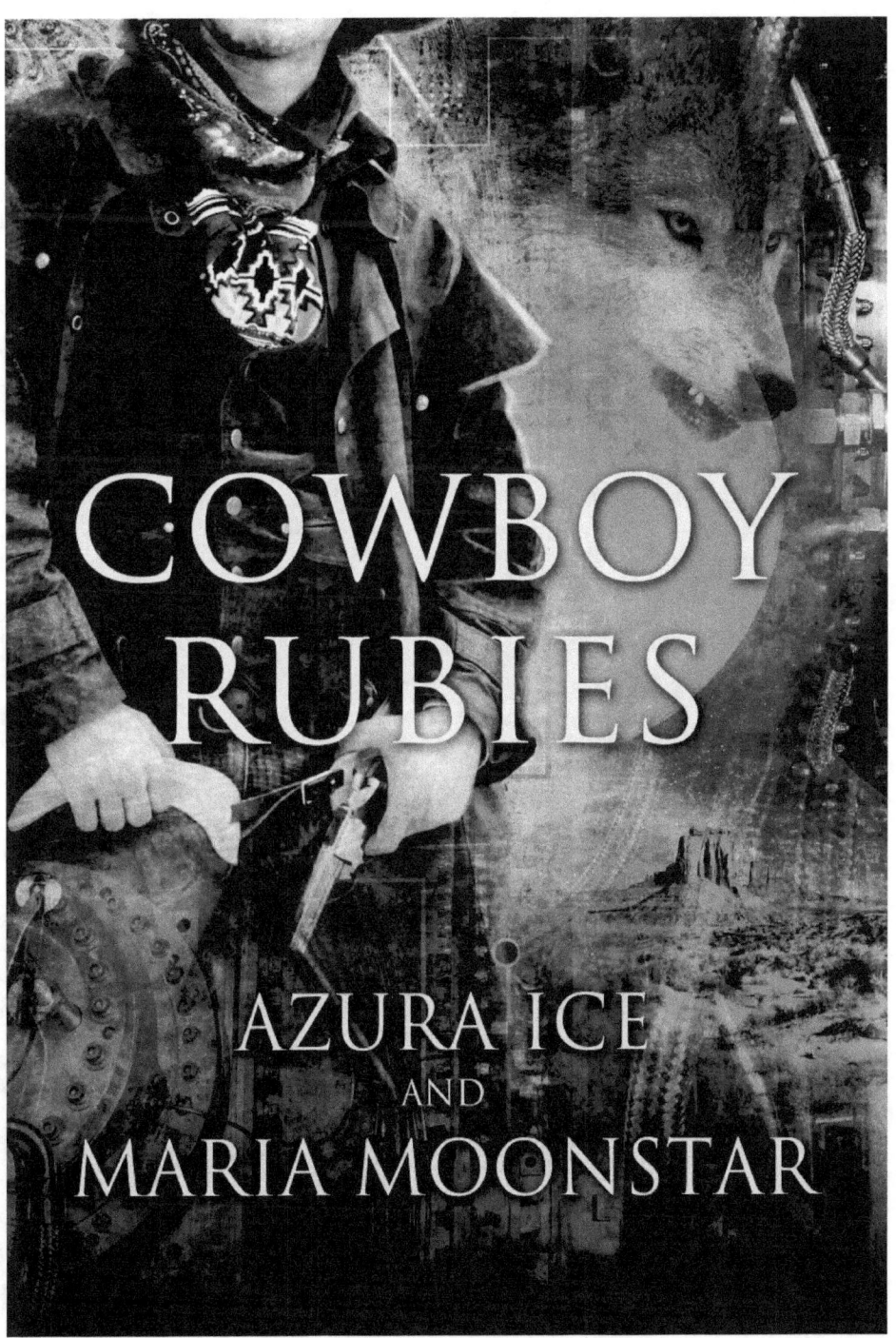

COWBOY RUBIES

AZURA ICE
AND
MARIA MOONSTAR

http://www.dreamspinnerpress.com

Genie's Wish

LIFTING THE VEIL 2

SUSAN LAINE

http://www.dreamspinnerpress.com

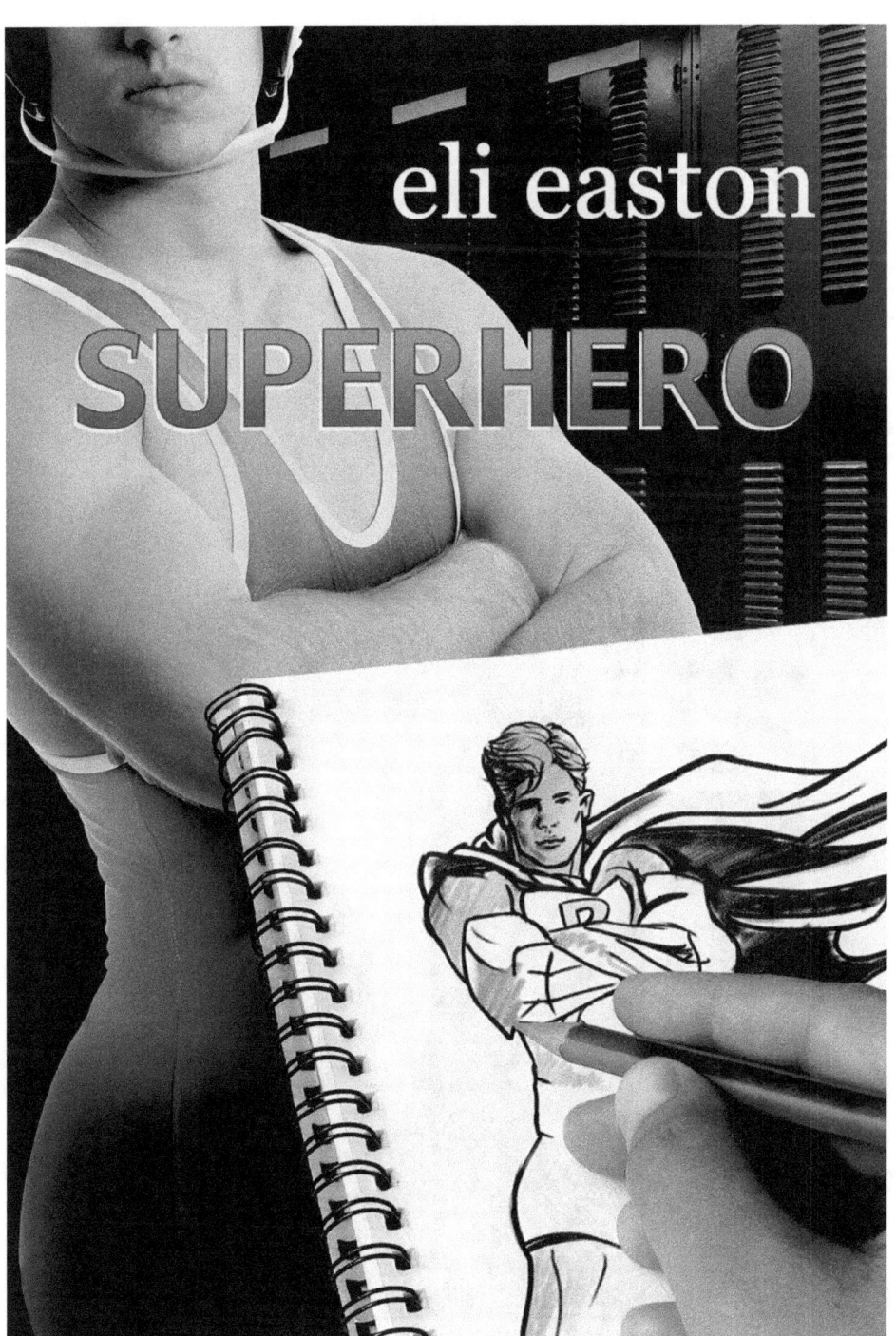

FOR **MORE** OF THE BEST **GAY** ROMANCE

Dreamspinner Press

DREAMSPINNERPRESS.COM

www.ingramcontent.com/pod-product-compliance
Lightning Source LLC
Chambersburg PA
CBHW050031030726
47506CB00001B/224